MY THIRD BOOK.

A Collection of Tales.

By LOUISE CHANDLER MOULTON,

AUTHOR OF "THIS, THAT, AND THE OTHER," AND "JUNO CLIFFORD."

NEW YORK:

HARPER & BROTHERS, PUBLISHERS,

FRANKLIN SQUARE.

1859.

PREFACE.

THERE is a pleasant legend which tells how the Hindoo maidens, in whose hearts love is beginning to dawn, go to the banks of the Ganges, and launch, each one, her little cocoa-shell boat with its lighted lamp. Kneeling on the river's brink, they watch till the light dies, or the boat, with its lamp still burning, goes out of sight, and from its fate they augur hope or despair.

Twice before I have made my venture, as doubtfully as they, on the tide of public opinion, and now I have come again to the river's brink to send forth "My Third Book." What the future will decree for it—genial airs, warmth, and sunlight, or adverse gales —I know not. I can but wait.

Hitherto I have found kind friends among my readers, and I hope the gift I bring to-day may prove a passport to their continued regard. Some of the tales herein embodied may be recognized by those familiar with the magazine literature of the past four years; but, I trust, their reappearance in a new garb will not be unwelcome. Other portions of the contents are entirely new; and of all, whatever their imperfections, I can but say, as those who proffer humble entertainment to distinguished guests,

"Still the poor mansion offers thee its best."

CONTENTS.

The Pride of Moses Grant.

Men
Can counsel, and speak comfort to that grief
Which they themselves not feel; but, tasting it,
Their counsel turns to passion, which before
Would give preceptial medicine to rage,
Fetter strong madness in a silken thread,
Charm ache with air, and agony with words.
A wretched soul, bruised with adversity,
We bid be quiet when we hear it cry;
But were we burdened with like weight of pain,
As much, or more, we should ourselves complain.

SHAKSPEARE (*Much ado about Nothing*).

THE PRIDE OF MOSES GRANT.

I.

IT was a wild, wet December night, full of tempest. Outside the red wooden house in the hollow, where Moses Grant had lived all his respectable life, the winds blew with an eerie sound, like a lost spirit's wail, and the snow fell steadily, folding the earth in great white shrouds.

Moses Grant and his wife sat before the fire. A cheerful glow came out from the blazing logs; a mug of cider was toasting unheeded on the hearth, and a few apples stood untouched on the stand between them. Every thing in this peaceful family sitting-room wore a snug and comfortable look, from the neat bed standing in a recess in the wall, with home-made blue woolen spread and snowy linen, to the brightly-polished pewter plates upon the dresser and the unsoiled sand on the white floor.

Outside, through the snow and the storm, tottered a single female figure—wearily, painfully, as if every step must be her last. Forsaken of God and man, the very elements seemed to do battle with her—the winds blew her feeble steps backward—the snow piled up higher and higher drifts before her feet, and yet those feeble feet tottered on—over the drifts, against the wind—steadily toward the red house in the hollow.

There was a strange shadow on the face of that meek woman, Moses Grant's wife. Her knitting had fallen from her busy fingers, her foot tapped the floor with a restless beat, and at last, as if she could endure the stillness no longer, she arose and began moving hurriedly about the room, giving a touch here and there to her domestic arrangements, and now and then going stealthily to the window to look forth into the night.

"Oh!" she cried, in a low voice, "God have mercy—this pitiless, pitiless storm!"

"You are thinking of Margaret," said the slow, firm tones of Moses Grant.

The woman started, and dropped the candlestick she held in her confusion. She turned ghastly pale, and grasped the dresser, near which she stood, for support. If a grave had opened at her very feet she would have been no more overwhelmed with wonder. For many months in that household that name—Margaret—had been dead and buried—a forbidden sound. Perhaps—her eyes gleamed with a wild hope, and the color came back to her cheeks—perhaps her husband had relented; perhaps he would forgive their child—their Margaret. She went toward him, that meek woman, and, kneeling at his feet, lifted up her pleading voice.

"Surely, father, I may speak of her, now you have called her name. It may be you are willing to forgive her—to let her come back again. Five-and-twenty years I have walked patiently by your side; I have tried to be a help-meet to you. God has given us seven children, and we have made their graves—all but one—behind the church on the hill-top. And now she is gone—the last—my one child—Margaret. Oh, husband, will you forgive her? Will you let her come back? What would even shame be to the loss of her? And perhaps she has not sinned as we have thought. She was a good child always, our Margaret. She loved the church and the Bible, and you used to say no one else learned their lessons in the catechism so well as she. We are getting old, father—may I have my girl back again?"

The old man's face had worked convulsively while she poured forth her pleading prayer, but it settled back now into stony, immovable calm. He looked sternly at the woman crouching at his knees, as if she, too, had some share in Margaret's sin. He said, in his cold, resolved tones,

"It is of no use. If we would take the child back we do not even know where to seek her. She is dead to us, now and forever. Hear me, Mary: if she lay at this moment outside that door, with this storm falling on her bare, unsheltered head, I would not open it one inch to let her in. She has made her bed; she shall lie in it. We have lived here many years—I, and my father, and my father's father—elders, one after another, in the church—and when did disgrace ever come to our humble, honest name, till she brought it? She chose that bad young man and his unholy love, and father and mother she has none. Hear me, Mary; we are childless. Let her name never pass your lips or mine."

The woman rose and groped blindly to her chair. She sat there with half-closed eyes, swaying herself to and fro, muttering now and then, "Oh, this pitiless storm!"

Outside, the figure tottered on.

Suddenly there was a cry borne upon the blast—a

wild, wailing human cry, rising high above the wind, piercing into the red house, piercing Moses Grant's firm, stony heart, as he sat before the fire. A weight seemed to fall helplessly against the outside door, and then there was silence.

The mother sprang up and mechanically threw open the door, and the snow tumbled in, and the wailing wind rushed in. What was it lying there, stiff and helpless, upon the stone step, lifting up, whiter than the snow, its ghastly human face? The old man sprang to his wife's side. He had overrated his own stoicism. He shook her arm, almost harshly.

"What are you thinking of, Mary?" he cried, passionately; "have you no mother's heart? will you let her die there before your eyes—our child, Margaret?"

He caught the prostrate figure in his arms—to his breast; he carried her in, to the warmth, the light, the father's house whence she had wandered; and then the cold, iron man wept over her like a helpless child; while the mother, fully herself now, worked with wild energy, collecting and applying restoratives, chafing the thin hands and the numb, half-frozen feet.

Her efforts were successful in so far that the girl, for she was not more than eighteen, opened her eyes and came back to life with a gasping shudder. She did not seem quite restored, however, to the full use of her faculties. She spoke by snatches, in a strange, wandering fashion.

"I thought I was dead," she said, "but I'm not. This is home, isn't it? and there's father! What do you cry so for, father? You never used to. I never saw you do so before. Oh! I know; you are crying about poor Margaret. You think, now, that she wasn't so bad, after all. You are glad she has come home."

"Margaret," broke in her mother's voice, "were you deceived? Did you think you were married to that man—that Gilbert Trumbull?"

It was pitiful to see such fierce passion in one so gentle as Margaret Grant, who, from childhood, had never known a thought save of loving submission to her parents' will, until that stronger love came and compelled her obedience in another direction. The blood mantled her pale cheek, and burned there in one round red spot. She rose up in the bed, and shrieked out, with her eyes gleaming, her frame trembling,

"You shall not, I say you shall not speak his name—you who hate him so. You shall not drive me into betraying his secret. Turn me out again into the storm, if you will. I can die there as well as here; but you shall not make me answer your questions."

"Hush, darling, darling, darling," murmured Mary Grant; the mother-love, the mother-tenderness, stronger than life, choking in her voice, thrilling in her touch, raining in tears from her eyes: "you shall not tell me if you do not wish to. Be satisfied. You shall never go out into the cold world again; you shall never suffer any more."

And Moses Grant wept on, the while, his proud, stony heart melted, for the time, quite into childishness; saying nothing, only looking now and then at the girl whom his anger had driven forth, and who had come back to him—alas! he knew it now, to die.

That night a babe was born in the red house in the

hollow. She came in the storm: was it a token of the life that awaited her? Outside were the snow, the darkness, the pitiless, wailing blast; within, only the girl, so young, so fair even in her ruin, and the two old people, tearless now and silent, keeping breathless watch over their one child.

The baby came into the world with a wail. Mary Grant brought forth from an old bureau, where they had lain for almost eighteen years, the tiny garments, soft and delicate in fabric, antique and simple in make, which her own fingers had fashioned, joyfully, hopefully, for her youngest-born, Margaret; and in them she robed Margaret's child.

But death was written on the young mother's brow, and the parents could not choose but read. She drew her little one to her arms, and, holding her on her bosom, she blessed her.

"She shall be called Elinor Trumbull, after the mother of her father." When she had said these words, in a firm, quiet tone of command, she seemed to sink in unconsciousness. After a time she roused herself with wild energy.

"Let no one defraud my child of her name," she cried out. "It is hers—she has a right to it. Father, mother, promise me that you will call her by this name—Elinor Trumbull?"

The two old people, with one consent, faltered the required promise, and then she said, in a humble tone,

"Before I die, forgive me, my parents. God knows I have loved you, in spite of all I have done to make you suffer. Tell me that you forgive me."

They forgave her without reproach or question. They blessed her with tender tears, and, sitting at her bed's head, they watched her as she sank again into a sort of drowse, still holding her babe on her breast. After that she never opened her eyes, but she murmured dreamily of green fields and fragrant blossoms, and the babblings of summer brooks, blent now and then with loving words or tender memories about her baby's father. Then all was very still, and they thought her sleeping; but somehow, I know not how, unseen and silently, from that calm her soul stole forth, and was translated to the great endless calm lying beyond. Margaret was dead!

For the next two days the storm raged with unabated violence. The snow, swept by the fierce wind from the mountain tops, was piled high in the valleys, and Moses Grant and his wife were all alone with their dead child and the living babe she had left them. In the interim much of his old sternness had come back to the elder's heart, the self-command and reticence to his outward life. I think he remembered his promise, that the little one should be called by the name of her father's family, with a kind of grim satisfaction in keeping with the silent pride of his character. The village where he lived was in the western part of Connecticut, under the shadows of the mountains, and Trumbull was an old and proud name in the far eastern portion. Gilbert Trumbull had won Margaret Grant's love during a shooting season among the hills, and, a few months after he left Mayfield, driven forth by her father's harshness and scorn, she had followed him. Trumbull was a name any woman might be proud to wear worthily, and Moses Grant was well resolved the world should never know, through him, that it did not legitimately belong to his infant grandchild.

For two days the elements did battle, but the third morning of Elinor Trumbull's life rose calm, and bright, and fair. Early in the day Moses Grant went forth to seek the pastor of the old Presbyterian church, in which he had been an elder for so many years, and arrange for his daughter's burial.

That afternoon, where the snow had been scooped away behind the church on the hill-top, they laid the elder's last child, beside her six brothers and sisters, in her narrow grave; and she, the youngest, the fairest, slept best, perhaps, of all, for the calm is most precious that comes after the wildest storms.

Very dear was she to the gray-haired pastor who had baptized her in infancy, and had always accounted her the gentlest and sweetest among the lambs of his flock—very dear to every heart among the many which beat around her grave that winter day. But they asked few questions concerning her death or her life. She had been the elder's favorite child, they all knew, but no one had ever heard him mention her name since the summer night when she went away from Mayfield—no one knew whether alone or in company. So they respected the old man's sorrow and silence.

It was not many months before over Margaret's grave there rose a simple head-stone, but no one's curiosity was gratified by the inscription. It only said,

MARGARET—AGED EIGHTEEN YEARS.

The child was duly christened. The country folk understood what an old and respectable name she bore; and at length the wonder died away, and she was left to grow up in the quiet stillness of the old red house.

Indeed, very few were brought into any near connection with her, for Moses Grant and his wife neither made nor received any visits now. Her only regular education was imparted by her grandparents, who taught her the three needfuls of an old-fashioned New England woman—to read, and write, and cipher. In addition, when she grew older, Parson Blake gave her a few books and a chance lesson now and then; and she learned early to form shrewd, self-reliant theories and opinions, which no one mistrusted, however, that she possessed.

Mary Grant often remarked that the little Elinor was her mother's own child. She had the same fair hair; the same clear blue eyes; the same slight figure; but beyond these was a difference rather to be felt than explained. About her mouth was a graver, more saint-like smile. A tenderer light shone in her blue eyes, and her voice did not ring out with quite such joyous music as made Margaret's tones in her early years such a cheery sound to hear. Elinor's were lower, quieter—she spoke more slowly, as if, even in childhood, to address others, she had to come out of an inner world where she oftenest dwelt—the world of thought and of dreams. Gentle, quiet child as she was, her name, her stately name, borne once by the proudest belle in Norwich, seemed not unsuited to the simple dignity of her nature.

Sunday after Sunday she sat by Moses Grant's side, in the old-fashioned Presbyterian church, bowing her graceful head through the long prayers, lifting up her clear voice to join in the well-known hymns. Sunday after Sunday—first as child, then as maiden; and the old pastor watched her lovingly—lovingly for her own sake—lovingly for the sake of a grave under the willow trees; and all the while, Sunday after Sunday, his own hair grew whiter and his step more feeble.

II.

Parson Blake was dead. His life, his kindly life, seventy summers and no winter, was ended. In the little church-yard on the hill-top they laid him gently and reverently to his long sleep—the little church-yard where he had faltered the last prayer over so many of his flock; where, sixteen years before, he had stood tearfully beside the bier of Margaret Grant.

Wife and children he had none. He had lived alone all his blameless life, and his people had been to him instead of kindred. Like his children they all mourned for him. Not a heart beat in Mayfield to which he was not dear—not an eye but was dim with tears at the pastor's burial. He had married the old folk, he had baptized their children, he had buried their dead, and now he was gone to receive the reward of his labors. More than forty years had he been in and out before them, and broken bread in their midst. Was it strange that his death left a great void, which never, thereafter, could be filled?

It was with saddened mien the elders met together to consult on the choice of his successor. No one could ever be to them in his stead, and perhaps it could hardly be expected of human nature that they should award due credit to the honest endeavors of a younger man. Thus Walter Fairfield came to them under a disadvantage. They were kind-hearted people naturally, but the new pastor must stand in a place which none but the dead could fill worthily to their minds; and, moreover, he was a young man, just fresh from his studies, not more than twenty-five.

On the first morning after his installation, Elder Moses Grant called Elinor to his side, and charged her to be ready in season for church—the young man wouldn't be Parson Blake, to be sure, but they must show his preaching due respect.

Elinor had grown, at sixteen, into a tall, graceful girl, promoted to a seat in the village choir now, and remarkable to all eyes but the accustomed ones of her grandparents for her rare beauty.

There had never been much outward demonstration of tenderness from Moses Grant to this girl, the child of shame, the seal of disgrace, as he sometimes called her in his accusing thoughts; and yet, almost unknown to himself, he did love her tenderly. Much of the love which had been Margaret's had come out of her grave and folded itself round her child, though in all her life the girl could never remember that he had kissed her or lifted her upon his knee.

One night his wife, alarmed for Elinor's health during the prevalence of an epidemic in the quiet town, had called him to look upon her while she slept. It was wonderful, the resemblance which she bore in her slumbers to her dead mother. Waking, the play of her features, the different expression of her eyes, was all her own; but sleeping, he could almost have thought Margaret was before him—Margaret, whom he loved more in death than in life, because he forgave her in dying.

Oh! how often the wave of death comes like a blessed baptismal, washing away all memories of wrong and strife—a new birth, making those born again into the world of spirits seem to us fair, and pure, and blameless as the infant just laid for the first time upon its mother's loving bosom.

Many times after that night Moses Grant, hard, stern man as he was, stole into his grandchild's room and watched her as she slept, thinking tender, softened thoughts of her dead young mother—always a girl, young and fair, in the old man's memory—and bitter, scornful, murderous thoughts, which, in a nature less restrained by rules of outward holiness, would have shaped themselves into curses on that Gilbert Trumbull, hated with an unforgiving, unresting hatred all these years.

It needs not to be told with what ceaseless, caressing tenderness Mary Grant loved her grandchild; and yet, woman-like, Elinor, dear as both were to her, loved most the old man, whose calm reserve seemed kindred with her own quiet, deep inherited nature. Going up the hill to church on this first morning of the new pastor's ministry, she walked by her grandfather's side, feeling with most tender sympathy the trial it would be to him to see a new face in the old pulpit.

When the hymn was sung that morning, Walter Fairfield, sitting back in his pulpit, screened by the high desk, leaning his head on his hands, was striving to compose his thoughts for his first sermon among his first parishioners.

He heard, as one in a dream, above and apart from all other tones, one clear, rich soprano voice, flooding the old-fashioned church with its melody. It strengthened him; bore up his soul to the very gates of heaven; and yet he scarcely knew, scarcely thought, whether the voice was mortal or angelic. He was contented to accept unquestioningly the help it brought. Elinor Trumbull little knew what influence her singing had on the sermon which followed.

It was such a discourse as had never before electrified the simple villagers of Mayfield—full of earnest thought, glowing with imagery, uttered with an eloquence to which they were strangers. To Elinor Trumbull it was a revelation. Full of sound religious truth though it was, its unwonted grace of diction carried her thoughts out—out from the quiet village among the mountains into the world where such polish must have been acquired—the gay, fascinating, far-off world, beaming upon her fancy in such wondrous hues. With her clear eyes fixed on the speaker, or now and then veiled modestly under their fringing lashes, unquiet, tumultuous thoughts were surging through her heart—thoughts of the wonders of nature and the wonders of art—brave men and beautiful women, and a full, strong existence, tasking all her capacities, quickening every pulse of her being, on which she longed to enter; going out from the peace, the quiet, the shadows of the mountains into the broad plain, where were bugles and trumpets calling strong souls onward to victory in the wonderful battle of life.

The young clergyman, absorbed in his subject, did not perceive her breathless interest—did not even consciously see her face, so remarkable among all others there for its patrician beauty; but yet he carried away with him that day a conception of loveliness more perfect than had ever dawned on him before—a sweet face which seemed to smile on him from the clouds, to meet him at every point of vision.

When the services were over, Walter Fairfield walked, like one overtasked and weary, quietly out of the church, and took the path leading through the field to his simple parsonage. A kindly, cordial smile was on his face, but he spoke to no one. The congregation allowed him to pass in respectful silence, not ill-pleased with the opportunity of discussing among themselves the wonderful sermon to which they had listened. Elinor Trumbull was faint and weak. The unwonted excitement had been too much for her delicate organization, and, telling her grandparents that she was not well, she stole quietly away and went home.

Moses Grant came from church in the afternoon, disposed to say but little of the young clergyman. He had spoken with him after church—he would visit them that week—it seemed that the Spirit of the Lord was with him, but they must wait and see.

It was Wednesday afternoon when Elinor Trumbull, busy among the stand of house-plants which were her chief winter amusement, saw, from the kitchen window, a figure coming down the hill. Her quick eye recognized at once the new minister, and her girlish heart thrilled with its first flutter of womanly vanity. Shyly she gathered from her monthly-rose-bush a bud just bursting into crimson bloom, and placed it in her bosom. Then, stealing to the little looking-glass, she smoothed down her already faultlessly smooth hair, hoping, with pretty womanly self-consciousness, that the two old people by the hearth would not notice her unusual anxiety about her appearance. Then she said, in her quiet, respectful voice,

"Hadn't I better light the fire in the parlor, grandfather? I see the new minister is coming down the hill."

The room which she entered, in accordance with her grandfather's "Certainly—make haste, child!" was simply, even humbly furnished, and yet there had been imparted to it an air of feminine grace and refinement during the last two years, since it had been Elinor's especial charge. Every thing was faultlessly neat. Snowy muslin curtains draped the windows; the arm-chairs were covered with crimson patch, and two corresponding footstools—Elinor's own workmanship—stood conveniently before them. A few books were strewn upon the table—Parson Blake's gift to Elinor—a Shakspeare, and the works of Pope and Milton, in handsome bindings. Not a speck of dust was visible, and yet Elinor, after lighting the fire, fidgeted nervously with her feather-brush from chair to table, and then, seized with a sudden impulse, sat down and appeared diligently engaged in reading.

That was an afternoon of new and exquisite delight in the girl's quiet life. Walter Fairfield possessed the rare gift of clothing lofty thoughts in simple words, and making himself alike agreeable to old and young. To him also came, that winter day, a new revelation. He recognized in Elinor's musical voice the clear tones which had strengthened him for his Sabbath duties—in her young, innocent face the vision he had carried away from church on the Sabbath morning as a new and superior type of loveliness. He had seen beautiful women before, arrayed in the manifold charms of style and fashion, but beside the unconscious grace of Elinor Trumbull they seemed to him like flaunting peonies contrasted with the fresh rose-bud she wore in her bosom.

There was something dearer in Elinor's beauty than the untroubled azure of her eyes, the golden flow of her hair, the clear tints of her complexion—a soul looking forth from the young wistful face, womanly, pure, strong, and true.

And she, with her imaginative, dreamy nature, her haunting visions of a perfect life, a refined and extended culture shut out from her reach by mountains of circumstances and destiny, listened to the new-comer's voice, making music through all the avenues of her being, and was content.

That night, when the supper was over—the supper prefaced by a blessing, the first one spoken in that house by Walter Fairfield, and whose prophecy to that household of good or ill only the after years could unseal—the simple supper which Elinor had made beautiful by the exquisite neatness and delicacy of her arrangement—when it was over, and the new minister had taken his departure, the elder sat alone in the best room, absorbed in thought; while his wife and her granddaughter were busy in the kitchen, clearing away the fragments and washing up the painted china.

Moses Grant was growing old. His hair was very white; and trouble, more than years, had dug deep furrows in his stern face. The habit was growing on him, as it does on so many old men, of talking to himself. As he sat there, leaning his head back in his chair, and looking thoughtfully into the fire, he murmured,

"Well, after all, the young man does seem full of the Spirit of the Lord. Yes, I really think the Lord is with him. But he can never be what Parson Blake was to Mary and me. He didn't marry us; he didn't bury our seven children; he didn't know and love Margaret. We are too old now for him to care for us —too old to make new ties—and yet, there's Elinor. The child needs a pastor's care. He will take an interest in her. I believe he does already: she's a good child. Through her, he may get attached to us—who knows? It's a blessed thing when folk can love their minister, and be loved back again, as in Parson Blake's time. And then this young man will be getting married one of these days. He'll be sure to marry a good woman, and she'll be a nice friend for Elinor when Mary and I are laid in the church-yard, with our seven children gone before. Yes, they'll be good friends for the child, and she'll need them then. Elinor!" he called, in a louder tone, and the girl came into the old parlor, and sat down on a stool in the firelight.

"I like this young man, Elinor. He isn't Parson Blake, to be sure; but I think he has the Spirit of God in his heart, and there's no reason why you shouldn't like him as well as another. You have not the memories of so many years to bind you to the dead. He told me this afternoon that he should start a Bible-class, and I want you to join it, and see if you can't keep up your reputation as Parson Blake's best scholar."

"Very well, grandpa;" and then the girl sat there in the silence, while her fancy made glowing pictures in the embers, out of which looked the dark, kindly eyes of the new minister. That she could ever be any thing to him never entered her dreams; she only hoped that, ignorant girl as she was, she might find such favor in his eyes that he would impart to her some of his wonderful knowledge; lend her books, perhaps, and now and then condescend to talk to her.

The next Sunday she joined his Bible-class; and that day, and for many quiet Sabbath-days thereafter, the clear tones of her singing renewed his strength, and carried his soul heavenward; and the approving light of her expressive eyes, never by any chance turned away from their steady gaze, filled him with calm, and yet not always calm, delight.

III.

The slow, reluctant feet of the New England spring came over the mountains. Her blue eyes shone over hill and meadow-land through many tears, and in her footprints sprang up crocuses and violets, to live their little day, and die their balmy death. The plowman turned up the rich, loamy soil of the valleys, whistling at his task. The larch hung forth her fragrant blossoms, the laburnum dropped her long sprays of gold. The old lilac-bushes, planted in Moses Grant's front yard when Margaret was a baby, put on once more their liveries of green, and coquettishly tossed up their purple blossoms, that the winds might rifle their perfume.

Walter Fairfield came very often, in these days, to the elder's house. He had undertaken to teach Elinor botany, and the study involved long, delightful walks over the hills. The old folks were well content that their grandchild should acquire a little of the learning they held in sincere reverence, but which they would never have sent her out into the world to obtain. She seemed to them so mere a child still, that they never thought of the danger that she might learn another lesson—that while she analyzed the blossoms that skirted hillside and brookside her own heart might be unfolding itself, petal by petal, even to the golden centre, whereon was written "love."

And Elinor was, like them, blissfully unconscious. She had never read a novel in her life. No one had ever talked to her of love or marriage. How should she, at sixteen, be able to translate aright the story which Walter Fairfield delighted to read in her blushes, her downcast eyes, to hear in her tremulous tones which replied to his questionings?

He was an honorable man, and he loved her with an honorable man's deathless love—a *man's* love, full of passion, stronger than life, and yet he shrank from telling her so—from awaking her heart from its maidenly repose—changing sweet hope into certainty—binding her by vows of betrothal.

The time when he could keep silence no longer came to him, as it does to most men, unexpectedly. They had been taking a long walk. The sun had scarcely set, but a young June moon was drifting, like a tiny, glittering cloud, up the blue sky, and they stood watching it together. At last Elinor turned her wet face toward him. He had never seen tears in her eyes before.

"I have been thinking," she said, "how lonely my life used to be before you came. What mysterious fancies, which I had none to explain, haunted me at twilight and moonrise, and how your coming changed all; and you found time to talk with me, and understand all my thoughts; and then, how this, too, must end some day, and you will be busy with other happiness, and I shall be all alone."

Then the words—the wild, loving, yet reverent words—gushed in a tide from his full heart, and overflowed his lips. The story was told—the old, ever-new story—old as our first parents, new as a new day. They loved one another. The veil was lifted from Elinor's heart, and she knew that, with all the quiet strength of her quiet nature, she loved Walter Fairfield. She was silent from very happiness.

As her lover drew her close to his side, and pressed his first kiss on her pure lips, he said, fervently,

"Elinor, you are all I ever asked—good, gifted, beautiful. You fulfill my every want. God in heaven bless you—the crown, the glory of my life, whom He has given me."

IV.

The next morning Elinor was with her grandparents in the little summer parlor. When the elder had read a chapter in the Bible, as was his wont, and finished his accustomed prayer, she said, timidly,

"Dear grandpa, I would like to speak to you a moment."

She had settled it with her lover that she should be the first to communicate to the grave old man the news of her betrothal. This was her own desire. She had thought it would be best so. She feared nothing more than that he might object to her extreme youth, and she hoped much from the strong esteem in which she knew he held their young minister.

Falteringly she told her story, and the old man listened in silence.

He did not answer her for some moments, but he was evidently deeply moved. Elinor was frightened at the convulsive workings of his face, and the tears that coursed like rain down her grandmother's withered cheeks. At length he spoke.

"God forgive me, I have done great wrong. I never thought of this. You were so young. Elinor, you can not marry this man. No, not to save your own life. Do you hear? I forbid it. It *shall not* be."

Elinor rose and stood before him. She was not Margaret's child merely—the old Trumbull blood fired her glance. Her face was as resolute, her tone as firm as Moses Grant's own.

"Grandfather," she said, "I love Walter Fairfield—he loves me. We are more than life to each other, and this question *shall not* be decided so. If you will separate us, I must know the reason, or, God helping me, I will go and pray him on my bended knees to take me away from you and make me his wife."

There was no pity in the elder's face now for the young creature who had dared to resist his decree, to rise up in the might of her love and oppose him. His face grew livid with rage.

"You must know my secret, then, young madam," he said, in the fierce tones of passion. "Well, mark it: you have no right even to the name you bear. Your mother, my child though she was, was not your father's wife. Don't you think Walter Fairfield, a minister of the Gospel, would be proud to marry you in disgrace?"

But the last taunting question fell on ears that could

not listen. With every faculty intensely aroused, she had heard the fatal truth, scorching her for the first time with its blight, and then she heard no more. Gradually she had sunk lower and lower at the old man's feet, until now she lay upon the floor, her white, death-like face cold as her young mother's under the June roses.

"Go into the kitchen, father," said Mary Grant, "for it'll throw her back again into her swoon to see you when she comes to."

The elder obeyed, and then his wife quietly busied herself in bringing back consciousness to Elinor. It was no very difficult task. The girl was young, and even so great a shock could not overcome her utterly. In a few moments she was able to sit down in an easy-chair by the open window, and the balmy air of the summer morning stole over her senses like a new life-draught.

Her face was very white and rigid still, and Mary Grant put back her soft hair and looked pityingly into her troubled eyes.

"Oh, my darling!" she murmured, "my poor darling! to think that your first sorrow should darken all your life!" But the voice was calm that answered her.

"It will not darken it, grandmother. I have full faith in Walter. He loves me, and he will not give me up, even because of this great shame. I shall tell him all, and I know he will marry me."

"God grant it, darling!" and the old woman dropped on the white, earnest face a very tender kiss. "You sit quietly here. I want to go and speak to your grandfather."

Moses Grant was sitting, though it was June, by the fireside, in the very spot where he had sat before, one memorable night. Absorbed in surging, bitter, tumultuous thought, he was indifferent to heat or cold, or any outward surrounding whatsoever. His wife went up to him; she knelt down by his side; she clasped her hands across his knee, and then she plead with him even as she had plead with him on a wild, wet night, more than sixteen years before—the night on which, amid storm and tempest, and the wail of restless winds, Elinor Trumbull's dawn of life was ushered in.

"Oh, father," she said, "she is all we have left. We are old now, and she is young; do not break her heart."

"Woman," said the elder's stern tones, "tempt me not. The minister shall not be deceived. I will not do this great sin against God."

"But you can let her tell him. She says he loves her, and she knows he will marry her, in spite of all. Let her tell him: only leave her this one hope."

Then the elder's wrath rose to a white heat.

"Yes, I have no doubt you would approve of that. Her mother did not shame me enough; you would bring another into this secret. Elinor!" he cried, with raised tones, and forth from the inner room the young girl tottered. Moses Grant's face was terrible to look upon in his rage, but Elinor confronted him calmly, though she was obliged to cling to the table for support.

"I have told you all; what do you propose to do now?" he asked, in tones of forced composure.

"There is but one thing, grandfather. I should feel

this disgrace more bitterly if Walter's love had not made me strong to bear any thing. I will tell him what you have told me. I would not deceive him any more than you would; but I will tell him all, and he will but love me the better because I need his pity. Oh, you don't know Walter. He has such a great heart. He will not care for the world. He fears nothing but sin. He will make me his wife."

The old man was silent for a moment. The girl's face beamed like one inspired. It awed him, it was so full of deathless, triumphant love and faith. But this emotion passed, and his tone, when he answered her, was firm as ever.

"Elinor, you shall not tell him this secret. I, your grandfather, forbid it. He himself would be the first one to say it was your duty to obey me. If you tell him, I will curse you; do you hear me? curse you with a curse that shall cling to you all your life. You shall *not* tell him. I bear a humble name, but an honorable one. Only this one shadow of disgrace has fallen on it. As God hears me, you shall not spread the shameful secret. Tell your lover that you can not marry him—that *I* forbid it. If he wants to know why, he can come to me."

Elinor had heard this outburst silently, growing stronger, as it seemed, under every stern, cruel word which fell on her ear, slaying her lifetime hope, blotting all the brightness out of her existence. When the last word, swift, crushing, remorseless, had died on his lips, she answered in such tones as he had never dreamed she could utter, so cold were they, so passionless.

"Give yourself no trouble, grandfather: I shall

obey you. I will not incur your curse, still less will I deceive Walter. Thank God, the time comes when you and I will go before Him together, and the wrongs of earth shall be righted by the immaculate justice of Heaven."

Mary Grant would fain have soothed her, but she seemed sufficient unto herself. Calmly she walked into the parlor and took her seat by the open window, where she could watch the road leading down the hill.

Soon she saw him coming—the young lover who could remain away from his betrothed no longer. Joyously he walked, with quick step and erect head. Hope was holding a cup to his lips beaded to the brim with bubbling drops of joy. She must dash it from them—she who loved him best, whom he best loved. She clasped her hands over her eyes, and prayed—a short, silent prayer which Heaven would answer. She heard his step upon the door-stone. He opened the little front door without knocking. He came to her side. He drew her close, close, as one who had a right to hold her on his heart forever, and she was silent: she could not break the spell.

At last she started from his arms—she stood before him with her white face and gleaming eyes.

"Walter!" she cried, eagerly, "you know I love you. You never can doubt that. I am very young; I have had no other fancies, no other dreams. You won all my heart. Hear me, Walter! I am yours—I will be yours till I die. Never shall any other man speak words of love to Elinor Trumbull. I give you all. I am yours—yours—yours—on earth and in heaven. But I can not be your wife. My grandfather has forbidden it. You yourself will counsel me to obedience. It is harder for me than for you. You have the great world to flee to—your high calling to follow. I must stay here—here, where light, and hope, and love came to my life—where they will go out, and leave me alone in the darkness. God forgive me, Walter, but death were better."

She had spoken with wild energy. She sank back exhausted now in her chair. Walter Fairfield stood struck dumb for the moment with sheer wonder. At length he faltered,

"You can not mean it; you do not know what you are saying, Elinor. Your grandfather may object to our marrying while you are still so young, but he can not mean that you must never be my wife."

The door had been open all this time between the parlor and the kitchen, and now Moses Grant himself came forward. The anger had passed away from his face, leaving a look of pity blent with stern resolve. He said gravely,

"I like you, Mr. Fairfield. I had not thought any one else could so fill Parson Blake's place in my love as you have filled it. If I could, Heaven knows I would gladly give you this girl, but it can not be. In all truthfulness, you must not marry her—you must never marry her. I, her grandfather, forbid it before the God whose servant you are. You will not dare to disobey me. It will go hard with you both; but if you knew the reason, you would *thank* me. It is my fault. I should not have put you in each other's way; but I thought she was only a child."

"Elder Grant," the young man said, respectfully, "will you come out of doors with me? I would like to speak to you for a few moments quite alone."

The particulars of that interview were never known, but the result was decisive. In a little while the young man came alone into the room where Elinor still sat by the open window. He closed the door. He went up to her and took her, for the last time, in his arms.

"The hand of God is in it, Elinor, as it is in every earthly thing, though we can not see it now. We must submit. Thank God, my beloved, that after life comes death, and after death heaven. And yet, how can I give you up, my poor, innocent darling—my one love?" And his voice broke down into low, agonized sobs—a strong man's sobs, very pitiful to hear.

That last half hour of love, and torture, and despair—that parting which they both felt was eternal—I may not dwell on it. When Walter Fairfield passed out of the wicket gate and walked up the hill along the winding road, Elinor Trumbull watched him with eyes in which there were no tears, with a pale face on which shone a hope purer than earthly love, holier than earthly happiness—a hope born in tears, in anguish, in desolation—of a meeting where all that remains of sorrow is the wings by which it has borne the soul upward—in the city without foundation, eternal in the heavens.

They parted on Saturday, and the next day more than one strong heart in Mayfield was moved to tears as the young minister read his mysterious, unexplained resignation of the pastoral charge. He had become strangely dear to them, this young man, whose coming had seemed such a doubtful experiment. He was not their father in the Lord as Parson Blake had been, but they cherished him equally in another way. He was their very own. He had come to them first. They were to him almost like a first love, the parish in whose service he had been first installed into the ministry. They had hoped he would live and die among them, and now they must give him up. There was scarcely a dry eye among the many which rested upon his face this last Sunday. Moses Grant sat, with sorrowful yet composed mien, in his accustomed seat, with his quiet old wife by his side, but Elinor's voice did not flood the church with its melody; Walter Fairfield preached his last sermon in Mayfield without the silent encouragement of her eyes.

The next morning, when he rode by the red house in the hollow on his way to take the stage at Cornwall, he gazed in vain at the windows. No small hand fluttered among the roses, no gentle face looked out from between the muslin curtains. It cost him much then not to spring from the wagon and seek one last farewell, one more blessing; but, for her sake, he rode on and made no sign.

And where was Elinor? Looking forth, herself unseen, from her chamber window, straining her eyes to catch one last glimpse of his too dear face, praying for him in her self-abnegation, praying that his life might be very full of joy, though over her own, with all the promised hopes of its future, rose, like the lettering on a monument, the one sorrowful inscription —"Never more."

V.

There came a new minister to Mayfield, a worthy man, who dwelt quietly in the parsonage with his wife and his six children. He had not old Parson Blake's place in their hearts, consecrated by the memories of a lifetime, nor had they pride in his eloquence and tenderness for his youth and enthusiasm, as during Walter Fairfield's brief sojourn among them; still there was mutual good feeling between pastor and people, and, save in one quiet household, all things went on as before.

This autumn and the winter which followed were a very trying time to Elinor Trumbull. She had a strong consciousness of duty. Earnestly she strove to be in all things the same to her grandparents as before her brief, bright dream of love; but something was wanting. The fullness of the old content would never come back again. For the second time in the red house in the hollow was a buried name. Walter Fairfield was never mentioned there. Mary Grant had once commenced to say a few words of comfort to her granddaughter, but the expression on Elinor's face stopped her — it was so full of hopeless suffering. After that she only silently pitied the sorrow she had no power to soothe.

Elinor never uttered a single complaint. She performed all the little housewifely duties which had formerly fallen to her share: she went regularly to the church on the hill-top—listened quietly to the new pastor's preaching. But Mary Grant's tears fell as she saw her silently taking in the few dresses which composed her simple wardrobe, that they might better fit the figure growing so very fragile and thin now. Her step lost its accustomed lightness; her voice never rang through the house with its old, gay melody. When her seventeenth birth-day was ushered in on the wings of storm and tempest, it found her no longer a girl, but a woman, prematurely grave, and thoughtful, and silent. The delicate summer bloom was gone from the blossom, the subtle fragrance vanished, and there was but a poor consolation in thinking life's autumn might ripen it into fruit.

One day Mary Grant called her husband's attention, when they were alone, to Elinor's languid step and wasting cheek. An expression of sudden pain crossed the elder's face for the moment—a look as if conscience were forcing upon him an unwelcome truth, and then he answered, with easy self-delusion,

"It's not strange. It's a hard winter. The girl will be herself again when the spring opens."

And so the months passed on, and once more the slow, reluctant feet of the New England spring stole over the mountains, and the crocus and the violet started up in her footprints. Once more the brooks, set free from their winter chains, began to babble—the plow-boy whistled at his task—the birch hung out her tassels, and the lilacs in Elder Grant's yard burst into purple bloom; but this time there were no long, pleasant walks over the hills. She had no strength for them—that pale, silent girl, whom the spring had surprised as she sat nursing her sorrow.

As the days grew longer and brighter, the blue sky overhead more intensely clear and blue, Mary Grant, watching her grandchild, could see her fade. Each day she seemed to move more feebly about the house, until at last she seldom moved any more, but lay all day on a lounge, which, perhaps, with a secret care for her comfort, the elder had bought at an auction sale. She did not seem unhappy, for the one hope, mightier than earthly love, stronger than earthly grief, was gently guiding her tired feet—so early tired with the crooked paths of life—toward the "distant hills" of heaven. And Moses Grant saw it at last; the great fear struck to his heart that his pride would have a second victim—that another young, fair face would lie beneath the drifting leaves of this year's autumn. Did not conscience speak to him then?

He came home one day with a strange look on his face. He held in his hand a large, business-like epistle. He beckoned his wife into the kitchen. She left Elinor lying upon the lounge in the best room, and closed the door after her.

"What is it, father?" she said, in pitying tones, going to her husband's side. "Has some great trouble come over us?"

"The hand of the Lord is laid upon me, Mary. I am punished for my sin. I killed Margaret, I have wellnigh killed her child, and yet, listen, wife, Margaret was true—Margaret was pure."

"Oh, thank God! thank God!" burst involuntarily from the mother's lips as she sank upon her knees. The vail of her life's greatest sorrow was rent away, and she seemed to see her child, her last child, her pure, innocent, blessed child, as she named her in her heart, waiting for her in heaven. But her cry of thanksgiving fell on unheeding ears.

Moses Grant spoke earnestly:

"Yes, Mary, God has suffered this knowledge to come to me in the eleventh hour, just to show me that I, who dared to call myself His servant, have been but a hard, unmerciful tyrant, after all; fearing earthly disgrace more than I feared him. Oh, Mary, is it too late to save our child?"

"God grant it may be in time," Mary Grant faltered; "but tell me how the knowledge came to you. Are you sure of its truth?"

"Look there! see with your own eyes Margaret's marriage certificate; and listen! I will read you this letter which I have received from Gilbert Trumbull. It seems his lawyer wrote it for him when he was dying. It says:

"'MR. GRANT,—I have not been a good man. I feel this now, lying here on my death-bed, and I confess it to you the more readily because I do not believe that at heart you are a one whit better one. I must speak plainly and bluntly, for I have no time for circumlocution. I have hardly strength enough left to dictate this to Richard Huntley, my attorney. I have made a brave effort to forgive every body; but it has been the hardest of all to forgive you; for your harshness, your sinful pride, killed my beautiful Margaret. You never loved as I loved her—I, her lover, her husband. There! you will start at that word, I foresee; you will start again at the marriage certificate enfolded in this letter. We were married secretly, as you will perceive, while I was in your very neighborhood. I bound Margaret, when I left her, by a solemn oath, not to make it known until she had my permission.

She was a gentle creature, as no one knows better than you, and never thought of disputing the will of any one she loved. My father was dead. I was dependent for all my hopes of future fortune and support on my mother, a very proud, resolute woman. She had a grand match in contemplation for me at that time. I knew it would be no easy matter to reconcile her to its failure, and if she should know just then that I had married as she would have thought so far below me, much as she loved me she would have cast me off forever. This, to a true man, would have been no great matter compared with causing Margaret one hour of trouble, one agony of humiliation. But I was not a true man. I was helpless and imbecile, for I had never been brought up to depend on myself. But I must hasten, for my strength is failing me.

"'I kept Margaret advised, through a friend, of all my movements, and when you crushed her with the weight of your scorn and contumely, she fled to me. I welcomed her. God knows I did, for I loved her! I took care of her in secret, and I should have made her happy had not your displeasure haunted her. Toward the last I was obliged to leave her for a few weeks. In that time she fled—fled because she was dying of a wild longing to throw herself at your feet and beg your forgiveness. She told me this in a note she left for me. It was full of love, stained with her tears, blotted with her kisses. In it she said she would not, in any extremity, betray our marriage until she had my permission. She must have walked nearly all the way to you, since, thinking all her needs were provided for, I had left her but a few dollars.

"'You know the rest. I have a friend in your

neighborhood who has kept me informed of all that concerned Margaret and her child. God in heaven knows how sincerely I mourned her. Had she lived, I should have acknowledged her as my wife. The child would have been brought up as Elinor Trumbull's namesake should have been; but, since Margaret was dead, I preferred to leave her baby to you. I had never seen the little one. It was not natural I should have any very strong love for her, and to give her up saved me a great deal of embarrassment. My mother died without knowing that I had ever been married, and I inherited her fortune. It will all be the child's. I leave her that and my name as the best amends I can make for the neglect of my lifetime.

"'Believe that I loved Margaret by this token: I have been faithful to her memory—I have lived alone all my days since I lost her.

"'After I am dead, Richard Huntley will send you this letter, along with a copy of my will, and a miniature I had painted of Margaret and myself by stealth, while she was with me. The child may like it. I suppose I am not good enough for my blessing to avail her much; but she has it, that young girl whom I have never seen—Margaret's child and mine. I die in peace with all men, even you. GILBERT TRUMBULL.'

"There are a few lines more in the lawyer's hand, to say that he died twenty-four hours after that letter was dictated; and the will is inclosed, by which Elinor falls heir to fifty thousand dollars."

"But how he insulted you. I can not bear that!" exclaimed the wife, her first wifely thought a jealous one of her husband's honor.

"Nay, Mary, he but spoke the truth. I have been a self-deceiver. The judgment of the Lord is visiting me now, and I see my sin. I killed her—he said truly—oh, Margaret—my child Margaret!"

"I want to see it, husband—the picture."

"Well, here, only don't show it to me. I don't want to see *her* eyes—poor Margaret."

The mother took it from his hand and looked at it in silence. It was Margaret, in her youth, her love, her beauty, only there was an unwonted shade of sadness in the clear eyes and about the flexible mouth. Beside her face Gilbert Trumbull's was painted—handsome, fascinating, brilliant—the face in which Margaret's eyes had seen heaven. Mary Grant looked at the two steadily for a few moments through her tears, and then, without saying a word, holding the picture still in her hand, she went in to Elinor.

"My child," she said, in faltering tones, "would you like to see your mother's picture?"

A hot flush rose to the girl's cheek, but she stretched out her hand for the miniature.

"That is your father, too, darling. Nay, Elinor, you needn't blush so to look on them; for, see this, child—here is something worth more to you than all the gold that comes with it, your mother's marriage certificate."

Elinor Trumbull clasped the paper with convulsive energy. She looked at it with eager gaze, reading it over and over again. Then it dropped from her nerveless fingers, her eyes shut together, and her stricken heart, for the first time, uttered the wail of its anguish.

"Oh, Walter, Walter!" was the low cry which rung helplessly through the room. Mary Grant knelt beside her, and folded her motherly arms around her. She was not repulsed. She drew that young head to her old, loving bosom, and Elinor wept there, at last, like a grieved child.

"Oh!" she murmured, after a time, "I might have married him—I should not have disgraced him, after all. What was it you said about gold, grandmother?"

"You have inherited fifty thousand dollars, dear child. Your father's will came with his letter and these things I have shown you."

"His letter! my father's letter! Why don't you give it to me?"

Mary Grant put the girl from her, and laid her tenderly back on the lounge. Then she went out, closing the door behind her.

"Father," she said, "Elinor wants to see that letter. I think she has a right to."

"Yes, Mary, take it. Her seeing it can not make my shame any greater. Leave me alone for a while; I am trying to see my way clear."

And so Mary Grant carried Gilbert Trumbull's letter in to his child. The girl read it, pausing tenderly over the passages where her father wrote of his love for her young mother, pressing the sheet to her lips where he invoked his blessing—a dying man's blessing—upon her. Then, folding it up, she put it in her bosom, and sank back again upon her pillow.

"You are very tired, darling," said her grandmother's gentle voice.

"Yes, very—but oh! so thankful. It is such a blessing that this knowledge came to me before I died, that I might reverence my dead mother's memory as much as I had always loved it."

"Before you die! Oh, Elinor, you must not say that; you will break my heart."

This was the first time any allusion had been made between them to the slow decay of Elinor's powers. Mary Grant had trembled long before the phantom of this very fear, but every nerve quivered when it took to itself a voice and stood unmasked before her. Elinor saw it, and soothingly laid her hand—alas! so very thin and white now—on the withered one of the old woman.

"Yes, dear grandmother, we may as well meet it bravely. I have known it a long time; but, thank God, I shall die happy now. You will explain all this mystery to Walter, and he will know I am worthy of his loving. He will be mine in heaven."

There were a few moments of solemn silence, and then Mary Grant murmured, falteringly,

"Elinor, will you, can you forgive your grandfather?"

"As I hope God will forgive me. His punishment will be heavy enough at the best. His sinful pride will soon lay a second victim beside my poor mother, and, seeing this, he will repent in dust and ashes. God forbid that a word or look of mine should add one pang to his self-reproach."

While these words were trembling on her lips, the door opened, and the old man came in, with his humbled, heart-stricken face, and his bowed head. He came up to her, and, for the first time in all his life, Moses Grant knelt by a woman's side.

"Elinor, child," he cried out, beseechingly, lifting up his withered, trembling hands, "God has shown me my crime as it is; can you, whom I have wronged, forgive me?"

"Fully, freely, and love you also, as your last child should."

He drew her close to him. He held her in his arms, as he had never done before, even in the days of her innocent babyhood. He murmured blessings over her —tender, caressing words, such as no one could have thought his stern lips would ever utter—and when he lifted up his head, Elinor's cheek was wet with tears which were not her own.

"I will go now and write to Walter," he said, in more hopeful tones.

The young girl turned her face toward the wall, to hide the anguish which convulsed her slight frame when the beloved name was uttered.

"It is of no use, now," she said, sadly; "we do not know where he is, and if we did, it is all too late."

"Oh, Elinor, you must not say that. God will not chasten me so heavily. It is not too late. It shall not be too late. You shall see him."

VI.

The letter which the elder wrote that afternoon told Walter Fairfield the whole story—the fearful wrong —the penitence which would fain make feeble restitution by confession. He laid bare in it his stricken, humbled heart.

No one at Mayfield knew Walter Fairfield's present location. There was but one hope of the letter's reaching him. The elder directed it, on the outside, to the care of the Principal of the Theological Seminary where the young man had been fitted for the ministry.

Then he sent it forth with wild, anguished prayers that God would speed it—that it might find him—might be in time to save the young life trembling in the balance.

That night, when Mary Grant told her granddaughter that the letter had been sent, and in what wise it had been directed, a longing hope took possession of Elinor that it would reach him, would bring him there before she died—that she might look once more into his loving eyes—that his voice, none but his, might murmur the last prayer over her grave. During the weeks that followed, this hope never left her, and, though unconsciously to herself, it seemed to be leading her feet backward a little from the brink of the dark river over whose waters she had thought so soon to journey to the country of everlasting life lying beyond.

Her step grew a little less weary and feeble. She lay less frequently, as days passed on, upon the lounge, and sat oftener in the arm-chair by the window, where she could watch the road winding down the hill. It had been four weeks since the receipt of her father's letter, and now it was midsummer. The little village among the mountains was gay with blossoms and verdure—vocal with bird-songs—sweet with the incense of summer flowers. How pleasantly the world looked to Elinor, sitting by the window; the world, which she thought so soon to leave, brightened now with the radiance of sunset. The landscape seemed, as she sat there, so calm and peaceful, with not a living thing to mar the perfectness of its repose.

But the quiet is broken now. A rider comes dashing down the hill, fast, fast, fast. It seemed dangerous. Elinor is very weak; she dares not look at him. She closes her eyes, and lays her head back against the chair, but she listens—she can not help that. The rider rides swiftly on. He has stopped now in front of the house. He opens the little wicket gate. He comes up the walk—into the door. Courage! trembling heart. Open your eyes, Elinor Trumbull. He springs to her side—he folds her close in his arms, calling her his poor little sorrow-stricken darling, his pride, his wife, his best-loved Elinor; thanking God that he can hold her now as he had never hoped to hold her again on earth.

Weak as Elinor was, she did not faint. There was power in that voice to rouse, instead, every faculty into its fullest life. Strength seemed to flow out from him into her own exhausted being. She clung to him in silent rapture.

When the passionate joy of meeting had grown calmer, Walter Fairfield told his story. The summons, he said, came to him in the far West. After leaving Mayfield he had gone there, and striven to absorb himself in the arduous duties of a missionary preacher. He had worked night and day: it was his only consolation. On his return from a three days' tramp in the woods he had found the elder's letter. At its first reading his heart had swelled with wrath. A Cain among all other men he had felt Moses Grant would be to him henceforth. His soul rebelled against the sinful, worldly pride which had sacrificed the whole life of two who loved one another to a selfish, cowardly fear of disgrace. Then he read it again, and the heartbroken tone of sincere penitence, of despairing, self-despising humility which pervaded it, moved him to pity; and then all thought of Moses Grant was lost in one agonizing fear lest he should not be in time to see his Elinor alive. He had traveled night and day. He was with her now, and she lived still—she *would* live. God would grant her life to his prayers. His love should call her back—she should be his own yet—his wife.

He was no professed worker of miracles, and yet, as she listened to his words, the crimson tint stole back into the fair cheek of his betrothed, and she seemed to feel a sense of returning strength, a faith in the reality of his prediction.

Moses Grant met the young minister with outward calmness. In his letter he had poured forth his remorse, his sorrow, his penitence. Neither of them ever alluded to it afterward. Only in the hand-clasp between them—full on the one side of timid self-abasement, on the other of pity, forgiveness, encouragement—there was a silent reconciliation. Mary Grant sobbed out her welcome with murmured blessings, and choking pauses, and many tears, and that night the four knelt together in *peace* before the throne of Him who looks on human weakness with the eyes of heavenly pity.

Elinor's health improved rapidly. Before the summer roses under the parlor window had faded, she twined from them a wreath for her bridal, and another garland, which she hung in the pleasant August morning—a daughter's reverent farewell—over the low head-stone which marked her mother's grave. She went there leaning upon her husband's arm, and, lifting to him her relying eyes, she murmured,

"I wonder if *she* knows, up in heaven, how happy her daughter is this hour?"

C

The farewell between the old people and their children was full of tender peace and love, and the elder and his wife stood together at the wicket gate, watching them with moist eyes as they rode up the hill. Moses Grant was not too proud to weep now.

The next Sunday, after the sermon was over, the congregation was requested to wait, and there, before them all, an old man, bowing his gray head in shame and sorrow, laid down his eldership in the Mayfield church, and bewailed the sin which made him unworthy, in his own eyes, to wear it longer. A very old book saith, "Whoso humbleth himself shall be exalted," and perchance that seemed to angel eyes the hour most worthy of pride of all Moses Grant's earthly life.

Walter Fairfield spent that winter at the South with his young wife; but cheerful letters came now and then, telling the old people of Elinor's renewed health and strength, and promising to bring her back blooming and happy.

In the early spring Parson Stevens received an unexpected call to a larger salary and wider sphere of usefulness, procured, some said, through Mr. Fairfield's influence. Accepting it, he went away with his wife and his six children. Walter Fairfield came back in good time to take his place. Elinor's fortune would more than satisfy all their wants, and they chose to settle down with the people of his first love—to live and die among them.

To Elinor no other spot could be half so dear as the quiet village among the mountains, where, for her, the star had risen which rises but once—the star of love, whose light was to bless all her happy life on earth, and sparkle still in the golden crown the angels were keeping for her in the Beyond.

And so, after all its pride, and pain, and passion, rest came at last to Moses Grant's life. The old man and his old wife live quietly still in the shadow of the mountains, in whose shadow they were born; and by-and-by, when their willing feet have drawn nigh to the fathomless river, kind hands will lay them gently down to their last sleep, beside Margaret's grave, in the little church-yard on the hill-top.

How One Woman came to Marry.

Love me, sweet, with all thou art,
   Feeling, thinking, seeing,
Love me in the lightest part,
   Love me in full being.

Love me with thine open youth,
   In its frank surrender;
With the vowing of thy mouth,
   With its silence tender.

Through all hopes that keep us brave,
   Farther off or nigher,
Love me for the house and grave,
   And for something higher.

Thus, if thou wilt prove me, dear,
   Woman's love no fable,
I will love *thee*—half a year—
   As a *man* is able.

ELIZABETH BARRETT BROWNING.

HOW ONE WOMAN CAME TO MARRY.

THE early summer morning is rising clear and bright, but chill, and yet, before these pages meet the reader's eye, over all will lie the midsummer pomp, and flush, and pride. I can think of no fitter emblem for one I knew in other days than this reluctant summer, cold, and still, and coy at first, only to burst forth, by-and-by, into more wonderful and tropical luxuriance of bloom.

In Hortense Greenwich there was, from her very childhood, though few knew it then, very much of pride, but never any littleness of vanity. She had been born to an assured position in society, for she was the only child of wealthy parents, moving in the upper circles of New York. Her mother, still young and very beautiful at the birth of this one child, was a woman of fashion. Dinner parties, balls, and morning visits filled up her life, so that she had no time to become acquainted with her daughter. She gave the little one a French governess, and left her to grow up as best she could. Even the governess had a lover in America, besides an extensive correspondence with certain old friends in *la belle France*, and, in her turn, neglected her duties.

Perhaps, however, this very neglect developed the child's soul more healthfully than a greater amount of attention from those two sources would have done. She learned readily all that was taught her, and much that was not. Acquisition of ideas was a passion with her, and her father's library, fashionably well filled and fashionably little used, was a perpetual delight to her dawning intellect. She might, perhaps, have been a beautiful child had due pains been taken in the cultivation of her natural graces. As it was, she was in no way remarkable. She was allowed to braid her hair closely back from her large, thoughtful brow; to sit carelessly, and to wear, ordinarily, what suited her best—a quiet robe of dark, shadowy, unbecoming gray. On state occasions, when her presence was required in the parlor, and she was bedizened in brighter hues and fashionable finery, she was too much embarrassed by the unusual costume to have it contribute at all to her beauty.

Circumstances early schooled her to content herself with no great amount of affection. Her father would have loved her, but what with early and late devotion to the business that maintained his splendid house and faultless equipage—to say nothing of bills at Stewart's and Madame D'Arblay's—he had very little time for the cultivation of home ties. Her mother—she must have had a mother's heart somewhere in her bosom, though its beatings were effectually smothered by silk and velvet—was too much absorbed in her beautiful self to remember the child, except with an occasional fear lest her growing up should be an unwelcome reminder of her own age. The governess understood this sentiment, and needed not to be told to keep the girl back as much as possible. As for Mademoiselle, she wrote her letters and chatted with her lover, consoling herself with the reflection that in neglecting her charge she was but following the example of the higher powers. And so Hortense Greenwich brought herself up.

At twenty she was little changed from what she had been at ten. It is true, some years before, Mademoiselle had married her American lover, and Miss Greenwich, deprived of her supervision, had been sent to a boarding-school, where she had learned a little French, a little Italian, and a good deal of music. At twenty she was introduced into society. She was not at all showy; indeed, her mother pronounced her, "after all that had been done for her, decidedly wanting in style," and, I think, was secretly rejoiced that her daughter was so little likely to dispute with her the palm of fashionable admiration.

At twenty Hortense Greenwich might easily have passed for fifteen. So little of passion or emotion had swept over the calm surface of her life, that her face was still placid and reticent as in childhood. It had no story to tell. Her only accomplishment was her music, and this with her was rather a passion than an art. She practiced it solely for her own gratification. Hour after hour, at her harp or her piano, she breathed out her very soul—all the mystery of her inner life—in thrilling, passionate improvisations. It was to her instead of father and mother love—instead of brothers and sisters—instead of friends.

She had been in society two years when she first met Rowland Chivers. Though only four years older than herself, he was already *blasé*. He had traveled in the Old World. He was well read in the book of beauty. He could tell a woman's fine points at a glance. His flirtations had been numerous abroad, but he had come home unfettered, and "Japonica-dom" welcomed him eagerly. For a wonder, his fortune, really large, was his smallest claim to distinction. He would have been a man of mark any where. His manners were emphatically, as Mrs. Greenwich expressed herself, *distingué*. He was handsome, and he had a mind well and richly stored, despite his flirtations and fooleries.

I said he could tell all a woman's charms at a glance. After a little, he made Mrs. Greenwich his mortal enemy by perceiving that her daughter was younger, and possessed finer points of beauty than herself. At her exhibitions of disdain, however, he only smiled. He was contented to let her love or hate him as she liked, and, with serene self-satisfaction, set himself at work to *bring out* Hortense Greenwich.

A little encouragement, a little graceful flattery, was all she needed. Soon the world began to perceive what a faultless figure she had, now that she had acquired a motive for dressing it becomingly. Then her fine eyes were noticed; the superb scorn of her daintily-cut mouth; her hair, so long, so luxuriant, now that a quick eye had perceived its capabilities, and a few artistic yet careless hints had guided her in its arrangement.

Miss Greenwich, accustomed to go into society as a sort of necessary sacrifice at the shrine of Mammon, without the least hope or expectation of finding pleasure therein, was at first surprised, then gratified, when Rowland Chivers, just then quite a centre of attraction, persistently sought her side. With his matchless tact, it was not difficult to make her feel, without once saying any thing to startle her susceptible pride, that he alone understood her—that he recognized her capacity to be more than she was—loftier than any of the social magnets glittering about her. To a nature like hers, this feeling, that she was appreciated—that she received her full deserts, was the most acceptable of incense. She inhaled it eagerly. Under its influence she not only learned how to make the most of all the graces which were already hers, but new charms came to her; a deeper color glowed in her cheek, a warmer light shone from her large, dark eye.

At first she thought only of friendship. Rowland Chivers never talked to her of love. He was lonely, he told her. Very few of those he met in the gay circle where his lot was cast had power to interest him for an hour. It had been like a new revelation to know her. She could feel with him—could share his thoughts. As much as ever sister could be to brother she should be to him. And this contented her. It was her first friendship; it seemed so pure, so sweet, so tender. It was something to be proud of, to have this man, sought of all, always at her side. His homage elevated her in the eyes of those who had been accustomed to consider her as a good, quiet girl, of no great importance in any way. She was grateful to him for gaining for her the position to which, in the sensitive pride of her proud nature, she felt entitled. For his sake she adorned herself. Her naturally fine taste was aroused. She must do justice to his choice of a friend.

From all this, in a character like hers, the step was not long to love. Soon she knew that, in spite of herself, he had become dearer to her than all the dreams of her girlhood. And now came a season of self-humiliation; a fear which stung her like a scorpion, lest she had given her love unsought; a longing, anxious questioning of his heart; a striving to read every expression of his haughty, handsome face.

And then, as if in answer to her doubts, his manner became tenderer than ever. More constantly he sought her side—more gentle was his voice—more full of love the songs he brought her, and sang with her by the hour together. One day he said to her,

"Hortense, I thought I knew women, but even I was deceived in my estimate of you. You have matured, this past year, into such a woman as my fancy never foreshadowed. It has been like the sudden bursting into bloom of the still century-plant, or the breathing radiant, glowing life into a perfect statue. What has changed you so?"

Rowland Chivers would have made a capital surgeon. He would have looked unmoved on the death-throes of a thousand victims. As it was, he delighted in nothing so much as in dissecting hearts. With keen relish he watched the color come and go in her cheeks, the lids droop downward to veil the shy responses of her radiant eyes. Her voice was very low as she answered,

"*You* have changed me by being my friend. No one had interest enough in me before to make it worth my while to be my best self."

But farther than this he never carried the conversation. He would break it off at this stage to read her some old legend of long-enduring love, or to make her sing for him his favorite songs. His actions told her, every day of his life, more eloquently than any words, that she was beloved, but his lips had never yet spoken it.

At length a new star rose in the firmament of New York society—a young widow, gay, beautiful, *piquante.* She possessed less dignity, less *hauteur*, less style, even, than Hortense Greenwich; but her versatility, her grace, her good-humor were infinite. She was a little fairy—a perfect flower of the tropics, with a passionate, fervid nature speaking in every look of her sparkling eyes, every flexible movement of her graceful figure. Rowland Chivers was charmed. Here was a new book—a fresh page. How would this bewitching little divinity look if *she* were in love? His attentions were divided now, and perhaps Mrs. Bellair received the largest share.

I do not think Hortense Greenwich ever could have been jealous. It was not in her nature. She could love and trust blindly up to a certain point; but when her trust was slain her love must die with it. So she looked on in evident unconcern while the widow danced, and sang, and flirted, and Rowland Chivers was ever at her side. I think he was disappointed. He was not noble enough to understand a nature above jealousy. He had expected Miss Greenwich would flatter his vanity by growing pale, sad, abstracted; that she would slight him a little at first, and by-and-by there would be a scene, and he—I believe he had not decided, even in his own mind, whether he meant to marry her. Her calmness disappointed him. It was not feigned. She never thought of doubting his love. She believed—when he had finished his game, his pretty little amusement of a flirtation—he would be as much her own as ever. She had no fears for the widow's heart, and she was too much accustomed to see such kind of trifling to realize how much it dimmed the bright perfectness she had loved to ascribe to her idol. So, when he did come to her side, she received him as cheerfully as ever. Her cheek lost nothing of its brilliant glow—her eye of its sparkling light. He began to fear that she did not love him, and this reawakened all his interest in her. To test the matter thoroughly, he flirted with the widow more desperately than ever.

One night, when Miss Greenwich was in full beauty, she was for a time the centre of attraction in Mrs. Livingstone's crowded *salon*. Gentlemen thronged round her, and ladies stood by in envy. Despite his doubts of her love, Rowland Chivers gloried in her. She was so queenly, so fair; to all but him, so unapproachable. He lingered near her, saying just enough to draw out her best powers.

At length a diversion was created by the widow's late entrance. This night Rowland Chivers was resolved to probe to the utmost the heart he had begun to doubt. He was among the first to seek Mrs. Bellair. He danced with her; he bent over her as she sat at the piano; he devoted himself to her with all the enthusiasm of a courtier. At length his keen eye detected Miss Greenwich for the moment alone. She had withdrawn herself a little from the gay company, and sat in a kind of recess watching the flash of the lights, the sparkle of the diamonds, the sheen of the floating silken robes, and now and then catching some chance word borne by her on the waves of sound. He sought her side, and was welcomed with her usual frankness. For a while they chatted indifferently, and then, as if moved to confidence by a sudden impulse, Rowland Chivers said,

"I do believe, Hortense, that you have a real friendly interest—a sister's interest—in my welfare; and something I can not explain impels me to ask your advice. You women judge each other more justly than a man can. Tell me, then, what you think of Mrs. Bellair. Would my life's happiness be safe if I should ask her, and she should consent, to be my wife?"

He had meant this should be the crowning test of her love. If she manifested one emotion of grief or anger, he would believe she loved him; perhaps—but the future must settle that—perhaps he would ask her to be Mrs. Chivers. He watched her keenly. Not a muscle of her face quivered; not a shade deeper was the rose-tint on her fair cheek; she did not even turn her calm eyes away. There was no tremor in her silvery voice. As if half musingly, she said,

"I do not quite know her well enough to answer; but I should think, nay, I am very sure, that your natures are much alike—that she would suit you admirably."

Her auditor had an uncomfortable impression that a hidden satire lurked in her remark. It galled him, and he winced under it; but she had given no sign of love for him. He had mistaken her all this while, and, roused to regret by this knowledge, he began to think that he loved her, and could not live without her.

Just then they were interrupted. Mr. Richmond Spendwell came to claim her hand for the next dance; and for the rest of that night Hortense Greenwich was more beautiful than ever, and, unlike her usual self, was the gayest of the gay.

When it was all over the reaction came. Leaning back in the carriage by her mother's side, she sat for a time in profound silence. But Mrs. Greenwich was sociably inclined; her eyes were sparkling; her cheeks glowing; her spirits were at high tide. They must find an outlet somehow. There was not often much conversation between these two women, they had so few thoughts in common; but Mrs. Greenwich must talk now.

"It *has* been a brilliant evening; but then Mrs. Livingstone's evenings always are. I haven't enjoyed myself more this winter. Why don't you speak, Hortense; didn't you like it?"

"I am very tired."

"Tired! Well, you look so; I can see by the street lamp how white your face is. Why, I should outlast three like you, mamma though I am. You will never do for a belle. But don't that little widow make herself ridiculous enough? One would suppose she thought there had never been another handsome woman in the world. There's Rowland Chivers, how she does draw him after her! Why, I really used to think he was attentive to you."

"Mother, *don't!* I can't talk; I am so tired—so sick."

There was a strange pathos in her voice. It would have reminded you of the moan of some stricken animal hunted to death. Mrs. Greenwich did not understand it: she was not a sympathetic or a quick-feeling woman at any time, but this cry of an unspoken sorrow hushed even her into silence.

After that, however, Miss Greenwich regained her self-command. Her good-night, as she went up stairs, was spoken in her usual cheerful tones; her step was firm, yet elastic, and her mother looking after her, thought what a strange, unsociable girl she was, and how little she cared for society any way.

In her own room her sleepy maid sat before the fire waiting for her. She was perfectly calm now—she did not even seem fatigued. The business of disrobing was quickly performed; the ornaments she had worn were restored to their proper places; the girl was dismissed, and Hortense Greenwich was alone, with no farther need for self-command. She sat down before the fire, and looked steadily into it. Was this the same world it had seemed when she sat there, five *hours before, dreaming blissful* dreams, in which one face ever shone, one voice made an eternal music? Gone forever was the sunlight which had gilded that fair world. No longer were the skies blue, and the very clouds rosy; no longer the future stretched out before her a green, sunny path, bordered with roses and bright with verdure. She had crowned herself, indeed, with those fair roses of Hope, but they had turned to thorns upon her forehead; and from those gaping wounds would not the life-blood ooze forever?

Then, in the stillness, Pride rose up like an avenger, and buffeted her sorely. She had loved unsought, it told her; given her heart to one who did not even think the gift worth the acceptance; trusted all things to one who had promised nothing. But Memory defended her warmly. Memory asserted that he *had* sought her love; Memory brought forth from her treasure-house looks and words of unmistakable tenderness; she recalled daily and long-continued care; manifold tokens of interest; constant attentions; all that could, more eloquently than any words, tell the story of absorbing love. And then Justice acquitted the proud heart accused.

Oh, Rowland Chivers, you would have known one woman better than you were ever likely to learn her, with all your study, if you could have sat by Hortense Greenwich's fire that night! I spare my reader the torture, the agony, the despair. Women like her love once, and, if deceived, never again thereafter. She had lost that night something dearer than life, something loftier than love—her faith in humanity. She had never had but one friend. Rowland Chivers was the first one who had ever read the pages of her woman's heart. She had gained a higher, truer estimate of her own powers, seeing them through his eyes. To this first tenderness she had given all. The full tide of her passionate yet reserved nature had set toward him, and now the deep waters must flow back again, flooding the waste country of her affections, uprooting every flower, destroying every fruit. Henceforth she must go on alone. Life stretched out before her bleak and barren of hope. Alas! there was no one to whisper of a narrower path, where the seed sown in tears might spring up in joy; where the blessings of those ready to perish would cheer the fainting traveler, whose goal was the Celestial City. Fashionable life —she knew no other—was the arena where she must struggle for the victor's palm. At least—her lip curled at the thought—Rowland Chivers had taught her something of her own value; she could touch him through his vanity; she could *shine.* Through all that night not one tear came to her proud eyes. The blight which had fallen upon her life was too deadly for any gentle dew of sorrow. She would not suffer the love which lay in its death-throes upon her heart's threshold to make a single moan, even in dying. Sternly she watched its agony until it was dead, then she took up the fair corse and buried it. It might haunt her sometimes; sometimes she might wake at midnight from feverish slumbers, and see at her bed's foot a still, white face, and the gleam of golden hair, but she would know it was but the illusion of fancy. The dead love should *not* arise—she rolled a stone to the mouth of the sepulchre.

It was thus that Hortense Greenwich became a belle in society. After that night she went forth into the world a changed woman. That world had never found her so charming before. She was prouder than ever; but society likes pride. Her words were keen with the two-edged sword of wit. Now and then a victim winced under them, but the by-standers applauded, and the sufferers from such wounds are the first to smile. Rowland Chivers wondered at her. He had never suspected, with all his appreciation of her character, such power as this. He left Mrs. Bellair to bite her pretty lips and break her Spanish fan in vexation, and actually haunted Miss Greenwich wherever she went. Her reception of him was precisely the same as she accorded to others; marked with a courtesy which no presumption could construe into more than courtesy.

She was become like the rest of the world now. She formed friendships in the fashionable sense of the word. Rowland Chivers called on her, and found other young ladies, graceful butterflies of fashion, whiling away the morning with her; or, at other times, some gentleman would be serenely making himself agreeable, where once *he* only had been the privileged guest. At other times still, he would call and be told that Miss Greenwich was out, and this piqued his vanity still more, for he shrewdly suspected that she was only "out" to him. He had roused his somewhat apathetic sensibilities by this time into what he believed an absorbing passion for her. He was quite convinced that all his happiness for the future depended upon persuading her to return his adoration.

At length he called on her one morning at an unfashionably early hour. She was in, and alone. He found her in the same room where they had passed so many hours together. He trusted to the old memories to assist him. Once more he asked for a favorite song. With thorough self-command she complied with his request. She manifested no emotion—there was no droop of the eyelids, no softening of the voice. The metaphysical dissector, the hero of a thousand flirtations, was at a loss. Perhaps he had never felt so deeply before. At all events, it had never before been so hard a task to make a declaration of love. But he managed it at length. For once in the world he might have gained credit for modesty. No one could have doubted but that he was sincere. With a humility as strange as it was new, he told her the high sense he entertained of her perfections, and besought her favorable hearing for his confession of love. His utmost experience with women could never have prepared him for her reply.

"I will not deceive you," she said, in her proud, yet quiet voice. "My own pride shall not tempt me to say that I never loved you. Little as I believe you deserve it, I did love you once with all the strength of my nature; or, rather, I loved something I believed was you. My life had been lonely before you came. I was indebted to you, I acknowledge that now, for a juster knowledge of myself. I believed that you loved me—your constant attentions gave me a right to believe it."

"I did—oh, God knows I did," faltered Rowland Chivers's voice. She went on without heeding the interruption.

"I trusted in your love so fully that, when Mrs. Bellair came, your flirtation with her gave me no concern. Only your own words could have undeceived me. They were not long wanting. You remember that night when you asked my advice about marrying her. Then I saw you as you were. Either you had never cared for me, and had but amused yourself with deceiving me; or having, after your own fashion, liked me, you were now experimenting upon my love, wantonly giving me pain. In either case I had been loving an ideal. The man I had supposed you to be could never have condescended to such trifling. You acted out your own nature. I do not complain. I rather thank you for letting me see you as you are. But, if it will solace your vanity, if it will give you any triumph to know that I suffered, I do not grudge you the satisfaction of that knowledge. I suffered in that one night such tortures as all the pulses of your lifetime could not measure out. But even then, if you could have knelt at my feet and poured out your soul in a prayer of forgiveness, it would not have comforted me—in my heart would have been no response to your voice. I had loved an ideal, which was *not* you.

You will understand now that our paths must lie very far apart. You have taken from me all that my life had of glory—my faith, my hope, my trust in human love. I shall marry some man for the position, the independence he will give me, but I can not marry you."

Rowland Chivers showed how far he was from comprehending her by persevering in his prayer. He knelt at her feet. He uttered a passionate cry for forgiveness—for love. He drew a picture of his desolate life without her. He told her that he had never loved before—that his only hold on a true, right life, was through her.

There was goodness enough in her nature to pity him, even then. Her great dark eyes rested upon him mournfully. Her voice was not proud now, but sorrowful.

"I *can not*, Rowland Chivers. Plead with me no longer. My heart is dumb. It makes no answer."

And he felt that it was indeed true. He bade her farewell with faltering tones, he pressed kiss after kiss upon her hand, and then he went out into the world, and Hortense Greenwich sent after him no regret—no sigh.

That very morning, scarcely an hour later, Mr. Richmond Spendwell sat beside her, in the seat which Rowland Chivers had filled. There could scarcely have been a greater contrast than between these two men. It was something more than the ordinary difference between twenty-six and forty. Mr. Spendwell was pompous, self-satisfied, almost arrogant. He had a far more definite idea of turtle-soup than of turtle-doves. Billing and cooing would not, at any time of life, have been in his line. He was better posted in stocks than in literature. As for sentiment, it was to him *terra incognita;* and he had no knowledge of hearts beyond a dim schoolboy recollection that they had something to do with the circulation of the blood.

Therefore he was saved from all embarrassment in the doing of his errand. In a manner most business-like and creditable he made Miss Greenwich an offer of his hand. Like her former suitor, he was quite unprepared for her reply:

"Mr. Spendwell, I would not marry you under false pretenses. I would not deceive you for the world. *If* I marry you, I shall be your faithful wife, for I know my duty; but I can not marry you because of love. That is forever past for me. I did love one man; or, rather, I loved the ideal which I called by his name. I found out the weak points of his character, and my love died a natural death. He left me this morning, a rejected suitor. Would you be satisfied with a wife who had no love to give you?"

Mr. Spendwell listened politely, but with a look which said, more expressively than words, that this was all Greek to him. He took advantage of the first pause to interrupt her.

"My dear young lady, I am too old, perhaps, and too prosaic to fully understand you. As nearly as I can make out, you once fancied yourself in love, but, finding your mistake, you rejected your suitor. Now I am not very exacting in these matters. You are graceful and beautiful beyond any woman of my acquaintance. I have confidence in your good sense and good principle. If you will be my wife, I think I may say I shall make a kind and indulgent husband."

"I am sensible of the honor you do me, sir, and I accept your proposal."

"Very right. Just the reply I expected from your good sense. I will see your father this afternoon."

This was Hortense Greenwich's plighting. Hortense Greenwich! dreamer, enthusiast, genius! Was it strange, as she sat alone after her very respectable affianced left her, that for one undisciplined moment the dead love seemed to stir in its unquiet grave, and her thoughts roamed backward once more into the enchanted country over which Hope's sun had set, and stood for that one moment pleading vainly at the closed gates of her Eden? That was all. After that she walked forward with firm footsteps in the path she had chosen; she said to her woman's heart, "I have no need of thee;" she received the congratulations of her friends, and went on superintending the preparations for her bridal.

The news of her betrothal came to Rowland Chivers with a keen pang. To such natures as his blessings brighten as they take their flight. By refusing to be his wife she had made herself his goddess. He sailed for Europe in the next steamer, and news comes of him now and then engaged in his old career of flirtation and foolery.

Alas! he had left behind him the greatest ruin he had ever wrought. In Hortense Greenwich he had found, perhaps for the first time in his life, a true, high-souled, self-contained, yet loving woman. There was more power in her nature, for good or for evil, than in twenty like Ernestine Bellair. He found her young, generous, susceptible, ready to give up all things for truth and right. He left her with her heart prematurely old, cold, glittering, scornful, suspicious. It was the wreck of a most noble nature. She was married; that is, Mr. Richmond Spendwell was legally pronounced her husband; but her unwed heart was left alone, alone—like an unquiet spirit making its moan in the darkness.

She was a splendid bride. Some envied her, some condemned her, some approved of her worldly prudence; and one quiet old book-keeper, looking out from the window of his *chateau en Espagne*, murmured, with sad sagacity,

"Once more Venus has married Vulcan."

The Tenant of the Old Brown House.

Life and Thought have gone away
  Side by side,
  Leaving door and windows wide:
Careless tenants they!
All within is dark as night:
In the windows is no light;
And no murmur at the door,
So frequent on its hinge before.
Close the door, the shutters close,
  Or through the windows we shall see
  The nakedness and vacancy
Of the dark, deserted house.
Come away; no more of mirth
  Is here, or merry-making sound.
The house was builded of the earth,
  And shall fall again to ground.

TENNYSON.

THE TENANT OF THE OLD BROWN HOUSE.

"Oh! do whate'er thou wilt, I will be silent."

THE old brown house on the hill was at last to have a tenant. A woman was coming to dwell in it. No one in Ryefield had ever seen her. By letter she had made the bargain, and she gave no clew to her fortune or circumstances, save, at the foot of the page, the strong, bold signature, "Hester Wilde." The property, which belonged to a distant owner, had been, ever since I could remember, in my grandfather's care. It had not been inhabited for years. There were strange stories about a murder which had once been committed there, though I believe there was no positive proof. Shrieks and groans, it was confidently reported, came forth from its windows at midnight; and strange forms, clad in the costume of long ago years, passed before them in ghostly conference. However this may have been, certain it is that the proprietor, Wilton Eldredge, had not visited it since he came of age; and the last family who inhabited it moved out at midnight, and came, as I have heard my mother say, to our house white with terror.

My grandfather, as in duty bound, had inserted an advertisement in the county paper at the beginning of every quarter, and, naturally anxious for the interests of his client, he was heartily glad to receive an application at length, and acceded to the proffers of Mistress Hester Wilde without troubling himself to make many inquiries concerning her character or circumstances.

She had written like a lady well bred and well educated, and yet the tone of her communications was hard and stern, and invited little freedom of reply. She had said she should bring no furniture, and requested that the house should be made habitable before the fifteenth of May.

"Put on your bonnet," said my grandfather, when he had finished the perusal of this letter, "put on your bonnet, Louise, and we will walk up the hill to the old house."

I obeyed him gladly. It was a delicious May-time afternoon, bright with opening leaves and blossoms, sunshine, and a cloudless expanse of blue sky. Only about the brown house seemed to lie a heavy shadow. It might have been the effect merely of the dark row of tall old poplars leading solemnly up to the door, but I fancied there was something in that unbroken silence, that still darkness, almost supernatural. With a half shudder I involuntarily murmured, "And what if there should be another removal—if the ghosts should drive out the strange lady?"

My grandfather was a God-fearing man of the straitest sect of Puritans, and had no terror of any thing out of heaven. In his strong, unimaginative mind there was no foothold for superstition, and he answered me almost sternly, "Mistress Hester Wilde, if I have read her letters rightly, is not a person to be driven out of house and home by imaginary fears, and I had hoped you, too, had more sense than to talk of ghosts."

I was quieted, but not subdued. To me there seemed, in spite of myself, a strange mystery in the shadows that lay so thick about the old mansion, and I looked up at its windows—I could not help it—with a thrill of something very much like fear.

It had gone a long way toward ruin during those uninhabited years. Here and there panes of glass were broken in; bats whizzed in and out at the windows, and swallows built their nests in the chimneys. The furniture belonging to the old proprietors was stored away under lock and key in an upper chamber, and we found it, though faded and rusty, in very tolerable repair. It had lain useless ever since the fair Margery Eldredge went to her rest, and now it was to be furbished up and arranged once more in the deserted rooms. In this task of arrangement I was to superintend the labors of my grandfather's trusty servant.

At length the repairs were completed. Bridget had put down the carpets the day before, and early in the morning we set out to prepare the house for the reception of its mistress. It was a large house, but Mistress Wilde had said she wanted little room, and so we only fitted up the most convenient apartments. There was a parlor—a stately parlor looking out upon the poplar walk. A rich but sombre carpet was upon the floor, and we arranged around the walls, at regular distances, the high-backed, embroidered chairs which graced the best room during the Eldredge dynasty, and which Margery Eldredge had herself worked in her days of youth and love. A few paintings, portraits of the dead, hung upon the wall—cold and lifeless they were, and suited well the grim aspect of the room: we left them there. The kitchen would be dining-room and sitting-room, if Mistress Wilde followed the country custom, and we took more pains to make that cheerful. The white floor was nicely sanded, and over the mantle I hung the only pleasant picture the house had to boast. This was the likeness of Margery Eldredge in the early days of her wifehood. She was the mother of Wilton Eldredge, the present proprietor, and the summer of her life never dawned—she died while it was yet spring. In the portrait she was fair, with a bright, bewitching, girlish beauty, very sweet and tender. When this picture was hung it seemed to brighten up the whole room. We put Margery's low sewing-chair and soft footstool of Berlin wool beside the little work-table; and when all else was set in order, I gathered a few early wild-flowers, and bestowed them in a dainty gilt-edged saucer on the white-covered toilet-table of the new mistress's bedroom.

She was expected that day; and in the afternoon my grandfather came over to remain with me and receive her. As the day drew toward its close and she did not come, I began to tremble at the quick approach of twilight, shutting in that long silent house. But I sat there, too proud to confess my undefined fears to the strong-minded man at my side. At length, and this time startling even him—we had not heard the stage stop at the distant gate—footsteps sounded on the graveled walk without, and a tall figure darkened the door-way.

"Mr. Cleveland, I suppose," she said, coldly and stiffly. My grandfather bowed. "I am Hester Wilde," she continued, bestowing a scrutinizing glance upon the premises.

She was a woman to whom I could not venture a

single word of the earnest, friendly welcome I had been planning in my own mind, so I sat still, and silently looked at her. She was very tall, with a certain angularity and stiffness pervading not only her figure, but all her motions. She was not in the least pretty, and she never could have been. Her hair was straight, black, and coarse, giving evidence of extraordinary powers of endurance. Her eyes were black and very stern; rigid lines lay about her mouth—lines which suffering must have furrowed; and her features were not only masculine, but irregular. She sat down, not in the easy sewing-chair I had left vacant for her, but at the other side of the table, in an arm-chair as hard and stiff as herself, exactly facing the picture of Margery Eldredge.

"Is that a portrait?" she asked, after a time, in her cold, quiet voice.

"It is—of the mother of Wilton Eldredge, the owner of your new home, which I trust may prove a happy one," replied my grandfather, with the courtly politeness of a gentleman of the old school.

She uttered a cold "Thank you," and once more relapsed into silence.

Her age might have varied any where from thirty to forty. I could not tell. There was something in her expression which moved me to a silent sympathy, notwithstanding it was so forbidding. It never softened, except once or twice, when she glanced involuntarily at the portrait over the mantle, and then for a moment her face fairly gleamed with something which, in her, I was forced to pronounce untranslatable, which yet resembled the look other faces wear when any trifling thing recalls the aspect of one tenderly, mournfully beloved. She did not seem at all disposed to make conversation, and after a few moments my grandfather rose to wish her good-evening.

"Will she not be afraid?" I whispered aside. He looked at me with a sternness which was meant to be final; but I could not heed him, I was so timid in those days. She was a woman, and I thought it terrible to leave her there alone.

"Miss Wilde," I said. She started. A flush even rose to her sallow face as if she had not always been accustomed to hearing herself addressed by that name. "You have no servant engaged. Shall we not send Bridget over to sleep in the house with you to-night?"

"By no means," she replied. "It was one thing I wished to say to you, Mr. Cleveland. I would like you to find me a trusty boy, who will come here at night and morning, and do little jobs and any errands I may wish about the village. It is all the help I shall need." My grandfather bowed, and promised to execute her commission on the morrow; but I could not leave her so.

"Miss Wilde," I said, "I can't help telling you. They *do* say this house is haunted! What if you should see a ghost? I wish Bridget might come over."

She smiled, not unkindly, and answered with a tone just a little thawed, "I am not afraid. There are no dead people who want any thing of me—and no living ones either," she added, after a moment, with a touch of something like sadness in her voice. She bade us good-evening—not rudely; though in her careless invitation to come again there was an evident intention to put its acceptance out of our power by her frigidity.

We went out. I turned round at the gate, and looked through the long row of poplars with an actual shudder. I met my grandfather's eyes fixed upon me with a curious twinkle. "Well, child," he said, "you have had your say; but you did not frighten Mistress Wilde. May you have as much sense some day. Ghosts indeed!"

"But, grandfather, wasn't there once a real murder committed in the house?"

"I do not know of any. Old George Eldredge died there very suddenly. The doctors called it apoplexy; only ignorant people said poison."

We walked the rest of the way in silence, but my thoughts were roaming up and down the poplar walk, or sitting in the silent house with Mistress Hester Wilde.

The next morning my grandfather found a boy suited to her needs, and I begged the privilege of taking him to his new mistress. She did not look as if she had closed her eyes.

"You did not sleep?" I queried, timidly.

"No;" then seeing my "I told-you-so" look, she added, with a queer kind of half smile, which I afterward found was peculiar to her, "but it was not ghosts—at least not such ghosts as *you* mean. If you live, child, you will find there are no spirits so potent as memories."

A verse came to my mind of a little fragment, written I never knew by whom. I murmured it aloud:

> "The dead are ingulfed beneath it,
> Sunk in the grassy waves;
> But we have more dead in our hearts to-day
> Than the earth in all her graves."

She looked at me curiously. "Poetical, I see!"

she muttered. I thought there was a sneer in her tone.

The more I saw of her, the more she interested me. As the weeks passed on, finding that no coldness would discourage me from visiting her, she began to receive me more cordially. But she saw very little of society. The boy, Thomas Wilson by name, was her chief organ of communication with the villagers. Many of the neighboring families had called upon her, but when they found she did not return their visits, or manifest any desire for their acquaintance, they abandoned her again to her solitude. My own perseverance formed the only exception.

None of our conversations, however, though at length they became quite numerous, ever gave me any light upon her past history, until one warm August afternoon, when I strolled over to the brown house, and found her busy in the arrangement of her drawers. She had folded up a packet of letters, and tied them with a black ribbon. She held them in her hand when I entered. She was so absorbed that she did not notice my approach. I could see that her face was very white and rigid, but her hands trembled, and her nerves were so overwrought that, on my coming to her side, a heavy miniature escaped from her hold, and fell, with its crimson-velvet case wide open. I looked upon the face only for an instant, but that was long enough to have it fully impressed upon my memory. It was that of a very handsome man. His bold, black eyes; his short, crisp, black curls; his mouth, passionate yet stern, were unlike any one I had ever seen; and yet, in the whole, there was a certain intangible something which associated itself in my mind with the fair, sweet lineaments of the peerless Margery Eldredge. I stooped to raise it, but she bent over me almost fiercely:

"You shall not!" she cried, sternly; "you shall not look upon my husband!"

I surrendered it, half in terror, and for the moment she seemed unconscious that she had betrayed her cherished secret; for this was the first intimation I had had that she was other than she seemed—a quiet, single woman, living alone. For an instant she looked upon the pictured face with an expression I could not quite translate. There was pride in it, passion, tenderness which softened even her hard features, and yet with all these was blended a look of intense pain.

"I did not mean to see that face now," she murmured rather to herself than me. There seemed a fascination in the proud lineaments on which she gazed, from which she could not bear to turn away; but at length she resolutely shut the case, and pushed it from her into the farther corner of the drawer. Then she looked at me, and said, in tones as sharp and imperative as ever,

"You have surprised me out of my secret. Now I hope you'll have honor enough to keep it. I would not have even your grandfather know that Hester Wilde is other than she appears."

I gave the promise which her words seemed to require, and then I lingered in the expectation that she would reveal more of her history. But I was disappointed. She was silent and thoughtful. She evidently wished to be left alone, and I very soon went away. As I went out of the door a strong perfume greeted me from a scarlet geranium standing there in the sun; and from that day to this the scent of scarlet geranium, no matter where I meet it, always brings before my eyes a picture—a glowing, glorious August afternoon; the brown house behind the poplars; the lone woman standing there in her proud silence; and, above all, that pictured face, seen but for a moment, yet never afterward to be forgotten.

Days braided themselves into weeks, and though I visited Mistress Hester Wilde very often, she never alluded to the scenes of that August afternoon. But I fancied, somehow, that we drew constantly nearer to each other. More recently I had made another discovery, quite as startling as the first: Hester was a student and a genius. I had found Greek and Latin authors in her closet; and gradually I had so far won her confidence, that she uttered in my hearing some of the thoughts which the woods, and the winds, and the everlasting sky were forever speaking to her solemn, solitary life; and I grew to hold her in strange reverence.

One wild November afternoon Tommy Wilson came for me. It was drawing toward night, and in the west a storm seemed rising. The wind blew outside a slow, monotonous dirge, and I sat by my window watching the red leaves it whirled along from the maple-trees. The boy made his awkward, shuffling bow at the door, and then, coming in, put a note into my hand. It was written in the stiff, regular chirography of Hester Wilde, and it said,

"Louise, will you come to me? I have not felt well for some time, and at last I am forced to yield to the illness so long resisted. I think a storm is coming up. If you do not fear to encounter it here, and if you can so far forget your old terror of the ghosts, will you stay all night with me?"

I smiled at her allusion to the ghosts. This one brave, solitary woman had lived so long unharmed in their immediate vicinity, that they had well-nigh lost their terror for me, and I tied on my bonnet and hurried up the hill, well pleased with the invitation. It seemed to me, as I approached, that every thing wore a look even more deserted than usual. The sentinel poplars along the walk lifted up their great naked boughs, and over the carpet of dry, faded leaves, on which my footfall made a crackling sound, the winds rustled slumbrously. I opened the door without knocking, and entered. Hester was not in her accustomed place in her neat kitchen, but her cold voice proceeded from the bedroom beyond, and summoned me. I went in, and she half sat, half reclined upon her bed, bolstered up with pillows. Her face seemed actually wan in the dim light, and I noticed that her hands clutched the bed-clothes tightly, as one in pain.

"I am glad you have come," she said, as I entered. "For the first time I was unwilling to be left here alone. Besides, I think I have not long to live, and I have resolved to tell you to-night the story of my life. You might hear false accounts of me when I am gone, and I would like to have you know the truth."

"But what is the matter?" I cried, in alarm. "What caused this sudden illness? What makes you look so wan and white?"

"The illness is not sudden. My heart has been terribly diseased for some time. When I came here I knew the blow had been struck, and that I had not long to live. So far, I have struggled against it, but now it has become too strong for me. But you must be quiet. I have a very painful task before me, and if I am to tell you my story I can not be interrupted. It is almost dark. You may light that wax candle yonder. It will require no care, and last the whole night."

I obeyed her; and then, drawing up an easy-chair, I settled myself in a comfortable position by the bedside, and she began:

"I was born in Georgia, though you would never think me a daughter of the soft, sunny South. My father, however, was a New Englander, and perhaps it was from this union of the North and South that I derived the very opposite qualities in my nature. I look like my father. He had the same coarse hair, the same stiff angularity of figure, and the same *hardness*, so to speak, of voice. From him also I inherited an energy very unusual in that enervating climate. From him I derived an intense, passionate love of study, particularly of languages and mathematics. But from my mother came an undercurrent of fire—smouldering, volcano-like, beneath the overlying hardness of my nature. From her came the quick perceptions, the passionate worship of the beautiful, the hidden sensitiveness, to which you, my friend, have given the name of genius.

"I was not more than twelve years old when, within two days of each other, an epidemic carried off both my parents. Different as they were, they had loved each other tenderly, and I, their only child, sympathized enough even then in the wonderful mystery of that love whose outward symbol is marriage, to rejoice that since one must be taken, the other was not left behind to mourn. I bore this great sorrow, outwardly, with a calm patience, far too old for my childish years; but inwardly, fierce flames of passionate grief swept over the child's heart, and left it arid and desolate.

"In the whole world there was no one to love me. I was not at all a prepossessing child—a shy, dark, silent girl, caring little for society, liking best to take some cherished book, and flee away into solitude and stillness. But my mother had understood me. In my nature were all those strong qualities so unlike herself, which, by some strange spell, had made my father the object of her worship, united to an underlying current of emotions so like her own that I scarcely needed to give my thoughts utterance in order to be comprehended. Her death had left me alone. There was no human being on all God's fair earth, it seemed to me, so utterly loveless and sorrow-stricken as myself. I was not a buoyant child. I had no far-reaching hopes, to sit all day, like golden-winged birds, and sing me siren strains of future love and joy. I expected to pass through life misunderstood and unloved, and I accepted my destiny with a kind of savage content.

"The guardian to whom my father had left me was a Mr. Randall, an old friend of his own, living in a handsome country house on the margin of the Hudson. He had a graceful, sweet-tempered wife, and three daughters, beautiful girls, the youngest a year younger than myself, and the eldest three years older. They received me very kindly, and, indeed, during my whole life with them, I had never any thing unkind to complain of. But they were not of my kind. Among those blue-eyed fair-haired girls I looked, with my straight black hair and dark skin, like some Indian waiting-maid; nor would my stiff, ungraceful motions have denoted any higher position or more careful training. I think this soured me in a degree. No outside observer could have perceived the contrast half so acutely as I, with my sensitive pride, my passionate love for the beautiful.

"I loved the *beauty* of the Misses Randall, but I do not think I always felt toward them as kindly as, considering they were my only friends in the world, would have seemed natural. In particular, I used to have a kind of instinctive dread of the elder, Miss Jessie Randall. She was called a very amiable, pleasant girl, and there was really about her an extreme softness, a certain pliancy of muscle, manner, and voice. To me, however, it always seemed a dangerous and deadly softness. The large bright blue eyes never fearlessly met your own. It is true, there was a semblance of great modesty in the way the golden lashes drooped over them, but the frank, uplifting eyes of her younger sister Anne pleased me a great deal better. By some strange association of ideas Jessie always seemed to me like a cat—an animal I held in the extremest abhorrence, from the gliding, stealthy motion, to the treacherous claws cased in velvet. A curious prophetic instinct made me look upon her as an enemy, and yet she was uniformly polite to me. She smilingly tolerated all my rudeness, apologized for my *brusquerie*, and appeared so amiable that every day she grew more and more out of my favor.

"We were educated at home by teachers. Miss Jessie's education was completed at eighteen, and an elegant wardrobe was provided, in which, under the care of an aunt residing in New York, she was to make her *début.* Nothing could have been more beautiful than Jessie Randall at that age. Her sisters were more than pretty, but she was, *par excellence*, the beauty, and on her, above all, was the ambition of her father and mother centred.

"She had been trained carefully in every accomplishment. Her snowy fingers discoursed ravishing music on the harp and piano; her voice was sweet and clear; her dancing had been pronounced, by our gallant French teacher, 'the very poetry of motion;' and her manners were considered faultless. We who were left behind heard of her triumphs—how joyously her days were floating on; of her appearance at party, theatre, and opera; and I, imbittered perchance by a consciousness of my own entire incapacity to attract, would inwardly cry out,

"'Oh, shame upon her for a woman! Does she think this dancing, and dressing, and reigning is all that there is of life? that for no better ends than these God has made her so beautiful?'

"For the next three years Miss Jessie was seldom at home; and when she did come, she would bring with her a train of her city friends, brightening up the house with their gay dresses and brilliant jewels, as if a flock of tropical birds had alighted there, pausing in their flight.

"In the mean time I grew up, as was the promise of my childhood, plain and shy. I bestowed all my suppressed enthusiasm on study; all my friendship on my black horse, Hercules. When I was eighteen our teachers were dismissed, and I came into possession of the liberal allowance which my father had assigned me from eighteen until I should be twenty-one, when my fortune, large at first, and greatly increased by accumulation during the comparatively inexpensive years of my minority, was to come into my possession unencumbered, and unfettered by a single restraint.

"About the period of my eighteenth birthday Jessie Randall came home for a much longer stay than usual. It was a beautiful autumn. I remember how glorious every thing looked to me. I was young, in high health, and had begun to be hopeful. I was not long in discovering that among the gay friends whom, as usual, Jessie had brought with her, was one, a Mr. Eldredge, the cynosure of all, the chief object of interest. He was the life and soul of their parties of pleasure. He rode, he danced, he jested—in short, he seemed crowned of all manly graces, natural and acquired. I had never before seen any one who so nearly approached my ideal of masculine perfection. I did not speak of him, even to Anne, who during this influx of visitors was my room-mate, but mentally I compared him to Apollo and Ulysses, my favorite heroes of the classic world, in which so much of my life had been spent.

"I was considered old enough now to go into society, and I was doomed to weary evenings of unoccupied, listless looking on, while the gay party sung, and danced, and acted charades. But the weariness was short-lived. I soon became intensely absorbed in the contemplation of this same Wilton Eldredge."

"What!" I exclaimed, interrupting her, "was it the owner of this house?" She went on without heeding me:

"Every development of his character, every expression of his face, was a welcome study to me. I soon perceived that in what I had at first thought perfection, there were many deficiencies. Physically, nothing was wanting. I have seen years of life since then, and yet I have never looked upon one more perfect in manly beauty. Intellectually, I discovered he possessed more brilliancy than depth. That is to say, intellectually he was indolent, and to a certain extent superficial. Morally, his want of energy was still more culpable. He would assent to a wrong opinion, countenance a wrong action, rather than arouse himself to the exertion of resistance. These spots upon my sun had troubled me greatly at first, for I had a nature inflexible in its stern love of right and justice; but I was rapidly losing the consciousness of them in my admiration for his beauty, for the strong sense, the glow, so to speak, of physical life that animated his face, and radiated over his whole being. I thought, too, and this conviction has never left me, that there were depths in his nature which needed only the angel's 'troubling wing' to bring the bright waters of healing to the brink.

"He had been there two weeks without addressing a single observation to me after our first introduction. It was a bright October morning; the leaves were just turning, and a thousand gorgeous tints, sparkling with dew-drops, flashed back the sunlight. A horseback ride had been arranged to some place of interest in the neighborhood, and my horse had been brought out among the rest. Going through the hall, I had caught the reflection of my face and figure in a full-length mirror hanging there, and, for the moment, I was impious. My wild thoughts arraigned God, who had made me so unlovely that to no human being could my face give pleasure. I went out into the sunshine, among that group of glad young creatures, every one of whom had her own distinctive charm, and I stood there, as I felt, like a black, ugly shadow—the only blot upon the landscape. Jessie, in particular, had never seemed so beautiful. Her slight, undulating figure showed to advantage in her close-fitting riding-habit of Marie Louise blue; her golden curls fell in a shower from beneath her beaver hat; and her face, oh! I thought at that moment she was radiant as Helen when she tempted Paris to his doom. They mounted their steeds among jests and silvery laughter, with courtly aid from their attendant cavaliers. As ever, Wilton Eldredge was close at Jessie's side; for, though there was no positive engagement, rumor said our fair 'eldest' would not long remain unwedded.

"Without assistance I vaulted upon the back of my own horse, and dashed off in an opposite direction from that which the party were to take. The fresh autumn wind blowing in my face restored my reason, and I repented of my momentary insanity, and began to bless God for life, when in the very sense of existence—of *being*—was so much joy. I remembered how much on earth was worth living for besides idle dreams of love—pleasure-palaces—gilded by youth and beauty.

"I had ridden perhaps a mile, when I heard the quick tramp of a horse behind me. I did not turn my head, and in a moment more Wilton Eldredge rode to my side.

"'Well,' he said, in his gay, ringing voice, 'well, runaway, I am commissioned to bring you back to the rest of our party.'

"'Thank you. I had rather not go.'

"'But why? Let me tell you, Miss Hester Wilde, it looks very ungirllike and unsociable to be riding off by yourself in this way. Will you tell me your reason?'

"I was one of those who never take a medium course—I must obey or disobey. Perfect truth was an element of my nature: I must answer honestly or not at all. I chose the former.

"'Because,' I said, 'I am very plain. I look out of character among those beauties. I don't want to go with them. It makes me feel wicked.'

"'A little envious, hey? You are honest in your confession, Miss Wilde.'

"'No, sir, *not* envious; but it makes me feel *wicked*—as if, somehow, God hadn't used me well in making me so plain nobody could ever love me.'

"I should have liked him less if he had insulted my common sense by contradicting or complimenting me. He did neither. He made no answer to my speech, and for a moment there was silence. Then he said,

"'You have been studying me closely for two weeks back, Miss Wilde. What have you made out?'

"A crimson glow suffused my face as he bent his laughing eyes upon me; but I answered, honestly still,

"'Well, sir, I have discovered that you love beauty almost as intensely as I do; that you love ease and pleasure better yet—mental ease I mean, for physically you are not lazy; that you would be thorough if being brilliant had not already satisfied your ambition, and good if it were not too much trouble.'

"'Well, Miss Wilde,' with a slightly disturbed face and a bow of mock courtesy, 'you are at least candid.

You have read me like a witch, as I suspect you are; and now, let me tell you, I too have studied you, though I'll wager you have never seen me look at you. I have found out several things. To begin with, you think *me* very handsome, and for that compliment your humble servant is much obliged.'

"I blushed more painfully than ever; but he went on:

"'You think your cousin Jessie little better than a beautiful butterfly. You come as near to envying her loveliness as your pride will allow you; and then you flatter yourself that you pity her for making what you call an unworthy use of it. Now I don't sympathize with you there. I neither envy nor pity the fair Jessie. I am contented to look at her. What has a star to do but to shine? You know more about books than people; you are honest, but too proud to be half as happy as you ought; and, finally, you and I are so very *unlike* that I think we shall be excellent friends.'

"Oh! how I hoped so in my heart, as I looked up at him, much as the Lady of Shalott might have looked at Sir Launcelot riding by with his 'Tirra—lirra.' We had both of us forgotten that he was to take me back to the gay company he had left, and we rode on in the bright autumn sunlight, while I drank in, at every pore of my being, such happiness as comes but seldom in a lifetime.

"After that our acquaintance progressed rapidly. Scarcely a day passed that he did not join me in my morning rides and rambles, and I think these meetings were as pleasant to him as to me. He said I was so different from the women he had known before, so unconventional and so honest; and I became conscious of a power to call into action all that was noblest in his nature and loftiest in his thoughts. It is one of the surest ways to awaken the highest elements of character to let their possessor feel that he is *expected* to be a giant and not a pigmy. It was many days before I realized how dangerous was this new acquaintance to my peace. Before I was aware, the whole tide of my being had set in one channel. I, who had never before felt other than the general and diffusive sympathies of humanity for any human being, *loved* now, unsought, unwooed, with all the silent, resistless might of my passionate but reserved nature. This knowledge came to me with a bitter pang.

"For the most part, all his attentions to me had been bestowed during our solitary rides and rambles, and in the evening he was Jessie's constant cavalier as before. At first, I had accepted the common rumor which coupled their future together without regret or questioning. Of late, when my glimpses into his inner nature had been more frequent, I had begun to doubt her ability to enchain his preference; and, finally, I had resolutely cast the Future from my mind altogether, and quaffed eagerly the wine of joy held to my lips by the rosy fingers of the Present.

"But one night he, my hero, was more attentive to her than usual—he seemed to hang upon her every look and word; and, finally, some plan for the coming winter was discussed, in which she seemed to turn to him for his approbation, and I heard his reply:

"'It matters little where you are, since, wherever you are, we shall be together.'

"For a moment my eyes were blinded, my limbs were paralyzed. Then, with an instinctive feeling that his gaze was upon me, I arose and went out. That night I never closed my eyes. No moan or cry escaped me. I suffered dumbly such pangs as her shallow nature never could have comprehended. But I could not submit. Once more I arraigned my Maker. I asked him why on my poor life had been poured out so much bitterness—why He had given me such power to love, when no kiss of husband or of children could ever bring the warmth to my cold lips? Why I must so worship beauty, when I possessed not one element to gratify this yearning? Thinking of it afterward, I wondered He whom I blasphemed in my madness had not struck me dumb; but He spared me. The face of the night was calm, the stars shone above my speechless agony, and the silent moon looked down lovingly upon even me.

"In the morning I rose. I bathed my tearless eyes, smoothed my disordered hair, and went out. Never was-there a brighter day. Dew-drops glistened like diamonds on every spray, and below me the blue river wound along, flashing gayly in the sunshine, and singing as it journeyed to the sea. Up to the loving, leaning sky I lifted my ghastly, defiant face, and then a voice fell on my ear, gay, mocking, yet tender:

"'Does the sky pity you, Hester?'

"Wilton Eldredge had followed me. He came to my side.

"'No, I don't think the sky *does* pity you. You don't look comforted. Perhaps I can do you more good. I see you have not been crying, hard girl that you are; but you haven't slept any all night. Now I shouldn't tell you how bad I have been if I didn't know, beforehand, you would forgive me. I made that remark to Miss Jessie last night on purpose for you to hear. I wanted to find out whether you loved me. You had been too proud to show it—I meant to make you. I saw it struck home when I said it. I don't think I meant to make you suffer quite so much, and yet it *is* flattering, Hester.'

"He looked into my face with a roguish smile. Ah! if his fault had been ten times as great, I could not have chosen but to forgive him. Can you fancy what it would be if you had been immured in a dark dungeon for life; if the days and the nights had come and gone above your misery till your soul sickened, and, just as your despair was growing absolute, one should throw open the iron door, and heaven's own bright sunshine should once more trance your life with its half-forgotten glory? But that would be nothing to the flood of light which broke upon my whole being.

"'Your face is transfigured, Hester,' said Wilton Eldredge, looking at me. Then he went on gayly: 'You ought to have known I loved you all the time, else why did I seek you? Jessie I do not love—that is, I do love her as I love all beautiful women, but not, oh, not as I love you! I want to marry you, Hester. Will you have me?"

"He drew nearer to me, and waited for my reply. I could not utter a word. The depths of my being were stirred, and the waves gushed to my lips in too full a tide. I put my hand in his, and—it was almost the first time in my life—the tears fell from my eyes, and glittered on the grass at my feet. For once all his lightness and gayety were gone. He said, solemnly,

"'I love you, Hester. Plain, and shy, and dark as you are, you are more to me than all other women.

You have appealed to all that is lofty in my nature. You have ennobled me, and I give you my life. If I am not faithful, Hester, may the Lord judge between us!"

"I believed him then; I knew that I was beloved; and, looking back now over all the years, I believe still that in that hour, heart and soul, he was mine. Our hearts were too full for farther speech. We walked back to the house in silence—my hand upon his arm, as became his betrothed. Jessie Randall smiled as she saw us coming up the steps—a kind of speculative, derisive smile; but that morning our engagement was announced, and she was first in her congratulations. Her vanity must have been piqued, and perhaps—I do not know—her heart was wounded; but she had far too much tact to show it. She danced, and sang, and flirted as gayly as ever.

"Soon after this, one little circumstance occurred which I must not forget to mention, as after years brought it back to my thoughts. My father's will provided that, if I married before I was twenty-one, I should come into the full possession of my property, though it was to be secured to myself. I mentioned this one day to my lover, saying playfully, in the fullness of my joy,

"'You didn't know what a golden treasure you had won. Confess, now, did you ever hear I was rich?'

"'Oh yes,' he said, with careless sincerity; 'I knew that always. I used to be very proud, Hester. You would call it a weakness, but I don't think, if you had been poor, we should ever have become acquainted.'

"I remember the remark thrilled me at the time with a sudden pang; but I reflected how natural was this feeling to one educated as he had been, and soon it passed from my mind.

"I do not think there had been any vanity in my desire for beauty; for, from the moment I knew that he was mine—he, my king, my eidolon of love—I ceased to repine that fate had not been more bountiful. He loved me—I was precious in his sight—that was enough. My very face became dear to me because of the radiance his glances reflected upon it. I would not have had a single feature changed. For the rest of the world I cared not. He was my universe.

"Some women might have thought his continued attentions to the fair Jessie—which she received with a kind of repellent raillery, irresistibly piquant and charming—were cause enough for jealousy. But that was not in my nature. I was too proud of my lover ever to doubt him, and I do not think he gave me any cause. Beyond a man's natural admiration for pretty women, I do think that he was true to me—that all his tenderest thoughts centred in the bride he had chosen.

"Our engagement was a short one. We were married in December, and we went immediately to reside on my paternal estate of Heath Cliffe, in Georgia. This was my wish, and Wilton seemed to unite in it. In truth, his wife was not charming enough to tempt him into society, that the world might appreciate the treasure he had won. I think now that he must have had an ever-present consciousness, which no love had power to soften, of my irredeemable want of beauty. Despite that, however, we were happy.

"Our Southern home was dowered with the rich gifts of nature, and we did all that art and wealth could do to enhance its natural loveliness. My life, for a time, seemed to overbrim with gladness. I had enough and to spare, and I scattered loving words and deeds on all around as carelessly as a rose sheds dew-drops.

"Three years passed, and a new joy grew into both our hearts. We were expecting God's sweetest gift—a little child—to nestle on our bosoms, and look up at us with its shy, sweet eyes. Around this vision we wove bright and beautiful fancies. In its presence our thoughts grew sweet, yet solemn as prayers.

"The day of trial came. There were a few hours of terrible suffering, and then they laid my baby girl upon my bosom, cold and dead. The eyes I had dreamed would meet my own opened only in heaven—the baby voice I had thought would coo out such murmurous music responded only to the symphonies of the angels. The Great Father had need of her. The mysterious instinct of motherhood had been aroused within me, stirring all my nature, and now the new chord was broken.

"For a little while I held her there—my dead child, my wonderful, beautiful mystery—and then they took her from my arms and buried her. They made her grave—I would have it so—in a bower of magnolias, where Wilton and I loved best to sit together, so that in our hours of tenderest intercourse her memory might blend, and all that earth held of her be near us. Had she lived, she must have been very lovely; for she was her father's own child, and her baby features seemed a reflection of his.

"God never gave me another child; but, hard as it was, at first, to resign myself to His will, I was very happy. And yet my husband would not have made some women so, even had their love for him been as true and fervent as my own. He was arbitrary in his disposition, absolute in his control over the minutest actions of my life. But, proud as I was to others, while I believed in his love I had no pride for him. Even this control was grateful to me. Love made the yoke easy to be borne. I had no troubles. Only once or twice, when he had been absent upon business a little longer than I thought necessary, I had been conscious of a passing twinge of fear lest my society was not so much life, air, sunshine to him as his was to me —lest I did not make his home so attractive as a more beautiful woman would have done. But when he came back, once more his kisses upon my lips would charm away my fears, and my life would be all brightness.

"We had been married ten years without so much as meeting any of my guardian's family. At last, one evening in early spring, my husband, opening the letter-bag, tossed into my lap a dainty, delicate-looking epistle, on the outside of which I at once recognized the smooth, flowing, characteristic chirography of Miss Jessie Randall—*still* Miss Jessie Randall after all these years. I broke the seal, and the letter informed me that she was *blasé*, as she said, ennuied of fashion, and folly, and New York. She smelled from afar the fragrance of my Southern roses. Might she come and gather a bouquet of them? I should find she had grown very good, she added. She was quite a different woman at thirty-one from what she had been at twenty, and she really thought we should get on nicely together, particularly if I would keep my satirical, too perfect husband out of the way. Indeed, she made so sure of a welcome that she should be with me almost as soon as her letter.

"I had always ridiculed presentiments, and yet, as I read that letter, I was seized with a mortal dread. A sudden spasm of blinding pain came and went, leaving my cheek blanched, my lips rigid. In the distance I seemed to hear the future wail out a warning of the events she was bringing me. I reasoned with myself a moment. What trouble *could* there be in store? My confidence in my husband was perfect. I should be selfish not to rejoice that some one else was coming to enliven the solitary life so much of which he passed alone with me. Besides, my guardian's daughter had a right to as warm a welcome as her father had given me when I went to his home a helpless orphan. So reasoning, I regained my self-command, overcame my undefined dread, and, handing the letter across to Wilton, said cheerfully,

"'Read that, dear. Jessie Randall is coming to us. It seems we may expect her any day now.'

"He took the letter and glanced over it.

"'What a graceful hand!' he said.

"Alas! those words cost me another pang. You know what my writing is. There never was any grace in that, or any other of my outward manifestations.

"'A pretty, piquant style,' he said, as he handed the letter back. 'This visit will be a fine thing to set you up, Hester. You are growing thin, and it's confoundedly dull here. Jessie must be a splendid woman by this time!' Then, seeing a look of pain upon my face, he added, 'My gifted wife, though, is worth a dozen such.' Then he kissed me gayly, and went out.

"That was our last evening alone together. He

had never been more tender, more thoughtful. The next day Jessie came. Wilton was out of the house when she arrived. I expressed my regret that he was not there to welcome her.

"'Nonsense!' she cried, with a kiss I shrank from, and did not return. 'I had quite as lief he would not see me in this chrysalis state,' pointing to her gray traveling-wrap, somewhat covered with dust, and the 'ugly' drawn over her straw bonnet.

"I conducted her to her room, and then, sending my own maid to unpack her trunks and assist her, I went down to give directions for my early tea. When the bell sounded she came, looking quite refreshed and radiant. Time had dealt lightly with her. She was even more beautiful than in her girlhood. Her proportions were more mature, her grace more queenly, her self-possession more perfect. Her taste, too, always exquisite, perfected by years of patient study, was now faultless. Wilton met her at the dining-room door. I saw him start back as if bewildered by this unexpected vision. He welcomed her cordially, and she came in and took her seat at the board. Sitting beside her, I forgot that I was a loved and loving wife, and once more, in my heart-sickness, I seemed to myself the black, ugly shadow, necessary and welcome to no one, which I had been in the days when I first knew her.

"Weeks passed on, however, without bringing me any thing of which to complain. It is true, I seldom saw my husband alone. Most of his time was occupied with our guest; walking with her, riding with her, or listening, in the pleasant evenings of early summer, to melody so entrancing that even I was charmed out of myself."

At this stage of her narrative I glanced at Hester's face. It was fearfully pale. Her nerves trembled, and her whole appearance gave signs of extreme exhaustion. I had been too much absorbed in her story to notice this before; now it frightened me.

"You are overtasking yourself," I said, earnestly. "Don't! You mustn't go on. It will kill you. You can not bear it."

"Yes, I must do what I do very quickly," she answered, solemnly. "Just hand me that glass of wine. It will strengthen me a little. There!

"I said at first I had nothing to complain of, and yet all this time a weary, desolate weight was settling down upon my heart. I went often alone to the little grave where they had buried my baby, and there only I could weep. Oh, what a blessed relief those tears were!

"One night they had gone out to take a walk, and I turned my footsteps toward the accustomed spot. As I drew near I heard voices. I stole noiselessly toward the bower, and, standing on one side, looked in through the leaves. There, above my child's grave, his child and mine, knelt my husband; on the seat beside him sat Jessie, her beautiful eyes beaming on him through a mist of tears, her hand clasped passionately in his. I thought not of propriety, or so-called honor, when my all was at stake. I listened—listened with strained ears, desperately, eagerly, as for my life.

"'She was rich, you know, and I was poor,' I heard him say, as I drew near, and then came shudderingly back to me the memory of how he himself had said, in the days of our engagement, that, had he not known I was rich, he should never have sought me. I bit my lip and held my breath. Her soft, purring, catlike tones came next:

"'Then you did love me?'

"'Love you! For what else did I go there but for love of you? There was not an hour before my marriage when you might not have drawn me to your feet, had you willed it. But what matters that? I did not love you then as I love you now—Jessie, Jessie!'

"He said her name over and over again, as if its syllables embodied all tenderness—and I, I listened. I can not tell you what else they said; light words of me—cold, sneering words; pledges of eternal love; and yet, notwithstanding she exchanged these vows, her firm refusal of even a single kiss—I understood it all. She wished him to contrive some pretext for divorcing me, and then she would be his wife—be revenged for the innocent wound I had once given to her vanity, nay, perhaps to her heart; for I think she must have loved him as well as such a nature could.

"I wonder I did not go mad. I wonder, roused to phrensy, I had not stood before them and denounced them—cursed them by my love and my wrongs. But I did not. I still retained the deep, undemonstrative nature of my childhood. I listened until I could listen no longer, and then, my hands tightly clasped, my lips resolutely sealed, I walked noiselessly toward the house. I gave myself no time for repining. I would not let my sick heart utter a single cry; I sat down and looked my grief steadily in the face. One thing I saw clearly—I was no longer loved. I stood in the way of *his* happiness whom I would have died to bless. I had promised to cleave to him for better, for worse, until death parted us; but now his own words had raised up between us a barrier more effectual than death ever could. I would depart and leave him free. I had one wild, irrepressible dread, and that was of meeting him again. How could I hear his voice, how look upon his face, I whom he loved no longer? Let me go any where, any where, was the wail of my heart—only let me get out of his way. A beautiful woman would not so have given him up, but I had no confidence in my own powers. Besides, from childhood I had learned to yield; and more than all, during the ten years of my married life, had I been daily and hourly learning the lesson that my happiness was nothing to his, and I never thought of putting them into competition. I made up a bundle of a few necessary things. In it I put a tress of his hair, a miniature which he had given me during our brief engagement, and the letters I had received from him in his short absences. Then I wrote him a few lines. I told him that I had listened to the scene in the arbor over my dead child's grave; that I knew all—and then I said,

"'Because I do know this I am going out of your sight. I have staid with you while I thought I was necessary to your happiness, but now that I am in your way, I love you too truly not to go. But oh, my husband! my heart's own husband! I leave you my blessing. Its fullness shall abide with you, even though her head should lie, where mine so often has rested, upon your bosom.'

"Then I ordered a trusty servant, who had been my mother's, and who loved nothing on earth so well as his mistress, to bring horses for himself and me.

In ten minutes we were on our way. I do not know whether any attempts were made to pursue us. At any rate, in three days we reached Savannah, and I went to my lawyer. One haunting fear had seized me, that my husband might seek a reconciliation with me for the sake of my fortune. There never could be a moment of my future life when I would not receive him with open arms; but if he came, it must be from love, and not from policy. With the assistance of Mr. Brief, I executed an instrument conveying to him, without incumbrance or restriction, all my property, reserving for myself but a mere pittance. Leaving a copy with the lawyer, I intrusted this instrument to Pompey's care, and dispatched him on his return to Heath Cliffe. The same night I started for the North. Fate or chance led my steps to a town about twenty miles from here, and I was soon established in a quiet boarding-place. What I suffered God only knows. I have made no moan; I will not.

"From that day to this—it is three years now—I have never heard from Wilton. My heart has been troubling me more and more, and I have felt that the struggle with death would be but brief. Last spring I read, by chance, your grandfather's advertisement. I recognized the house as being my husband's early home, and I at once applied for it. I loved him as fondly as ever. I yearned with irrepressible yearning for the tones of his voice, the touch of his hand, or the sound of his foot upon the stair. I longed to come here—to dwell in solitude and silence where he had played, a young, innocent boy, pillowing his head upon his mother's breast. I thought these fancies would be company for me. Besides, there was another reason, which I scarcely owned to myself. I thought perhaps this might lead to my seeing him once more. I could not put aside the belief that he had loved me once. I knew he had had no means of learning the place of my abode since we parted; that he could not have found me had he sought me even with tears. Now I thought he would learn from your grandfather that one Hester Wilde, a lone woman, was his tenant, and perchance he would come to me.

"I have waited, vainly; but, ten days ago, the cloud began to lift, and I could see the faint dawn of day. I read the announcement of Jessie Randall's marriage to a rich old man in New York. I knew then that my husband was not with her. At the same moment I felt that the hand of death was on me; that I had but a few days more to live. In the might of my dying life and my undying love I sent my soul forth to summon him. I prayed, I wrestled with God that I might look upon his face once more this side of heaven, and since then I have been waiting."

She sank back as she said this in utter prostration, and lay there, her face growing fearfully deathlike in the steady light of the wax-candle. I drew my watch from my belt; it was almost midnight. Suddenly she started up.

"Listen!" she cried, with wild energy, "listen!"

My first thought was of the ghosts. I listened breathlessly, but I heard nothing save the storm—which, having come on at nightfall, had risen now to a gale, and was bursting wildly against the windows, and rocking the old brown house to its foundations.

"Don't you hear it?" she cried, eagerly—"a horse, coming here?"

I could hear it now, plainly enough—the tramp of a horse ridden furiously. It came in at the gate, up the long poplar walk. It stopped, and the rider dismounted before our very door. Hester had risen up in bed now. Her head was bent forward, and every wan feature was aglow with longing anticipation. The door opened, he sprang in, and in a moment the original of Mistress Hester Wilde's miniature stood before me; but sadly worn and wasted, as if by long sorrow, was the proud, noble face now. He did not seem even to see me. He sank on his knees by Hester's bedside, and, gathering her up, folded her to his bosom. Her arms were closely clasped about his neck, her head sank on his shoulder, and a low murmur of ineffable peace floated from her lips.

"Wife—saint—idol—blessed one!" he cried, holding her there, "you shall not kiss me, you shall not even utter that forgiveness for want of which, for three long years, I have been slowly dying, until you hear my story. I did love you, Hester, God knows. I did love you, and no other. I went into the house that fatal night. I sought you in our own room. I found your note, and read it. Oh, Hester! its uncomplaining, patient tenderness thrilled me as no reproaches could have done. I felt then that your heart was broken. How I longed to cast myself at your feet, to pray for your forgiveness! I loved you so unutterably. You had never been so dear; and I loathed with deadliest loathing the beautiful Evil who had tempted me from you. Before light the next morning I had left Heath Cliffe and started in pursuit of you. I left behind me a few lines for Miss Randall, in which I inclosed a copy of your note. I told her I had awaked from my mad dream, and how inexpressibly dear beyond all earthly objects was the wife I had lost. I reached Savannah the day after you had left. Your deed of all your property to me was another stab, piercing my very heart. I had no clew by which to trace you, and so I staid there until I heard that Miss Blair had left Heath Cliffe, and was *en route* for the North. Then I went home and waited. Oh, Hester! I sometimes thought you would come back, but as time passed on this hope faded. It was only three months since that I learned you were living here; and then you seemed so pure, so perfect, so far removed from me, that I dared not come to you. But ten days ago, at noonday, I heard, or fancied that I heard, a voice. The tones were like yours, but it seemed to come from very far off. It uttered a wail, a pleading cry that I should come to you before you died. I have traveled, since then, night and day. Here I am; Hester, mine only one, will you forgive me?"

Her voice was broken now and faltering, very thick with tears.

"You, too, have much to forgive," she murmured. "I did wrong. I was your wife. I should have kept my place and striven to win you back; but yet, God knoweth, I did what I thought would make you happiest."

His arms clasped her tighter. Feebly she raised her head. Their lips clung together in one long, passionate kiss, and in that, I know not how, her spirit was exhaled. The kiss of forgiveness was the kiss of death.

The storm lulled, and the wind only wailed now like the tender, sorrowful notes of a solemn psalm. We lifted her up and laid her head back upon the pillow. A smile was upon her dead face.

Three days later we buried her in the family burying-ground, behind the stately poplars, and it was not many weeks before Wilton Eldredge lay down beside her, to sleep in the same grave his long, dreamless slumber. The Eldredge family were left without an heir. No one cared to live in the old brown house. It is going to decay.

But the dead rest well. At "moonless midnight or matin prime" they lift not up their covering of verdure. Suns rise and moons set for them in vain; but I know there is another country where the long-enduring love will receive its reward—where the roses are eternal, and the tenants of the everlasting mansions shall never die.

Uncle Roger's Story and Mine.

I loved you, Evelyn, all the while;
  My heart seemed full as it could hold—
There was place and to spare for the frank young smile,
  And the red young mouth, and the hair's young gold.
So hush! I will give you this leaf to keep;
  See, I shut it inside the sweet, cold hand.
There, that is our secret! go to sleep;
  You will wake, and remember, and understand.

ROBERT BROWNING.

UNCLE ROGER'S STORY AND MINE.

WE were sitting on the upper piazza—my Uncle Roger Apthorpe and I. It was at his house in Hingham—a country house, yet looking out upon the distant ocean, with its countless white wings of sails, "its million lips of shells," the cliffs upon its margin, the islands on its bosom. I had been talking to Uncle Roger. He was my mother's brother; the house in which he lived was his inheritance from my grandfather, and here I spent with him the summer months, to me the happiest portion of the year.

My mother had died when I was very young. My father was immersed in the cares of business, and between my stepmother and myself was always a thin ice of reserve—perhaps a courteous and unexpressed hostility. Therefore Uncle Roger was my only confidant.

I had been telling him of a visit I had received that morning. Young Harry Holt had ridden out from town, and, in a few manly words, had offered me his heart and his name. Uncle Roger had listened to my story with even more than his usual interest. Harry was one of his prime favorites.

"And you accepted him, Ethel?" he said, inquiringly, as I paused.

"No, Uncle Roger; why should I? It was my first offer. I might see fifty men I like better, yet—"

Here my conscience gave me a twinge, and I added, "Or, if I shouldn't, he knows women too well to take my first 'no' for final; he will ask me again."

Uncle Roger made no reply. I lifted the glass which lay in my lap, and looked listlessly, yet wistfully, over the sea at the great ships going out and coming in. Whence were they? Where did they go, carrying all their freight of unquiet human souls—weary souls that could not stay at home, and so traversed the wide earth over, seeking rest and finding none? It seemed to me that travel was the forlorn hope of desperation. Those who were denied happiness were roaming after excitement. I felt a sadness I could not explain or define. In its shadow every thing wore an expression of hopelessness. And yet that June afternoon was gilding land and sea. A golden haze, mellow as autumn, warm as summer, lay in the air. A tender dreaminess brooded over the whole face of nature. I could hear no sounds, save the swell of the sea breaking upon the distant beach. The tide was coming in. Every now and then a tenth wave broke loftily over the others, scattering its spray of green, and gold, and violet; its diamonds, amethysts, and emeralds, perishing, yet how glittering. The sun was not painfully bright; its garish beams were tempered by the haze in the atmosphere, the fine, imperceptible mist rising from the water, and it seemed to hang in mid air as if conscious that it was the longest day in the year, and there was no need of hurry in its journey to the west. The hour and the scene were both bright. Why was it that my heart could see in them only images of sadness and unrest!

At length I became conscious that Uncle Roger was

watching me. I looked at him. There was a strange gleam, a flash of youthful fire in the tempered and quiet sadness of his gray eyes. A flush had risen to his withered cheeks, and the fingers he had unconsciously knitted together were tremulous. At any other time I should have inquired the cause of his emotion; but my thoughts were preoccupied, and he was the first to speak.

"And so you have refused Harry Holt, as I take it, from a mere wanton caprice—a feminine desire to say 'no.' Well, I believe happiness is offered to every one of us, at least once in life, but not one in a hundred is wise enough to take it. I thought you would have been. You are a good girl in the main, Ethel; a kind heart, not much vanity, but you are a woman. Human nature will be human nature."

He drew a long sigh. I looked at him in silent expectation. I had always felt that his life had a mystery; that he, with his shrewd mind, his loving heart, his keen intellect, had not lived alone without a more than ordinary reason, and I believed the time had come when he would return my confidence with his own. I was not disappointed. He was silent for a while, and his face wore the look of one absorbed in self-communion, painful but intense. At length he spoke:

"They say every life has its own romance, Ethel; I have often meant to tell you mine. At my age the world would say the dreams of youth should have long since been forgotten, and yet they are not. Old, and gray, and sober as I am, there is one name I can not utter, even to myself, without quickened pulses.

"Caroline Windham was no angel. I think, if she

had been, my imperfect human nature, standing afar off, would have seen in her no charm. She was not even one of those saint-like beings whom some men worship—marble without a flaw, faultless perfection. She was a woman—a girl rather, full of passion, of pride, of quick, ungoverned impulses. There was a dainty grace in her movements, a pretty petulance in her manner. She was one to be loved with fervid, jealous exactingness, once and forever. She was one to love, but I did not know that then.

"Her very beauty was peculiar and all her own. She had a face like a gipsy, with strong lights and shades, framed in heavy bands of jet-black hair, with large black eyes flashing out upon you one moment their subtle electricity, the next veiled by the inky lashes which swept their penciled shadows over her crimson cheeks. Her mouth was small, though full—at once proud and fond. Her figure was rounded and symmetrical. A physiognomist would, perhaps, have pronounced her wanting in ideality in the spiritual element, but he would have told you that her undisciplined heart was warm; her untried soul, as yet a stranger to itself, was true.

"I remember to this day every circumstance of our first meeting. She was the one intimate friend whom your mother, like all other young ladies, had made at school; and I came home, from a couple of years of foreign travel, to find her domesticated for a long visit in this very house. I had seen many charming women at home and abroad; many, perhaps, far more strictly and regularly beautiful than she; but never, before or since, have I seen one at all like her. I used to think her piquant, irresistibly fascinating face should have belonged to some Moorish Circe, some gipsy queen, rather than to Miss Caroline Windham, daughter of Jonathan Windham, Esq., merchant, of New York.

"I can see her now just as she looked when I was introduced to her first—the dark, bright face; the small head, bound round with a wreath of blood-red garden roses; the negligent folds of her white muslin dress, flowing loosely about her figure, and gathered in at the waist with a crimson girdle. I do not know but her manner—half careless, half disdainful—would have repelled me in another. It did not in her; it seemed perfectly appropriate.

"From that hour I worshiped her, and yet I think the closest observer would have failed to detect my adoration. My nature was both proud and reserved, and my quiet manners seldom gave outward indications of my feelings. Possibly this very reticence and apparent stoicism attracted her. At all events, our acquaintance soon ripened into an intimacy which might have been friendship, but for the concealed passion which I had determined not at that time to express, and which effectually prevented a response on my part to the friendly and assured familiarity of her demeanor toward me.

"She seemed to me as winning and as artless as a child. She uttered all her thoughts frankly, and joined in every country pleasure with a zest, the natural result of her city life and education, but which seemed singular enough to one accustomed to country life as I had always been.

"That was a happy summer. We sailed, we drove upon the beach, we fished, we rode, and the long summer day seemed not long enough for our merriment. Two or three times we went, at nightfall, to watch the sunset at Nantucket Beach. Once, I remember, the tide was just coming in. The sun had set gloriously, kindling the western sky with coruscations of rainbow-colored flame. The moon was rising, and threw a long line of silver over the waters. We had sat down together, Caroline Windham and I, on the wreck of an old ship that had been cast on the shore by some of the wild storms so frequent on the rocky New England coast. Your mother was at a little distance, looking with dreamy eyes at the sunset clouds. Poor Ellen, she had her own Spanish castles then—hers was a loving heart, and it was that summer that she first met your father. I had never seen Caroline so quiet, almost sad. She sat there leaning her head on her hand, watching the billows chasing each other restlessly toward the shore.

"At last she lifted her face toward me. 'There is no pause for them,' she said; 'they go on, one after another, forever and forever. Are they never tired?'

"I answered her question by another. 'Are you ever tired, Caroline? You are always gay. You go from one pleasure to another, a sort of human humming-bird. Do you ever weary of flowers?'

"Tears, which yet did not fall, gathered heavily on her lashes. She looked at me wishfully, and then turned her eyes away.

"'Yes, ah! yes,' she said, with a low sigh; 'I am tired often; but what can I do? People look for nothing in me but gayety. Who loves me? Who cares to find out the secrets of my heart? Nay, who dreams that I have a heart? And yet I have one, and it is flame.'

"Then was my hour. Fate and fortune favored me. Happiness held her cup to my lips. I spilled her proffered wine on the sand. I hardly know why I did not, then and there, show her my heart—offer her my life and my love. I thought I had reason for my self-control. I did not believe that she loved me. I had hope that her love might be mine in the future, but I feared to startle her by asking it too soon. She was too young, I thought, to know herself; besides, I had a sort of quixotic hesitation about endeavoring to draw her into an engagement while she was my sister's guest; ignorant, as I was, whether it would at all meet her father's approval. I silenced the words which were rising to my lips. I answered her quietly, almost coldly,

"'I do not think you do your friends justice. Ellen, I am sure, loves you, and—'

"I do not know what other commonplace I was about to add, for she sprang up from my side, her quick, petulant manner all restored, the sad tenderness gone from her expression, the pathos from her voice.

"'Yes,' she said, lightly, 'Ellen loves me. She is a good girl, but she loves John Hammond a good deal better, and I—what could I do with love, after all? I could not wear it, or spend it; it is not even tangible to touch or sight.'

"The next moment she was shattering the fair, frail turrets of Ellen's castle in the air, pulling at her curls, and declaring that it was time to go—that she hated the sea; it made her feel blue and stupid—she liked driving, and she should drive those two horses standing there, so impatiently, all the way home.

"She did drive us home. She insisted on sitting alone on the front seat, while I occupied the back one with Ellen, and, as we dashed over the sands at a rattling pace, she would now and then look round at us, and laugh and shake her head, threatening us with all manner of calamities. Every trace of that sad sensibility, which had puzzled and enchanted me an hour before, was gone from her manner, and I began to wonder whether her character was not more of an enigma than I had supposed.

"Soon after this she left us. Her father came for her one evening, and took her away with him in the morning. I did not like him. He was a stiff, stately, somewhat pompous man. I could not understand how his daughter had grown up to be the free, natural, impulsive girl she was, under his shadow.

"We were separated without my having said one word to her of more than ordinary friendship. Her father was standing by her side when she bade me good-by. I thought her hand trembled as I held it, and her eyes were humid, but then she had just parted from Ellen.

"It was six months before I saw, or sought to see her again. I know, in this, my conduct will seem entirely at variance with what I have told you of my love; and yet, was it any stranger than that of many a girl who turns, in apparent coldness, from the very man whose voice quickens every throb of her pulses?

"I believe I placed too much faith in her youth. I thought her so young no one would be likely to seek her. She seemed to me a mere school-girl, an impulsive child. I thought I might wait with safety.

"It was early spring when I, at length, went to New

York. As I rang the bell at her father's door, a shiver of emotion passed over me—an emotion born of love, of hope, of a vague doubt, in itself almost as delicious as love. I sent up my name, and was shown into a little morning-room, leading from the parlors, through which I followed the polite footman.

"Caroline rose to meet me as I entered the door, her face flushed with welcome, her lips parted, her eyes sparkling. I believe I did not speak. She was self-possessed; women always are. She made some inquiries after Ellen, welcomed me gracefully to town, and then silence fell between us. I had leisure to note now what, in the eagerness of her welcome, I had not observed. A winter of fashionable life had wrought its effects upon her. She was thinner. The crimson of her cheeks and lips was less brilliant; her dark complexion was less clear. There was a sad droop to her eyelids, an intangible element of melancholy in her very smile. It made my heart ache to see her. 'Decidedly,' I thought, 'this kind of life is not good for her. There is too much of the wandering Ishmaelite in her nature to bear this conventional confinement. I wish I had her in the country, now, for a good race over the hills. It would bring back color and flavor to her life.'

"I commenced by telling her this. I ended by telling her, I know not in what phrase, that I loved her—that I had loved her from the first moment I had ever seen her—that my one hope in the future was to win her for my wife.

"I was not prepared for her answer. I had expected, perhaps, a little embarrassment, a tender confession, or an uncertainty almost equally encouraging;

possibly, though I had not looked at the case much in this aspect, a proud refusal. I got neither.

"She looked at me long and earnestly, as if reading my soul. She must have seen my truth in my eyes. The passionate tears gushed in torrents from hers. Then her words came, low, but distinct and firm.

"'You have done me great wrong, Roger Apthorpe, me and yourself too. Had you told me this last summer I would have given you my love and my life. Nay, I did love you. Did you not know it? did you not see it, when we sat together on the wreck, and you turned from me so coldly? But now it is too late. I must not talk with you about it. I shall be married in six weeks to a good man—a man who loves me.'

"'And whom you do *not* love,' I said. 'Oh, Caroline, can you do this great wickedness? You will blight your own life and his, and mine too, if that were any thing to you.'

"I had roused her temper, which was never gentle. Perhaps her anger flamed against me all the more fiercely for her very love.

"'For shame!' she cried; 'for shame, Roger Apthorpe! It is like you to tempt me now to break my word. If you loved me, why did you not tell me? No, I will not marry you. I will marry a man who does love me—who was not too proud to say so—who did not think me too young or too foolish to be his wife. Do not say any more; you can not move me. I shall not make my husband's life miserable. I tell you he loves me, and I will be a good wife to him.'

"I tried entreaty and persuasion, but she would not be moved. Underneath her gay, careless exterior was the firmest will I have ever met. She had given her promise, and she was as tenacious as a Bedouin of her plighted word."

"But, Uncle Roger," I interposed here—it was the first time I had spoken since he commenced his recital—"how could you continue to love her if she was so proud and so passionate; if she would commit such a sin as to marry another when her heart and soul were full of you?"

Uncle Roger shook his gray head and smiled sadly.

"I am fifty-four years old, Ethel. Twenty-two years of life have passed over me since that morning; and, with my faculties sharpened by suffering, I have read many hearts. We talk and write of virtues with high-sounding names, but when we love they make very little difference. The woman at whose shrine we worship may or may not have them. No matter! What enchains us is not tangible, can not be defined; it is a certain something which links soul to soul; a subtle electricity to which all submit while they deride it. I knew well enough that Caroline Windham was haughty, self-willed, and passionate; that a character would have been, theoretically, more noble than hers, by force of which its possessor, finding or fancying that she was not beloved by the man to whom her heart was given, would have resolved to remain single for life. Such was not Caroline; and yet, just as she was, I would not have bartered one of her faults for any other woman's virtues. To have conquered that proud will, to have subdued that haughty heart, would have been a sweeter triumph than a thousand easier conquests.

"I did not quite abandon all hope, though I left New York the next day without having made an attempt to see her again. For six weeks after I haunted the post-office. I had faith that her love would yet overmaster her pride. Sleeping or waking, I seemed to see the very shape and handwriting of the little note which I daily expected would come to me, with a sentence of invitation and encouragement.

"At last came—not that, but a letter from a friend who knew of my sister's intimacy with Miss Windham, but had no idea of my own attachment. In it he inclosed for Ellen a notice of her friend's marriage to Mr. Robert Eastman; and he added the information that they were to spend the summer in traveling for the benefit of the bride's health, which was delicate.

"It would be idle to dwell upon the bitterness of my despair. Such epochs are indescribable—fraught with a suffering beyond words. I sought no sympathy; I desired none. Even your mother never dreamed that my love for her cherished friend had transcended and outgrown her own. She wondered a little that Caroline had not written to her about her wedding, but she was too much absorbed in her own happiness to pay much heed to the circumstance. Her marriage was arranged for that fall; and, dear as she was to me, I could not bear to look upon her face with the transfiguring light of happy love flooding her quiet eyes, glorifying her whole expression. I have sometimes thought the very effort it cost me to conceal my misery was good for my soul's health. If we sit down weakly under a blow, and call upon others and ourselves for pity, we lose the recuperative power which self-control, taken as a tonic, never fails to give us. I always admired the Spartan boy who let the fierce wild fox gnaw at his vitals, and made no cry or moan.

"Early in the autumn I received a letter superscribed in a bold, manly hand with which I was not familiar. I broke the seal, and glanced first at the signature — Robert Eastman — the name of Caroline Windham's husband. It was, indeed, from him. He told me, in a few words, that Caroline's health had been failing ever since their marriage; that he was convinced she had but a few days to live, and he begged me to lose no time in coming to her. She had told him, he said, of our friendship, and expressed a strong desire to see me.

"There was not one word by aid of which I could determine whether he knew of the past relations which had existed between her and me. One thing I noticed, that he spoke of her as Caroline, not once as his wife. I did not waste time in conjecture. Caroline, my love, lay dying. Oh, to be in time to see her once more, to hear her voice, to hold her hand! The railroad from Boston to Providence had been built the year before. It was the quickest route to New York then open. I was in time for the steam-boat train. I reached New York the next morning, and hurried at once to the address given me in Mr. Eastman's letter. I asked for him, and presently he came to me in the parlor, whither I had been shown. He was a noble-looking man. Every lineament of his fine face expressed benevolence, gentleness, kindness. He looked pale and worn with watching and anxiety. He took my hand in an earnest clasp.

"'Thank God you have come,' he said, in a voice tremulous with emotion. 'Poor Caroline! she has told me all. She is more truly your wife than mine. It was a terrible mistake. I would give the universe if I had never married her. She might have lived then, and been happy, but—I loved her. Come, we are losing precious time. She is worse this morning, but she is buoyed up now by excitement. I told her you were here.'

"I begged him to be present at our interview; I felt I had no right to see her alone. Caroline, he told me, had made the same request, but he thought it better to leave us to ourselves. We, who had been parted in life, might surely snatch a few moments from death and the grave.

"He led me to the door. He opened it, and closed it again behind me. I was alone with her. She raised herself from her pillow. Her wan face was illumined with a glow and a glory as of a dying day. She stretched out her arms. I sprang to her bedside, and those thin, wasted arms fell about my neck. Her lips met mine for the first time, and there I held her, with death watching and waiting beside us. I know not how long it was before either of us spoke. At length Caroline raised her head and looked at me. Her eyes were the same, large, bright, and full of tenderness, though in all else she was terribly changed.

"'This is not wrong, Roger,' she said; 'it can not be wrong to love you now. Before the sun sets I shall be where they neither marry nor are given in marriage. I have told Robert all, and he forgives me freely. He will not even let me blame myself. I am so glad, so thankful that I am going to die. If I had lived, to know, as he must have known, that I did not love him, would have blighted all his life. Now he will be happy again; I know his nature. He will mourn for me a while, and then some one else will console him. I thank God for this. It is a terrible thing to wrong a man as I wronged him. The only atonement I can make is in dying. We always pity the dead and forgive them, no matter what their faults are. I do not ask *you* to forgive me, Roger.'

"I can not tell you in what words I answered her; how I poured into her dying ears the fullness of a love no human utterance could measure. She understood me. I did not say it, but she looked into my heart, and knew, even as I did in that hour, that for me only heaven could bring consolation—that my first love would be my last.

"I think we must have been together two hours. Much of this time had been passed in solemn silence, much in grave and earnest talk concerning the stern realities to which she was hastening; and blended with all this was the strong cry, from the living to the dying, of a love which death itself could not subdue.

"At length a swift and ghastly change passed over her face. In a faint voice she bade me call her husband. He hurried in, followed by the nurse and the physician. She lifted her eyes to his with a sweet and tender smile. In a tone so low that only he and I could hear it, she said,

"'I have loved you dearly, Robert—dearly, though not best. You have been very good to me. No one could have been kinder or more tender. It will comfort you to remember this when I am gone. Some time, I am glad to think, you will love again, and be loved in return as this wayward heart could never have loved you.'

"He sat down on the bed beside her, and lifted her head on his bosom. She was dear to him, I could see that, as his own life. She rested there, tranquilly lapsing away into death, 'going out with the tide.' I knelt by the bedside, and her hand was clasped in mine. For a time she looked at me steadily, with eyes full of clinging tenderness; then the lids closed over them, but she did not sleep. From time to time we could catch scarcely audible snatches of prayer; and once she murmured, 'He shall wipe away all tears from their eyes.'

"At length she quite ceased to speak. We watched her still, as her breathing grew slower and slower; at last I bent my face to hers; I felt a chill, faint breath cross my cheek. Was it the token of her passing soul?—that moment the doctor said, 'She is dead.' Her husband laid her tenderly and reverently from his arms, and I can remember nothing more. For months I had borne up against my grief; I had set the seal of silence upon my lips; I had striven with calm front to fight the battle of life. At last my over-tasked energies had sunk under this continual pressure. Merciful unconsciousness seized upon my faculties.

"When I awoke from this stupor it was late in the night. I was lying in a comfortable chamber, and Caroline's husband was watching over me. He said gently,

"'You have been unconscious a long time. The doctor says it was only over-excitement. You will do very well now, but at first we thought you would follow her.'

"'Would that I had! would to God that I had!' I cried, in mad insubordination.

"He gave me a strange, dreary look, as if he scarcely understood why *I* should sorrow. 'She loved *you*,' he faltered, with a quiet pathos, which softened my stricken heart to sympathy with a woe yet more hopeless than my own.

"He was the noblest man I ever knew, this Robert Eastman. In his place, how many would have pursued me, all my life through, with vengeful hate; but to him the very love which Caroline had borne me rendered me sacred. Caroline had understood him well. He had loved her deeply; he mourned for her truly. Had he been, as I was, the beloved of her soul, he would have consecrated all his life to her memory. But he knew that she had never loved him; that, in the most sacred sense, she had never been his wife; and, after a few years, he married again, this time a pale, blonde beauty; a gentle, quiet woman, very unlike Caroline. They are happy. They have passed fifteen years of their life together. It has been like a perfect day, growing brighter toward its afternoon. I think it is one of those heaven-made marriages which death only makes eternal.

"For myself, after the first shock was over, I think Caroline's death was almost a comfort to me. She had never seemed so truly mine as when I stood beside her grave. I am technically no spiritualist. I do not believe in physical demonstrations; I have had none of her presence; and yet I know that many a midnight she has watched over my slumbers, that her free soul walks through life at my side. I believe, as truly as I believe in heaven, that she will be mine hereafter; that, when the messenger comes for me who comes for all, she will guide me across the tideless, fathomless waters, and be mine on the other side; mine in all the changeless radiance of her beauty, the glory of her immortal love, and her immortal youth. *I* shall be young again *there.*"

I looked at him as he ceased speaking. A great light, as of a mighty hope, sat on his face. In its transfiguring glow he looked no longer old and withered. I could see a foretaste of the youth which death was to bring to him. He sat for a long time silently gazing on the distant sea. I thought the fire which shone in his eyes must be such as had kindled them when he looked on *her.*

At length he rose, and, drawing a miniature-case from his breast, put it into my hand.

"Look at that, Ethel, and judge if I have exaggerated her charms. It was taken when she was your age—just seventeen."

He left me, and when he was gone into the house I opened the case. The face was that of a most beautiful woman. There was a flush, a glow of buoyant, physical life upon it, which made its loveliness seem beyond the reach of time or death. It was not a face to grow old, and yet, if she had lived, she must have been past middle age now. Perhaps death was better than life, and its stern discipline of trials and changes.

I did not see Uncle Roger again that night. The next morning I gave the miniature back to him. As I did so I made my own confession of wrong.

"Uncle Roger," I said, "you were right. I love Harry Holt almost as you loved *her.* I refused him from foolish vanity. I was vexed with his hasty wooing. I wished to make him more submissive, more humble; and now, perhaps, I have lost him. Is he too proud ever to come back?"

Uncle Roger soothed me with sympathy gentle as a woman's. It was strange how well we two understood each other. Most men in his place would have proposed to recall the banished lover; but he knew the pride of my nature too well. Indeed, his pride for me was as lofty as my own, and I would have died sooner than make one effort to bring the banished suitor back.

Weeks passed on, and I neither saw nor heard of him. For a long time I comforted myself with delusive hopes. Morning after morning I more than half expected to see his horse at the gate. But it never came. Perhaps, wayward girl that I was, I should have liked him less if he had forgotten his own dignity and humbled himself to seek me again.

Never once since I gave him the miniature had either his heart's loss or mine been mentioned between Uncle Roger and myself. But all this time I could feel that he gave me his tenderest sympathy. Trouble had never hardened his heart, only made it more earnest and more loving. He strove to gratify all my wishes. His care over me was inexpressibly soothing and watchful. I strove bravely against any weak indulgence in regret or repining. I tried to make my outer life cheerful and useful, and I think, in some good degree, I succeeded, but in my heart was a great void.

At length, one afternoon, I asked Uncle Roger to drive me down to the beach. I wanted to see the tide come in. It was a glorious August day. The sea was still, and the ripples only broke lazily on the shore and retreated. I was disappointed at the calmness. The dash and roar of the wildest breakers would have suited me better. I longed for excitement. Soon it came, in a manner widely different from my wishes.

I had been watching for some time the different vessels, when my attention was attracted by a little skiff, quite far out at sea, and rowed by two persons.

"What a perilous thing it looks," I remarked to Uncle Roger, "to put forth on the ocean. It reminds me of the three wise men of the nursery rhyme, who went to sea in a bowl."

It quite interested me, it was so frail, and yet so well managed. It skipped over the waves like a sea-bird. It was coming toward the shore, and soon I could distinguish the forms and faces of its occupants. One was Harry Holt. My heart beat wildly when I saw him. It was the first time since the morning on which he had told me that he loved me. Would they come on shore near us? Would he see me? Would he speak to me? Would he ever, ever seek again the love I had refused him once?

I was asking myself these questions, when I saw Harry make some sudden, incautious movement. The boat careened. He threw his arms up, seeking to preserve his balance, but in vain. They were both in the deep water. A thought flashed into my mind, instantaneous, terrible—Harry could not swim. He had told me so. He sank. I saw his companion strike out to aid him. He rose. Will his friend reach him? No; he has sunk again. A second time to the surface. His comrade seizes him now, and pushes gallantly for the shore. Will he ever gain it? The water is deep and the burden heavy, but—on they come. Nearer and nearer. Uncle Roger and I wade out into the waves to meet them. We are strong now, in our excitement. We stretch out our hands and seize them. I do not know how, or by whom, but they are drawn upon the beach. I see Harry lying there, pale, ghastly, the water dripping from his hair, but—safe! I bend over him, helpless, exhausted, and my excited feelings find vent in a passionate flood of tears. His arms closed round me. We cared not for the friendly eyes which were watching us. I heard nothing but his fond, fervent whisper,

"Ethel, Ethel, my own at last. Did you love me all this time?"

I could say nothing but, "Oh, Harry, what if you had died?"

There is no need of farther words. My story ends here. Harry Holt has been for just six months my husband. I have told you how the waves brought him back again to my feet.

The Mist over the Valley.

God pity them both! and pity us all
Who vainly the dreams of youth recall.

For of all sad words of tongue or pen,
The saddest are these: "It might have been!"

Ah well! for us all some sweet hope lies
Deeply buried from human eyes;

And, in the hereafter, angels may
Roll the stone from its grave away!

WHITTIER.

THE MIST OVER THE VALLEY.

MY wife was dead. I had never loved her—I may as well speak frankly—never loved her; and yet, for her sake, I cast away the one priceless pearl of my life. I think every human existence has its moment of fate—its moment when the golden apple of the Hesperides hangs ready upon the bough—how is it that so few of us are wise enough to pluck it? The decision of a single hour may open for us the gate of the enchanted gardens, where are flowers, and sunshine, and air purer than any breezes of earth; or it may condemn us, Tantalus-like, to reach evermore after some far-off, unattainable good—make us slaves of the lamp forever and forever. And yet we seek no counsel. We stretch forth our hands and grasp blindly at the future, forgetting that we have only ourselves to blame when we draw them back pierced sorely with thorns.

My life, like all others, had its hour of destiny; and it is of that hour, its perils, its temptations, its sin, that I am about to tell you.

I had known Bertha Payson from my infancy. She was only a year younger than I. I can remember her face, far away back among the misty visions of my boyhood. It looked then, as it does now, pure and pale, yet proud. Her eyes were calm as a full lake underneath the summer moon, deep as the sea—a clear, untroubled gray. Her hair was soft, and smooth, and dark. She wore it plainly banded away from her large, thoughtful forehead. The pure yet healthful white of her complexion contrasted only with her eyes, her hair, her clearly-defined, arching brows, and one line of red marking the thin, flexible lips. It was relieved by no other trace of color, even in the cheeks.

I have not painted for you a beauty, and yet I think now that Bertha Payson had the noblest female face my eyes ever rested on.

Her figure was tall, and lithe, and slender; her voice clear, low, and musical. From my earliest boyhood she had seemed to me like some guardian saint, pure enough for worship, but, for a long time I had thought, not warm enough for love.

She was twenty before I began to understand her better. I had just graduated at Harvard, and I came home—perhaps a little less dogmatic and conceited than the majority of newly-fledged A.B.'s—full of lofty aspirations, generous purposes, and romantic dreams. I was prepared to fall in love, but I never thought of loving quiet Bertha Payson, my next neighbor's daughter. The ideal lady of my fancy was far prettier—a dainty creature, with the golden hair and starry eyes of Tennyson's dream—an

> "Airy, fairy Lilian,
> Flitting, fairy Lilian."

And yet, in the mean time, I looked forward with pleasure to Bertha's companionship. To talk with her always brought out "the most of heaven I had in me." There was nothing in art or nature so glorious that it did not take new glory when the glances of her eyes kindled over it. My mind never scaled any height of lofty purpose or heroic thought which her far-reaching soul had not conquered before me, and so the best purposes of my life grew better and stronger in the serene atmosphere of her approval.

Thus it came about that we were daily together. Long before I thought of looking at that pale, proud face with a lover's passion, I think I had given her reason to believe that I loved her. What other interpretation could a woman like her, so pure, so single-hearted, so true, have put upon the eagerness with which I continually sought her society? I passed the largest portion of every day in her presence. She was an early riser, and often, even before the summer sunrise, I went through the narrow path and little gate which divided our garden from hers, to persuade her to join me in a ramble in the delicious morning twilight.

There was one scene of which we never tired. I have never seen it any where but in Ryefield. In the valley of the Quinebaug the mist rises so blue and dense that, from the hills overtopping it at a mile's distance, it looks like some strange inland sea, whereon, perchance, Curtis's *Flying Dutchman* might take his long and wonderful cruise, or a phantom *Maid of the Mist*, sailing at dawn out of some silent cove, might cut the phantom sea with her phantom keel, and go back with the sunrise into silence and shadows. On one of those o'ertopping hills Bertha and I watched the slow coming of many a summer morning. It was in one of these enchanted hours that I first learned that a woman's heart, strong and passionate as it was pure, slumbered beneath the calm reticence of her external life.

We had been watching, as usual, the sea of mist, and speculating idly about the phantom bark and its strange crew. Then we stood silent for a moment, Bertha looking out over the mist, and I looking at her dilating eyes, growing so large, so solemn, so full of thought. At last she turned with a sudden motion—

"Who would think, Frank, to see this prospect now, that underneath this seeming sea lay smiling the greenest and loveliest valley in Connecticut? I was thinking how like it was to some human existences—men and women whose outward life is a veil denser and more impenetrable than the mist over the valley, screening the throbbing, passionate, yet silent heart from human vision. And yet there comes a time when the veiled heart will assert itself. See, the sun is rising now; the mist looks like a soundless sea no longer; it is beginning to curl away in golden wreaths; soon we shall see the fair valley, with its three white houses, its waving trees, and its little becks of bright waters. Some time, even thus, from all proud hearts the mist will roll goldenly away, and we shall see as we are seen, and know as we are known—if not here, there."

She paused, and I looked at her inspired face. I did not wish to break the silence which followed her words. I started and led the way down the steep hill. After a little I looked round to see if the morning sunrise still lingered in her eyes. I caught my foot, in some incautious step, against the roots of a tree from which the spring rains had washed away the earth. I was thrown headlong and violently to the ground. I was stunned for a moment. My first sensation of returning consciousness was a pleasant one. I felt Bertha's cool hand upon my forehead. She had run swiftly to a neighboring spring, and, with quick presence of mind, had saturated her handkerchief and mine, and now she was bathing my brow with the water. I did not open my eyes at first, it was so pleasant to lie there and receive her gentle ministrations. At length I felt her place her ear close to my lips. By a resolute effort I held my breath. I wished to try her. She thought I was dead. She did not shriek or moan; only, as if against her will, a single cry, low and sorrowful, escaped her—

"Oh, Frank, darling! darling!"

I slowly opened my eyes and met hers. There was a look in them I have never seen in any other woman's. Then I knew that Bertha Payson could love; that she did love me with a love that not one woman in a thousand could even understand. I saw that underneath the marble her heart, her passionate woman's heart, was flame; but it was flame as pure as the heaven-kindled fires on the altar of the God of the Hebrews. I knew that she loved me, and, in the same moment, I knew that with all tho might of my heart I loved her—that she alone was the one woman to whom mind and soul could do homage and say, "I have found my queen." But I did not speak of love then. I know she must have read my glance as I had read hers; but she only said, very quietly,

"Thank God that you are alive. I must leave you now to see about getting some one to take you home."

"No, I can walk, if you will help me."

I made the effort, but I could not rise. The least attempt to move caused me such exquisite pain that I began to think my injuries must be severe. I said, reluctantly,

"I am very sorry, Bertha. I shall have to let you go. I see it is impossible for me to walk."

She drew a shawl from her shoulders and arranged it so as to make the position in which my head was lying a little easier. Then she tripped away, and, lying there, I watched, half dreamily, her light figure go out of sight down the hill-side. The time of her absence seemed to me very short. Except when I attempted to move I felt little pain, and never had my soul been so flooded with happiness. I was too weak to speculate about the future. I only rejoiced in the present.

Soon Bertha returned with the village doctor and two or three sturdy assistants. Arranging a hastily-constructed litter, they started to bear me down the hill. At the first jolt the motion caused me intense pain. With a longing for sympathy, I stretched out my hand. Bertha understood me, and laid her own in it; and so, with her walking beside me, I was borne home.

No bones had been broken by my fall. My injuries were all internal, though not dangerous; but my convalescence was long and tedious. In all this time Bertha was like an angel of light. She shared with my mother the labor of nursing me. She read to me, sang to me; or, when I liked it better, sat by me in silence. It was six weeks before I was again able to walk out; but in all this time we had never spoken of love. My passion was too reverent for light or hasty utterance. I resolved to wait until I could stand with her again upon the hill-top where I had read my heart's answer in her eyes.

When at length I could go out, my first visit was made to Dr. Greene. He had been so kind and attentive, he seemed to take so much pride in his success, that I could not refuse his invitation to take my first walk to his house, and drink a cup of tea with his wife and a friend she had staying with her. It is with this friend only that my story has to do.

God knows I did not willingly put myself in the way of temptation. How could I tell that, sitting that summer afternoon in Dr. Greene's quiet parlor, I should find a Circe?

"Miss Ireton," said the doctor's deep, sonorous voice as I entered the room, and before me rose a young, slight figure, robed in white, with roses on her bosom, roses on her cheek, roses in the golden hair that lay in long ringlets upon her dainty shoulders, and clustered around her head. Her eyes were bright and full of smiles; dimples played at hide-and-seek among her cheeks' roses; her lips were full and red, and her complexion clear, with a quick, changing color, infinitely charming. Sometimes—even now, out of the darkness of death and the grave—that face rises up to me, and I see her stand before me once more, in all her witching loveliness, as she stood that summer afternoon. If you had seen her then you would have thought that she was immortal—that death and change could never come to that form of grace, those eyes of light.

Miss Nellie Ireton was a practiced flirt. It was not in the nature of things that any man could love her as reverently as I loved Bertha. She could not have comprehended Bertha's self-denial, her heroism, her entire freedom from all vanity, all desire for triumph. And yet her dominion over the senses was absolute. I was a born worshiper of beauty. I could not help admiring the airy grace of her movements, the sparkling changes of her face, the smiles which hovered so archly about her lips. Days passed, and no fly was ever more hopelessly entangled in a spider's net than I in the meshes of her golden hair. At first I could see that Bertha was simply incredulous and astonished. Then a wild trouble began to darken the clear gray of her eyes. All this time I loved her. A single tone of her voice had more power over my highest nature than all the enchantments of the other, and yet I could not break away from the fatal spell which bound me. My senses were intoxicated—steeped in delirium by the Circe. Can you comprehend the enigma? Its solution involves the history of many a man's marriage besides my own.

Just at the right time Miss Ireton brought a new competitor into the field. In a young law-student then visiting in the place I found a rival. Nellie was a good tactician. She played us off against each other most adroitly, until we were both inspired with all a gamester's eagerness to win. Bertha had now withdrawn herself from my society almost wholly. Indeed, I seldom visited her; but when I did I only saw her in the presence of her mother. Every evening I passed at Dr. Greene's. At last, in one fatal hour, I found Miss Ireton alone. I proposed and was accepted. So far had my madness lasted; but when I heard her faltering "Yes," when her head sank with fully as much triumph as tenderness upon my shoulder, when I would have pressed the kiss of betrothal upon her lips, a cold shudder ran through all my veins. I closed my eyes for a moment in the struggle to regain my self-command, and there, before me, I saw Bertha stand as she stood *that* morning. I saw her pale, rapt face, her eyes dilated with thought, fixed on the mist over the valley. I heard her inspired voice—

"Some time, even thus, from all proud hearts the mist will roll goldenly away, and we shall see as we are seen, and know as we are known."

Alas! in vain had the mist rolled away from that proud heart of Bertha Payson, showing me its hidden treasures. I had rejected the golden fruit of the Hesperides, lured by the fair-seeming apple of Sodom, and now I must wait vainly at the closed gates of Eden. We have but one birth and one death, and the charmed hour of fate comes but once to life.

My betrothed was speaking; I roused myself to listen.

"I liked you the very first time I saw you, Mr. Osborne, and I meant to make you like me. You see I thought it would be more difficult, for Dr. Greene told me you were half in love with that pale, proud Bertha Payson, and I meant to see if I couldn't make you fancy me in spite of all."

"You succeeded only too well, little charmer."

There was a mournful truth in my answer, which her light heart did not penetrate. I do think Nellie loved me, or, as she said, liked me, as well as she was capable of liking. Her freely-expressed preference was fully sincere. I should have a true wife, as the world reckons truth; and yet, in God's sight, I should be unmarried still. We *two* could never be made *one*.

I made haste to announce my engagement. I hurried the preparations for my nuptials. I felt that my only safety would lie in leaving Ryefield as soon as possible. Now that the excitement of the love-chase was over, and the young law-student had subsided into the quiet friend of my affianced, I could not conceal from myself that I had set the seal to my own mad folly, and condemned myself to an eternal yet unavailing despair. I carefully avoided any opportunity of seeing Bertha. I would not have dared to trust myself in her presence.

It was the day before my bridal. So far had I traversed my path of thorns. I rose early and went out of doors. One more walk I would have to the hill where the knowledge of Bertha's love had come to me—down whose slopes I had been borne with her hand in mine. It was September, but it had been a cool, damp summer, and the verdure along the hillside was still fresh as in June. I climbed it rapidly. When I was within a few rods of the summit I looked up. A tall, slight figure was clearly defined against the sky. Should I go on? Dared I meet Bertha then and there? I answered these questions to myself by climbing on silently and quickly. I could not help it.

In five minutes I stood at Bertha's side. She had not heard my approach. Proud woman as she was, she had not been too proud to weep. The tears glittered heavily on her long lashes. She made no vain attempt to conceal them. She met my glance steadfastly.

"Bertha," I said, in a choking voice, "I did not think to find you here."

"Or I you," she answered. "See, the mist lies as heavily over the valley as when we stood here last. How little the scene is changed!"

"And how much every thing else is!" I interrupted her, wildly. "Bertha, it may be madness, but I must speak. I love you better than my own soul. I always did love you, but never with such passion, such despair, as now. Is it too late? Must it be too late?"

She looked at me a moment in wonder, in sorrow. Her dark, searching eyes questioned me. Then her lip curled.

"Would you be twice a traitor, Frank Osborne?"

"No," I answered, impetuously. "I would but return to my only true allegiance. Nellie's pride would be wounded, but her heart would not suffer much. And you, oh! Bertha, you did love me—you do love me. Do not wreck your own life and mine."

"Frank," she said, quietly, yet earnestly, "this is worse than folly—it is sin. To-morrow you will be the husband of another. What right have you to speak to me of love? True, I did love you once, but that dream is past. If you were free to-day I could not trust my happiness to your keeping. Forget me, or think of me only as a kind, well-wishing friend."

"Is there no hope, Bertha?"

"None."

But I could not so give her up. The hour had come I had dreamed of through my long convalescence. I stood with Bertha again upon the hill-top where I had meant to tell her my love. I must plead with her a little longer. Scarcely knowing what I said, I assailed her with wild prayers. I poured out my very soul at her feet. But she only looked at me with her dark, wistful eyes, and returned the same firm, reproachful No. At last I was silent. I saw it was of no use. I had myself cast away my pearl of great price. I must be contented hereafter with the glitter of my paste brilliant.

"Well," I said, humbly and sorrowfully enough, "I do not deserve you. You are right, Bertha. But give me your hand once more, as you did that morning. Friends claim that much."

She laid her fingers in mine. They did not tremble, but they were very cold. She said, with a deep, pathetic earnestness,

"God bless you, Frank Osborne! I, who know you so well, believe that you are sincere in the words you have spoken to me this morning. But you must think such thoughts no longer. Happiness only comes to us in the right. Your duty now is to Miss Ireton. Fulfill it, I conjure you. You have a woman's happiness in your keeping. You must answer to God for it. I conjure you to make her future bright. Trust nothing to her light-heartedness. I tell you no woman's heart is light enough to bear up under any want of love from the man for whom she has given up all things. Do your duty, and you will find comfort even yet. Good-by."

She turned away, and once more, as on that other morning, I watched her light figure tripping down the hill. Her step was firm. Her heart must have been strong. She did not once look back. I watched her till I could see her no longer, and then I turned and looked moodily over the valley. Already the mist had parted, and before the sun's fiery eye the valley lay unshrouded, undisguised, as our souls must stand some day before His eye at whose word the first sun rose and the last sun will set. I thought of the solemn import of Bertha's words. I had indeed a duty to do. I could lay my burden of sin and punishment on no other shoulders. It was not Nellie Ireton's fault that I had turned away from Bertha and asked her to be my wife. I owed her my life now. She should have it. I knelt upon the hill-side. I bared my forehead to the cool breeze of the September morning. I cried out to Heaven for strength. I think my prayer was heard.

The next day I was married. We left Ryefield at once, and for three years I did not return there.

I do believe—thank God for this gleam of comfort—that I made Nellie happy. In her own way she was very fond of me. She loved society, mirth, and fashion. She had them all. I placed no restraint upon her pleasures, though I seldom accompanied her. Often she has returned from some gay party late at night, and found me sitting alone in my study. She would bound into my lap at such times with her old, childlike *abandon;* tell me what a fine time she had had; who had talked to her, and who complimented her, and then ask, with a comical air of self-satisfaction, if I was not proud of such a handsome little wife.

"You know I *am* handsome, you provoking, teasing, clever old fellow—now don't you?" was usually the conclusion to her harangue; and I would always give her the confirmation she coveted. Thank God, she never knew how lonely my soul was in those days—how my heart pined for companionship—how my spirit panted for a kindred spirit to share its doubts, its triumphs, its seekings after the Infinite! Thank God that the lark in the meadow was not gladder or merrier than she!

She had been my wife more than two years when she went out, one bitterly cold night, with her fair neck and arms uncovered, and only an opera cloak thrown over them, as she drove to a gay party. I had remonstrated, but she had pleaded to be allowed to have her own way, and I never could bring myself to cross her in any thing—I, who could never look at her without a remorseful consciousness that the heart which should have been hers only, shrined in secret the image of another. I strove, by the most lavish indulgence even to her whims, to make what compensation I could for the heart devotion I could never give her, and so this night, as usual, she had her will. She did, indeed, look lovely with her azure satin dress falling in such graceful folds about her—the golden curls just veiling, but not concealing, the snow of her neck, and her arms gleaming through misty lace. Most men would have been proud of her; but I had known one woman whose simple superiority to all outside decorations so far transcended all the aids of dress and fashion that I could not triumph in the mere beauty of the external.

For once the consequences of my indulgence were disastrous. That night Nellie took a severe cold. In a few days it settled upon her lungs, and then medical skill was of no avail. She grew rapidly worse, and they made her grave beneath the cold, gray sky of March. Through her illness I had been a patient nurse. She died with her head on my bosom. With almost her last breath she told me that I had made her very happy. When I stood over her grave I mourned for her sincerely. I would have given much to call her back to life; nay, I would have been willing—life was not very precious to me—to have taken her place under the mould, so that she could have walked forth again in her youth and beauty. And yet, as weeks passed on, God, who judgeth not as man judgeth, will forgive me if a secret thrill of joy did sometimes make my heart-strings quiver when I thought of the love of my youth and remembered that I was free.

After a time I went home to Ryefield. I sought Bertha's society. At first it seemed to me that she tried to avoid me; but I persevered. I know she must have felt to the core of her heart the sincerity of my love. Would she ever again return it?

At last, one night, I asked her to go with me the next morning to the hill overlooking the valley, where we had stood together so many times in other days. She consented.

We went up the hill almost in silence, and when we reached its summit we still stood silently for a time.

At length I turned to her.

"Bertha, there was a time when, as the morning mist rolled away from over the valley, the mist rolled away from your heart, and I saw its hidden treasure, your love for me. I have sinned since then; but oh! Bertha, I have suffered. I loved you first, last, always. With all the might of my soul I love you now. Will you take me, and weave the broken threads of my life into brightness at last?"

She looked at me steadfastly and sorrowfully.

"Frank," she said, with a gentle, pitying aspect, "I came up here with you because I knew you wanted to ask me that question. I could see that you were cherishing hopes about me that I ought not to let you cherish any longer. It is all in vain. I will be your friend, your warm, tender friend; but the day for any thing more is past. There was a time when I would have gone with you to the world's end; but you yourself made my love a sin. I could not cherish it for the husband of another. I conquered it, and on earth it can have no resurrection. By the wild agony of its death-throes I know that it is dead—dead utterly. You can never again kindle the life in its cold corpse. If you wronged me once, I forgive you. If you are unhappy, I pity you. On earth I can never have a dearer friend than you, but the flame on my heart's altar is burned to white ashes. I can never be your wife."

I looked in her clear, friendly eyes. An angel's pity softened their glance, but they were not once cast down. I could see in them no shadow of hope. I turned away from their wistful look. I uttered no more prayers. I only clasped her hand in mine, and some tears I was not ashamed to shed fell over it. Then I let her go. Once more she went down the hill alone, and I was left upon its brow to struggle with the anguish of my despair. Oh, Bertha, Bertha!

Look out, my friend. From this eastern window, even now, you can see the mist rolling goldenly away from the valley of the Quinebaug. Just so, I have sometimes thought, I shall one day see it roll away from the valleys of the Upper Country, and, perchance, the love that was dead, when I would have awakened it on earth, will have its own resurrection in heaven. God knows!

Joseph Thorne—his Calling.

Oh that I were
The viewless spirit of a lovely sound,
A living voice, a breathing harmony,
A bodiless enjoyment—born and dying
With the bless'd tone that made me!

BYRON (*Manfred*).

Touch the chords gently;
Those strings are heart-strings, and the sounds they utter—
Be silent when you hear them—are the groanings
Of uttermost pain, the sighings of great sorrow,
Voices from out the depths.

ANONYMOUS.

JOSEPH THORNE—HIS CALLING.

NEVER have I heard any thing so like to the musical, half-uttered wails of a prisoned spirit, as the sad, sweet complaints of Ole Bull's violin. Sometimes the spirit lingers tenderly over the memories of old hopes—hopes that long ago faded into memories—and its tones are not all mournful, for a thrill from the past joy trembles through them. Then again the spirit is tortured. It sobs. It shrieks. Fain it would be delivered from its prison-house. Then, hopeless, it sighs itself into silence.

In one of these pauses a story came back to me; a mournful tale of one who died young; a story I used to like to dream over in other days, imagining to myself how every word that told of a dead hope and a dead love had been spoken. The very scent of lilacs and laburnums haunted my fancy. I saw the old farmyard; the June twilight, so long and bright; the dew-beaded flowers and grass, and the trees, all in blossom, shaking their odorous boughs downward, over the heads of Joseph Thorne and pretty Mabel Emerson.

Can any one describe a lovely woman? Say that she has blue eyes, and light hair, and a sweet mouth, and it might apply equally to fifty blondes whom you may chance to know, of entirely varying character. I think one gains a truer estimate of the nature of beauty by being told what thoughts it awakens. Joseph Thorne, unknown to himself, was a poet. He had known Mabel all his life, and he said that seeing her made him think of long summer days, when the blue sky looks not only bright, but deep, and still, and solemn; of lovely flowers, growing all alone in desert places; of a rippling stream, with the stars shining on it; but most, oh, most of all, of sweet music. Perhaps, however, he was the only one who had ever looked into her heart; ever seen, beneath her gay, smiling exterior, the deep-flowing fountains of tenderness and self-sacrifice. Most persons thought her merely a pleasant, light-hearted maiden, whose presence, like a sunbeam, always carried brightness with it, and to whom sorrow and weariness were unknown.

Her mother had died in her infancy, and her father, the richest and busiest farmer in all Westvale, had never found time to learn any thing of her inner nature. Perhaps he was not even capable of appreciating her. It was enough for him that she was well clothed and well schooled; that her bright face was always ready to welcome him home at night, her dextrous hands to preside over his early breakfast. Nor had Mabel any female confidants. Kindly and gentle to all, there was a maidenly shyness and reserve underlying her nature which made it impossible for her to unveil to careless eyes the altar of her heart, the very holy of holies, where the love of which she was capable, the dreams and fancies so brightly tinged with the glory of her youth, all lay an unclaimed sacrifice, till the heaven-elected priest should come, and her whole being should acknowledge him and do him reverence.

Like herself, Joseph Thorne was bereft of one parent, but his mother, a true, pure woman, had been spared to him. He had grown up from childhood with one strong, all-absorbing passion. He worshiped music. The earliest delight he could remember was the low, plaintive interludes of the flute and viol between the singing at church, or his mother's voice as she caroled the ballads of her girlhood.

The first purchase he ever made, with money for which he had worked indefatigably at odd jobs, was a small violin. He had a marvelous delicacy and aptitude of touch, and, as he grew older, a singular power of improvisation. He *talked* through his violin. It uttered all the griefs of his lonely boyhood; all those vague longings that trouble the heart of an imaginative youth after power and fame, or a dim, undefinable greatness and goodness shining afar off, like the pale beauty of a half-hidden statue.

In all these dreams he was to be a musician. In that way he was to draw near the far-off good. His little violin was to talk to many hearts. The world should hear its cry and obey its teaching. He would do a good work—be a master among men. With all these visions his mother fully sympathized; nay, her simple, unworldly heart was as fully imbued with faith in them as his own. They were poor, but she managed to send him to school all through his boyhood, and afterward to keep herself so neat and comfortable that he should never see she wanted for any thing, that no care for her might ever disturb his progress.

As I said, he had always known Mabel Emerson. As a child he had led her to and from school, or drawn her over the drifts on his little sled. She was dearer to him then than any thing else, save his mother and his violin. She was not yet seventeen when he had learned to place her even before these. As a child, she clung to him with caressing, childish fondness; as a maiden, she loved him with all the strength of her heart. She recognized in him the consecrated high-priest of her life. For him the altar was unveiled, and he looked unchidden upon all the thoughts and fancies of her innocent soul. She possessed, what to such a nature as his was more than all things else, entire faith in him. She believed in his power to do great things; to be not only the noblest of men, but the first of musicians; and it was very soothing to him, so poor, so proud, so sensitive, to turn from the world to her; to be comforted by the singleness of her devotion, the implicitness of her trust. Yet it was many months, even after they each believed themselves dearer to the other than any thing else on earth, before any binding vows of love were spoken. Such utterances are of slow growth in a mind so dreamy and sensitive as Joseph Thorne's. The uncertainty of her girlish ways was so sweet—the coming and going of her delicate color—the fluttering of her fingers when he took them in his own. He hesitated to exchange all this even for the assurance that she would be his wife.

But the charmed hour came at last. I think every human life that is worth living has its hour of destiny; its one golden number in the twenty-four, at whose chiming is ushered in every important change, whether of joy or sorrow. To some it is morning, rosy and bright with sunrise and sparkling dew, and vocal with bird-songs. Others find it at high noon—the zenith of power, and pride, and passion, when the sun woos the earth with his most fiery kisses—the hour in which bold and daring souls recognize a peculiar heritage. For others still—men and women of sober, thoughtful, mysterious lives, half superstitious, owning a ready allegiance to the unseen—the hour of fate is the solemn noon of night. For Joseph Thorne, and such as he, it was twilight. On a summer twilight had he been born, and on a summer twilight he told his love.

They stood—those two young things, for whom life and sorrow were still invested with a sweet, serious, half-melancholy charm—for whom the dark days had not yet risen—under the trees of Farmer Emerson's old front yard. The balmy summer air was burdened with the fragrance of blossoms. The sunset clouds were like that hour of their two lives, all *couleur de rose*, and the chimes of the village bells, mellowed by distance, rung out a pleasant chorus—a sort of consecrated amen to their plighted vows. In that hour no new tale was told—both had been fully satisfied before that they were beloved; the very words were the sweet old words that have trembled all along the discords of so many centuries of years upon so many loved and loving lips.

But their utterance changed the whole current of Joseph Thorne's life. They made it necessary to him, for he possessed a high sense of honor, to go the next day into the presence of Farmer Emerson, and, telling his story this time to ears that would not be sympathetic, to ask for his Mabel's hand.

It was a terrible ordeal to the young, sensitive musician. He had an intuitive knowledge of the farmer's character. Instinctively he felt that this busy, energetic, matter-of-fact man would look upon him and his music with distrust, perhaps disapprobation. But, fortified by Mabel's solemn pledge that nothing on earth should ever have power to change her love, fortified anew by the soft touch of his mother's fingers upon his hair—his mother, to whom he confided every thing—and her whispered, "God bless you, my son, for you have been a good boy all the days of your life," he sought the man in whose hands lay his destiny.

It was just after dinner. He knew Mr. Emerson would be resting, as was his habit, on the wooden settee, under the porch at his front door. He walked into the yard with desperate courage and approached him. He was kindly received, and invited to sit down.

"I wanted to speak to you, Mr. Emerson."

"Well, my young friend, what is it? Any assistance about getting into business? I will do all I can for you, gladly, were it only for the sake of your dead father, as good a neighbor and as honest a man as ever sat in Westvale meeting-house."

"No, sir, it is not that;" and Joseph plunged bravely *in medias res.* "I love your daughter, and she loves me; will you consent that she shall be my wife?"

Wide opened the farmer's eyes in wonder. "Your wife! my daughter Mabel! What are your prospects? What is your business? What would you keep her on?"

Joseph's tones faltered. "I did not mean just at present, sir. We will be satisfied now with your consent to our engagement. I hope to be a musician. I think that is my true calling. For nothing else have I so much talent; in nothing else am I so happy."

There was silence for a few moments, and then the

old man broke it. His voice was firm and clear, and yet it seemed almost sad.

"I am sorry—I am truly sorry. Mabel is like her mother, and if she loves you she will not love lightly; but, if such is the life you have marked out, I can not give her to you. I do not care so much for money. It is a good thing, though I would let her marry without it; but a musician! a fiddler! It is an idle, wandering, useless life: I speak to you frankly. No good will come of it. I can not give her to you."

A wandering, useless life! Alas! Joseph Thorne, where were your lofty dreams, your high hopes now? You that had aspired to talk to the world through your instrument, to sound upon its delicate strings the awakening calls to a higher, purer life—you to whom this had seemed the noblest of missions. Small wonder your voice faltered as you asked,

"Can you, then, give me no hope?"

"Yes, I can give you one hope—one test of your love for Mabel. She is my only child; I would not cross her lightly. If you will give up these vagaries about music, and become a practical working-man, you shall have her. I will take you on my own land, under my own eye, and when I think you competent to manage for yourself, you shall marry her, and I will give you the Widow Sikes's farm for a wedding-portion. There isn't a snugger little place, or one under better cultivation in the state; and you'll be close by home too. But I am a man of my word; and, unless you give up this foolery about the music, you shall never have Mabel. If you want time to decide, you can take three days."

"I will give you my answer in that time;" and, bowing gravely, Joseph Thorne went out of Farmer Emerson's yard with crushed hopes.

He made no attempt to see Mabel. He went home. His mother read the sorrow on his face, but she was one of those rare women who know when to keep silence. Heavy as her heart was, she asked no questions. He went into his own room and sat down by the window. He took his violin, which lay upon a stand beside him. He had been accustomed to translate into music all his griefs, but now that the first real trial of his life had come upon him, its chords seemed dumb and powerless to comfort. He bowed his head over it, and tried to think.

Mabel and music—twin inspirations of his life—how could he give either of them up? No one knew—no one could know—what this gift, which he had fondly deemed his calling, had been to him. Something else he might, indeed, make his business, his profession, but it would be only a *profession*—a living falsehood. To this only God had *called* him. His soul was full of a light, a heaven-bestowed revelation. The world had need of it. How, save through this voice of music, could he give it utterance?

At one moment he had well-nigh resolved to cling to his chosen vocation through every thing. He would go out into the world, and do his duty manfully. This great world should recognize him. He would do it good. But he must grow old; and there rose before him a picture of a lonely, loveless old age; a hearth which no woman's care made bright; a fireside where no wife's sweet presence, no calm brow and holy eyes would linger beside him; a silent house, where no children's light footfall pattered along the floor, no little faces reflected back the vanished light of his own youth. At this picture the humanity of his nature veiled its face, and uttered a wail which would not be quieted. His love was mightier than his genius. He could not give himself wholly to the world. He had a heart that only human tenderness could satisfy. Then Mabel's face rose before him in the still, summer afternoon—the calm brow, the holy eyes of his fondest dream. He thought of her as his wife—the mother of his children—in bridehood, wifehood, motherhood; and growing old, at length, by his side, yet never old to him, with the smile which age had no power to dim lingering still about her lips, till death should freeze them into the last and sweetest smile of all, and they should be young once more in heaven. And, thinking thus, his soul seemed to clasp and tighten round her image, and involuntarily his lips cried out,

"Oh, Mabel, Mabel! Mine own—mine own!"

All the afternoon he sat there, lost in troubled thought, his fingers now and then wandering listlessly over the chords of his violin. At twilight he rose, and went silently down stairs and out of doors. Standing at the window, his mother watched him as he walked with rapid step toward Farmer Emerson's house. The knowledge had come, at first, to this gentle woman with a sharp pang, that her son loved another better than his mother, but for his sake she had conquered it; and now she said to herself, thankfully,

"I am glad he is going over there. Poor lad, he is in heavy trouble, but God grant Mabel may be able to console him."

Mabel was standing under the trees at the gate. He saw her waiting for him as he drew nigh, but he had never seen her face so sad before. He took her trembling fingers in his own. They were icy cold.

"I know it all," she said, with sorrowful calmness, through which thrilled the smothered cry of a breaking heart; "father has told me. I know you can not give up your music, and I can't disobey my father. We must—"

She could not finish the sentence. Her voice broke up into sobs, and Joseph Thorne drew her shivering form to his bosom. Swift as lightning, the thought flashed through his mind that thus Heaven had taught him his duty. He had not considered her suffering before. What claim had the world on him, what claim his beloved music, that could be weighed for one instant with this breaking heart—this pure, woman's heart, which was all his own? He pressed his lips to the forehead lying against his breast. He said, very tenderly,

"Hush, Mabel—hush, darling! I have decided for us both. God has joined us together, and nothing can put us asunder. I shall accept your father's proposal. What would music be to me without you—you, my soul's best music? If I went forth without you into the world, the thought of Mabel alone and suffering would unnerve me and make me powerless. What could I give forth but utterances of despair? No; God calls me to stay here. Look up, my darling, my sweet Mabel. You do not fear I should ever tire of you?"

She raised her eyes, and looked long and earnestly into his face.

"No, Joseph, no; I do not fear you will tire of me, for I know your steadfast nature. I know God has made us one. But it will break your heart to give up your fame, your calling, your beloved music. Better give up Mabel. Go, Joseph; I am not selfish. I will believe that you love me always. It shall be the glory of my life. You *must* go to your career, your duty."

"My career is here. My duty is here. My world is in your heart, your priceless heart. Nay, Mabel, I have decided. Urge me not. How could my heart break for music when the clinging tendrils of your love bound it together? Be satisfied and smile, for I shall be happy."

With these words, and such as these, he soothed her; in some measure he won her from her sorrow; and yet, though the smiles came to her lips at his bidding, in her heart was a prophetic silence of fear, lest, in giving up his music, her lover gave up the best half of himself.

They went together at length to her father, and, holding in his the hand of his betrothed, Joseph Thorne said,

"I require no longer time, Mr. Emerson. I have decided. Your daughter is more to me than all things else. I give up all for her. I accept your offer with thanks. To-morrow I will come and place my time at your disposal."

And then he went home to his mother. It was dark, but there was no light. She had been sitting alone, absorbed in her anxious thoughts. He knelt at her feet as in his early boyhood days, and told her his story.

"All is settled now," he said, steadily. "I go to work at Mr. Emerson's to-morrow. Mabel will be mine. Music must be given up—my dreams—my ambition."

His mother interrupted him with her sobs. She clasped him in her arms. She wept over him; she, who had gloried so in his gift, who, ever since he had been laid, her first-born, upon her breast, had understood him and lived in his life. And he wept with her. He was not too proud, with his mother's arms around him, to weep for the far-off fame-wreaths of which his ambition had vainly dreamed—wreaths which he must never more hope to gather. That night neither of them slept. He laid his head, as in boyhood, upon her motherly heart. He breathed into her sympathetic ears all the hopes and longings which this decision had crushed; and all the other hopes and longings, which were blooming now brighter than ever, which clustered around Mabel's name. And his mother comforted him.

The next morning he commenced his task under Farmer Emerson. His heart was almost buoyant, despite all he had resigned, for he had had a few moment's conversation with Mabel—Mabel, who was to be all his own. She looked so lovely in her fresh calico morning dress. The light of hope sparkled in her eyes, and sat serenely upon her brow. Surely that smile would have power to brighten any fate.

But the task which was set him, light as it seemed, taxed all his energies. The delicate, study-loving youth was not used to labor. The sun scorched his slender hands pitilessly; the sweat stood in great, bead-like drops upon his brow. It was a comfort when the horn sounded for dinner. It was a sorely-needed refreshment to sit in the farmer's porch, while Mabel brought cool, sparkling water to lave his burning, dusty face.

Day after day passed on, and he never faltered. With steady, unflagging industry he performed whatever tasks were appointed, and as rapidly as possible made himself master of all the mysteries of farming. But he drooped under his uncongenial toil. Even Mr. Emerson could see this; but he predicted "the boy would grow stronger and get used to it in time." Mabel saw more clearly, and the hope in her eyes grew less steadfast. Often, when he came to her in the evening, tired and worn, she would say,

"It is no use. You will have to give it up, or it will kill you."

And he would strive to answer cheerfully.

"Nonsense! I *am* tired, but you know, dear, it will be so much easier when we get a place of our own. I need only do the lightest work then."

But he could not blind Mabel's clear eyes.

It was during Ole Bull's first visit to this country, and, as the autumn grew into winter, the papers were full of his success. They often read of him together; of his tall, swaying figure, his face so calm and spiritual, and the wonderful music which seemed the voice of his soul. One morning, with a paper in his hand, Joseph Thorne came to Mabel. His face was kindled with enthusiasm. His eyes flashed, and his manner was eager and hurried.

"See here, Mabel," he said; "he plays at New Haven to-night. Only thirty miles off. I can resist the temptation no longer. I must go. There is not much to do on the farm, and I can borrow your father's horse. Oh, Mabel! it will give me new life."

She entered eagerly into his plans. Her father did not oppose them, and in half an hour he had started.

Most tenderly had he bidden his betrothed the good-by which was to be so brief, and she stood at the gate and watched him with a cheerful smile until his eyes, looking back, could discern her no longer. Then she went into the house, and the grief smothered, woman-like, for his sake burst forth.

"Oh," she murmured, "he will never be the same to me again—I feel it. This music will speak to him like a clarion. It will awake him from dreams. His life-work will rise up before him, and the necessity to go forth and do it will be upon his soul. And I—woe is me!—how shall I learn to live without him? Hush, selfish heart? Wouldst thou hold him back from his true life, weak spirit?"

But the chidden agony *would* come back again. The veil was rent away from the pale brow of the future. Swift and sure she saw her fate coming toward her. All that day, all that night, all the next day, she wrestled with it, but still its face was set resolutely toward her—still its steps were onward.

It was almost nightfall when the watched-for figure came in sight. She went to the gate to meet him. He sprang from the horse and folded her in his arms. His kisses thrilled upon her lips, yet even then she felt there had been a change. She drew him into the house and questioned him eagerly. It had been as she expected. The wonderful music had troubled all the depths of his nature. It had bound him captive. In vain he struggled against the chain.

Unfalteringly she gave her counsel.

"Go!" she said; "you *must* go! I told you it would break your heart to give it up; and see, already in these few months you have grown prematurely old, and weary, and feeble. Go: you will be false to the highest part of your nature if you do not serve your soul's master. It is the task God himself has set you; it is not yours to deliberate whether you will accept it."

"But you, Mabel, my life's life—I can not give you up."

For one moment the white face grew whiter. But there came no quiver into her quiet tones.

"You *need* not give me up. I shall be yours only, till I die; nor need we despair. If you succeed, perhaps my father will give me to you. I *believe* he will, he loves me so. And you *will* succeed, you must succeed. For such as you there is no such word as fail. Go, Joseph; it is right."

A troubled, anxious week intervened before he had decided, but Mabel saw how it would be all along. Not for an instant did she beguile herself with false hopes. He went. The farewell kisses of two pure women, mother and betrothed, were upon his lips. Their blessings were the last sound in his ears. Their prayers followed him. He *seemed* to suffer more than Mabel in the prolonged agony of their parting. Twenty times he was on the point of giving up his career, his future, to stay with her, but she would not suffer it. She sustained him, she cheered him; she, who knew better than himself how impossible for him was any other life than the one which had haunted all the dreams of his boyhood. When he was gone at length —when anxious eyes, strained ever so widely, could not catch another glimpse of the beloved form—the two women, both bereft of their dearest thing in life, went in silence, each into her own home, to struggle alone with her sorrow. In that hour there could be no partnership of grief.

Mabel suffered most. It was natural for the mother to wish her son to go out into the world, to do and be all that God gave him power; and, whatever change came to him, the one tie could never be broken—he would be her son always. But to Mabel, despite her strong faith in him, the light of her life seemed to have gone out, and her soul shuddered—alone in the darkness. She had exhausted all her energy in soothing and encouraging him; she had none left to struggle with the grim presentiment which oppressed her own spirit.

She had always been strong, in spite of the extreme delicacy of her figure, and she did not grow feeble even now. All her accustomed duties were performed with her usual energy. There was no visible change, save that her lips smiled a little more seldom, and her cheek was white as marble. She seemed to strive to be continually occupied, as if fearful if she gave herself time to confront her grief it would overmaster her.

Her face always brightened after a letter from her betrothed. They were not very frequent, but when they did come they overflowed with love and hope. She felt that now, indeed, was he living his true life. Nor had success been so very difficult to him. Ole Bull had been his friend. He had sought, at once, the gifted Norwegian. In secret, for he was not one to bestow his benefactions in public, the master performer had given him a few hints, a few instructions, that he might know better how to translate his soul's depths into his music.

Soon Mabel heard of him. He was making a tour under an assumed name, to which only those who loved him best had the key, and every where he was —as Mabel had felt he must ever be—successful. The small country places which witnessed his first trial of strength were moved as they had never been before. No mind so dull but his tones made themselves understood. The country press was full of his praises. This young performer—they wrote—so delicate, so almost boyish, but with such a wonderful genius! They told of his face beaming as if inspired; the eyes sweet and bright, yet sad; the slender figure; the almost transparent hands; and, as she read, the prophetic fear in Mabel's heart grew heavier. His letters became more and more rare. It was not that he loved her less. Mabel had never doubted him for a moment. But he was doing his work, and it absorbed all his energies. If it were brief, it must be mighty.

One afternoon in May she sat alone under the trees where they had so often sat together. Her thoughts went back over all her life—that young, innocent life, where were no blighting plague-spots of willful sin, few even of unintentional wrongs, and yet where, of late, so many tears had fallen. She remembered the long-ago time when Joseph Thorne had been her childish friend and confidant; she retraced the days, unquiet yet so blissful in their uncertainty, when her heart awoke from its maiden sleep, and she knew that she had given him the love for which his words had not yet sued. Then she lived again the evening of their betrothal, and whispered over and over to herself every tender word which had fallen from his lips. Her father's step along the highway disturbed her reverie. She looked up as he entered the gate, and something in his face startled her. There were tears in his eyes, and his whole expression was full of an unwonted, sorrowful tenderness. She sprang to his side.

"Poor Mabel!" he said, as if speaking to himself, "how hard it will fall on her!" Then, folding his arm about her, as if in terror lest she should be overcome by the shock, he said,

"I have seen Joseph Thorne. He came home this afternoon, as I think, to die. He wants you. Go to him, Mabel. I give you free leave to stay with him to the last. Poor child, it's all the consolation you can have now."

Mabel did not faint. "Thank you," she whispered gratefully, as she withdrew from her father's arm and went into the house. The blow had come so suddenly that she did not realize its force. Mechanically, as one moving in a dream, she put on her bonnet and walked out toward the Widow Thorne's cottage. The door was open, and she stood in it for one moment, silently watching her lover. He lay upon a lounge. His face was very thin and white, and his eyes seemed supernaturally large and brilliant. His mother was kneeling by his side, with her face buried in his bosom. A solemn awe was upon Mabel's soul. She dared not go forward or break the silence. Already he seemed to her like an angel. He was the first to speak.

"Mabel! Thank God! Come to me, darling!"

His mother rose, and, almost without her own volition, Mabel had crossed the room; her arms were folded about his neck, her lips clung to his in a long kiss of love and despair.

For six weeks she was his constant nurse, sharing her duties only with his mother. During many hours of every day they were alone together, and in them all his soul was revealed to her. She shared his triumphs, his successes; success whose contemplation deepened the hectic on his wasting cheek even now.

"But it has been too much for me," he would say, with a sad smile; "the excitement, and, worst of all, the being parted from you—it has worn me out."

All that his art had done, all that his genius had comprehended and struggled to express in his music, his lips whispered to her in those long, bright days, when she was going down by his side to the darkness of death; down to the river's brink, whence she must turn back in loneliness and sorrow. Unspeakably precious were those last hours of soul communion. Mabel felt then how truly she was part of himself—that their two souls, separated though they might be for years, must be reunited before either could be a symmetrical and perfect whole.

His summons came on a June twilight. On that day, twenty-two years before, he had been born into the world of mortals; on that day God saw fit that he should be born again into the world of spirits. The two women, of both whose lives he was the dearest portion, were alone with him. An unspeakable tenderness breathed in his farewell. His last words were,

"Mother, your son will know you in heaven. Mabel, my life's angel, I will wait for you there."

After that he lay, looking earnestly at his betrothed, as if he would fain carry her features with him to the land of the angels. His violin, beloved even in death, lay on the bed beside him. It had been placed there by his request. Listlessly his fingers began to wander over the strings, and beneath their touch grew, somehow, a strange, wild melody, as if spirits were playing upon the chords. It was like the story of his life. It began in feeble, uncertain cadence. It swelled into love, ambition, hope. Then it grew feebler, slower, more mournful. Low, and sweet, and tremulous, yet wild, it thrilled along the strings, until, at last, with a long sob, it grew mute. With the soul of the music had departed the soul of Joseph Thorne.

His mother soon followed him. Their graves are green under the sunshine of this peaceful summer. Mabel Emerson's work is not yet done. She is wedded to a hope and a memory. Bold, indeed, must the man be who would dare to speak to her of love. Wherever trouble is, wherever hearts are struggling with sorrow, her presence is at the door; and she whom Joseph Thorne used to call the angel of his life, will go to her last rest crowned with the blessings of those ready to perish. "Her works they shall follow her."

Olive Winchester Wight.

Nothing but lifeless flesh and bone,
  That could not do me ill;
And yet I feared him all the more
  For lying there so still.

HOOD.

Oh! thou dead
And everlasting witness! whose unsinking
Blood darkens earth and heaven! what thou now art
I know not! but if thou see'st what I am,
I think thou wilt forgive him, whom his God
Can ne'er forgive, nor his own soul—farewell!

BYRON (*Cain*).

OLIVE WINCHESTER WIGHT.

THE story began far away back among the dim mists of my boyhood. I was not more than fourteen, and my brother William was just sixteen when Olive Winchester first came among us.

My father was dead, and had left his large property to be pretty equally divided between myself and my elder brother. William was to have, on coming of age, the old ancestral hôme—La Plaisance; my mother, who was a French woman, had named it, cherishing, among the rocks and hills of New England, the memory of her French birth-place. I was to receive for my share, in bank stocks and other kindred investments, a sum nearly equivalent. My mother's jointure being sufficient for our present support, the estate was, during our minority, steadily increasing in value.

My mother, who clung to us passionately in her lonely widowhood, could not bear to send us from her, and so we received our educations at home, reciting daily to the rector of our village church. By these lessons my brother William profited more than myself. He was a studious youth, not sickly, but never very strong. Nothing in the world had such charms for him as books; while I, on the other hand, honestly detested study, and found my pleasure, even in boyhood, in athletic exercises—riding, climbing, and swimming.

No two brothers were ever more widely different in personal appearance as well as in mental organization. I had a full, yet firmly-knit figure, ruddy cheeks, sunburned hair, and thoroughly masculine countenance. William was slight and pale; his features were delicate and regular; his eyes a clear gray, full of softness and tenderness; his hair dark and wavy, and his hands small and fair as a woman's. From my earliest recollection I had exercised a sort of protecting care over him. In all disputes with the village boys I had been his champion, and he, in turn, had labored faithfully to assist my duller comprehension in mastering the mysteries of science. God knows that, in those days, we loved each other, ay, and we should have always, had not Olive Winchester come.

My mother was summoned, on the April in which my fourteenth birthday fell, to the death-bed of the most cherished friend of her youth, and she returned, bringing with her that friend's orphan daughter. The girl's father and mother were both dead, and, but for us at La Plaisance, she was, at twelve years, utterly alone in the world.

It was a sullen, stormy April day, the one on which we saw her first. We had had no intimation of the time of my mother's return, and I came back from a long gallop over the hills, in the very teeth of the storm, and found her quietly seated in the parlor, with my brother beside her. At a window stood a tiny figure dressed in the deepest mourning—a child she seemed—looking out there, watching the wind and the rain. She turned and came forward when my mother, after her affectionate greeting to me, called her by name.

"This, my son Roscoe, is Olive Winchester, whom I have brought here to be your sister."

The little thing laid her bit of a hand in mine, and shyly lifted her eyes to my face with a look appealing so pathetically for tenderness and sympathy that I was only restrained by boyish bashfulness from clasping her in my arms.

"I have no other friends," she said, simply, in a voice which, though clear, was very low and sorrowful. "I have no other friends, and Mrs. Wight says you will be kind to me."

"And so we will, by Jupiter!" I cried, with rough, boyish sincerity; and I wondered why the tears sprang into her eyes at words which I meant to be so very comforting.

She was a shy, pale little thing, with nothing very remarkable in her face except her hazel eyes, sorrowful, yet bright, but they were the twin magnets to draw all my existence after them from that hour.

Of course, at fourteen, I had never thought of love. I do not think the visions of possible love and marriage ever come to boys as early as to the stiller and more introverted natures of girls—certainly not to boys who read and think so little, who are so full of exuberant animal life as I was. And yet, looking back, I can recall many a pang, which I know now was of boyish jealousy, when she seemed to prefer my brother's society to my own. These occasions were not infrequent, for he was more of her kind than I. She, like him, loved books and study, and he was in great part her teacher. She looked up to him from the first with real reverence.

As she grew older he could talk with her, but I had

no faith in my power to interest her. They used to sit together long summer days upon the grass, under the great oak trees, and read old tales and tragedies, whose theme turned always on woman's beauty and man's devotion. Often they asked me to join them, but I had no enjoyment in their pursuits, and I used to take my solitary way to the woods, and lie for hours on the bank of some forest stream, catching glimpses of the blue sky as the wind lifted the boughs above me, or watching the sunshine sifting down through the leaves like fine gold poured into the very heart of the still wood. I would lie there and wonder why I was so wretched—I, with friends, youth, home, while the birds sang and the winds blew, and every thing was glad around me.

I was eighteen before I had answered this question even to my own heart. One day I was sitting with my mother at the library window. My eyes followed the direction of hers, and rested on my brother and Olive, walking to and fro among the shrubbery, and talking earnestly together.

"There they are, as usual," my mother said, musingly. "I shouldn't wonder if William were to love her some day. I think I should like that. It would be so much better for him to marry her than to bring a stranger in, to break up the quiet of our home."

I believe I, more than William, was my mother's confidant. She was very proud of his acquirements, and loved him dearly; but I was her youngest, and had always remained her pet: to me she confided all her hopes and speculations.

For once, however, I was not ready with my answer. Her words had revealed to me my own heart—had taught me that I loved Olive Winchester with no calm tenderness, which would be content to call her sister—to see her my brother's wife, the mother of his children.

My mother had spoken as if all that would be necessary would be for William to love her; as if her affection for him was not at all a thing to be questioned. I would not accept this verdict at once. I would watch her narrowly. She was sixteen—old enough to know her own heart—as old as my mother had been when she became my father's wife.

I staid at home more now. I walked and sat with them under the trees, and listened while William read or Olive sang; and, at times, I was almost convinced that they were made for each other. But sometimes I doubted. She blushed now and then when I looked at her, or sat down by her side, as she never blushed at any of William's attentions; but then she was more used to his presence than to mine. I brought her, one day, a curious flower from the depths of the forest, and she wore it on her bosom till it faded. Years afterward I found it in a secret drawer of her writing-desk, and then I knew how she had cherished it.

Well, I am making this episode of doubt and suspense too long, because I am dreading to reach the certainty that came after it. It lasted a year. During all that time, looking back, I can see that I gave her no reason to believe that I loved her, while William was constant in his attentions. I was waiting. She seemed to me so young that I ought not to trouble the calm, maidenly current of her life; and then, besides, I had so little hope.

At last she had completed her seventeenth year.

William was twenty-one. They were old enough for love. One day my mother asked me to walk with her. She wore a happy face, and, as she seated herself beside me on a rustic bench, she said,

"I have something pleasant to tell you, Roscoe."

A sudden presentiment struck home to my heart, but I mastered it, and asked, with outward calmness,

"What is it, mother?"

"My hopes are accomplished. Your brother loves Olive. They were betrothed this morning."

I felt the blood rush to my heart in a whelming tide. My brain reeled. The cry of my soul would be heard.

I threw myself on the ground at her feet—my mother's, who loved me as no other ever could—in whose heart I was always sure of room.

"Mother," I said, slowly, "do you think that *I* could love?"

My tone startled her.

"Surely, my son. Why do you ask?"

"Do you think my love would be as deep as William's?" I persisted.

"It should be deeper. Your nature is at the same time more ardent and more steadfast than his."

I sprang to my feet. I stood before her, and looked straight into her eyes.

"Mother, you say well; I *could* love, and with all the love of my lifetime I do love Olive Winchester. Pity me, mother; for what you have told me this hour has blighted every hope of my future."

She understood me. My words, she said afterward, sounded cold and quiet when she saw the passion of anguish and despair which swept over my face. She made me sit down beside her; she put her arms round my neck; she laid her pitying face against mine, so flushed and fevered.

"My son—my dearest son," she said, over and over again, in tender tones, and when I grew a little calmer she tried to reason with me. She persuaded me that Olive's love was never likely to have been mine. She prophesied joys that would yet dawn on my life; but my heart mocked at such vain hopes in sullen silence. Only one thing she suggested which I accepted eagerly—the relief which it would be to me to leave home—not to be present at my brother's wedding. It was something to escape the torture of seeing Olive given to another. I clung desperately to the idea.

My mother managed all for me so that my real motives were suspected by no one. In two weeks I left for Europe—to be gone, as was generally understood, three years—but to remain, as I promised my own heart, until I had conquered my mad passion for Olive Winchester.

My brother—I fear I have hardly done him justice in this story—had a nature noble, though calm. He loved me faithfully. Utterly unconscious of my feelings, he tried to persuade me to remain at home until after his marriage. His joy, he said, would not be half complete unless I could share it. Of course I resisted all his persuasions. Olive said nothing. I thought, though I could imagine no reason, that she rather preferred I should go.

On the morning of my departure I found her alone in the garden. I went to her side, and I could see that she had been weeping. I struggled to command myself.

"Olive," I said, "dear Olive, I am going. I will

bid you good-by here. I want to tell you, while we are all alone, how dear you have always been to me —how fervently I shall pray, when I am far away, that you may be as happy as you deserve—as you are sure to be. I want you should think of me once even on your wedding-day. Will you, Olive?"

She did not answer. She lifted those magnetic hazel eyes, and flashed into my soul one look—a look full of something I knew not what—which made my heart beat with a wild, tumultuous thrill of hope. But the next moment this vanished. I knew well that she did not love me—she, my brother's betrothed. I opened my arms.

"Come, and let me give you one kiss, Olive—my sister that is to be—whose face I may, perchance, never live to look upon again."

She came close to me. She suffered me to fold her in my arms. I had meant to kiss her calmly as a brother should, but the passion which surged in my heart found a language in spite of myself. I pressed on her lips a kiss which said more than I had any right to utter. With a sudden sense of guilt, trembling at my own rashness, I released her. Her expression was half-frightened, full of a sorrow which seemed strange to me even then, but in it was no anger. I left her there.

Three months later news came to me, in Italy, of the marriage of my brother.

After that two years passed on calmly, and in them my character, under the stern discipline of suffering, had undergone a great change. It is a mistake to suppose that sorrow comes to every one as an angel of regeneration. To more it plays the part of a tempting demon. I think it was such to me. I hardened under it. I grew cold, worldly, ambitious. My intellect was not naturally dull, and I now bestowed all my energy on its cultivation. I said to myself that it was only to divert my attention—to prevent my mind from dwelling on my sorrow; but I believe I was conscious all the time of a lurking motive, which I was unwilling boldly to confront—an undercurrent of thought. I longed, secretly, to rival my brother at his own weapons—to show Olive that I was something more than a fine animal—that I could do more than ride, and hunt, and swim. I progressed rapidly, for my will was firm, and my iron constitution, of itself, gave me great advantages. I could have been eagerly welcomed into society. My income was ample, and I think I was just enough of a satirist and a cynic to have been popular. But society had few charms for me. I saw many brilliant women, but not one who seemed to me worthy a moment's comparison with my lost love.

I was in Paris, but just preparing for a trip into Egypt, when a letter came to me from my brother, summoning me home, and begging me to use all possible dispatch if I would see my mother alive. It had gone first to Rome, and from thence been sent after me to Paris. It was doubtful if I could reach home in season. For the time all passion was swallowed up in the thought of my mother. I did not think of Olive; or, if I remembered her at all, it was as a gentle sister—the wife of that brother who was sharing with me now one common sorrow. It was strange how the old, boyhood affection revived in this season of trouble. William, toward whom my heart had so long been hardened and cold, was once again, to my fancy, the loved and loving brother Will of our boyish days, whose battles I fought, and who learned my lessons. My heart thrilled, my eyes moistened at these memories. What was woman's love, I asked myself, as I hurried to Havre on the night express, that it should come between two who had so loved each other—who had shared one home, one name, one mother's heart and bosom. I felt strong to go home a man—to meet my sister Olive with only a brother's calm affection—to receive my mother's blessing. But there my thought faltered. What if those lips should be beyond the power to bless me? What if those tender eyes were closed? What if I had looked my last on that mother's gentle face?

The train seemed to fly over the level road, but it did not keep pace with my thought. I felt like shouting "Faster!" to its swiftest speed.

It was twilight when the wagon in which I had ridden from the dépôt stopped before the gate of La Plaisance. I sprang from the vehicle and hurried up the walk. My brother met me at the door. He threw his arms around me, and I felt his tears upon my face. Then I knew all, as well as when his words came, slow and choked with grief.

"You are too late, Roscoe. We buried her yesterday. She struggled hard with death. She said she could not die until she had seen you once more, but at length her resistance gave way, and she lapsed into sleep. We kept her a week, but at last, as we did not know when you would come, we buried her."

I did not weep; I think my sorrow was too deep

for any outward expression; but William told me afterward that my face looked as ghastly in the moonlight as that other face on which, the day before, they had closed down the coffin-lid.

He led me into the parlor. I had a momentary glimpse of a figure dressed in the deepest black, standing at the window and looking out in precisely the same attitude in which little twelve-years-old Olive Winchester had stood there years before. She heard our footsteps, and came at once to meet me. At that moment I did not perceive, what I saw afterward, how ripe, and rare, and perfect in its beauty was the full blossoming of that flower whose bud had been so sweet. It soothed me to hear the low tones of her sympathizing voice, and I sat until a late hour, with her on one side and my brother Will on the other, listening to every detail of my blessed mother's illness—to every message, every word of parting tenderness which she had left for me.

I had loved my mother with no common love, and I mourned for her with no common sorrow. It was months before any unhallowed thought could find entrance into the heart so full of that sacred memory. But after a time, I know not how, my old passion began to rise up and assert itself—the old temptation came back in its full force. I began to realize what a beautiful woman Olive had become. I loved her as an undeveloped girl, and, now that she had ripened into womanly loveliness, is it strange that I worshiped her? Do not think that ever, under any circumstances, I could have revealed this to her. There was an atmosphere of saintly purity about her which I would have died sooner than taint with the faintest utterance of an unlawful love. But this very restraint deepened the intensity of my passion.

I felt all my renewed tenderness for my brother dying out. He had come between me and the love which might have been my life's crown. I am not sure that I did not hate him. Outwardly I was very calm. I strove to make myself agreeable. I surprised them both by my acquirements and the change in my tastes. I could see Olive's innocent pleasure in my society.

I felt that I ought to go away. Every morning my good angel whispered to me to depart, and I rose resolved to obey his monitions. Every evening found me lingering still. It seemed impossible to wrench away the seven-fold cable which bound me. There was such a charm in Olive's very unconsciousness—in watching all her movements—the lithe shape of her slender figure, the graceful flow of her garments. You smile. You were never in love; you do not understand the rhapsodies of a lover's passion. I hated myself for being subject to the dominion of mine, but I could not wrestle with it. It had grown with my growth unperceived, until it had become too mighty for me.

I had been there all winter, and now it was spring. I sat by my window with the fiend and the angel struggling in my heart as usual, when my brother came in and asked me to ride with him.

"I have had the horses saddled," he said. "The morning is fine, and we'll have a grand canter through the woods. You don't know how much better I like horseback exercise than I used. You've been getting my old taste for books, and I yours for out-door sports."

I felt disinclined at first to go, but I had no excuse,

so I laid down the book I had been holding in my hand for an ostensible occupation, and followed him down stairs. The horses stood before the door, noble fellows! pawing the earth in their impatience, with arched necks and fiery eyes.

Olive had come out to see us off. Just as William was going to mount, he went back, as if moved by a sudden, irresistible impulse of tenderness, took his wife in his arms, and kissed her. The sight of any caress between them, which, however, was very infrequent in my presence, always tortured me beyond endurance. I sprang into the saddle, and, without waiting for Will, galloped away. After a few moments I came to my senses, slackened my speed, and he came up with me.

"Halloo, Roscoe, what do you mean? Here I've been tearing after you like mad. I wanted to go the other way through the forest. The woodmen have cleared a path there to drag their logs home, and the scenery is so beautiful and grand."

"As you like," I answered, turning my horse's head indifferently. There was a keen, exhilarating sense of life, however, to which I could not remain insensible, as I dashed on over the forest road, with the trees just bursting into leaf above our heads, the water babbling from a thousand tiny springs, and the violets and anemones blooming in every nook. We did not talk much. I was busy with my own thoughts, and William was content to enjoy the scene in silence.

I must hurry on. I am nearing the hour which has made my life a curse. We came, suddenly emerging from a dense thicket, to a turbulent stream—the "Mad Rapids" it had been called ever since I could remember. A rustic bridge had been thrown over it, and across this the timber-road which we were traversing led. As we approached we saw that the stream, swollen by the spring rains, had swept away the bridge, and some of its timbers were lodged among the rocks which formed its bottom.

The question was whether to leap the stream or to turn back. The waters were very deep and the banks high, but it was narrow, not by any means a difficult or a dangerous leap for a good horse. I proposed that we should try it—not, God knows, with any worse motive than the desire of a little excitement. Bad as I was, Heaven bears me witness that it was with no thought, no faintest foreshadowing of the terrible consequences.

William agreed to my proposal. He touched his horse, and the noble creature sprang forward, but he had taken the leap at the wrong place. When his feet touched the other side the earth gave way under them, and horse and rider both fell into the rapids. Quicker than thought William had loosened his feet from the stirrups, and I saw that he had fallen, not underneath, but on one side of the horse. The animal fell directly upon a sharp rock, and, I believe, died instantly; but I saw my brother's ghastly, imploring face looking up at me from the rushing waters.

I sprang from my horse. I knew I could save him, but— O God! did the struggle last an hour, or can one moment contain such fierce, terrible thoughts?

On one hand, I saw his face, the brother whom my good angel was beckoning me to save; I knew that he could not swim—that he was utterly helpless; on the other, I saw Olive. The fiend in my heart tempted me with the memory of her maddening beauty—

her beauty, which only death, his death, could give to my arms. I saw her as I had seen her that morning —ripe, dewy lips, slender, delicate figure, eyes full of love and truth—only thus could I win her. And then the good angel whispered again,

"Would you go forth with the brand of Cain upon your forehead? Would you be your brother's murderer?" and I saw yet another face pleading with me; my mother's face, so white and still under the turf springing with blossoms.

I dashed wildly into the water. I drew my brother up. With a desperate struggle I landed him upon the bank. It was too late! The tempter had triumphed —I had waited the one moment too long. He was dead! I felt myself his murderer. Murderer! a ghastly word, but one which must underlie forever all the voices of my life.

With frantic energy, I tried every means to restore him; but he grew colder and colder. He was dead utterly; only it seemed to me that those glassy eyes, which would not close, were turned on me with an eternal reproach. Oh, I could never shut that out. They are looking at me still.

When I had convinced myself that he was gone beyond the reach of human aid, I left him lying there, and hurried on to a clearing nearly half a mile away, where a few woodmen were chopping. I told them my story—that my brother, in attempting to leap the stream, had fallen into the water—that I had jumped in after him, but before I could get him out he was dead. I asked their assistance to carry his body home. With a few planks they constructed a hasty bridge, a little farther down the stream, and then those stalwart men took the body up, and bore it solemnly over the fatal waters and back along the forest road.

My faithful horse, in the mean while, had been waiting me patiently. I mounted him, and rode onward to break the news to Olive.

In that moment I would have given, so I thought, all the hopes of my future, even Olive herself, but to have seen the light come back into those glassy, haunting eyes; to hear my brother's voice; to have the blight and curse of a murderer's doom uplifted from my soul.

I had been riding swiftly, but I slackened my rein as I drew near the house. How could I go in and tell Olive that she was a widow—I, whom the haunting voice accused as her husband's murderer? "I did not kill him," I cried, wildly; "I did not kill him. I only did not save his life." It was in vain. The inexorable voice would not be silenced. "Murderer!" it cried out still; "your brother's murderer." But I saw the necessity for self-control. I dismounted at the gate, and went slowly up the walk and into the house. Olive sat there by a table. A few flowers she had gathered were in a vase before her; her canary had come out of its cage and perched on her shoulder; a smile hovered about her lips. Oh, how innocent, and youthful, and lovely she looked, this young woman, scarcely yet twenty. In that moment I had no space for repentance. I was willing to accept my doom.

"Olive," I said.

She turned and looked at me. I suppose the wildness of my expression startled her. The color retreated from her face. I could see her tremble.

"Roscoe," she cried, "brother Roscoe, tell me what is the matter. Why are you here alone? Where is William?"

I had meant to spare her a sudden shock, to prepare her gradually for my evil tidings; but I lost all control over myself.

"They are bringing him home," I said. "William is dead. He tried to leap the Mad Rapids, his horse fell, and he was drowned. I plunged in after him, but when I drew him out he was dead."

I had looked at her steadily while I spoke. Perhaps I had some undefined hope that his death would be a relief to her as to myself. But no; her anguish was unmistakable.

"My husband—my good, kind husband!" she gasped, in a strange, faint voice, and then she sank upon the floor, not insensible, but prostrated as one felled to the ground by a heavy blow. I sprang forward. I was about to raise her up, to try to console her, but she repulsed me with a sort of terror which I understood better afterward.

"Go away!" she cried; "I can have no help, no comfort. I want none." Then she seemed to repent. A change passed over her face, and she said, gently and humbly as a little child,

"Forgive me, Roscoe; I do not mean to wound you. I forgot; you are his brother, and you will mourn for him with me. And you risked your life to save his. God bless you!"

No curse could have seemed to me half so fearful as that blessing. And then to listen to her praises for trying to save his life—I, who had stood by and let him perish, when I might so easily, with no danger to myself, have saved him. I withdrew from her side, and turned away my eyes, which dared not meet her own. As I did so I glanced from the window, and saw them approaching with the litter on which the dead man lay. I regained, with a strong effort, my self-command.

"Olive," I said, "they are bringing him into the yard. I will go and meet them."

She rose from the floor.

"I will go too—I, his wife. When did he ever come home that I did not welcome him? He used to put his hands on my head and call me his little Olive—his darling. But he'll not speak now!"

There was a wild pathos in her tone. I fancied her reason was departing, and looked at her searchingly.

"No," she said, "I am not mad, though madness might be merciful. See, I am quite myself."

I drew near her, and she leaned heavily on my arm, and we went forth together to meet the husband coming home.

I do not think Olive perceived any thing supernatural in that dead face; but I could see, turn which way I would, that those eyes haunted me, followed me, sought me out, upbraided me with their everlasting reproach. Well, the world, complain of it as we all do, is almost always more charitable to us than we deserve; and if there was any thing strange or unnatural in my manner, the lookers-on imputed it to my excessive grief at my brother's sudden and terrible end.

Olive was calm. She gave all the directions in a steady voice. A few neighbors were hurriedly assembled, and William was laid out on his own bed in the chamber they had shared together. When all had been done, with a sad sweetness that moved some of those strong men to tears, she thanked them for their kindness in this her hour of mortal sorrow, and then she begged that she might be left alone with the dead.

I dared not intrude upon her. Indeed, I would not willingly go into the presence of those eyes, which still, wherever I went, pierced through the distance and haunted me. At first I remained outside the closed door to listen for the sounds from within; but I could hear nothing. Her grief was as silent as I knew it was deep.

We kept him four days before we buried him. But I will not linger on those days when that shrouded terror, still, though terrible, lay in our midst. It is needless torture. When I followed him to the grave, with that wife, so young to be a widow, leaning upon my arm—when I saw the earth heaped over his coffin, I almost expected a voice would cry out from the depths of the tomb and denounce me. But the dead man told no tales. There was no sound save the sullen fall of the earth, the low words of the clergyman, and the stifled sobs of the bystanders.

I took Olive home. As she entered the house, she turned to me and laid her hand in mine just as she had done years before, a little child. How well I remembered it!

"Roscoe," she said, "God has taken all my other friends from me. My parents are gone, your mother is gone, and now He has taken my husband—my tender, good husband, who loved me so. I have only you left. Be kind to me, Roscoe."

I would have given worlds to take her to my heart

—to lavish upon her the wild idolatry of my love; but I restrained myself. Not yet, not yet; I must bide my time.

It was a whole year before I said to her one word which any brother might not have uttered. That year was one long fever, made up of alternate paroxysms of remorse and joy. Sometimes, in her presence, I would forget the past, with its sin, its despair, and live a tranced life, beholding bewildering visions of future happiness. I would believe that she would yet be mine—that she lived for me. I liked to watch her—to note every change of her moods—to see how the first utter desolation of her grief passed slowly away, and she began to find interest in her favorite pursuits, a charm in life. Then I strove to make myself necessary to her. I shared her readings, her walks, her drives. I invented new pleasures for her. Hardest of all, I listened, with gentle sympathy, to all her reminiscences of her dead husband—the thousand ways in which he had petted and indulged her, and the fond names which he had called her.

Out of her sight I passed hours of misery—hours when the accusing voices drowned out every harmony of life; when those pursuing eyes, which coffin and turf could not cover, or grave-stone seal together, looked into mine, till I longed to take refuge from them in the still land of shadows and silence. But the months wore away at last; and, a little more than a year after my brother's death, I revealed my love to Olive. I did not commence boldly. I told her a story, which I did not represent as my own, of two brothers who both loved one woman. The elder brother won her, and the younger fled from her presence. At length the husband died, and the brother, loving her more wildly than ever, yet dared not confess it, lest there should be no pity for him in her eyes—lest her heart was in the grave.

Before I was half through I saw that she understood me, but she listened in silence. I think my words touched a chord in her heart, whose vibrations she could not at once still.

When I paused she rose. I thought there was a shy tenderness in her eyes, but she spoke resolutely.

"I know what you mean; but you must not say such things to me. It is very wrong. I am William's wife. I have no right to listen to them."

She went from the room. I was not at all discouraged. My words had been received precisely as I had expected. I knew that the very thought of a second marriage would startle her, at first, as a phantom of evil. But I had her constantly with me. There was no danger of a rival. I was cautious and prudent. I could afford to wait.

It was not a month before I had won from her a confession which even transcended my hopes. Her first love had been mine. She did not dream, as indeed I had never given her any reason, that I loved her; but, unsought, she had given to me the wealth of her innocent young heart. When my brother proposed to her, she had felt so deeply her obligations to our family, that she had no courage to refuse to yield to his pleadings and the evident wishes of my mother. With maidenly modesty she had concealed her love for me, but she had told William that her regard for him was only a sister's calm, dispassionate tenderness. "That is enough, until you shall be my wife," he had answered, silencing her with caresses, and she had suffered herself to be persuaded.

She had never had the faintest suspicion of my regard until the morning on which I bade her farewell before leaving home, and even then she had felt no certainty of it. Besides, it was, or she thought it, too late to recede. After her marriage she had striven to conquer and stifle even the memory of her girlish dream, and had so far succeeded that she had faithfully believed my brother was dearer to her than any one else ever was or could have been. When the news of his death had come to her, she had at first repulsed me in the midst of her grief, because the memory of her former love for me came back to her conscience in that hour as a sin against the departed. Poor child! if she sinned in loving me, I believe it was the only sin of her lifetime.

That autumn my entreaties and her own secret wishes triumphed. She became my wife. Dear as William had been to her heart, I knew well that I only had ever entered into its inner temple—that the keys which responded to my touch had never been struck by other fingers.

I neither knew nor cared whether any condemned our marriage. I was satisfied. She was mine, whom I had sold heaven to win. It was something more than joy to share with her every moment of my life; to wake at night and find her beloved head lying on my bosom; her sweet breath coming and going in slumber peaceful as a child's, within the shelter of my arms. Oh, how I used to gloat over my treasure, when not even her eyes could witness my raptures.

I suppose the fallen angels, sitting in chains, remember the hosannas, and the incense, and the transports of heaven. They had their space of joy—joy as intense as their fall was terrible. Well, for months I had mine. The haunting eyes could not find me—the accusing voice could not waken me from my long trance of love. But, after a time, this mood passed. I worshiped her as madly as ever. Sometimes still I forgot all things else and was happy, but oftener my remorse was terrible—the remorse that I could not share even with her—that human love, be it ever so faithful, could not lighten. I began to be pursued by a fear, as terrible as it was vague, that in some form the retribution for my sin would fall on her, because so would the blow come most heavily to me. Sometimes, when I was with her, every fond word, every innocent caress would pierce through me like a sword. I could not shut out the thought that if she knew me as I was her love would be changed to loathing—that she would fly from me, hereafter, in the land of spirits, where the mysteries of all hearts and all lives shall be revealed. A thousand times I was on the very point of unburdening to her my load of sin, and then I would choke back the words; I could not summon resolution enough to utter what I thought must shut me out from her heart forever.

At length our boy was born. How I had looked forward to his birth! I had thought that his first cry—the voice of my first-born—would exorcise the phantoms from my life—that his baby lips would smile down care and trouble.

Oh God! no sooner had I taken him in my arms than I saw the fatal likeness. My brother's face had been sent again on earth to haunt me. It did not look like my child or Olive's. It had William's delicate features; his dark, wavy hair; his clear gray eyes, full, even in this infant, of soft, subdued tenderness. I put him from me with a shudder.

His mother noticed the likeness and wondered at it, but with all the fullness of her true woman's heart she loved and cherished her child. I think even mothers seldom love as she loved; her nature was so intense, and so few objects had been given her on which to lavish its wealth of passionate devotion.

Every week, as the child grew, this fateful likeness was stronger and more undeniable. He seemed to me more William's child than mine, and I consented, with an involuntary thrill of dread, when his mother expressed a wish to call him by William's name. And yet, sometimes, a father's yearnings rose up in my heart and overflowed, till I was fain to snatch him to my bosom. At such times I thought—it might have been fancy, or but the natural effect of my violence—but I thought he shrank from me, and I recognized in this turning away from me of my own flesh and blood Heaven's righteous retribution.

He was never a strong child, but he lived to be more than a year old. He learned to call his mother by her name, to mouth a few other pretty, childish words, and Olive loved him more and more, and rejoiced over him with an intensity which I trembled to see. More and more, haunted by this child's face, the likeness of my brother's, was I possessed by an almost irresistible impulse to pour into my wife's faithful bosom all the madness, the despair of my life; but still I mastered it, and was silent.

At last the child sickened suddenly and died. In

the morning I saw him lying as well as usual in his mother's arms, searching her face with those weird, unchildlike, yet loving eyes. At noon he was violently sick, and at night she held him as she held him in the morning, but he was cold and dead, though the eyes she had vainly tried to close were open still. Those eyes—William's own had never haunted me more remorselessly—and yet I kept silence. I said nothing until after we had laid him in a little grave by William's side. Then, when we came back from the funeral, and my wife turned to me for comfort, my terrible secret burst forth.

"Olive," I cried, "curse me as your child's murderer! I can keep it from you no longer. You stretch out to me your empty arms, where your baby used to lie, and I tell you that his death was the just punishment for my sin. He was sent on earth to haunt me with his strange likeness to the dead, and now he has been taken to smite me by piercing through your heart!"

She looked at me in blank terror—in utter wonder. I sank at her feet; I hid my face on her knees; she did not shrink from me even then. I poured out there, not daring to meet her eyes, my guilt—my long and terrible remorse. I told her in full the story of William's death. Then I paused, waiting her judgment. I expected she would banish me from her presence forever, but she raised my face in her gentle hands. She looked at me with an angel's pity and a woman's love. Then she spoke; oh, no angel, only a loving woman, could have uttered such words! She thanked me for sharing with her my secret. She told me that she had long suspected, from words uttered in my restless sleep

—from the strange alternations of my manner from joy to despair—that some fearful memory was preying upon my life, though she had never conjectured its nature. She thanked God that it was no worse. She told me it was wrong for me to call myself a murderer—that I had not been responsible for being tempted, and reminded me that I had overcome the temptation and plunged into the water at last. She believed that William must have died before any efforts of mine could have saved him—that the fall which had killed his horse could not have spared him. She told me, moreover, that, whatever I had done, it was the most fatal sin of all to despair of the almighty mercy of God.

Her reasoning did not convince me. Not even she had power to lift the burden from my soul. But oh! you can never conceive the inexpressible relief it was to have shared this secret with her—to feel that she knew me as I was.

Never, until then, had I fully understood the height and depth, the heroic strength of that woman's love. She put aside at once her sorrow for her dead child, whom no mourning could bring back, and devoted herself to soothe the despair of her living husband.

And then, just as I began, through her, to believe in the possibility of future hope and forgiveness, as if there was to be no rest for my troubled soul this side of the Infinite, God took her also. Never strong, and weaker than ever since her baby's birth, the shock of his death, followed by my terrible disclosure, had been too severe for her. After that she never saw another hour of health. Slowly, but steadily, she faded away. Tenderest care could not wrestle with the Destroyer.

To the last I do not think she ever thought of me

with a single reproach. And yet I have sometimes believed that the knowledge of my guilt killed her—that, though she never confessed it to me, the shadow which she strove to lift from my life settled upon her own. But she died blessing me, and pointing me to a future of peace and union in heaven, where, she bade me believe, the All-Father would forgive me and receive me. Oh, can Heaven be as merciful as she was?

When she died the sun of my life set forever. For me there could be no morning after the night. I buried her—my life's one treasure—beside her child, and on her tombstone is graven the name of her wifehood—

OLIVE WINCHESTER WIGHT.

AGED XXIII.

I never go to that grave; they tell me the weeds have grown over it. The Olive of my love is not there. I know that before this she has seen the Father's face. My heart tells me that she is praying in that heavenly country for him whose love for her, despite all his other sins, was faithful unto death. But can even her prayers be answered?

I am left alone with two memories—one of blessing, the other of bane. I am groping onward to the country of the shadows; and when my soul goes forth alone to cross the surging waters which lie between us and the beyond, I can not tell whether the pale hands of my beloved will be stretched out to help me to climb the banks of eternal flowers, or my brother's soul, seeking there, there, the revenge denied on earth, will plunge me, struggling vainly, downward, ever downward, into the depths heaven's highest archangel could never fathom.

My Inheritance.

Deep is the solitude in life of millions upon millions who, with hearts welling forth love, have none to love them. Deep is the solitude of those who, with secret griefs, have none to pity them.

DE QUINCEY.

Mine! God, I thank Thee that Thou hast given
Something all mine on this side heaven;
Something as much myself to be
As this my soul which I lift to Thee:
　　Flesh of my flesh, bone of my bone,
Life of my life—us, whom Thou dost make
Two to the world, for the world's work's sake,
　　But each unto each, as in Thy sight, one.

ANONYMOUS.

MY INHERITANCE.

I.

MY great-uncle, Mr. Gerard Sunderland, was dead; and I, his heir, Gerard Sunderland the second, had just stepped upon the cars to go and take possession of his estate in Woolwich, a pleasant little village not far from the Connecticut River. He had been a strange man in many respects, this dead great-uncle of mine. In his early youth he was a diligent student, a man of rare genius, devoting himself only to study. He had traveled over many lands, and came back with much learning, a polished, stately gentleman. He was over thirty when he fell in love. I use advisedly this hackneyed expression. It was with him a desperate, unthinking plunge. He staked his all upon one throw. With such a nature as his there could be no calling back the heart—no after-growth of tenderness.

He loved, as such men oftenest do, a woman remarkable for nothing beyond her peers, and yet he made of her a goddess. She was sweet and blithesome rather than very beautiful. She had little fondness for study. She would rather gather roses than read poems, and made pies oftener than periods. She was very young too, scarcely half his own age; and yet, to his fancy, she was the one stately and most perfect lady, whom no woman could ever equal, whose name no man's voice must ever utter without homage. He approached her, I have been told, with a reverent humility very wonderful in his proud nature, and perhaps that kind of wooing was not the one best suited to enchain her wayward fancy. At all events, his love was not returned, and before many months pretty Amy Mansfield, with her sweet brown eyes and her bonny brown hair, became Mistress Amy Deane.

After this my uncle Gerard shunned the world. He settled down at Woolwich, where his lady-love continued to reside; and though his stately house and pleasant grounds were the finest in the whole county—though he was the best of neighbors, and his early grapes and ripe peaches were freely sent to every sufferer who chanced to fall sick in their season of bearing, he yet avoided all society. He lived alone, with a housekeeper as reserved as himself, a maid-of-all-work, and a gardener.

My father, who was his favorite nephew, resided at that time in New York, and was about marrying. He tried vainly to persuade his uncle to remove to the city, or at least to settle near him. The invariable answer expressed a quiet but resolute preference for Woolwich. When I was born, two years after, my father wrote again, begging him to come to my christening, and telling him that I was to be called for him —Gerard Sunderland. I believe my mother, Heaven bless her tender heart! had selected a lovely young girl to stand sponsor by his side, hoping, with her womanly tact, that so the lost Amy might be replaced, and another smile make rainbows about his lonely life. But in reply came the same quiet refusal to visit New York, even for a day; and the letter also stated that he had made his will, bequeathing to his infant grand-nephew, Gerard Sunderland, all his property.

I had only seen him twice. Twice, during my early boyhood, I had been sent—rather with his permission than by his request—to visit him at Woolwich. Once my parents wished—because of my dear mother's health, which was then delicate—to travel without the care which taking me would have involved; the second time New York was visited by an epidemic, before which all fled who could. Business kept my father in the city; and my mother, caring nothing for life unless he might share it, determined to remain with him; while, to ease her mother-heart of its anxiety, I was sent again to Woolwich.

Sitting in the cars, while the quiet villages through which we passed, the tall trees, and the very fences by the wayside, seemed to fly from us with lightning speed, I recalled those two visits. I had traveled then by stage. The journey had been a very fatiguing one, lasting from the gray of the early morning until ten at night.

My welcome had been kind, but grave; and the weeks I passed there had appeared strangely solitary to a child accustomed to the restless bustle of New York. It seemed to me almost as if I were in one of the enchanted castles I had read of in my story-books, where all the beautiful things would vanish if one spoke above a whisper. But this very stillness had not been without its own exceeding charm to my childish imagination. It was happiness enough for me to walk through the garden when the morning dew trembled, tear-like, in the hearts of the blossoms; to gather the magical roses, and see the gardener train the climbing honey-suckle, so tall that I used to wonder if there was a giant living in wicked state at the top of it. It was best of all to watch the wonderful panorama of sunset. It was to me—city born and bred—as if the breath of God had created a new world; had called to quick and beautiful life wonders of which I had never heard or dreamed.

Uncle Gerard, too, was very good to me, in his own stately way. He used to tell me wonderful stories of the foreign countries he had visited, and sometimes to show me paintings which he had made—for he was no mean artist—of some of those far-off scenes.

There was one picture which hung in his study—the only one there—and I had never seen it, for a crimson curtain always hung before it. One day I boldly asked him if he had painted it, and why I might not see it, as I had seen the rest. A look which I could not interpret passed over his face. His voice trembled, but he was not angry.

"Surely," he said; "why not? You shall see it, Gerard."

He drew away the curtain, and a woman's face was there. Gentle brown eyes smiled on me; brown hair of precisely the same hue rippled in waves over the delicate shoulders; the mouth was arch and bright, yet sweet, and looked as if it was just going to speak to me. I was too much pleased to be demonstrative. I think the tears even came to my eyes. They had a trick of doing so in childhood whenever any thing appealed strongly to my quick, æsthetic nature. I only said,

"Oh, Uncle Gerard, I never saw any thing half so beautiful!"

"You think so," was the gentle answer; "but *her* face was ten times fairer than any painter's art could make it."

With a long, perhaps unconscious sigh, he replaced the curtain, and during my visit I never saw that face again. But its memory returned to me vividly as I rode on now toward Woolwich. How those far-off childhood days came back, shedding their glamour over my spirit—came back, with their strange radiance of sunsets and sunrises, their wonderful fragrance of flowers, their far hills and bright waters. I was twenty-eight now. It had been eighteen years since I last saw Uncle Gerard. I had not known him well enough to have his loss come home to me as a real sorrow; still a sort of tender, poetic melancholy invested the memory of this solitary man, grown old alone, clinging to a by-gone love which had never known response; alone with his artist gifts, his genius, his rare learning.

I had been too far away from home to be summoned in time for his funeral, but my parents had gone; and my mother told me, with tears in her eyes, how death had seemed to still tho long sorrow of his life—to give back youth and hope to his worn face—and how marvelously sweet was the still, dead smile into which his lips were frozen. Absorbed in these thoughts, I had not heeded the stopping of the cars or the name of the station, and I roused myself with a sudden start when the conductor, touching my arm, said politely,

"I believe you wish to stop here. This is Woolwich, sir."

I got out. My memory of places was always extremely tenacious. Much as Woolwich had in many respects changed since I had visited it, I knew my way at once to the house which was now mine. Leaving my baggage at the station, I walked onward. Before long I came to the spot where my uncle's grounds—I had not learned to say my grounds as yet—commenced. They lay on both sides of the road, or rather drive—for it was not public property—leading up to the mansion. The pine-trees on either side of the way were not many years old when I saw them last, but they had grown so tall now that their branches met over my head, and, looking up through their greenery, they seemed to lift their odorous boughs almost to the sky. The drive itself flashed white, as if strewn with snowy, glittering shells, in the summer sunshine. The grass was fresh and green, with the long afternoon shadows trailing over it. Soon I turned a corner, and there before me was the house which the trees had till now concealed—a stately, old-fashioned mansion, with an upright three-story centre, and long, rambling wings on each side. Around these wings, whose windows opened to the ground, were pleasant verandas. A flight of stone steps led up to the principal front entrance. The whole place was tasteful, well-appointed, beautifully kept, with a kind of hospitable face, which roused in me a certain pride and joy of ownership, for which I reproached myself the moment after.

I would have pushed open the door and gone in, but it was fastened, and I was obliged to have recourse to a ponderous knocker in the shape of a lion's head. The old housekeeper of eighteen years before came to the door. I had sundry grateful recollections of delicious little pies and cakes with which she had surfeited my boyhood. I was glad to see her kindly face again. She had not changed much. Her figure was hale and buxom as ever, though years had certainly frosted her hair, which used to be thick and black. I extended my hand:

"Ho do you do, Mrs. Tabitha?"

She did not answer at first; she seemed trying to recollect me. Her face wore a puzzled expression which presently cleared up.

"Belike you'll be our young master?"

"The same."

"Well, I'm sure we'll be heartily glad to see you, sir; only, if you'd just sent word you was coming, we'd have been all ready for you, and Mike would have gone after you with the carriage."

I suppose it always remained a mystery to the good old lady why I should have preferred walking quietly over the road to my new possessions, rather than coming to them with due honors, drawn in state by Uncle Gerard's sleek gray horses. However, I soon managed to put her on a right footing—to become the master instead of the visitor—and in due time I was quietly installed in my new home.

For the first day or two there was pleasure enough in rambling about the grounds; but the third morning was rainy, and I shut myself up in my uncle's study. The picture hung there still. I felt almost as if I were committing sacrilege when I drew away the curtain, but I had a strong desire to see how faithfully my memory had reproduced it. It was the same face that I had carried with me all these years, only there was a look of self-renunciation about it, a look like a prayer, which I had not remembered; which I was puzzled to reconcile, at first, with what I had been told of Amy Mansfield's sunny, joyous nature; her disposition to take every thing at its best—to live in the present. My uncle must have painted her as she had seemed to his imagination. All the lofty traits with which his fancy had dowered her he had brought out upon the canvas. But, even without that expression, which seemed the look of a pitying angel, she must have been very lovely. I could imagine how a man might well have worshiped her, and asked her to be nothing that she was not. I looked at her a long time.

I was not romantic. I had been engaged in commerce, and it had not been without its usual hardening effect upon me. I must marry some time, I took that for granted. I was equally resolved that the future Mrs. Gerard Sunderland must be a lady of fortune and position, and yet I could not help thinking, as I gazed upon the picture, that I should like very much to have her eyes look at me like those eyes of bonny Amy Mansfield. And then I smiled at the thought of getting so enthusiastic about a woman who must be old and gray now, even if she were still living. And here a curiosity—I wish I could dignify it by a worthier name—took possession of me to learn her after fate. All I had heard was that she became Amy Deane and lived in Woolwich. Who was this "gude mon" who was her husband—this successful rival of my refined, stately great-uncle? Nothing would be easier than to call Mrs. Tabitha and make the necessary inquiries, but I had a sort of romantic wish to find out in a different manner. It might be my uncle's papers would tell her story. Nothing more likely than for this man, reserved, yet painstaking and patient, who had no human confidant, to write down on paper such things as troubled the current of his life. I began a studious search among the papers in his desk.

I was not disappointed. In a compartment by itself I found a book which had evidently been a sort of journal. It was not dated, or kept with any attempt at regularity. It seemed as if, when he could no longer hush the cry of his soul, it had found vent there.

At first, however, it was joyous. He had just come to Woolwich—he had seen *her*. The words which dwelt upon her beauty seemed touched with flame. To him she was not the pretty, light-hearted girl which only she seemed to other eyes, but the elect woman, crowned, to his thought, with all that there was on earth of nobleness, purity, and religion—a woman such as must have inspired the poets of those old classic days when they wrote of goddesses.

His timid wooing was detailed there; the delicate, poetical attentions by which he sought to make known his homage; and, at last, he told in words, every one of which seemed an embodied agony, how he had asked her love and asked in vain. There was no reproach coupled with her name. He seemed to think it nothing strange that she had not been able to love one who seemed to her youth so grave and old; his only marvel was that he should ever have been presumptuous enough to ask her. She had not fallen ever so slightly from the pedestal on which he had placed her—she was his goddess still.

A few pages farther on her betrothal was chronicled to one Everhard Deane, the young rector of Woolwich—a man, my uncle wrote, whom she could worthily love—who, God grant, might love and cherish her forever! Of her marriage there was nothing written, but by-and-by there came a leaf from which it appeared that he had been painting her portrait. It said,

"I have been to church to day. Everhard Deane preached for the first time since his marriage. They have returned from their short bridal tour. They are living in the rectory. I knew I should see her at church, but I could not stay away, though every moment was torture. I went early. I took my seat where, if she sat in the minister's pew, I could watch every expression of her face, catch every inflection of her voice. Soon they came in. She was leaning on his arm, as I had once hoped, Heaven help me, she would lean on mine. Love made her face radiant. She had never seemed to me so beautiful as now, when she had given herself forever to another. My portrait does not do her justice. I must give to her eyes a tenderer light; I must paint an added nobleness in the still calm of her mouth. Did I covet her? If I did, God will forgive me; God, who knows I would not deprive her of one moment of happiness, even to make her mine forever.

"Oh, how her low voice thrilled me as she joined in the prayers! *Can* Everhard Deane love her as I do? He seemed, indeed, very content, very proud, as who might not be content with her? Well, I shall learn calmness in time. It is something to have loved her—to have dreamed, once in life, a happy dream."

Then came other pages, sometimes with intervals of years between them. Once he had seen her with her first-born child in her arms, a noble boy.

Then that brave boy had died, and it was beautiful to see how every sorrow that came nigh this Amy of his love brought out the still, deep tenderness of Uncle Gerard's nature.

There were many such sorrows. Five children, one after another, she had followed to their quiet resting-places in the church-yard, underneath the rectory windows—the church-yard where, all summer long, suns shone, winds blew, and birds sang above her darlings, and round them, every spring-time, went on the new birth of nature; the wondrous spring-time miracle of earth's resurrection, typical of the mortal putting on immortality—Nature's own seal to the divine promise, "Thy dead shall live again."

It seemed that, despite these many sorrows, the fair Amy was very happy in her husband. Nor was her middle age left desolate. The youngest of all her children, her daughter Rachel, was spared to her; was growing up by her mother's side, with her mother's gentle voice, and eyes which were Amy's own.

The last page of all was stained with that stain which from heart or paper can never be effaced—a strong man's tears. Amy was dead. The grave had closed upon that head, still brown and shining—that smile which had never grown old to his loving eyes. She had never been his, and yet, now she was gone, a light, a music, a glory had been swept forever from earth and life. Happy Everhard Deane! He has a right to plant roses over her grave—a right to mourn her—a blessed heritage for all his lifetime in the memory that that dainty form has thrilled in his clasping arms; those lips pressed upon his their first kisses—uttered for him their last prayer. The grave has closed over her. It wanted but this to make Uncle Gerard's lone life lonelier. It was something to see her—to watch, on Sundays and saint days, for the chance gleam of her sad and tender smile, or the tremulous music of her voice joining in prayer and psalm. Now he has watched and listened for the last time—Amy is dead! Happy Everhard Deane! *He* was beloved—therefore, for him, all the beauty and glory of life are immortal. Beyond the grave he can claim his bride, young and fair again in heaven. For him fond arms are waiting —for him one heart beats lonely, even in the light of that day which hath no end, with longings for his coming; but for Gerard Sunderland there must be solitude —so whispers his despairing heart—even in heaven.

After this page all the leaves were blank. With this record of sorrow, the journal of Uncle Gerard's life came to a full stop. There was no date—I could not tell how long ago it had been written; but I wondered if that had not been his death-stroke—if, after this great sorrow, his life had not begun to ebb.

That night, while Mrs. Tabitha poured my tea, I took occasion to inquire who was the present rector of Woolwich.

"Mr. Everhard Deane," was the reply. "He's getting an old man now, and since his wife died he seems sadly broken; but we all like him, and as long as he can say a prayer we would not change him away."

"How long since his wife died?" was my next question. The answer startled me.

"Just one year to a day before our dead master. He never held up his head after her death. Some said he took it harder than her husband. Belike you have not heard the story, but the master loved Mistress

Deane when she was Amy Mansfield. They say she was a pretty girl, and her eyes were wondrous sweet and bright, but nobody else saw such great things in her as your uncle. She said nay to his suit. Mr. Deane was a younger man, and he had her heart. But it darkened all Mr. Sunderland's life. He always seemed to feel every trouble that came upon her as if it was his own, and when she died he never got over it."

The next day was Sunday, and I went early to church, more anxious, I must confess, to see the husband and child of this dead Amy than to join in the service, which I had not then learned to love. That morning I saw Rachel Deane for the first time.

The rector seemed a quiet yet deep-feeling old man, bowed down by sorrow. There was something singularly beautiful in his benign face, and in the pathos of his low yet thrilling voice. His utterance charmed my ear, it was so distinct and musical, despite the tremulousness it had caught from age and sorrow. But I did not hear his sermon. I was too much absorbed in looking at the saintly face which was uplifted toward him from the minister's pew.

Rachel Deane, at sixteen, was the very image of her mother's portrait in my Uncle Gerard's study, save that the expression of holiness, of self-renunciation, was even deepened in her young face. She was, I could see, all that my uncle's imagination had made of her mother. Her voice—somehow I always notice voices—was so clear that I could easily single out its low tones whenever she joined in the service. Had I only heard that, without looking upon her face, I could have almost divined her character. I should have said that it must be the utterance of a true, pure soul, strong to do and to suffer; yet a cheerful, kindly soul, moreover, carrying light and blessing with it every where.

It was not long before I made her acquaintance. Mr. Deane came to call upon me, and, very naturally, I returned his visit. I soon found that his daughter possessed a vigorous, inquiring mind, already stored with all the available contents of her father's library. But these works, for the most part books of science, history, and theology, had by no means satisfied her. She had read a few volumes of poems, and one or two of Scott's novels, which had been her mother's, and these had opened to her vision the enchanted realm of song and fiction, through which she longed to wander. I had it in my power to gratify this longing. Uncle Gerard's library, which had come down to me with the rest of his possessions, was large and well selected. Himself a poet, his shelves were rich in the works of all the masters of song. I transferred volume after volume to Rachel Deane's table. Her earnest thanks, the glow of pleasure on her sweet young face, were my reward. I was daily more and more astonished at the rare, intuitive quickness of her intellect. It stood her in good stead of rules and precedents, so that I have seldom met with a finer critic.

I was a genuine book-lover myself. Even commerce and business had not been able to wean me from poetry and fiction, and it called back more than my early enthusiasm to share the deep, quiet, yet sometimes rapturous appreciation of this young girl. I often told her she brought back my youth.

I know now that I loved her even then, but I never acknowledged it to myself—I never thought of marrying her. It was, as I have said, a fixed fact in my mind, that the future Mrs. Gerard Sunderland was to be a lady of wealth and position. I never dreamed of finding her in the shy, quiet daughter of a village clergyman. So I went on, with this future settled in my thoughts, going to see Rachel daily, lending her books, rambling with her over the fields, and learning to watch for her smiles, and listen to the music of her voice, with an interest for which I never tried to account.

I think she inherited her poetical tendencies from her father. There was something very touching in this old man's quiet, self-contained life. Every night, all through the long summer sunsetting and twilight, he would sit at his western window and look forth over the church-yard, with its white tomb-stones bathed in the sunset gold. I thought he was calling the past days back again—sitting in fancy beside the Amy of his youth and his love—that he saw not the green grave where he had laid her, but was looking over and beyond it, through the golden glory of the clouds, to a far-off shore, where his eyes—none but his—could see the gleam of a white brow, the fall of chestnut hair.

One night, when he had been sitting there a long time, he turned away with a radiant look. Somewhat of inspiration had chased the gray shadow from his worn and aged face. Rachel and I sat together, in silence, at the other end of the room, but he seemed unconscious of a witness. His voice was clear and hopeful. In a steadfast tone he said,

"I shall go to her, though she can not come to me. Blessed be God—the God of Abraham, and Isaac, and Jacob!"

As he left the room I looked at Rachel. Through the twilight I could see the tears shining in her eyes.

"He loved her so faithfully," she said, "so many years; and now she is dead he loves her still. Oh, it was worth living and worth dying for; I know my mother thought so."

I remembered afterward a suggestion which came to me then—a wonder as to how *she* would love—this young girl, so shy, so tender, yet, it seemed to me, so faithful. I remember thinking how blessed the man would be who should win her pure heart; but I never thought of seeking this love, of which I believed her nature capable, for the crown of my own life.

That was a long, bright summer. I had come to Woolwich weary of the world, of fashion, of business, of care. I had found there rest, pleasant companionship, quiet. I was satisfied. I had scarcely perceived that autumn was tinting the forest trees, ripening the fruit in the orchard, the grain upon the hill, and sending forth his lawless winds to gather up the spoil of summer. I was too happy to heed the flight of time. Rachel and Rachel's father were enough of society; Mrs. Tabitha managed my housekeeping concerns admirably, and I was content. But the spell was broken one fine morning, late in October, by the receipt of a letter from my only sister, Flora. She was two years younger than I, and yet for seven years she had been Mrs. Maxwell Grafton.

She was a brilliant and fashionable woman, but a good sister notwithstanding, and, as the world goes, a devoted wife. It had never ceased to be a mystery how little Flora, the pet of my boyish days, could ever have matured into this stately matron, so unlike my gentle, retiring mother; and a stranger mystery still how she, younger than myself, and a woman, had ever acquired so much mastery over me, an independent bachelor. The solution of this last half of the riddle lay, I suspect, in three words—*strength of will.*

I remember wondering, as I broke the seal of her stylish-looking letter, what she had marked out for me to do, feeling a half-vexed consciousness that I should obey her, though the purport of her missive should be to dispatch me to the North Pole. Low be it spoken, I have a horror of arguing with a woman. They will talk so fast, they have such a feminine gift for making the worse appear the better reason, that I would far rather lay down my arms in despair than stand the shock of such a volley of words. I suspect Flora had found out this weak point, and grown tyrannical on the strength of it.

The letter opened with an account of a brilliant summer. I hurried over this, getting only a vague and confused idea, which rung through my brain a dozen changes on such formidable key-notes as "Saratoga," "Newport," "splendid creature," "pistols," "despair." I hurried on to what more immediately concerned me. I was a sad, provoking fellow to have buried myself all summer in Woolwich. So she thought; so Maxwell thought; so some one else thought, whose name I didn't deserve to know. However, if I would come at once to New York she would forgive me. I *must* come—that was certain—I must be there in time for her great party, which was coming off next week—the first of the season. She had a friend to show me—one who was just my ideal—elegant, stately, beautiful, and very rich. Yes, she knew Anastasia St. John would just suit me, but perhaps I wouldn't suit her; she couldn't tell. Anastasia wasn't a woman to be won without wooing. But there! she was busy; she had wasted time enough on me; only I must come next Monday.

It never entered into my head to disappoint her. Perhaps the promised introduction had something to do with my ready obedience. Anastasia St. John—I liked the stately name. Flora's description pleased me too. This was just the kind of woman I had always meant to marry, and it was nearly time now—I had passed my twenty-ninth birthday this very summer. I commenced my preparations for leaving home.

That night—did I tell you it was Saturday?—I went to bid Rachel good-by. I carried her a few books which she had expressed a wish to read, and offered her the use of my library during my absence. Was I mistaken? It seemed to me that a look of pain crossed her face when I spoke of leaving Woolwich. I even thought there was a suspicious mistiness in her eyes. The time came afterward when memory reproduced that look of tender sorrow. She did not speak for some moments. She sat silent, while her father answered me; but her voice was clear and gentle as usual when she wished me a pleasant winter and bade me good-by. I listened sharply, but there was no quiver of pain it.

I never went to the rectory on Sundays, but the next day I saw Rachel once more in church. If she had grieved at parting with me her face did not show it now. The faint rose-hue on her cheek was no deeper; there was no faltering in her tones as she joined in the singing; no suspicious dew in her clear yet tender eyes. The rector's sermon that day moved me strangely. It was about heaven—that heaven where his beloved waited for him; toward which his aged, trembling feet were hastening *fast*. There was I know not what of power and majesty in the old man's tones, so that all who heard him felt that he testified of that which he did know. As I listened, how vain it seemed to grope for happiness among the rubbish of earth. All of life looked empty and worthless save the one narrow path which he pictured in faltering tones—the path leading sometimes over rugged hills, where sharp stones goad the weary feet; sometimes through green pastures and beside still waters of peace. I remember, as I heard him, the thought came to me whether that saintly young girl, lifting such meek eyes to her father's face, was not a fitter companion for one whose feet should walk in this narrow path than Anastasia St. John, whose proud name seemed to conjure up a shape of earthly, not heavenly beauty, gleaming with gold and diamonds; a rustling of silken drapery; an embodiment of pomp, and pride, and worldliness. But this reflection was only momentary; I was scarcely conscious of its existence; and with the benediction that followed the rector's prayer it faded from my mind.

Of Rachel Deane I thought as a dear sister—nothing more; and yet, it was strange, the last night of my stay in Woolwich, I drew no pictures of New York gayety and splendor; my fancy summoned no stately Miss St. John to bear me company; but my eyes seemed to see, instead, an ancient gray-stone rectory — an old man sitting by the western window watching the sunset and the graves—a young girl pacing back and forth among the shadows, with tender, thoughtful eyes of brown, singing to herself now and then snatches of those grand old hymns which seem to have been set for martyrs to die by. I went to sleep with this cadence coming, or seeming to come, to haunt my slumbers, low, and sweet, and very sorrowful.

The next morning I left Woolwich.

II.

My first three days in New York were not very eventful ones. There was Flora's careless yet good-natured welcome, my mother's tender greeting for her only boy; and then I found my way to the offices and counting-rooms of half a dozen good fellows, old friends, whose society somehow gave me less pleasure than formerly. I think a certain peace and quietness had grown into my spirit during that long, still summer in the country, on which the bustle and confusion of this great, busy town jarred, at first, with a sense of pain.

My sister's grand party came off on Thursday night. I stood by her side at one end of her brilliant drawing-room while she received her guests. Her reunions were always very successful. It was an amusement to me to watch the different faces—the varying expressions of those handsomely-dressed men and women whom she called her "set." At last her quick whisper in my ear aroused me from my half-listless mood. I turned eagerly toward the door. It was Anastasia St. John.

The expression "a stately woman" had always, from some old, boyish association, conveyed to my mind the idea of a brunette. I had pictured Miss St. John, therefore, with flashing black eyes, with olive face, framed in shining raven hair. I had been mistaken; and yet she became, forever after, my standard of stately beauty.

She was the proudest woman I have ever met. There was pride in her thin nostril, her curling lip; pride sat serene and regnant on her smooth brow. She was tall, and faultlessly formed. Her skin was marble white, save where, in the cheek, a faint dash of crimson broke up through it, cold yet clear as a winter's sunrise. Her long, thick hair was of a pale gold color. It was folded back from her forehead in heavy waves, and wound about her small, erect head like a coronal. Her eyes were blue and brilliant, but there was no warmth in them. Her dress suited her. It was a robe of some costly lace, floating cloud-like over azure satin. Rachel Deane may have been lovelier, but this Anastasia St. John was the most beautiful woman I ever saw.

There was a kind of *empressement* in my sister's tones as she introduced us which convinced me that my name was not unknown to this cold goddess, but her manner was careless, and yet polished as glittering steel.

From that night I had an interest in New York. I had coolly made up my mind to marry Miss St. John, if I could win her. There was an intense excitement, a keen zest, in trying to conquer this cold indifference, this haughty calmness. That winter was to me like a long game of chess. Warily, carefully, I planned every move. Self-complacently I said, "I am playing I well."

In this subtle trial of strength Woolwich was well-nigh forgotten. Sometimes I saw in my dreams a gray rectory; a saintly girl, with calm, holy eyes, sitting alone in the shadows; an old man, looking out toward heaven. But in the daytime my whole thoughts centred in this lovely maid of ice—this Mrs. Gerard Sunderland that was to be. And yet I was forced to acknowledge to myself that I made little progress. I was much in Miss St. John's society. Her mother was an invalid, and my sister was her chaperon to balls, and drives, and operas. She accepted my attentions, or rather she endured them without seeming scarcely to be aware of them. She wore my bouquets, played my music, read my new books, and yet I grew no nearer to her. This piqued me, and I became more earnest in the pursuit.

Lounging in my sister's room one morning, I said, with assumed carelessness, as I unwound a roll of ribbon,

"I give you credit for good taste, Flora, but I don't see what you think a man could marry in Anastasia St. John. One wants a woman whose heart beats once in a while, just often enough to show its existence; but Miss St. John—I'd as soon think of kissing life into a statue."

Flora came up to me, and deliberately took the ribbon out of my profane fingers.

"Three dollars a yard, Mr. Gerard Sunderland. I can not have you spoil it. As for Anastasia, you don't know her, and I do. She has got too much heart instead of too little; you may not be the one to discover it, but it's there. If she does love, it will be worth winning."

I did not believe my sister at the time, and yet her words led me to observe Miss St. John more closely.

I began to see that she was weary sometimes. More than once I detected an expression in her fine eyes when they met mine which said, just as plainly as any words could have done,

"I should like you for a friend, Mr. Sunderland, if you would content yourself without trying to be my lover. You do not deserve me, because you do not understand me. I should gratify no part of your nature but your ambition."

But after a time I ceased to perceive this expression. I began to believe that I loved her; that that marble face, the clear blue of those eyes, the pale gold of that hair, were each and all dear and necessary to my happiness. I thought, too, that she seemed to soften toward me. Her voice grew lower. Sometimes I saw a strange tenderness in her eyes. Fool that I was, I thought it was evoked by my voice. I had indeed played well, I said to myself in these days. The checkmate was near at hand. Already the game had lasted through the winter.

It was on an April morning that I thought to win my crowning triumph. I went early to see Miss St. John. I found her alone, but I looked in vain for the tenderness I had fancied was growing habitual to those clear eyes. Had I, then, mistaken their expression before? I had intended this morning to ask her to be my wife, but the words did not come easily. I sat still for a time and looked at her.

"Could that proud woman ever *love?*" I once more asked myself, doubtingly. "Would any husband's brow find rest on that pulseless bosom? Would any children dare to climb that silken knee?" There was no answer in the cold pride of her face. But another voice spoke to me—a voice which no ear could hear but mine.

What were you, Rachel Deane—you, so shy, so small, so quiet—that you could shut out that proud beauty from my vision? By what strange might of your deep nature did you follow me, call me, draw me toward you? Never did mortal eyes rest upon your face more clearly than my spirit saw you then. Fearlessly your pure soul spoke to mine.

"Sin not," it said, "against your own best nature. Your love is mightier than your pride."

Every pulse leaped, every nerve in my body thrilled, as those words rung through my heart's chambers. She seemed to stand before me like an accusing spirit. Oh, I knew then that I loved Rachel Deane. I believed—how sweet the hope was—that she loved me; that, apart, earth held for either of us no true happiness. In my heart I blessed her for rising up before me: I called her my salvation. Her presence seemed very real to me. I lifted my eyes, and they then fell on Anastasia St. John, sitting there calm, and proud, and very beautiful, her great eyes seeming to look at something far away—something that was not me. I had never loved her; she had never loved me. Something within me forced me to speak to her—a new emotion I had for her—a calm, quiet esteem, a friendly regard, of which I knew now she was worthy. By this moved, I went up to her. I extended my hand. I said,

"I am here, Miss St. John, to bid you good-by. I leave New York this afternoon. Your society has made this winter very pleasant to me. We began it as strangers; I feel that we shall part as *true* friends."

She understood me. She had never looked so good to me as then. She put her hand in mine. Did I see rightly? I think the tears gathered in her eyes. Her voice was very gentle.

"I thank you," she said, warmly. "We *are* true friends—we will be. I am not so careless or so happy as the world calls me. I have my griefs; but when I think of you, I will remember that I have one friend."

"God bless you!" I said, with a fervent prayer for her in my heart. I left her with such tenderness as I had never thought she could inspire. I never saw her again.

My sister met me upon the stairs. She had known of my intention to visit Miss St. John.

"How sped your wooing?" she asked, gayly.

"Flora," I answered, "you were right. You understood your friend better than I did. Miss St. John could love with a love that would be worth winning, but I am not the one."

I believe she thought I had been rejected. At any rate, she made no opposition to my plan of returning to Woolwich that afternoon, and three o'clock saw me upon the cars.

III.

Oh, how fast we whizzed along. I had heard some one say we had started a little behind time, but it was not half fast enough for me. I felt like crying out to the conductor for more speed. My spirits were at their flood. I was going to Rachel. I knew my own heart now. With the hope of her love in my mind I grew quieter. I sank into a reverie. I sat back in my seat and drew my hat over my eyes, and then I strove to recall all the tokens she had given me of her regard. The expression which I had seen upon her face the night before I left Woolwich came back to me. I remembered her timid pleasure at my coming. How charming she seemed to me in her beauty, her grace, her innocent youth. I pictured her as my wife. I thought how bright would be the stately house behind the pine-trees when her light figure glided up and down the stairs, or sat, in household quiet, by the hearth-stone. I gloried in the thought of protecting her—of keeping all sorrow and care away from her life—of leading her footsteps out of the shadow into the light.

Absorbed in thoughts like these, time sped rapidly. We were nearing Woolwich. I looked from the window, and the fields by the wayside were familiar. My heart bounded. Soon I should see Rachel. I would tell her that I loved her—I would know my fate from her own lips. I fancied how her eyes would droop—how the color would come and go in her cheeks—how shyly her little hand would flutter into mine.

Just then came a sudden, quivering motion running along all the train—a crash—a loud, prolonged, wailing shriek, and after that I remembered nothing more.

It was a warm morning in May when my consciousness came back to me. My first emotion was that of pleasure in the balmy air; the blossoms upon the trees which brushed in at the open window; the spring sunshine over all. Next came a curious feeling of, not exactly pain, but *goneness.* My senses were hardly yet fully aroused. I put my hand where this sensation most oppressed me. My right leg seemed to have been cut off above the knee. I should have thought I must be dreaming, but that the maimed limb was exquisitely tender and sensitive to the touch. I looked around the room where I was lying. It was not in my own house. It bore strange resemblance to an apartment in the rectory. I was quite alone, but some feminine piece of work lay upon a stand by the window. A few spring flowers stood there also, in a delicate vase.

Soon I heard footsteps approaching. I closed my eyes and lay very still. The footsteps came into the room. Then I heard Rachel's voice, in a tone of sad, almost pleading inquiry:

"You *do* think, Dr. Smith, that his reason will come back to him? He won't rave so always?"

"No fear of that, Rachel. No head could stand such a blow as his got without being dazed for a while. Poor fellow! when his senses *do* come, it'll be a sorry awakening. A young, rich, good-looking man like him to have to carry a cork leg with him all his life."

I heard Rachel sigh, but she did not answer, and Dr. Smith left the room, saying he would be back in half an hour to dress the leg. Rachel came to the bedside. I knew she was standing beside me; I knew, as well as if I had seen her, that her tears were falling silently. I opened my eyes and looked at her.

"Come, Rachel," I said, "I heard what Dr. Smith told you, and now I want you to sit down beside me and tell me all about it. How long ago was it?"

She struggled hard to control herself.

"About four weeks," she said; "the cars—" but here she broke down utterly and hurried from the room. I lay there, wrestling with an agony before which any mere physical suffering sank into insignificance. It was not that my pride was humbled—not that I must go through life a lame, to some degree a helpless man, but it was that I felt I could never ask Rachel to be a cripple's wife—to mate her loveliness with my deformity. I strove in vain to choke back the cry which my longing heart *would* utter. My grief o'ermastered me. But I will not write out the sorrow on which only God and my own soul have ever looked.

When Dr. Smith came back I drew from him an account of the accident. I shudder to recall the frightful story now. So many souls called, unthinking, before their Maker. Such groans, such tumult, such helpless cries of agony. Dr. Smith pictured it vividly, but there is no need that I should write out its horrors here. I had been taken up, at first, for dead, stunned by a severe blow upon my head. In all this, the doctor said, Rachel had been the most wonderful nurse. I believed him.

During the two tedious months of convalescence which followed, there was often, in the midst of my agony, a troubled joy. Sometimes it seemed happiness enough to have Rachel in my sight; her gentle hands ministering about me. Sometimes, too, there was a look in her eyes whose meaning I dared not meet, lest it should make me selfish. I had resolved, firmly, that I would never seek her love. I would not impose upon her tenderness, her pity, to win any pledge which she might regret afterward. No, I must live alone all my life; but I turned from these thoughts to rejoice in her smile, in the tender tones of her voice.

It was midsummer before I went to my own house. In the mean time I had learned to walk in the poor crippled fashion in which I must make up my mind always to move about hereafter. Several times I had proposed to go home, but neither Mr. Deane nor his daughter would allow it. I must stay with them until I was quite well. I had been brought to them when I was first hurt. They had nursed me through my delirium; they had claims upon me, and I must obey them. I confess I staid with them willingly. But at last the time was fixed for my final removal. The day before, I was to drive to my home and give Mrs. Tabitha a few directions. I had sent for Mike to come with the carriage.

When it arrived, I entreated Rachel to do her patient one more good turn, and go home with me for an hour. She consented, and we took the short drive in silence. When I reached the house I wanted to walk a little about the grounds, and she made me lean upon her arm. How strangely it reminded me of my fancies, that sad day in April, about how tenderly *I* would protect *her*. Now this frail, delicate girl at my side was helping to guide my steps. I could not bear it; I hurried her into the house.

I do not know how it chanced that we sat down, not in the drawing-room, but in my Uncle Gerard's study. For a time I looked at her in outward silence, but my soul was crying out in its agony. So many hopes came back to mock me. I had thought once how her light feet would flit in girlish glee up and down those walks lying so white and gleaming in the summer sunshine; that she would sit by my fireside, the glory of my home and my life. The great pangs became too mighty for me. In spite of myself they found a voice. I rose and walked across the room. I put back the curtain from before her mother's picture.

"There," I said, and my tones were almost stern with the effort to keep back the grief surging in my heart, "there, Rachel Deane, is the picture my Uncle Gerard painted of your mother. You are like it. I am not the inheritor alone of my uncle's wealth, but of his hopeless love. *This* is my inheritance. To live here, as he lived, alone. To love as he loved. To long vainly as he longed. Nay, Rachel, do not turn your eyes away. I did not mean to tell you, but you *must* hear me now. Even as my uncle loved your mother and loved in vain, so must I, till my death day, love you. I was coming to Woolwich that day to tell you this love, to ask you to be my wife. I thought then I could win you; but God interposed, and we are separated."

She came across the room. She laid her hands, her little, woman's hands, upon my arm. The truth shone out of her clear eyes into my very soul. Her voice was firm but tearful. I can never forget her dear, dear words:

"We are *not* separated. We never can be. Take me, Gerard, if you love me. I love you; I have loved you long. I do not care for life unless I can pass it with you."

I could not gainsay her. I felt that she spoke truly, and thus the great joy and blessedness of love drifted into my heart—flooded my full life. I could not speak. I opened my arms and took her—thank God, I took my betrothed close to my heart. I know not how long we sat there. It was almost night before we returned. As I led her up the rectory steps, I said, not because I doubted her, but because I longed to hear her reply,

"Are you sure, my beloved, that you will never regret this—that you will be quite content with an ugly, crippled man, so many years older than yourself?"

Her brimming eyes answered me, and then her voice came to my heart, freighted with words too full of blessing to write here. They satisfied me forever.

We went together to her father as he sat at the western window. We told him of our love and asked his blessing. He rose and laid his aged, trembling hands upon our heads. He blessed us. As we turned away we heard him murmur,

"Now, Lord, lettest thou thy servant depart in peace."

We turned back as we reached the door to look at him. He sat again at the window, and his far-seeing eyes were fixed, not on his Amy's grave, but on the golden clouds far, far away. We left him there.

We had much to say to each other. I told Rachel of Miss St. John, and how she herself had been present to my fancy—had come after me and brought me back, when I would have done my own heart wrong; and she answered me with smiles and with tears. That first twilight after our betrothal was a blessed hour.

When we went in the moon had risen. The old man sat there still. Rachel went up to him, and laid her hand upon his brow.

"Oh, how cold he is!" she cried. "Father, father, wake up! *Don't* you hear me, father?"

I went toward her. Her father could never more hear any sound of earthly tones. He was gone to Amy. Who can tell what voice had called him? what fair hand had beckoned from the sunset clouds?

We laid him by Amy's side in the quiet church-yard, where the snow-flakes would drop, a white mantle of peace, above them in the winter; where the summer winds would blow, and the summer birds would sing. Even in their death they were not long divided.

Rachel bore it well, for she knew that joy had dawned for the reunited ones in heaven; and on earth my love comforted her. It was not many weeks before she became my wife. She dwelt in peace in the stately mansion where her mother's portrait had waited for her so many years. My life was rounded into full and beautiful symmetry. I asked no more of fate. I was content with my crippled form, my halting gait, for my soul's life was bright and blissful; the path wherein Rachel and I were walking onward to the world lying beyond was lightened by Heaven's own sunshine.

The summer was not over when an unusually long letter came to me, in my sister's hand. She had written previously her congratulations on my marriage, and an invitation to bring my bride to New York. As she was not a frequent letter-writer, I broke the seal with considerable curiosity. The contents were sad, but they gave me the key to a character I had ardently desired to comprehend.

"We know now," she wrote, "why Anastasia St.

John did not care for you. A little while ago, a young man, the supercargo of a vessel, was reported as lost at sea, and then it came out. She had known him when her father was poorer—when they were both children, indeed, and had loved him faithfully all her life. He was poor, and her father opposed it; but she was content to forego wealth and luxury for his sake. They were waiting till he could make enough to marry respectably. This was why she was always so cold in society. You know how she kept every one at a distance. It seems she saw his death in a paper, and it literally broke her heart. She was found with the blood flowing in a crimson tide from her mouth, and the paper clutched in her hand. In three days she was dead. They buried her yesterday. Poor, proud broken heart! Poor Anastasia St. John!"

My darling had read the letter over my shoulder. I felt her tears upon my cheek as she murmured, in her tender, pitying voice, this fragment from a ballad that she loved:

> "And they called her cold. God knows......
> Underneath the winter snows,
> The invisible hearts of flowers grow ripe for blossoming!
> And the lives that look so cold,
> If their stories could be told,
> Would seem cast in gentler mould—
> Would seem full of Love and Spring."

Behold, I have told you the story of My Inheritance. Vale!

Number 101.

A face that had a story to tell. How different faces are in this particular! Some of them speak not. They are books in which not a line is written, save perhaps a date. Others are great family Bibles, with both the Old and the New Testament written in them. Others are Mother Goose and nursery tales; others, bad tragedies or pickle-herring farces; and others, like that of the landlady's daughter at the Star, sweet love anthologies and songs of the affections.

LONGFELLOW.

NUMBER 101.

IT was a head—a woman's head.

The Art Union was unusually full that year, and No. 101 hung in an out-of-the-way corner. I had been there several times without noticing it, but that day my eyes chanced to rest on it, and I could not withdraw them.

The features were not entirely regular, but lofty, and with strong lines of power. The complexion was a dark, clear olive. The heavy black hair had been put back, as if impatiently, behind the ears, and was twisted in coils about the head. The expression was most remarkable. I had never seen any thing like it in a painting. There was fortitude and strong will in the lines about the mouth, and much of conscious strength and patient suffering sat on the broad forehead; but it was reserved to the eyes to tell the story. Those dark, melancholy, despairing eyes, whose glance seemed turned inward, seeking after lost joys. They were wild, they were stern, and yet they were melting with a woman's pain. Far down in their depths was a gleam of love—it must have been a mother's love, for no other could have throned itself on the desolation of such a sorrow. I looked at it silently a few moments, and then I said aloud, "Hagar." I had no catalogue, but I needed none to know to whom that face must have belonged.

"Yes," said a voice at my side, "you have understood my picture. That is Hagar—the Egyptian Hagar, after she was sent forth into the desert. Ishmael was with her, and the mother-love lived still, while all other human affections were swept away by the fierce hurricane of passion."

It was a low, rich voice which spoke to me. Its music thrilled all along the pulses of my being. I turned and looked at the speaker.

I do not suppose she would have been called a beautiful woman—her face was too faded for that—but once she must have been beautiful exceedingly. I could see, looking into her own eyes, how she had painted the Hagar. She too must have suffered and despaired. Her face was very pale, her eyebrows jet black and finely arched. These, with her jetty hair and eyes, enhanced the apparent fairness of her complexion. But, though fair, she was not fresh. As I said, she looked faded, and yet she could not have been old—at the most not more than thirty. There was on her face an expression which made me think that in other days she had wept much, but she looked too proud to weep often now. Genius sat on her forehead, and she seemed to me like one who had grown strong and pure through much suffering.

There was something so singular and unconventional in her speaking to me at all that I hardly knew how to reply. Perhaps some men might, for this, have esteemed her less, but it was not so with me. I was no stickler for etiquette—a man no longer young, who was poor, and a worker; who had been poor all the days of his life; who must always be poor. I was an artist too, in my own humble way; that is, I was employed by several publishers in New York to design illustrations for books and papers. I was interested to know this fellow-laborer. I thought I would relieve her embarrassment by appearing as if we had met before. I bowed.

"I do not remember your name," I said, in a tone as if I were trying to recall something which had slipped from my mind. A queer, half-satirical smile, in which was some kindliness but no mirth, crossed her face.

"That is most probable, since you never knew it. No matter; I am Margaret Welch, and you—"

"Robert Payson, madam. I wish very much that I could be properly introduced to you, but that seems impossible. Need the fact of our chance meeting be any bar to our farther acquaintance? I am a designer. I like to know artists, and there is something in your picture which makes me long to be your friend. May I?"

It was a moment before she answered me. She seemed weighing the question in her own mind. At length she said, slowly,

"I don't see any objection. I have no friends to be troubled at my forming an acquaintance in an eccentric manner. I am very lonely, and I have a human liking for occasional companionship. I am grateful to you, moreover, for understanding my picture. I had some trouble to get it admitted here, and until you came I have never seen any one stop to look at it."

"You come here often, then?"

"Yes, I have been here every day since my picture was hung. But I can stay no longer now. This is where you will find me."

She handed me, as she spoke, a catalogue on which she had been writing for a moment with her pencil. Her name was written in a careless, graceful hand, followed by a street and number which I recognized as the location of a respectable lodging-house not far from my own place of abode.

I thanked her, and she went out, leaving me standing alone before the head of Hagar. I was deeply interested in her. I confessed it to myself. It was not strange, for that was almost the first adventure I had ever met with. I was over forty, and yet, measuring my life by its pleasures or its events, it was a very short one. My parents had died before I could remember them. I had been brought up by an uncle living in the country. He had no children and was kind to me after a fashion of his own. But he was a self-willed man. He had resolved that I should be a carpenter, and, though no pursuit could have been less agreeable to me, I submitted, and went to my trade with scarcely a remonstrance. During my apprenticeship, however, I had drawn a great many vignettes on the smooth boards with my pencil, in the hour given us for dinner, and I had covered the back of my uncle's red house with outline sketches in chalk, and so had made up my mind that this was my true life. Submissive as I was to any necessity against which I saw no hope of successful contention, I had yet a strong will of my own, a dogged persistency in a purpose once formed.

I finished my trade the day before I was twenty-one, and the next morning I told my uncle that I was going to the city to learn to be a designer. His anger was strong yet quiet, for his nature was not wholly unlike my own. He told me that if I left him then it must be forever. He should be sorry to lose me, yet—with a grim smile—he guessed he could bear it; any way, he would have no vagabond picture-makers around him. I did not waver in my purpose. We parted that day. I heard of his death years afterward, but we never met again.

Fortune certainly favored me. I was not long, after reaching the city, in procuring work—humble work indeed—but still it brought me enough to supply my humble wants. I had never fancied myself a genius. I could never have learned to color, or, knowing how, I could never have painted a Hagar; but I loved to use my pencil, and by its use I had lived now for twenty-one years.

I had very few acquaintances—two or three artists, who were not ashamed of my friendship, and one or two men whom I had pleased by my illustrations to their books, were all, if I except the publishers who employed me, and whom I only knew in the way of business. I had never been on terms of familiar acquaintanceship with any woman. At forty-two my heart was as fresh and my life as pure as a girl's. Of love and marriage I had seldom thought, and when I did think, it was not to reckon them among the probabilities which might befall myself, but merely to contemplate them afar off, without envy or longing, as I did wealth and station, which might be for others, but not for me.

I do not think it was strange that, in such a man, the lady I had met should awaken a peculiar interest. Her face, no longer beautiful, was yet magnetic in its power of fascinating the attention. Her voice and manners revealed her, even to my slight knowledge of the world, as having been born and bred a lady. The strange beginning of my acquaintance with her was the first bit of romance that had ever shot its rosy threads through the sombre gray woof of my forty-two years of life.

I went home that night, but I could not sleep. All night long my mind was wide awake; I was making mental sketches, in which every female figure wore the pale, sad face of my new friend. With the first beams of dawn I sprang from my pillow, lighted my fire, and went to work. I never thought of food. I forgot, almost, my own existence. I worked on until after midday. I had succeeded. This was my sketch:

Morning breaking after a night of storm—a turbulent sea—fragments of broken masts and spars scattered along a desolate coast; but, in sight, only one living thing—a woman, looking steadfastly toward the waters. The waves had washed on shore her only, but in "the billows' joyous dash of death" had gone down friends, hopes, fortune; she had only herself left—only her own living soul. The face was that of Margaret Welch, but a little younger, and her expression was, if possible, intensified.

I was utterly exhausted when the last touch was given. I went out and got a cup of strong coffee and some food. Then, with my nerves steadied, I came back and looked at my labor. Was I a genius after all? I asked myself. There was unmistakable power in the sketch, but then *she* had been my inspiration. I put it away. I would not have had any eyes gaze on it save mine. I had no presentiment of the influence it was to exert on my after-destiny, but I was happier that I had executed it.

I went out soon afterward to the rooms of the Art Union, and there, standing before the Hagar whose conception seemed to me so matchless, I lost my dawning faith in my own power. I waited there for a time, thinking that the stranger might make her appearance; but she did not come, and after a while I started out and went to the street and number indicated on the catalogue which she had given me.

On my way I passed a florist's, where the windows were filled with bouquets and pots of flowers. My first thought was to take her a bouquet. It seemed to me it might give her pleasure; at least, I wanted to know if she retained gentleness enough, after all the sorrow which had left its traces on her face, to love flowers. But soon I changed my mind. I would give her nothing so frail as these cut blossoms. It should be a gift better suited to one whose means would not let him purchase often; something more durable and yet not unhandsome. I selected a tea-rose, growing in a little earthen pot. It had two buds on it and one full blooming flower.

I had but a few blocks to carry it before I reached her house. I paused a moment at the door. I did not know whether she were wife, maiden, or widow. Never mind; I would inquire for *Miss* Welch, at a venture.

I rang the bell. I asked the girl who answered my summons if Miss Welch lived there. She evidently took me for the employé of some horticultural establishment carrying home a purchase. She replied, with a careless toss of her head,

"Yes; you must go up four flights of stairs, and the door at your right hand will be hers."

The stairs were long and steep.

"What a weary way," I thought, as I climbed them, "for that delicate woman!"

I knocked, and instantly I heard a tread quick and firm, yet not heavy. She opened the door, and stood holding it until she had looked full in my face. Then she said,

"Oh, it is you! I hardly thought you would come. Will you walk in?"

It was a humble place in which I found myself, though scrupulously neat, and not without some marks of comfort. There was a lounge, which must have done duty for a bed also, two or three chairs, a stove, a table, and, in one corner, a painter's easel. But it was utterly devoid of ornament, save a few pictures that hung upon the wall, in which I recognized the same hand that had painted the Hagar. They were all more or less wild, gloomy, despairing. There was not a single gleam of hope in any—not a bird or a flower, or any thing bright and happy. Stern portraitures, they seemed, of human passion.

On the table were water-colors, drawing materials, and a few volumes of such designs as are used for printing calicoes and de laines. These were the only books in the room. She was dressed, as she had been the day before, in a plain, somewhat worn black silk, with no ornament or superfluity.

She sat down at the table after motioning me to a chair, and went on with her work with busy fingers.

I took up one of the patterns.

"So you, who can paint Hagar, do these things?" I

asked, with some reproach in my voice; for it seemed to me like a desecration of her genius. She understood my tone.

"Yes—why not? I can not sell my pictures. I must live, and I can get pretty good pay for these."

"Not sell your pictures—such pictures as Hagar? Will you let me try?"

She smiled.

"I have no objection, save that I wouldn't like you to undertake for me such a thankless task. People have sorrow enough of their own. They won't buy it in a painting. They want bright faces and pleasant landscapes—birds and flowers."

I had held the rose-pot in my hand all this time. Now I set it upon the table.

"Speaking of flowers," I said, "I have brought you this rose. Will you please me by taking it? I love flowers, and I should like to think you had this one to keep you company."

A look swept over her face such as I hope few faces ever wore. It was so lost a look—so hopeless, so despairing. She put forth her hands to take the flower. Then, shuddering, she drew them back and covered her eyes with them for a moment.

"Oh, no, no, no," she said, with such a wail in her tones as I never heard ring through the cadences of any other voice. "It is not for me—roses are not for me. I wore them once, when I was young. I had not suffered then, or sinned. I gathered them in my mother's garden when I was a child—a little, innocent, happy child—before I had broken her heart. Oh, do not give me roses now—my touch would blast them."

I did not say a single word. I sat there, stricken

dumb before her unfathomable despair. Soon she went on in a lower tone—if possible, fuller of pathos than before.

"You meant kindly. I thank you just as much as if I took them. But you do not know what roses mean to me. You can not tell what it is to lose all you ever cared for in life, and sit waiting for death, keeping company with ghosts. When I look at those buds I can not see these chamber walls around me, or you sitting there. I am walking again through fields of thyme and clover. The sky is blue over my head, and the robin's song pulses downward like a cry of joy. Roses bloom in the hedges, and one by my side gathers them and puts them in my hair. But between those days and these there is a great gulf fixed. I am not what I was when I walked in the meadows, and gathered flowers; and heard the village bells ring in the Sunday morning air."

She stopped; but the despairing look had begun to fade out of her face, and her voice was gentler. I thought the roses were, after all, doing her good. I could not bear to take them away. An expedient struck me. I rose.

"I must go now. Forgive me that I brought the flower; but will you not give it shelter for to-night? I can come for it to-morrow; but to-night I have a good way farther to go. Will you let me leave it till another day? I'll be sure to call for it."

She looked reluctant to comply with my request; but the habitual courtesy of her manners did not fail her. She assented to my wish, and I bowed to her and went out.

I wandered about the streets for an hour or two,

thinking of her. She had spoken of sinning and suffering—breaking her mother's heart—and yet I would have staked my life on her purity. Suffering, wronged, reckless she might have been, but I felt to the core of my heart that her womanhood was unstained. My interest in her had only grown stronger with this interview. I resolved to know her better.

The next day I worked with impatient heart—impatient fingers—at a task I had promised to complete. It was three o'clock in the short winter afternoon before I was at liberty to go to her. I think she had already learned to know my footstep; for, when I knocked at her door, she did not move to open it, but said "Come in."

I obeyed her. She was sitting at her easel, evidently very busy, but she glanced at me with a smile of welcome as I entered. I looked around for my rose-bush. It had been placed on the window-ledge. Evidently it had been watered and tended. One of the buds was already bursting into bloom. Her eyes followed the direction of mine.

"I have changed my mind," she said. "I should be glad to keep it, if you will let me. It has done me good, I think. See, already I am working differently."

I went to her side. The unfinished picture upon the easel was only an outline sketch, but it was infused with spirit, power, and life. Its subject was very different from any thing I had previously seen of hers. It was a clover-field, with a clear sky overhead. One side was bordered by a hedge full of blossoms, and along this hedge a young girl walked alone. About her mouth was a look of sweetness—of youthful buoyancy; but the expression of her dark eyes was informed with a most touching melancholy—a sort of prophecy of sorrow.

"It is beautiful," I said; praising her, I think, more with my eyes and the tones of my voice than my words.

"Better than the old, hopeless ones?" she asked.

"Yes, a thousand times better, because it will do more good. I think it has fully as much genius, too."

"Well, if you like it better, you may thank your roses for the change. At first I thought they would drive me mad with the memories they evoked, but after a while they softened my heart. I wept. I had not done that before for years."

I looked at her. I could see the traces of tears on her thin cheek.

I did not stay with her long. She was absorbed in her work, and I was more contented to leave her, because a little of the old, hopeless sorrow seemed to have faded from her face.

After that months passed, until winter had died its tearful death 'neath the blue eyes of spring, and the bier of May had been crowned, in turn, by the roses of the summer. Our acquaintance had progressed rapidly, and we had not been long in becoming firm, established friends. I worked all day more diligently than ever, for I had acquired a fresh inspiration, a new incentive, the presence of which, however, I did not yet acknowledge to myself. It was my reward, after each day's labor, to go to her—to carry her whatever I had done, and receive sometimes her praises, sometimes her censures.

It seemed to me, when I thought about it, a strange, unhoped-for blessing, that I, Robert Payson, should have such a friend; that for me, who had lived with such a lonely heart forty-two years of my life, in one unlooked-for hour a sun of warmth and hope should have arisen. I asked nothing better of Heaven. Just as she was, my friend suited me. The dim smile on her worn and faded face was more to me, more and fairer, than the brightest glory of any younger woman's beauty. Every outline of her shadowy yet graceful figure; every expression on her sad yet tender face; every inflection of her low, musical voice, possessed for me its own unexplained yet exceeding charm.

And so, unconsciously, love grew into my life, until, one summer night, like Venus rising from the sea, it stood up full-nurtured before me, and I knew that my heart was my own no longer. It happened thus:

I had just completed a design which I liked unusually well. It was for the vignette title-page of a book of poems—an angel bearing through space a lyre and a crown. The angel's eyes and hair were light, according to the generally-accepted tradition, but her face was that of Margaret Welch, only the expression was different. It was such as I had fancied Margaret's might be when joy had triumphed over the long sorrow of her life. It was a prophecy of all I had hoped for her. I was impatient to show it to her. I walked with hurried steps to her dwelling, thinking by the way whether it would bring her comfort—what she would say of it. Eagerly I mounted the four steep flights of stairs. I stood before her door, but outside it was pinned a piece of paper on which these words were traced:

"My friend, I can not see you to-day. I am ill; scarcely able to sit up at all."

Of course, there was no questioning such a decree. I turned sorrowfully away. I went home more unhappy than I had ever been in my life. It was not over my own disappointment, though that was not slight, but I could not bear to fancy her alone and suffering. I longed with inexpressible longing for a *right* to go to her—to sit by her side—to soothe her pains—to bathe her head—to nurse her, as I felt I could, with a woman's tenderness and a man's untiring strength. Then it was that my passion rose up and confronted me. I looked into my own heart—that heart which had so strangely outgrown my knowledge. I saw that no friend's place by her side would content me—that I must win her to be all my own, or from henceforth my life must be empty and barren of joy.

I knew nothing of her past history. She had never volunteered any information, and, respecting her silence, I had never asked any questions. But for this I did not care. I loved her as I knew her. I had faith in her. I know in this I was unlike most men, but I would have been contented to call her my wife—to hold her head on my heart forever, and know no more of her than I knew now.

But would she ever be mine? Could I ever hope—I, whose lot had been so lonely hitherto—to have that worshiped woman for my very own, my household angel, the best half of my existence. Hitherto I should have thought myself too poor to marry; but her tastes were simple like my own. I should have enough for her. I could not sleep that night. To a man who had seen forty-two years without having his pulse quickened by a woman's voice, love comes at last, if come it ever does, with a strength of which younger men never dream. It maintains its empire with a terrible tyranny.

The next morning, as soon as I dared, I stood again at the door of Margaret Welch. The paper had been removed. I knocked, and she came herself to answer my summons. She looked worn and ill, but her brush was in her hand. She held the door so that there was no room for me to enter.

"May I not come in, then?" I asked.

"No, not at this hour. I am busy, and so should you be. I am better. I know you came because you thought me ill. It was good of you to be so anxious. You may come again at the usual hour to-night. Perhaps I will go to walk with you. I should like a breath of sea-air on the Battery, but you must not stay any longer now."

So saying, she closed the door, and, half unwillingly, I obeyed her and went away. I felt happier all day, however, because I had seen her — because I should soon see her again. I was growing miserly. I could not bear she should be out of my sight. I did not work much that day. The pictures I made were fancy ones. I seemed to see a room pleasant, though humble; a cheerful carpet upon the floor; a few books; a few pictures; a few flowers. In one corner, at an easel, sat a woman with slight yet graceful figure. Her head, so regal with its crown of hair, was bent toward her work; and, sitting opposite to her at my own task, I could catch, now and then, the gleam of her earnest eyes. How sweet it would be to work together. Margaret had been more successful of late. Since I had known her many gleams of hope and happiness had brightened under her pencil, and I had been able to find for several of her pictures a ready sale.

How thankful I was that evening when the clock struck seven. Then I was at liberty to go to her. Her door was standing open, that the July air, which even in the hot city is not wholly without its breath of balm, might enter. She was sitting idly by the window, picking one or two faded leaves from the rose-bush I had given her, which was now full of blossoms. For once she was not clad in her accustomed black. A dress of some summer fabric, of a quiet, dim hue, fell around her in soft, fleecy folds. She had gathered one of the sweet tea-roses, and placed it in her hair. I thought I had never seen her look so lovely.

When she saw me at the door she looked up with such a glow of warmth and light upon her face as I had never seen there before.

"I am glad you have come," she said. "I feel better than I have for months. Yesterday I was sick. I fought a great battle, too, with a foe in my own heart, and conquered. To-day, my friend, you look upon a victor. See, I am wearing one of your roses on my forehead—the first flower I have worn in years. It is my token of victory."

I went in and sat down beside her. I tried to make some commonplace remark, but I could not. I sat watching her. She was in a strange, joyous mood. She seemed impatient of silence. Soon she said,

"Shall I get my bonnet? Are you ready to walk now?"

"No, not yet. Sit down, Margaret." And then

my love found words. She grew very pale as she listened. Oh, what a look overswept her face! In it were anguish, despair, pride, and love. Yes, I knew love was there. Cast me off—turn from me, if she would—I knew that she loved me. She listened to me in silence; and then a cry burst from her lips—a passionate cry—

"O God, my burden is heavier than I can bear!" Then she looked at me with dark, sorrowful eyes.

"Oh, could I not have been spared your friendship?" she went on. "Must I tear up by the roots every joy of my life? I thought I was secure of that always."

I interrupted her. I tried to tell her, in my poor way, which no passion could make eloquent, how I had not ceased to be her friend, but how I could not help loving her better than friends love—better than life; how I would gladly die for her. But she scarcely seemed to hear me. When I entreated her to answer me, she begged me to go away—to give her time to think. I had frightened her. Come to her to-morrow night, and I should know; but I must promise not to come before. I promised. I rose to leave her, but when I had reached the door I turned back.

"Margaret," I cried, "give me some hope. I know you will deal justly with me; but if you care for me at all, give me a little hope."

I could see the effort she made to control herself.

"Yes, my friend," she faltered, "I *will* deal justly with you. I have not listened to your words with an unmoved heart, but not till to-morrow can I answer you. I must have time to think. But I will give you this."

She took the rose from her hair, and laid it in my hand with a regal grace. I have it still. I went down stairs and groped my way home, for there was a mist before my eyes; and though the evening was still, and the sunset clouds were bright, I could not see.

I will not write of the next twenty-four hours. Hard as it was to keep away from her, I obeyed her wishes. I did not even enter, that day, the street where she lived, though I could not stay in-doors. I paced restlessly through and through the most crowded thoroughfares, striving to drown, in the confusion, the longing cry of my anxious, uncertain heart.

That night, when I had climbed the stairs, I found Margaret's door open as before. But where was she whose smile had so often transformed for me into Eden the little circumference bounded by those four walls? The room bore no trace of her presence. The pictures were gone from the walls—the easel from the corner—the rose-bush from the window. I write these things calmly now, but I did not look upon them calmly then. On the table lay a letter, superscribed with my name. This, then, would explain the mystery. I seized it. I never knew how I got down the stairs, or how I found my way home; but I broke the seal of that letter in my own room. I will copy it, word for word; but I can not tell you how I read it—with what tears, what prayers, what passion of love and despair. It told her story in these words:

"My friend, my life's one friend, I said I would deal justly with you, and I will, though it should break my heart. I will force my mind to be calm, my memory to be clear, my hand steady. I will give you the confidence you were too generous to ask. I will unveil for you my past life.

"Thirty-three years ago a baby was born in a pleasant country home in England. It was the first child, after seven years of marriage. It came to two who loved each other dearly—who received it with joy and thanksgiving. It grew up, so I have heard, into a beautiful child. I can remember, even now, the praises and caresses which were lavished on me in those early years—the green fields, and the blossoms about my home, the singing birds, and the blue sky which arched over my happy life. My parents were not wealthy, but my mother had been bred a lady, and I grew up surrounded by all the refinements of life.

"When I was only sixteen—a child still, in my impulsiveness—a stranger came to the neighborhood of my home—a young man. Oh, how handsome he was, and what a flattering tongue he had. It might have wiled away a seraph out of Paradise. I learned soon to love him. My nature was never one that could love lightly, and soon I yielded up my heart to him, with all its fullness of tenderness and youthful trust. My parents strove to break off our acquaintance. He was called wild and dissolute, and they forbade me to see him. But I thought they wronged him, and clung to him only the more resolutely. I met him by stealth; and it was not long before he had persuaded me to consent to a secret marriage. I fled with him, without a word of farewell to my father or my mother. I left only a note behind me, explaining the motives of my flight.

"Well, he established me far away, in a pleasant home; and here, for two years, I was happy. For a long time his devotion continued unabated; and when, after a year had passed, he seemed to get a little weary of being alone with me, and wished to make journeys now and then, and sometimes to gather his friends about him, I thought it but natural, and did not repine. I bore his absence the better, for on my breast lay a baby-girl, who looked at me with her father's eyes. With her in my arms, I was never sad or lonely. I thought, too, that her father loved me. Fear that he would change, or suspicion of his truth, had never crossed my mind.

"Did I tell you he was rich? In spite of this, however, we lived very quietly with only two servants. One day he had a friend to dine with him. I did not like the man's face, and I excused myself from joining them. Indeed, my baby needed my care. After an hour she grew restless in her sleep, and seemed feverish. I was always very anxious where she was concerned, and I thought I would go down and ask her father to look at her.

"When I reached the dining-room, I could tell by the sound that they were through dinner and sitting over their wine. I was about to open the door, when I heard my name—my maiden name—spoken by the visitor in a sneering tone. I paused, with a natural impulse to listen. Oh heaven! how shall I tell you the discovery I made in that hour? The man I had called my husband was telling by what means he had inveigled me into his power by a mock marriage. Oh, do not scorn me too bitterly, Robert Payson, but I learned then and there that I was a mother and no wife. Nor was this all. The man whom I had so loved—whom, God help me, I did so love still, was planning how to dispose of me so that I would not be an encumbrance in the way of his marrying one Lady

Elinor, a rich heiress, whom, it seemed, he had been wooing, and nearly won.

"My first thought was to burst into the room and denounce him for his treachery. But how, then, could I escape from him—from this shame which was turning my heart to stone? Once in his presence, and I should be in his power, for I knew myself and the mad love I bore him. No, I must never look upon his face again. Never again should he hear my voice until its echo should haunt him, as I knew it would, on his death day. I gave myself no time for moans or tears. I would not look in the face my anguish, my despair. I went quickly up stairs. My little girl was sleeping more quietly. I did not disturb her. Hurriedly I put together a few necessary changes of of raiment. I was unwilling to take any thing from him; but for my child's sake, his child and mine, I must not heed such scruples. I had a set of diamonds, the only very expensive present he had ever made me. I knew that he had given something over four hundred pounds for them. These I secreted about my person. I had, besides, a small purse of money. I wrote on a slip of paper these words:

"'I have heard your confession. I relieve you of my presence. You will never see either of us again, me or your child. Marry the Lady Elinor, and may the Lord deal more kindly with you than you have dealt with me.'

"I placed this where it would meet his eye, perhaps not at once, but before many hours. Then my preparations were complete. I took up my darling very carefully, so as not to waken her. I stole down stairs with her folded close to my bosom. Do you wonder now that I could paint Hagar—I, who went forth a more lonely wanderer than she, with no angel of the Lord to minister unto me?

"But I must not linger by the way. I do not know whether he whom I had thought my husband pursued me. I never saw his face again. It was five days before I reached my home. All day I walked onward, footsore and weary, and then at night I would procure a lodging from some kind cottager. My baby had seemed to improve during all this time, despite the fatigue. The fresh air, the sunshine, and the sweet breath of the summer meadows had been to her like a draught of life. But not even her head pressed against my heart, her little hands wandering over my bosom, could still the passionate pulses of my despair. Cast out and forsaken of men I felt myself. I had but one wish in life—every hour it grew stronger—a wild longing to get home—only to get home; to drag myself to my mother's side; to pray for her forgiveness; to see once more her kind eyes; to hear her gentle voice; to lay on her bosom my helpless baby, and then die. Ever, in fancy, I seemed to see the pleasant country church-yard. Wooingly its yew-trees stretched their green arms toward me. How I panted to lie down under them in a long and dreamless sleep.

"The fifth night found me still six miles from home. I was so worn-out and exhausted I could drag my weary limbs no farther. I sought, as usual, a humble lodging, and, with my baby on my breast, sank into the deep sleep of fatigue. A little after midnight I awoke. The close air of the room seemed to stifle me. I could sleep no more. I was too restless to lie still. At last the home-longing became irresistible.

I rose, dressed myself and my child, and started once more on the high road toward the little village which was the goal of my pilgrimage. When I arrived there it was the early morning. The sun had not yet risen, but clouds of gold, and crimson, and purple were heralding his coming. The village was still. At a little distance I could see the white chimneys of my father's house rising through the surrounding greenery. I turned my steps that way. 'Courage, darling!' I murmured to the sleeping baby upon my bosom; 'soon we shall be at home.'

"All at once, involuntarily, my feet were stayed. I heard a voice as plainly as I shall ever hear the Archangel's summons when the day of the Lord shall come. It said,

"'Go to the church-yard. It is there she waits for you.'

"Mechanically I turned and entered the place of graves. Tremblingly I sought the sheltered nook where my grandparents were sleeping. There was another mound beside them. For a moment I was dizzy. I could see nothing. Then the mist cleared from my eyes, and I sank on my knees beside the new head-stone. O God! it bore my mother's name, and under it these words of maddening reproach:

"'Her heart broke, and she died.'

"O mother, sainted mother, even from the grave your blood called upward to accuse me. Thus was my longing answered. The mother eyes, whose pity I had thought to meet, forever closed—the mother voice, whose forgiveness I had prayed to hear, forever hushed—the mother bosom, where I had thought my babe should find a home, cold as the head-stone over it. For one moment I sank down in dumb and helpless despair. Then a cry burst from my lips—

"'O God, let us both die here—I and my child!'

"Just then the sun burst through the morning clouds. Its first rays fell upon the head-stone, and revealed to me, on its other side, what I had not before seen—a sculptured angel, its wings poised as if for flight, its eyes uplifted to heaven, and underneath it the words,

"'Our loss was her gain.'

"Through them stole the first ray of comfort to my darkened soul. She was happy now, my mother who had lived and died for me. I, too, was a mother. I, too, had a child to live for. There was no one on earth now to take my responsibility from me. Well, for the little one's sake, I must endure life. I gathered her close to me. I breathed a silent yet fervent prayer to heaven. Then I arose. I would not seek my father. I would spare him a meeting with his child who had broken her mother's heart. There was nothing more for me in the little country village. I gathered a daisy and a few spears of grass which had already sprung above my mother's heart, and placed them in my bosom; and then, drawing my veil over my face, I went back into the highway and walked rapidly out of the village. An hour after I sat down under a beech-tree, and drew my purse from my pocket. Hitherto I had performed my journey on foot, determined that my small means should suffice to keep me, even in case of accidental delays, until I reached home. This was the more necessary, as I did not wish to turn my diamonds into money until I could send or carry them to London, where I thought I should be more likely to receive their just value.

"Now I had turned my back on home forever. I might as well go at once to London as any where. Three quarters of a mile away was a post station where I could take the coach. I counted my money. I had enough to pay for an outside passage. I walked hurriedly on. I had a little fear lest the driver might recognize me, and was relieved, as the coach came up, to see that a stranger held the reins.

"That afternoon I reached London. I went to a quiet lodging-house, and, having procured a room, put on the spare suit I had carried with me. Dressed thus in habiliments suited to a lady, I went out, leaving my babe in the landlady's care, and effected the sale of my diamonds for three hundred pounds. I had enough practical knowledge to be aware that this sum would soon be exhausted if I did not contrive to eke it out by some resources of my own. The only one which suggested itself was my brush. My natural talent for art had been carefully cultivated by the best masters during the time I had lived with the man whose wife I had supposed myself. But I could not stay in London and paint. I could never rest until the ocean rolled between me and my babe's father. Oh, how I loved that man still! My heart clung to him with a mad, passionate grasp, but I would not have looked upon his face for worlds.

"I ran my eye over the advertisements in the evening paper. A vessel was to start in three days for America. I would go in her. What mattered it to what strange shores I drifted—I, a lonely human wreck?

"Thus it chanced that I found myself in the late autumn in New York. You, my friend, know something of the struggles of an unaided stranger who would win food and shelter by art. It was only now and then that I could sell a picture. But I contrived to live, and to make my little Grace comfortable and happy. Can you believe it? I was myself almost happy sometimes in those days. The burning sense of shame, of disgrace, never left me, and the old love haunted me night and day with mocking whispers; but when my little girl could call me mother, when her young, merry voice cooed out such music to my life, I could not be wholly desolate. Something of the balm and healing of motherhood came home to me; her kisses charmed, sometimes, my throbbing, lamenting heart into silence.

"Alas! I know not why God saw fit to make me wholly desolate. When she was not yet three years old she sickened suddenly and died. During the three days of her illness I prayed as I had never prayed before, but there came no answer. I watched the light die out of her eyes; her limbs stiffen into marble; her fluttering heart grow still and cease to beat, and then I no longer prayed or wept. I was calm, Robert Payson, calm, but it was a calmness more pitiful than the wildest passion. I followed her to the grave. I saw the earth heaped over her, and then I came home—home, where I was all alone, where her voice would make no more music, her smile would make no more light: my arms were empty, my heart frozen.

"The next day I read in an English newspaper an account of her father's marriage to Lady Elinor Howard, but it moved me only to a scornful smile.

"I have lived alone twelve years since that day,

and in that time I have never had a friend until I knew you. I painted with more power than ever, but my pictures were like my life, wild and despairing. No one would buy them. I was willing enough to die, but a memory of two whom I held dear in heaven—my mother and my child—kept me from voluntary suicide. So I procured the pattern drawing of which you complained. It kept me alive.

"You know most of my life since our first meeting. You have done me good. You have melted the frozen heart, and convinced me that there is yet honor and truth in the world.

"I told you that yesterday I fought a battle with a foe in my own heart and conquered. I will explain all to you now.

"Yesterday was the anniversary of my mock marriage. Yesterday morning, by some strange coincidence of fate or chance, I learned the death of the man I had once loved. It did not move me as it would have done even one year ago. I examined my own heart. I found that the love which had survived betrayal, anguish, and separation, was now dead utterly. I had forgiven Arthur Hastings fully and freely, but I did not love him. In the same hour another truth stood unmasked before me. I did love you—you, who had never asked for my love. But I knew, I know not by what electric chord of sympathy, that your heart was mine. I did not blush for my love, but I strove to conquer its longings. I thought I had succeeded. But the struggle was a hard one. My life had been so dark, so lonely, how could I resolve, now that a cup of happiness was held to my panting lips, with my own hands to put it from me?

"And yet I must make the sacrifice. I loved you too well to ally you with my shame, to give you the mere wreck and ruin of a life. Nay, when you knew all, you would perhaps yourself turn from me; and yet a secret instinct in my heart tells me you would cling to me still. No matter; I will not linger over the contest. The right triumphed. I resolved that I would keep you from ever asking me to love you. I would retain you my firm, faithful friend. Your friendship should brighten the sunset of my day. This thought gave me inexpressible comfort. You found me joyous, triumphant. You told me your love, and by so doing you have separated us.

"I have been all night lingering over this letter. The new day which is breaking now brings with it work for me to do. I can not trust myself to see you again. When you come, at evening, for my answer, you will find this letter here, and not me. Do not mourn for me. I am not worth your sorrow. Waste no time in seeking me. It will be impossible for you to find me. Indeed, were it possible, it would be worse than useless, for I would then put sea and land between us. It would only bring upon me a new trial. Now I shall please myself by thinking that only a few streets separate us. Nay, sometimes I may even pass you in the street. I may see your eyes and hear your voice. And you will never be far away from me. When I am dying I will send for you. You shall have my last prayer, my last blessing. Until then we must not meet.

"Oh, Robert, how can I say good-by, even on this paper, which seems, while I am writing, to link me with you? And yet I must say it in its fullest sense. God be with you, Robert Payson; God be with you!"

This was all. She had loved me, and I had lost her. No, not lost her. She was pure as one of heaven's angel's in my eyes, dearer to me than ever. I would not allow myself to despair. Could a few streets separate two souls which belonged to each other? I would find her, and she should not again tear herself from me. Her own heart, her loving woman's heart, would second my prayers.

The next day I commenced my search. For three months I continued it. Sometimes I would see a figure far in advance of me which I thought was hers. I would hurry on breathlessly and overtake it, and some cold, strange face would meet my anxious look. I sought her every where. I asked after her at every picture-store and exhibition-room. No one answering my description had been seen in any of them.

At last, one evening, I sat alone in my room, thinking of her as usual. It was late autumn now, and a fire had been kindled. While I sat looking musingly into the embers, with the suddenness of an inspiration a new device came to me. This it was:

I would take the sketch which I executed the day after I saw her first, and place it in the window of a well-known picture-dealer on Broadway, with my name under it. She had never seen it, but I knew its subject could not fail to move her deeply. There was true genius in it. Even I was convinced of that. The turbulent stretch of waters—the one lone woman, white and despairing, upon the beach—the woman with a face so like Margaret's own that I could not bear to look at her—she could not see that picture unmoved. I would wait day after day within that shop till she should come, as I never doubted she would come at last. Thus I would regain my lost treasure. When I think now what a wild, almost impossible scheme of chance was this which I adopted with such implicit faith, I wonder at myself; but it did not even seem strange to me then.

Early next morning I went to the picture-dealer. Without any explanation of my motives, I easily procured permission to exhibit the sketch in his window, and to spend as much time as I wished in his establishment. Providing myself with a book of engravings for an ostensible occupation, I stationed myself where I could see all the passers-by without being observed by them, and there I sat from morning till night. Not until the middle of the third day was any particular interest excited by the picture. Then a woman stopped to look at it. She seemed bent by age and infirmity. Through her thick veil I could see that her hair was silver white. Any where else I should not have questioned for a moment that she was an old lady of at least sixty. But her emotion was unequivocal. She gazed with absorbing interest upon the picture. I could see that she trembled visibly, and grasped a railing in front of the window for support. Was it Margaret? Had I penetrated her disguise at last? My heart beat audibly. At length she tottered away. I sprang to the door and looked out after her. She moved on for a few steps, and then she sank, fainting and helpless, upon the pavement. I called to the driver of an empty carriage which was passing slowly by. I sprang to her side, lifted her up, and put her into the vehicle, giving the coachman the number of my lodgings. He shut the door, mounted the box, and drove away.

I think I was scarcely less pale than she, but my excitement gave me strength. I untied her veil and removed her bonnet. With it fell off the silver hair. It was indeed my darling, my life's darling, whom I held in my arms; but oh how changed, and worn, and wasted was her face now! All this time she had not opened her eyes, nor could I discover that she breathed. Had I recovered her but to see her die? I shouted to the coachman to drive faster. Almost before I had spoken the words we were at home. I tossed the man his fare. I lifted her out and carried her up the steps. My landlady herself answered my impatient ring. I told her, in a few words, that the lady was a near and dear friend who had fainted in the street. Her womanly sympathy was aroused, and she joined me in efforts to restore her consciousness. Soon she drew a long, deep breath. I whispered Mrs. Barker to leave us alone, lest the sight of a strange face might startle her. She obeyed.

When my beloved opened her eyes they met mine. I do not know what story she read in them, but she turned her own away, and a quick crimson overspread her pale face.

"Where am I, Robert?" she asked, in feeble tones. I told her the story of my search, and in what manner I had at last found her, and then I cried out, triumphantly,

"And now God himself has given you to me, you shall never leave me again. You have no other friend. You have no home in all the world but in my heart. My beloved, my beloved!"

She did not answer me. I saw that she had relapsed again almost into insensibility. I hurried to Mrs. Barker, and explained her story in a few words, begging her to send at once for a physician. She was a good, kind creature, and she proved, in my hour of need, a faithful friend.

After that a long, slow fever followed, which brought Margaret very near to the gates of death. The doctor said that only untiring care could have saved her. I did not know what fatigue was in those days. Night and day I watched over her. She was what Mrs. Barker called light-headed, and during three weeks she did not seem to recognize me. At length the fever turned, and the calm light of reason came back to her eyes. As soon as I thought she could bear it I plead with her again, not for her love—she had assured me that was mine long ago—but for her hand in marriage. I showed her how utterly joyless and lonely my life was without her—how she could be its crown and its glory. I told her how faultless and how pure she was in my sight, and then I prayed her, wildly, passionately, to be my wife. A smile broke over her pallid, wasted face; a smile of perfect trust, of unutterable love. She put her thin hand into mine. She murmured,

"You have saved my life, Robert; you have a right to dispose of it. If it is worth any thing to you now, you shall have it."

I sank on my knees beside her. I bowed my head to conceal the rush of glad, heart-relieving tears that would come, and then her feeble arms dropped around my neck and clung to me closely. I felt her lips press upon mine her first kiss.

Thus love triumphed.

A few days after she became my wife. I had asked only this of heaven, and it was granted me. I had reached the goal of my life.

In the years that followed, all the pictures I had made for myself of life with her were realized fully. We lived humbly, but happily. Sunny landscapes and joyous faces smiled on my wife's canvas, and even in my efforts she found something of which to be proud.

At length Old Age stole upon us, and turned our hair white; our eyes lost their power; our hands forgot their cunning. But he could not chill or make old our hearts.

Then Death surprised us. He stilled my wife's pulses, and hushed the voice I loved to hear. He led her before me into the country of shadows; but our love triumphed over even him. Night and day, though I see her not, I know she walks or sits beside me; and before many months, kind friends—I have friends now—will lay down "what once was me" to a long sleep beneath the trees of Greenwood, beside the grave in which her worn frame lies mouldering. But somewhere, far away, she and I shall rejoice together in immortal love and immortal youth. Some patient reader will pause, perchance, over this record of our two lives, but

> "We shall be gone, past night, past day,
> Over the hills and far away."

Leona: a Blind Man's Story.

Ye have a world of light,
Where love in the loved rejoices;
But the blind man's home is the home of night,
And its beings are empty voices.

BULWER LYTTON.

I ken the night and day,
For all ye may believe,
And often in my spirit lies
A clear light as of midday skies;
And splendors on my vision rise
Like gorgeous hues of eve.

MARY HOWITT.

LEONA: A BLIND MAN'S STORY.

I HAD not been blind from my birth. Sitting alone in the utter darkness, my closed eyes could make pictures. I could call back glories of nature and glories of art, blue sky, and wind-swept fields; and, above all, dear faces—faces whose very memory lightened my nighttime—my father, my gentle mother, my young, dark-eyed brother. There was another, too, not of our blood, whose face I saw oftener than any. This was strange, for Leona Ashland, the daughter of my mother's most intimate friend, was but a child of ten, six years younger than myself. She was very dear to me, however. She had been in and out of our house as familiarly as a daughter. She was the pet of every one save me; but, child as she was, my own feeling for her was too tender and reverent to admit of gay familiarity. I had never heard any one call her beautiful, but to me her face always seemed that of an angel. I used to tremble lest, some day of summer, God should give her wings, and we should see her no more forever—her features, framed in those long brown curls, seemed so spiritual, so delicate. When I looked into her thoughtful eyes, at school or at church, life seemed a holier, a more earnest thing. But the time came when I could see them no longer.

For fifteen years the world had been visible to me,

with its beauty, its mystery, its romance. Then darkness began to steal gradually over me. It was a whole year before the last ray of light had faded. I was stone-blind at sixteen. I was thankful that it was not a sudden stroke. Day after day I had sought in vain for some cherished object of vision. Once it had been the blue range of the far-off hills; again the familiar outline of a distant tree. After a time the darkness came nearer. Day after day some tender grace would fade out from a beloved face, and I could only reproduce it in my fancy. At length I seemed to dwell in a world of shadows. Shapes, whose dim outline I could only faintly catch, floated by me; but still I could tell day from night; still heaven's blessed light was welcome. But what shall I say of the anguish of desolation when the last ray was gone—when they told me the midday sun was shining clear and bright, and I, alas! sat in blindest, deepest midnight! no light, no hope?

I had so much to give up. It was not alone the joy of sight, the dear faces, the beautiful world, but all my high hopes, my plans for the future, my ambition, my pride. I had meant to be a student. I had had visions of fame. There were months of stormy, surging discontent before I could settle calmly down to my destiny. I secluded myself even from those dearest to me on earth. The very sound of their voices maddened me, for it made more intense the longing to look upon their faces. Day after day I sat alone in my room, where I had besought them not to come to me.

Sometimes my mother, who loved me more than ever in my sorrow and my helplessness, would steal into the room, and sit for an hour beside me in silence. She was so still I could scarcely hear her breathe; but I knew that at these times she wept much. Once, in an irresistible impulse of maternal tenderness, she folded her arms around me, and drew my head to her bosom. "Oh, my child!" she cried; "my dear child, be comforted! Believe that there is something left in life, or this blow will kill us both."

But my rebellious spirit would *not* struggle with its despair, even though I felt that it was breaking my mother's heart.

Once—and I think this did me more good than any thing—Leona came to me. She had so long entreated to see me that at length my mother consented. She came in alone. I knew her footstep as soon as it crossed the threshold, but I did not speak. She came to my side. She laid her hand—her little child's hand—upon mine. I knew, as well as if I had seen it, the sorrowful pity with which her eyes were lifted to my face. She seemed striving to gather self-command enough to speak calmly. At length, low and quiet, yet earnest, her words fell upon my ear:

"Oh, Mr. Allen, the rector says God knows just what is best for every one. He is our father, and he does not love to make us sorry. This is the passage Mr. Green told me to say to you: 'Like as a father pitieth his children, so the Lord pitieth them that fear him.'"

Her childish voice had deepened into a thrilling energy as she recited the words of inspiration. Then she turned to leave me; but I detained her. Already she had comforted me.

"How came Mr. Green to tell you to say that to me?" I asked.

"You are not vexed, Mr. Allen?"

"No, I am grateful. I only wished to know how it happened."

"He was at our house last night, and he spoke of you. He pitied you very much; but he said you had a great deal left in life yet, if you would not be in despair. After a while mother went out of the room, and I told him you had been very good to me, and I wanted to tell you something to make you feel better. Then he said I might repeat that verse to you. Does it do you good?"

"Much good, blessed child! Your words have helped me more than you can ever know."

She left me then. I did not strive to keep her. I felt the need of solitude to receive reverently the light, brighter than earthly dawning, which was rising upon my spirit. Her words had thrilled me as if they had dropped downward from some angel's lips, leaning from the far watch-towers of the celestial city. "A great deal left for me yet in life!" And, as I repeated those words, my blessings seemed to rise up before me and reproach me. For me Agur's prayer had been answered. I had neither poverty nor riches; but a competence was mine in my own right, which would secure me against want. I had health and strength, and many friends. The paths about our little village were all familiar to me. I could traverse them without a guide; I could feel the free winds sweep my brow; I could inhale the sweet breath of the flowers; I could hear the beloved voices of home. Verily, God had not forsaken me. I had been willfully shutting his mercies out of my heart. I knelt now, and thanked him for what had been left—prayed him to teach me to bear patiently the loss of what had been taken.

When the bell rang for supper, I rose, and went quietly down stairs. They gave no noisy greeting to the son who had not sat beside them there since the spring flowers had blossomed, though now the summer lay green and luxuriant upon hill and woodland. But I understood my father's welcome—the unuttered tenderness which deepened my mother's voice—the eager grasp in which my brother Richard held my hand. I found my plate and my chair in their old place. After that, I never secluded myself from them again.

When supper was over, I went out to go to evening prayers at the church. I had not thought I could ever go there again. I had dwelt morbidly on the curiosity with which the congregation would look at me. I never thought of that now. God had opened the eyes of my spirit. I went there to thank Him for this great mercy. I had never before been so deeply thrilled with the church music. Hearing seemed to me like a new sense. Through it, I drank in deep draughts of pleasure. I had sat in the choir; and, when prayers were over, I entreated the organist to play for me again. Soon we became fast friends. I think that my enthusiasm pleased him, for twilight after twilight found us alone in the church, with only the little boy who blew the bellows—John Cunningham playing, and I listening and dreaming.

But I soon felt—I think an intuitive sense of power revealed it to me—that the organist was no artist. Sometimes I longed to sweep him off the stool, and interpret with my own fingers the music that was in my soul. This idea that I could be a musician dawned upon me slowly; but day by day the sense of power strengthened.

At length I asked him to let me try. I think he was astonished. My soul was flooded with harmony. Wild, sweet strains came to me like the whispers of angels. From that night I was the master, he my pupil. Sometimes I would persuade my brother to go with me to the church, and then, for hour after hour, the organ would indeed be the voice of my soul. I breathed out in music all the dreams of my long, dreaming boyhood, before the one stern stroke had come, under which I bowed my head, and rose up a man. God was very merciful. With this resource, I could never be entirely lonely, wholly desolate.

When I was twenty-one John Cunningham had left Ryefield, and I had been chosen the organist of our village church. It was my business, for which a small salary was paid me. This was all I was, all I ever could be; but I was content.

My brother was in college. He was taking my place; he would realize my early dreams. The world called him a brilliant young man. At home there was little change, save that Leona's light footfall less often crossed our threshold. For some years she had been at school in Boston. In the vacations she came home, and then I could tell by her voice that she was good and innocent as ever. The next spring—it was winter now—her schooldays would be over. At last the time arrived. I welcomed her joyfully, though I scarcely knew why her presence seemed so infinitely precious. We wandered together into the fields; and she told me how fresh and green the grass was springing under foot—how blue and bright was the May-time sky. I could smell the bloom of the fruit-trees, which were dropping their fragrant blossoms in our path. She never wearied of making all things visible to me. She would tell me how the mist was lying white and purple in the valley—how the far, hazy hills were sleeping in the sunshine; and, seeing with her eyes, I scarcely realized that I was blind.

But this dream also had an awakening. My brother Richard came home. He had finished his course at the University with high honors, and his advent in Ryefield was the signal for a series of parties, and picnics, and merry-makings, in which I did not join, and which took Leona from my side. I heard from all quarters the praises of my handsome, manly brother. He was only nineteen now, but he was six feet tall, and, they said, looked older than his years. I was not surprised to hear that his wit and his manly graces were making sad havoc with the hearts of the village girls. Already over my soul had begun to steal a presentiment of sorrow.

I think my brother was very fond of me. He had always made me his confidant. One night he came to my room, and said, with a hesitation which seemed very singular in his frank, fearless nature, that he had something to tell me. Then he talked of indifferent subjects for a while; and at length, suddenly—alas! it seemed to me pitilessly—the blow fell. He loved Leona Ashland!

Oh, heaven pity me! God have mercy on me! I knew in that moment that I, too, loved her. I, blind, helpless fool that I was, had made her my idol. I had not known before what was the spell which bound me to her, or, rather, I had resolutely closed my heart against the conviction. The veil was ruthlessly rent away. I could not choose but look on my own stupid imbecility. A voice in my soul mocked me. It cried, "You cowardly idiot! You thought, did you? to darken her life by fastening yourself upon her, a blind, helpless shadow! You thought that young girl could love you—that girl, radiant with youth and hope, all the glory and brightness of life, before whose feet the future stretches out green, and fresh, and smiling. You thought you could win her. Selfish! insensate! mad!"

I bade the voice cease its upbraidings. I shut my ears against it; I ordered my brother from the room. For the first time in my life I was harsh and stern with him. He had a generous temper. I do not think he blamed me. He reproached himself, rather, for speaking to me of a love from which he thought my misfortune had shut me out forever. Begging me to forgive him, he went out.

I closed the door behind him. I locked it. The key turned with a sharp click. Then I threw myself down upon the floor, as a traveler might prostrate himself before the poison wind of the desert. Lying there, this fierce, scorching simoon swept over me. Unknown to myself, I had been cherishing one sweet flower in my heart, watering it day and night with the dew of hope. It lay there now, torn up by the roots, its buds blighted, its fair blossom withered.

Blind, helpless idiot! So the voice in my heart had called me. Ay; but the blind idiot could *love*. Who else could pour such wealth of tenderness on one who could never grow old to his sightless eyes—whose brow would always be smooth—whose hair would never lose its brightness—whose eye would never grow dim, because forever he could clothe her with the fair garment of his fancy? And a new voice in my heart answered, "I *am* worthy, for I love."

With those words strength came to me, and I rose up, and stood erect in my darkened world, lonely and grief-stricken, but still a man. I was not one to inflict my sorrow upon others. I strove to go out among my fellows with a cheerful face. But I listened with tremulous eagerness to every inflection of Leona's voice when she talked with my brother. I knew she must love him; but there was a curious fascination in watching how this passion would spring up in her pure heart—how the tenderness which could never be for me would grow into her beloved voice. Day after day it seemed to me to become full of a sweeter pathos. Richard was constantly by her side. Often they roamed together over the fields. Sometimes they asked me to go with them; but I was too sensitive to intrude. I always refused. Once or twice, when I had declined going, Leona insisted on remaining with me. Then she would be so cruelly kind to me, read to me, talk to me, bewilder me with torturing glimpses of an impossible happiness. Then Richard would come back with a floral offering—a spray of honeysuckle or a bunch of wild roses; and, sitting beside her afterward, I smelt all day the fragrance of his flowers upon her bosom.

One night she asked me if she might go alone with me to evening prayers, as she used before Richard came. It was a pleasant walk, that half mile between our house and the church, in the summer sunset, with the trees over our heads all odorous with bloom. There was a curious joy, which was more than half compounded of pain, in knowing that she was by my side, in feeling the light pressure of her hand upon my arm.

When the services were over, she asked me to stay a little longer, and play for her, as I had often done before. Hitherto, at such times, she had chosen the tunes; but now the fever fit of inspiration was upon me. I poured forth the story of my hopeless love. I used no words; but the music explained itself. It thrilled, it trembled, it pleaded, it despaired, it struggled, it hoped; then, as if for the dead, it wailed, and died out, at last, in a long, helpless cry of sorrow. I heard Leona sobbing. She stood, at a little distance, alone in the darkness. I left my seat. I went to her and took her hands. In the darkness she laid her tender, pitying arms around my neck. I felt her wet cheek against my own. Alas! I knew the language of that silent caress. She loved Richard; but, with all the fullness of her angelic nature, she pitied me. She would be my sister.

No word was spoken by either of us. We went out of the church, and went home, under the night and the trees.

Soon after this Richard was obliged to leave us for two or three weeks on some business for my father. I did not know whether he had declared his love previous to his departure. I watched Leona's voice jealously for signs of sorrow, but it was clear and full of music as ever. Indeed, I thought it more joyous than was its wont. I said to myself, "How certain she must be of his love, to bear his absence so calmly. The joy of knowing that he is her own forever makes her insensible to sorrow."

Oh, how kind she was to me during those two

weeks. It was almost like the old days before Richard came, save that a barbed arrow was rankling in my heart. The unconscious hope I had cherished in those other days could never return again.

At last the time came for Richard's return. Leona was with us. Frankly, as one who has nothing to conceal, she talked of the pleasure there would be in having him back. At noon he arrived. With eager step he entered the room; but his voice trembled when he spoke to Leona. I could only tell by that token how his heart thrilled to be once more by her side. She was not demonstrative. The tone with which she replied to his greeting was very quiet; but I had never known Richard's manner so eager, so restless as that afternoon.

In the evening we three were alone in the long parlor. I sat at one end among the shadows. Richard and Leona were at the other, where the moon—for I heard them talking of it—shone in at the open window. Perhaps Richard thought I could not hear, or that I slept. He did not know what a second sight hearing is to the blind. Not a murmur, not a quiver of their voices escaped me. It seems that he had never told her of his love before. He poured it forth now with passionate, fervid eloquence. I listened breathlessly for her answer; I held tight to the chair where I was sitting; I commanded every nerve to do its duty; I bade my self-control to be vigilant at its post; I would bear the torture without a moan; I waited to hear her low words of love. Her voice fell on my ear. Hush, rebellious heart, thou hadst no business to throb so wildly.

"I can not," she says; "oh, I can not! I thought

you knew—I thought you must have known—" And here the tender, troubled voice breaks up into pitiful sobs, as she beseeches him to leave her—only to leave her. Richard makes no attempt to comfort her. I hear him go out. Then I cross the room; I kneel beside her; I tell her I have heard all; and then a mad impulse seizes me: I pour out at her feet the libation of my love. I can not help it. Blind, and poor, and helpless as I was, I had dared to love her. I did not mean to tell her. I knew she could never return it. But when I had heard her grieve, I had longed so to comfort her; I had wanted her to know how gladly I would die to give her peace.

Oh! how can I tell the story? She did not spurn me. Once more, in the darkness, her tender arms were laid about my neck. For the first time I felt upon my mouth the kisses of her fresh, pure lips. Her words were solemn and earnest: "Do not die for me. Live, live, dear Allen! and, if you love me, let me be your wife."

When our betrothal was made known, there was a struggle in my brother's heart. He loved me; he strove to rejoice in my happiness; but he could not stay to witness it. I, who knew Leona's worth, did not blame him. He left home the next week for a year of foreign travel; and, three weeks after, Leona became my wife.

Our wedding was a very simple one. We chose to be married in the old church at twilight, for to us that had been the blessed hour of destiny. When the ceremony was over, and the witnesses had departed, we walked slowly homeward under the trees. Leona told me the moon was flooding all things with a silver rain of peace, and we felt that it would be the emblem of our future.

My wife insisted on a short bridal tour. She must take her blind husband to Boston. I was a little sensitive about exposing my misfortune to strangers. This step seemed unlike Leona; but I wished to please her, and I consented.

The next morning after our arrival we sat alone in our room at the Winthrop House. I wanted to talk to my wife, but she could scarcely listen. She fluttered around the apartment, arranged and disarranged the furniture a dozen times. I had never known her so restless. Every now and then she would drop for a moment upon my knee, and, lifting up my face, would cover it with kisses; but even there she would not sit still.

At length there came a tap upon the door, and she sprang hurriedly to open it. There were a few whispered words with the new-comer, and then Leona said, gravely,

"My love, this is Dr. Williams. I have heard much of his skill, and I brought you here because I longed, for my own satisfaction, to have him examine your eyes. I did not wish to mention it at home, for there was no use in making any one else a sharer of my suspense."

Dr. Williams' voice was very kind. I liked that. He proceeded gently with his examination. For five moments I was in an agony of hope. In fancy I saw again earth and sky, and, dearer still, the sweet face of my bride. Leona held my hand tightly.

At length the doctor's verdict came. I know he pitied us, two poor young things, looking to him to crush or confirm a hope as precious as life. His voice trembled. He said, in low, earnest tones, "God soften it to you! There is *no* hope!"

He went out of the room. Leona closed the door after him, and then came back, and threw herself into my arms. I could feel her heart throbbing tumultuously against my side. But she commanded herself, and strove to comfort me. "My poor, poor darling!" she said, tenderly, "can you forgive me for disturbing you with this vain trial? I did so long to know the worst. I could not help hoping before. Now we shall be at rest. It will not be like a doubtful sorrow."

"And you, Leona, can you indeed be content to share a blind man's darkened life?"

She stopped my words with her kisses.

"Hush, beloved! I will be your light—your eyes."

She has kept her word. I miss no pleasant sights or sounds of nature, for in her I have all things. I do not even need to look on her beloved face, for I see it in my heart forever, fresh, and young, and fair as when my eyes last beheld it. She was but a child when she first aroused me from my blind despair. She was my comforter then. She will be all the days of my life. The two years since our bridal have been full of joy. My heart has hardly space for more.

A month ago Richard brought home his bride. They call her more beautiful than Leona, but her voice is not so thrilling in its music. I do not believe so much soul looks from the eyes they call so dark and bright. I am full of content. I know, when God's own angels shall unseal my vision—when, in the everlasting light of heaven, the blind shall see again—fairest among women, fairest and truest will stand by my side my God-given—my wife LEONA.

The Mountain Road.

I will work him
To an exploit, now ripe in my device,
Under the which he shall not choose but fall;
And for his death no wind of blame shall breathe;
But even his mother shall uncharge the practice,
And call it accident.

SHAKSPEARE (*Hamlet*).

Other sins only speak, murder shrieks out.
The element of water moistens the earth,
But blood flies upward and bedews the heavens.

WEBSTER.

THE MOUNTAIN ROAD.

I CAN not write the story with my own hands, but I shall dictate it to a tried and trusty friend, for I must have the public know all that I can tell respecting that strange and mysterious death. My name is Henry Wilde, and I was present when *it* happened. It was a week ago, and in body I have been utterly helpless since that day. I do not think that my intellect was much disordered by the shock; and yet I seem to have lost, in some degree, control over my mind—the power of condensation. Therefore I must tell this story in my own way. If I am prolix—if I linger too much over detail not connected with the act itself, it must be pardoned me.

I am not a young man. I have known Steven Cranston for more than forty years—ever since he and I went to school together in our pinafores. I am forty-eight now. Last week I should have said that he was two years younger; but he stands to-day where they do not reckon ages by earthly measurement. Many who will read these words know what he was as a man—stern, dark-browed, silent, and mysterious. He was all this even as a boy.

At the district school we attended together he seemed to like no one. He might have been a favorite if he would, for he had the most physical courage

I ever knew any boy to possess. He literally feared nothing. He had no equal in the various athletic games with which we whiled away our noonings; and these two traits, of daring and agility, are potent to win the suffrages of boys. Any one else possessing them to such extent would have become a loved and recognized leader; but Steven Cranston was too silent, too forbidding and unsocial. No one would have dared in any wise to interfere with him; but he had none of those dear boy-friendships, those brotherhoods of the soul, whose memory, in after years, has power to thrill so many old men's hearts, and make them happy boys again.

I said he seemed to like no one. I should have made one exception. Nearly opposite to him, on the "girls' side" of the long red school-house, sat Lucia Reynolds, the daughter of one of our wealthiest men. She did not owe her popularity to this circumstance, however. Looking back through the mists of twenty-eight years, I can see Lucia Reynolds as she was at fifteen, and I know that I never saw a fairer face. I met her the other day—a woman of forty-three she is now, and older than her years, with a look of patient waiting in her eyes, a settled sorrow round her lips—a woman to whom you would not even pay that saddest compliment, "She must have been beautiful once;" and I turned my eyes away, and back through the fair country of the past, till I could see her, as I saw her twenty-eight years ago, bending over her desk in Ryefield school-house.

Slight, girlish figure; small but perfect features; eyes of the bluest; delicate rose-tint on the dimpled cheeks; full, smiling mouth—I saw them all in the light and glory of youth, untouched by time. She had a clear, ringing voice, a dancing step, and, better than all, a heart full of love for every living creature; and so every body loved her, and every body included misanthropic Steven Cranston. Indeed, his sentiment for her seemed no mere childish liking. It was more the blind devotion of a Romanist for his patron saint. He would sit and watch her for hours with a look of rapt adoration. Lucia had the heart of a woman, and she could not help recognizing and liking this homage. She accepted, with the graciousness of a gentle queen, the rare flowers and fruit he used constantly to seek for her, and she befriended him in her turn. She was his warm defender when any one censured his coldness and misanthropy, and more than one predicted he would some day win her for his wife.

I never thought so, however. I was five years older than Lucia, and I think I understood her. I felt certain that *he* must be very different from Cranston who would arouse her heart from its long, delicious, dreaming girlhood, and quicken it into womanhood's passionate yet steadfast love. And yet I used sometimes to fancy that he loved her with a man's passion even then. If she could have returned it how different might have been the current of his future! Does it not seem as if there were some lives to which Destiny is pitiless? lips from which the only cup in all the spheres which could work their healing is dashed remorselessly?

When Lucia Reynolds was sixteen I left the place, and for many years I went back there but seldom. I kept up, however, a constant correspondence with my sister Bell, and through her was made *au courant* in all the gossip of Ryefield.

Two years after I left a stranger came to live there—a Colonel Eastman, whose family consisted of an invalid wife and a son, a young man who had nearly finished his collegiate course. When this latter personage came home for his first long summer vacation after the establishment of the family, Bell's letters were quite full of him—he was so handsome, so gallant, so generous and gentlemanly. Soon she wrote that he had made the acquaintance of Lucia Reynolds. She believed that it was nearly a case of love at first sight on both sides. She wrote me that they were always together; that they seemed just suited to each other; and Lucia was growing prettier than ever in her happiness. To one of these descriptions she added, playfully,

"I suppose I'm too bad to break your heart, brother Harry! I remember your old admiration for Lucia; but I seriously hope you won't look as glum as Steve Cranston did when Robert Eastman first came. You would have thought he'd lost his last friend; but he seems to have gotten bravely over it now, and is more cheerful and good-humored than I've ever seen him before. Indeed, I don't know but I shall lay siege to his heart myself."

I don't remember that I thought much of what Bell said of Steven's glum looks, but I did smile at her allusion to breaking my heart. I could afford to laugh at such things in those days. I loved—no matter; I am not telling my own story. There is a little white stone in Weymouth church-yard, and it is the sole memorial of the only dream I ever dreamed of love and woman. Yet I have not lived a sad or gloomy life. After death comes heaven, and I shall find my virgin bride *there*.

It was early autumn when I received a letter from Bell, full of tragic gloom—of sorrow—of desolation. Young Robert Eastman, whom every body liked, had been found dead in the Mountain Road, near the Black Pool—murdered, evidently. No blood had been spilled, but the marks around his throat showed that he had been strangled. He was robbed also, and had doubtless been killed for the sake of a considerable sum of money which he had drawn from the bank the day before, and was carrying home to his father. As yet, she said, suspicion was directed to no one; but it was so sad—so terrible—just as he had become engaged to Lucia! It would break her heart; and his poor sick mother had not spoken since.

I was too happy in those days for the story of this tragedy to sadden me as deeply as it might have done at another time; still I felt it keenly for the sake of Lucia, my dear friend and schoolmate.

From time to time Bell wrote me of the apprehension of several persons faintly suspected of the dreadful crime, but no evidence could be brought against any of them, and they were all discharged. It was not long before I heard that the poor young man's mother had followed him to his long home in Ryefield church-yard; and, soon after, Colonel Eastman, unable to live on and bear his sorrow in the scene of his double bereavement, sold out and moved away.

It was not till three years after, when my own life's trouble had already come to me, that I saw Lucia Reynolds again. She seemed nearly as old then as she does now. Her mouth was rigid; the look of patient waiting had grown into her far-seeing blue eyes. She never laughed, and she spoke low and seldom.

At the same time I saw Steven Cranston. Over him too had passed some inexplicable change. More glum, forbidding, and unsocial than of old he could scarcely be, and yet there was something in his face, in his manner, which seemed to say that, whereas Hope and he knew each other once, they had parted company forever now.

I did not see much of him or Lucia after that until this summer. I came to my old home last June an invalid. I felt that the free winds blowing over the Connecticut hills would bring me health and healing; and, though my dearest hope is in the Beyond, still I love life—I cherish no misanthropic longing for death. Coming back to Ryefield, I found Lucia Reynolds and Steven Cranston the only ones of all my schoolmates who were unmarried and in their old homes. You must bear in mind that nearly twenty-five years had gone by since young Eastman's sudden and terrible death. Lucia had passed all these very quietly. She had not mingled at all in society so called, but her face was known in the abodes of the poor, the sick, and the sorrowful. She had done much good in her own unobtrusive way.

Steven Cranston had led, rumor said, a wild life during these twenty-five years. A little more than three years after Robert Eastman's death he had gone to sea, and most of his life since had been passed on the ocean and in the different ports to which he had sailed. He had grown rich, though I heard hints of unlawful gain, to which I did not pay much heed. Country neighborhoods are usually more or less given to gossip, and ours was no exception to the rule.

At all events, he had come back the autumn before

my return to Ryefield, and given out that he had been to sea long enough, and was going to settle down now and end his days among his own townsfolk and kindred. I think people liked him somewhat better than they used. He was a trifle more communicative and neighborly. I can't say that I, however, felt much real regard for him. Yet he entertained me sometimes by his reminiscences of hair-breadth escapes on the high seas and in far-away lands. He was a link between memory and the dead and buried boyhood days, and so we were a good deal together.

It is just a week ago to-day that he rode into the yard on his strong bay horse. I was sitting under the apple-tree.

"Come, Harry," he called to me, "get your horse saddled, and ride out on the Mountain Road. I've a story to tell you, madder, and jollier, and merrier than any of 'em. It's a nice time to tell it, this September morning. Let me see, September the 17th, 1858, isn't it? Yes, it's the best time in the world to tell *that* story."

It struck me that his manner was very peculiar. It was said that he was a hard drinker, though I had never seen any signs of it before. I thought the brandy might have flown to his head. However, I got ready, and we started on our ride.

If any, unfamiliar with the locality, should read this story, perhaps they would like to understand better the physiognomy of the Mountain Road. In the northwestern part of the town is a very high hill, known in that region as "The Mountain." A road was laid out, in the town's infancy, along the base of this hill. It was the nearest cut then to some of the neighboring towns, but a better one was made a few years ago on the other side of the hill. In some portions of the way it is as utterly solitary as a wilderness. To the right hand rises the mountain, overhanging it, high, and steep, and frowning. To the left stretch away rugged pasture lots, used only for sheep, rocky, and here and there interspersed with wood. On this road there is little travel, and for nearly two miles there is not a single house save one, ruinous and dilapidated enough now, but which used to be, in my boyish days, the residence of a solitary man called old Wrath Spaulding—a bad and reckless man, in whose very name lurked terror. He died long ago, and I have never heard but that he sleeps quietly enough in his lonely grave in the rear of his old tumble-down house. A little beyond this place — the half-way house in those desolate two miles—and just concealed from it by a turn in the road, is a deep pool at the base of the hill, known to all the townspeople as the "Black Pool." It looks as if it might have been dug out by the giants of dead centuries. Its waters seem fathomless in depth, and one can not gaze down on them as they lie there, black, still, treacherous, without a shudder. It used in other days to be separated from the road by a sort of paling, but this has fallen down now, and the way is so seldom traveled that no one has taken the trouble to replace it. There is a strange charm in the ruggedness of the scenery, the very desolation of this untrodden road, and I looked around me with a keen sense of pleasure as we slackened our reins and turned into it.

Though it was September, the landscape was still as fresh and verdurous as in July. You could understand the poetical license of the term "living green" as you looked at it. You could almost see the trees grow and the grass spring up. The sky was blue, deep, cloudless, untroubled. The mist—golden, and white, and rosy—was melting away over the hill-tops, and, it seemed to me, earth, air, and sky were as glorious as when the Father first pronounced them "good." Absorbed in my own thoughts, I had almost forgotten Cranston's presence until he spoke.

"I promised you a story," he said, riding up close to my side. "It'll be a queer one—a love story about murder," and he grinned a ghastly grin. "I don't think you ever heard just such a one—a tale with its hero for the teller."

He paused a moment, and the September morning seemed to grow very cold; I think his manner chilled me. Pretty soon he spoke again.

"I don't know as you ever mistrusted that I loved Lucia Reynolds. There was a time, I think, when people imagined that we took a kind of fancy to one another, but nothing came of it, and they gave up the idea. Perhaps there was never any foundation for it on her side. She must have returned such devotion as mine was with at least a kindly liking. I think she did like me, and on that I built wild hopes. Love does not at all express what I felt for her. I worshiped her. Sullen, and morose, and gloomy as every body thought me, one smile of hers would make a light bright as heaven in my heart. I would have died, I used to think, for the sole hope that she would weep over my grave. I have kissed, when no one saw me, the very grass that had bent under her light footsteps. I have treasured, like something sacred, a flower that had dropped out of her pretty hair. It was nothing short of madness; but if she *could* have loved me back again I might have been a good man. With her for my guardian angel, I believe I could have won through and scaled heaven. Well, now, I suppose, I shall go to company that's more of my kind than saints and angels.

"I went to see her one day when she wasn't quite eighteen, and told her what she had been to me all my life, ever since the days when she used to sit opposite to me in school, a little eight years old child, in her red dresses and white aprons. I tried to show her the height, and breadth, and depth of my love. I think I made her understand it, as well as her gentle nature could understand the strong passion of mine. She heard me all through, and then she began to cry. I have heard of women weeping at such times for joy and bashfulness, but I knew well enough her tears were not of that kind. They fell fast. They were born of her tender pity—her sorrow at giving me pain—and they answered me as well as words.

"Soon she commanded herself and spoke. She talked like an angel. She told me how much she had always thought of me, and always should. She would be my sister, she said—a fond, loving sister; but such love as I asked for she could not give me.

"*I* wept then too. It was the last time any tears ever fell from my eyes; but I bowed my head on her lap—I was kneeling at her feet—and the flood broke loose.

"Even after that I did not quite give up all hope. Time, I thought, might work wonders. Any way, she had been the life of my life too long for me to shut her out of my heart. I went on worshiping her, and I comforted myself—it was the only comfort I had—with thinking that even if she did not love me she loved no other. It was just before then that Colonel Eastman had moved to Ryefield, and very soon his son Robert came home to pass the summer. He met Lucia, and they seemed at once greatly interested in one another. It was not strange. He was of her kind—generous, genial, and loving. I suppose they were just suited to each other. Well, I hated him. That was not strange, either. I hated his handsome face, his social manners. I gave to every one of his good qualities a distinct and separate hate; and, because her eyes looked on him with favor, this still, deadly hate grew daily deadlier and more murderous. But I dissembled. I even cultivated his friendship. I was more social and good-humored than I had ever been before, and I began to gain popularity. But the smiles I wore were like flowers growing over a volcano.

"After a while I heard that he and Lucia were engaged, and then I resolved that he should die. I met him just as usual, with this purpose in my heart. I even congratulated him on his happiness. But I watched his every movement — close, close. Soon there came a time which placed him in my power. He was to come from Windham one day with five hundred dollars he had drawn from the bank the day before. He would come this way. I resolved to meet him here. He was not expected until afternoon, but I came early in the morning: I was determined he should not escape me. I stationed myself behind that clump of poplars, near the Black Pool. Lightning has blasted them since. No wonder. I had not been there very long before I heard a horse's footsteps. I looked out cautiously. It was he. He had started early—perhaps to make the journey in the coolness of morning; perhaps—I gnashed my teeth in silent fury at the thought—perhaps he was in haste to see again his fair betrothed.

"I had laid my plans as coolly as I tell them to you now. I had armed myself, and resolved, as soon as he should reach me, to spring from my concealment, fell him from his horse, and murder him then and there. Of course there was always the chance that he should defend himself and master me—the yet more dreadful chance that, if I killed him, I should expiate my crime upon the gallows; but, physically, I am no coward. I had made up my mind, and there was no fear that I should flinch.

"It happened better than I had planned. For once Satan favored his own. Before he reached me he dismounted and tied his horse to the fence on the other side of the way. The animal looked tired, and, I suppose, his master was in the mood to be merciful. Then he came across the road, and sat down in the very shadow of the poplars behind which I, his deadly enemy, was hid. He took off his cap and bared his forehead to the September morning air. Then he drew from his pocket a miniature, and bent over it lovingly. I was almost near enough to hear him breathe. I could see the features as well as he. Lucia was there—Lucia, with her soft hair, her eyes of violet blue, her bewildering smile. After a moment he pressed it passionately to his lips, murmuring, fondly,

"'Oh, Lucia, my bride, my darling, my dear, dear love!'

"If I had meant to spare his life before, I should have killed him then. *I* might never win her, but *he* should not live to bask in her smiles—to claim her—to hold her in his arms.

"Softly as a cat I stole from my concealment. Absorbed in his happy thoughts, he neither saw nor heard me until I stood behind him, and my hands were clasped around his throat — tight, tight. Then, indeed, he struggled for his life. But I never relaxed my hold. Soon he fell down at my feet—still and stiff, struggling no longer—*dead.*

"I was calm still. I rifled his pockets. I took the five hundred dollars and his watch, and tied them, together with a heavy stone, in his pocket-handkerchief, and dropped them into the Black Pool. They cleft the dark waters and sank heavily. In an instant they were lost to sight forever. I left the miniature—which I longed but did not dare to keep—upon his person. I gave him, as he lay there, one long, triumphant gaze, and then quietly walked away home.

"But not even yet was my hatred satisfied. The dead man lying there, stark and cold, with his face upturned to the September sun, was yet, to my thinking, better off than I. Gladly, ay, gladly would I have taken his place, and lain there dead, but to have once heard *her* lips call me the beloved of her soul—to have carried the memory of her kisses into the hereafter of spirits.

"For a time I half expected to suffer for my crime a felon's doom; but suspicion never seemed to point my way. That afternoon his horse, which I had left as he had tied it, broke from its fastening, and rushed, riderless, home. Then they found his body. The robbery which had been committed seemed to indicate the money he had with him as the motive of the deed, and led to the apprehension of two or three persons hitherto suspected of theft. But they were all discharged; and after Mrs. Eastman had died, and the colonel moved away, the matter pretty much ceased to be talked of.

"The first pang of remorse I suffered was when I saw Lucia standing at Mrs. Eastman's grave. I had not seen her before since *that* day. She had changed in those few weeks so that you would hardly have known her. Her cheek and lips were ashen; the smiles had faded forever from her face; the joyous light from her eyes. I loved her so that I would have died, even then, to bring back to her happiness; but I would have seen her die before, if the power had been mine, I would have restored her lover to life.

"Three years after that I went to see her. In all this time I had never once seen her alone. Now I could wait no longer. I had not much hope, yet I longed to tell her again of my love. She came into the room where I waited for her, and stood before me. A mortal terror seized upon me, and seemed to chill the blood in my veins. I read in her cold eyes that she knew my secret.

"'Listen to me, Steven Cranston,' she said, in her low yet distinct voice. 'You have come here to ask my love. Hear what I have to say, and consider whether I am likely to give it. I loved Robert Eastman better than my own life. Every hope I had for all the future centred in him. I saw heaven itself through his eyes. If lightning had struck him, if sudden fever had drunk up his life, or slow disease wasted it, I would have been faithful to his memory forever. How much more now? You—you, who professed to love me and care for my happiness, you murdered him. You took away all the hope I had in the world. I know this from my own sure instinct—the instinct which makes every pulse quiver with loathing at the sight of your face or the sound of your voice. But I could not have proved it against you. Even if I could I would not. I had rather you should live, that, perchance, in some eleventh hour, even your soul may find mercy of God. Besides, the time will come when worse than any mere physical death will be the torture of your spirit. He will be avenged by the remorse which shall dog your footsteps like a fiend.'

"As she said these words her cold gray eyes flashed fire upon me, as you have sometimes seen the lightning flash from the cold gray depths of a winter's cloud. I did not answer her a word—contrite confession, bold denial, were alike impossible. I slunk out of the house like a coward. I have never entered it since.

"Soon after that I went to sea, and I have followed it for more than twenty years. Oh! could I ever tell you what I have suffered? Nights, when I would look into the waters and see, plain as I see it now, this Mountain Road, always with Robert Eastman lying dead and ghastly under the poplars—noons, when the winds going by me would shriek with frantic, accusing voices in my ears, and I would wonder that those around me did not hear that pursuing cry, and hang me in their midst as a murderer. Sometimes, where the figure-head of the vessel should have been, I seemed to see Lucia stand—that same withering fire in her cold eyes, and her thin hand pointing down, ever down, to the depths below, and the tortures that waited for me there. Do you wonder I fled from such visions? I came here for rest and quiet, but *he* pursues me still.

"I have told you my story because I could not die with my crime unconfessed, and I am too tired of life to keep my secret any longer. Now you may go and deliver me up to the Philistines."

He stopped. His voice had risen, in the latter part of his confession, to a fierce shriek. A glare as of madness was in his eyes. It seemed to me that it would be but a short step from this excitement to utter phrensy. I strove to soothe him.

"No," I said, "I will not betray you. Heaven is infinite, and there may be mercy yet, even for you. *She* spared you, and so will I. Cry to God, and He may yet hear you."

A wild gleam shot across his face.

"No," he cried, "God's mercy I ask not for—man's mercy I will not have. My hour of doom has come. Fiends wait for me. Twenty-and-five years ago this seventeenth of September Robert Eastman died by my hand. To-day—to-day his unquiet ghost shall be avenged!"

Our horses had been standing still for half an hour under the trees; but, as the last words fell from his lips, he struck the one he rode a sharp, quick blow, and dashed away from me. Breathless with terror, I hurried after him. I was only in time to see him throw himself from his horse and plunge into the Black Pool. I sprang to the ground and rushed to the chasm's brink. As I looked in I had one momentary glimpse of a white, ghastly face, on which sat the impress of everlasting despair; I heard one cry, "Lost—lost—lost!" and the waters closed over him forever.

I hurried to the proper authorities and told my story. No one dreamed of questioning it. Then I came home and threw myself on this bed, from which I may not soon arise. There are few who could bear such a scene unmoved; and to me, with my nerves already weakened and disordered by illness, it had well-nigh proved fatal. It will be long before I shall cease to see that despairing face—to hear that last cry of mortal agony; but calmness will come back to me in time—if not in this life, in the land where there is no work and no device—where the yew and the willow wave forever over the great city of the silent.

The Story of a Man of Business.

Come not, when I am dead,
  To drop thy foolish tears upon my grave,
To trample round my fallen head,
  And vex the unhappy dust thou would'st not save.
There let the wind sweep and the plover cry;
    But thou, go by.

TENNYSON.

THE STORY OF A MAN OF BUSINESS.

I DID not wait to hear the messenger conclude his sentence. Before the last word had died on his lips I was in the saddle, and, putting the spurs to my horse, I dashed away. Only one thought was in my heart, and yet I could not help, even in that mad gallop over the hills, drinking in, through my senses, my fill of beauty. White and still lay the moonlight over the fields on either side. I could see my shadow stretch, Centaur-like, upon the green sward. Not a breath of air was stirring: it was one of those rare nights such as sometimes the late fall gives us—pearls snatched from the necklace of the summer. Pure, and white, and silent was the matchless hour; and yet I was riding on through its stillness toward the home where the woman lay dying who was to die for me.

Involuntarily I slacked my rein as I approached it. This was my old habit when Lilias had stood at the gate to meet me, and I had paused a little to look upon her exceeding beauty, and heighten, by a moment's delay, the rapture of her welcome. It was all a delusion, I know, but I almost thought she stood there now. Under the lilacs by the gate I saw, or seemed to see, the gleam of a white robe; to catch the outlines of a slight, girlish figure; the light of a waiting, expectant face. But it was not she. Lilias Hunt would stand there never again. In that upper chamber, on whose windows the mocking moonlight shone, I knew well that she lay dying. Never again, in all time, would those light feet spring to meet me. Never again should I hear the glad echoes of that voice, sweeter and merrier than all the birds of the forest, as she tripped beside me along the steep paths of the woodland. How could I go in and look upon her now? I stayed my feet at the very gateway.

Again that curious sense took possession of me by means of which the mind, utterly absorbed in one great danger or sorrow, yet takes note of the minutest particulars of surrounding objects. I saw how peaceful was the scene; how the old brown farm-house, battered and stained by the winds and rains of a whole century of years, looked now, in the white moonlight, like a sentient thing, weary and gone to sleep. A faint, sweet scent came from the almost leafless boughs of the sweet-brier at the door. Along the path leading up to it from the gate were autumn blossoms—asters and dahlias; I could even distinguish their colors.

It might have been five minutes, or five seconds, in which I saw all this—I can not tell. Suddenly a voice seemed to say to me,

"Go in there now, you who have killed Lilias! Go in and look upon her before she dies. Wipe the death-sweat from her forehead, and ask her to forgive you, now she is going where the rich and the poor shall all be alike."

I turned, but no one was near. There was nothing round me but the stillness of that beautiful night; only, far off, from among a clump of fir-trees in a distant corner of the yard, came again the last words of the sentence, sighed out like the low refrain of some tune—sorrowful, yet triumphant:

"Where the rich and the poor shall all be alike."

My heart gave one strong, tumultuous throb of anguish. I pushed open the outer door, which was already ajar, and went in. Her mother met me at the foot of the stairs—not weeping, but with a pale, speechless sorrow upon her worn face, more pitiful than any tears.

"I know the way, Mrs. Hunt; let me go to her alone."

She did not speak—she made a motion for me to proceed. Quick as thought I sped up the stairs, and stood within the room where Lilias lay. It was lighted only by the moon-rays. I could see how like herself it looked—pure and neat, and very, very quiet. She was all alone. I went up to her and would have spoken, but something in her face stopped me. A smile sat upon it of ineffable peace. Her dark hair fell heavily over the pillows. Her lips were closed, and one hand lay outstretched upon the coverlet. Tremblingly I touched it. Oh heaven! how cold it was. Those fingers that had been wont to thrill at my lightest touch lay like ice in my clasp. O God! was I then too late? In all the anguish of that wild night-ride this worst fear had never once come to me.

No need now to rain repentant tears—to press throbbing kisses upon that marble brow; and yet the tears fell, and the kisses—fond enough almost to have awakened from the long sleep of death her who had so loved me—were dropped upon her forehead; and yet she stirred not. Crushed and broken was my lily, drooping in this world's cold soil; and the great Gardener had only lifted her up to bloom forever in the fields of the upper country. It availed me nothing now to know that she was gone where the world's cold breath could never again chill her. I would have given more than my life but to have seen those pale lips unclose for one moment—but to have heard her voice say just once, "Harry, I forgive you."

I *loved* Lilias Hunt. Standing this moonlight night—just such a night as that one was, twenty years ago—standing in memory by that death-bed, I tell you I loved her as I never loved another—as man seldom loves woman. And yet my cruelty broke her heart. God forgive me! I can never forgive myself.

She and I were children together. Both our parents were poor. We had walked to school through the flowery lanes, and shared together all our childish sports. When she grew up to innocent and beautiful maidenhood, the love of our childhood had strengthened with our years. I saw in her the ideal woman who was to crown my life. A creature purer or more beautiful never walked forth under the light of heaven than Lilias Hunt, in her glad, innocent youth. I never asked her to marry me. Bad as I am, I never could have broken my plighted troth. My parents had contrived, by severe toil and strict economy, to assist me in obtaining a very good education, and at twenty I left home to study law with a distinguished attorney in a neighboring county. My parting with Lilias was playful, and yet, in my heart, was the hardest struggle I had ever undergone. I had resolved not to tell her my love, and yet it seemed almost impossible to leave her without. I told her she must give me a lock of her hair—a keepsake for the memory of the old school-days. After a little entreaty she consented, and then she said, in a laughing tone, assumed—as I knew it was—to conceal deeper feeling,

"And now, Sir Absolute, you shall lose one of your own brown curls, just by way of retaliation. What a wound your vanity will get, to be sure, for I shall take the very prettiest one, and you'll miss it in your morning devotions before the mirror!"

I submitted laughingly to her illustration of the *lex talionis*, and I went away with her tress of hair lying close to my heart. I have been looking at it to-day. It is dark, and soft, and shining as ever, though the white brow round which it used to wave has been still and pulseless for twenty years under the daisies of the church-yard.

When I left Mayfield that morning, despite my sorrow, a lover's hopes lay warm and strong at my heart. I was young, vigorous, and possessed a fair share of talent. I was sure to succeed, so Hope whispered. I would win a name and a position, and then I would come back to my dove-eyed Lilias. All my struggles should be ennobled by her memory—should have her for their reward.

It was no wonder that I made rapid strides. I think Judge Wentworth was pleased with me. He used to tell me that my future was certain, if I could but hold out as I had begun. I have told you that I was poor. I had neither time nor money to spare for frequent visits to Mayfield. I had resolved to remain six months in Windham before going home even for a day. In the mean time I did not allow myself the luxury of writing to Lilias. It would not be right, I thought, until I could ask her to share my life. She had never said that she loved me; but I had seen her cheek flush and her soft eye kindle at my coming, and I knew that I could trust her. I was contented to wait.

Three months of my absence had passed away, when, one morning, Judge Wentworth said to me,

"You have heard of my niece, Clara Barton? Mrs. Wentworth and I have long considered her as an adopted daughter. She has filled the place of our own children, whom God saw fit to take away. She has been absent on a visit ever since you came here; but this morning we expect her back, and I want you to join us at tea to-night, and make her acquaintance. There is very little society here at all suited to her taste, but you and she will have many things in common."

I had heard, through other sources, of Judge Wentworth's orphan niece—of her pride, her wealth, her beauty. I could hardly expect to be received into her society on a footing of equality, but I was very curious to see her. All I had heard of her, however, had not prepared me for the vision which greeted me when I entered the judge's parlor.

Among all the women I have ever met I have never seen Clara Barton's peer. Lilias was quite as beautiful; but between them was a difference not unlike that which exists between a wild rose, hanging fair, and fragrant, and wet with dew upon its parent stem, and some regal blossom of the tropics, lifting its proud head in lonely grandeur under the fiery beams of southern suns, and filling the air with a fragrance subtle, intoxicating, dangerous. I stood still for a moment at the door, forgetful of courtesy and propriety, and looked at her.

She was a woman not much more than twenty, but her form was full, mature, regal. She was above the medium height, and yet not exactly tall. She wore a plain white dress, with no ornaments save a band of curiously-wrought African gold on each rounded arm, a bunch of crimson roses upon her bosom, and another drooping low in her jet-black hair. Her forehead was low and smooth, with the hair waving away from it, and gathered, Grecian fashion, in heavy coils at the back of her neck. Her complexion was a clear, dark olive, with a rich crimson tint that came and went in the cheeks. Her mouth was small and proud. Her face indicated a strong and positive will, and her great black eyes were full of slumbering fire and power. Nothing, I repeat, could have been more unlike Lilias. In cultivating the acquaintance of this haughty beauty I apprehended no danger to my heart.

She did interest me exceedingly. Her conversation was brilliant; her thoughts were fresh and original, and she reserved most of them for me, seldom exerting herself to talk much with others—a tacit compliment to which no man's vanity is ever insensible.

The history of the events that followed, in one blind, dizzy whirl, my first introduction to Clara Barton, is so incomprehensible, even to myself, that I despair of ever making it clear to another.

I had not known Miss Barton long before I discovered—how, I can not to this day tell, for she never descended for one moment from the pedestal of her own dignity—that she loved me, and was resolved to be my wife. I was flattered by her preference, as, I think, any man would have been; but for a long while every beat of my heart was faithful to Lilias. I was daily invited to the judge's on one pretext or another. Sometimes it was a book I was to bring; a song I was to practice with Clara; a rare flower I was to examine; and sometimes I went because it had become my habit to go, and I was lonely away. After a time I began to listen to the voice of ambition. I was proud and poor. Next to love, ambition was the regnant passion of my nature; for a time it overpowered even love itself. I had known what poverty was. From my childhood it had stung me, crushing out warmth and light from my life. If I married Lilias we must both suffer its stings together. Our children must grow up to struggle with it as I had done. No leisure for the æsthetic part of life; no means to surround one's self with works of art, choice books, rare pictures. And in return for these privations what should I have? A low, soft voice, like Lilias Hunt's own, spoke in my heart, and answered, "Love;" but the tones of ambition hushed it into silence. Tauntingly they said to me,

"You have seen love and poverty in the home of your childhood. Did love make poverty less grim? Did it keep your mother's eye bright and her cheek young? Did it shed a silken lustre over her faded calico gown? Marry your pale, fair Lilias, if you will, and see her eyes grow dim with care, her hands grow coarse, her slender figure bowed and thin; and then look into those eyes, and try to recall the bright young Lilias of your love till your tears come at the very contrast. Or, marry Clara Barton; be Judge Wentworth's partner and adopted son; be the husband of a wife, rich not only, but cultivated, graceful, accomplished—loving you, too, with all the might of her tropical heart. Leave Lilias in maiden peace. You do not know that she loves you—you have never asked her—and by-and-by some other will woo and win her, one rich enough to set worthily the gem of her bright young beauty—to make her happier than you ever could."

Alas! even then the thought that any other should ever make the happiness of Lilias Hunt smote my heart with a sudden, deathly pang. To stifle it I went out of the house—it was an afternoon in the late summer—and walked hurriedly toward Judge Wentworth's. I had no purpose in this visit beyond the wish to divert my mind from unwelcome thoughts; and yet it must have been fate or Providence which led my steps there at that hour. I pushed open the door without knocking, as was my habit since I had become such a familiar visitor, and went into the parlor. Clara Barton was its only occupant. She raised her head from the arm of the sofa as I went toward her. She had been weeping. A bright red spot burned on either cheek, and round, shining tears still glittered upon her heavy lashes. Her eyes flashed, and her voice was full of pride and passion.

"I did not want to see you, Mr. Lincoln. You had no right—you of all others—to come stealing upon me thus—to surprise me in my weakness."

Was it I, or some demon voice within me, which answered her? In that hour my soul fell from its high estate. I sat down beside her, and put my arm around her. I said,

"Give me the right—me of all others—Clara, to

share all your sorrows—to shield you from grief, as far as in me lies, through the whole of our two lives."

I had crossed the Rubicon. There was no longer any room for repentance, though I might seek it with tears and anguish.

Her answer was a burst of weeping. That proud head sank upon my shoulder—that little hand, flashing with jewels, was laid in mine—and, almost before I knew it, I was betrothed to Clara Barton. And yet never had my love for Lilias surged in my heart more wildly than in this very moment, when I had raised up between us an invincible barrier forever! I saw her then as I had seen her last, standing in the shadow of the lilacs at the farm-house gate, her tender eyes sad and misty with the sorrow of parting; her sweet, pale face uplifted to the summer sky. But she was my Lilias no longer, even in hope. Forever must roll between us the inexorable tide of a destiny of my own creating. Ah! I wonder if Clara Barton felt the passionate beats of the heart against which her head was resting, and thought they were for her?

Well, in three months more I was a married man. I never knew exactly how this happened. I certainly had not expected it myself. I think it all originated with Clara, whose influence with the judge was unbounded. At all events, he sounded me on the subject, and gave the plan his warmest approbation. He did not believe in long engagements, he said; Clara's fortune would be enough for us both; I might as well be married, and continue my studies afterward. And so, one warm November day, I walked up the church aisle with a stately figure, robed in bridal satin, upon my arm, and went out again—a husband. I wonder if there was a single hour of real happiness in the winter which followed? I had striven to cast the memory of Lilias Hunt out of my heart, and sometimes, with my wife's head lying upon my breast, looking into her eyes, toying with her hair, I cheated myself into believing that I was happy. My ambition was satisfied; my taste for wealth and splendor was fully gratified; I was no longer the poor student, with his uncertain way to work out alone. Rich and influential friends were around me; power and fortune were in my grasp; and for these things I had given up love and Lilias.

I think Clara loved me truly, but it was with a passion like her nature, self-willed and imperious. She had little in her character of self-abnegation or silent fortitude.

I did not carry her to Mayfield until the next spring. My parents did not rejoice in my good fortuno as earnestly as I had expected. In especial, I could see something of disappointment in my mother. I think she had suspected my love for Lilias Hunt, and she would have far rather seen me married to a gentle woman, in my own rank in life, than the possessor of Clara Barton's fortune. Still, she received my wife lovingly, for my sake; but I could see that my humble home was a dull place for Clara, and I determined to cut our visit short.

The day before we left I was driving through the town in my own luxurious carriage, with my wife beside me. Going slowly along a well-known road, I met Lilias Hunt and her father, face to face. They, too, were riding in their humble, old-fashioned wagon, and as they slowly drew near, I could see them distinctly. Oh heaven! that white, white face! Was that my Lilias? As she saw me she crimsoned to her very temples, and then turned pale as death. Slowly I saw her head sink and sink, till she lay, like one dead, across her trembling old father's knees. I would have given all the world but to have snatched that fair head to my bosom—to have covered that pale brow with my kisses; but I was a slave, as is every man or woman who sells heart and hand for wealth and a name. I drove on, and left Lilias Hunt lying there in her father's arms, without one word.

"Poor thing, I should think she had the consumption!" said my wife, carelessly, as we passed along. "Do you know her, Harry?"

I do not think the finest alchemy of even the most jealous love could have detected any change in my voice as I answered,

"I used to; her name is Hunt."

The next day we left Mayfield. Oh, how glad I was to go back to business—to drown, or strive to drown, in the great turbulent battle of life, one weak woman's voice, whose tones must haunt me forever; to bury myself in study, closing doors and windows, and shut out the gleam of one pale, still face. And yet there were hours when memory was omnipotent—when I looked on my wife's beauty, or listened to her words, as one in a dream—and my heart kept its sorrowful tryst beside the lilac-trees with Lilias Hunt. All that summer I never heard from her, except that once this brief sentence, in the postscript to one of my mother's letters, filled my heart with a vague sense of dread:

"Lilias Hunt is very feeble, and they doubt if she will ever recover."

It was the late autumn before I again visited Mayfield. This time my wife did not accompany me. The old farm-house was never much to her taste, and I was willing enough to leave her behind.

Almost my first inquiry was for Lilias Hunt. I was told that for some time she had been considered in a decline, but, my mother added, she thought her malady was of the heart rather than the flesh. I had been home only three days when the messenger came who told me she was dying. She had heard of my presence in the village—she wanted to see me.

I have told you of my mad night-ride over the hills, and how, when I stood by her bedside, it was too late. I could only kneel beside her, and rain my repentant tears on eyes that would not open—pour out my agonized prayers for forgiveness to ears that would never again listen. And yet sometimes I think that she heard me, even then, my dead Lilias; that from heaven she has forgiven me, and is waiting for my coming. God knows!

When they robed her for the burial, her mother found, lying upon her innocent heart, a locket, such as her small means could purchase, containing the curl she had severed from my head the last time I ever heard her voice. They left it there.

Twenty years have passed since then. Honor and fame have come to me. My stately, fashionable wife has walked or sat by my side. Merry children have sported round my knee, and grown up to manhood and womanhood; but Lilias has slept on through the years very quietly, with willows waving above her grave, and my hair lying still upon her virgin breast. Ah! I have sometimes thought they buried my heart with it.

The Cottage on the Hill.

An old woman, in an old farm-house, sitting in an old high-backed chair, and knitting by the fire, is made so, probably. There is scarcely a boy in the barn-yard or a girl in the kitchen who suspects for a moment she was ever any thing else than an old woman knitting in a high-backed chair. * * * * The table on which you write was part of a tree once. Heavens! how merrily it swung in the great March winds, in the wild December storms! How it bloomed in May and reddened in October, and was as sensitive and responsive to the touch of light and breeze as a girl's cheek to her lover's look and whisper! Would you believe it? Steady old table! it holds your dinner, your books, your coffin, but it tells no tales.

GEORGE WILLIAM CURTIS (*Trumps*).

THE COTTAGE ON THE HILL.

I WISH I were an artist, that I might preface my story with a vignette. It should be a little brown cottage, with low, sloping eaves, and the moss thick and gray upon its shingled roof. There should be trees in front, and a rambling, carelessly-built stone wall, overgrown with sweet-brier and woodbine, shutting it off from the highway. On the eastern side I would paint a garden—not a great, well-kept garden, full of gay flowers and thrifty vegetables, such as you often see beside a substantial country farm-house, but one with a few blossoms, and herbs, and berries, such as a woman's hand could keep in order. In front of the garden I would draw the same rambling-looking wall, only, instead of sweet-brier and woodbine, gooseberry and currant bushes should grow thick and green behind it, and, in their midst, you should see, as I did one July morning, years ago, old Mother Margery, as the villagers called her, busily gathering the ripe red currants, and dropping them, sprig by sprig, into her tin basin.

I was going to school with a companion, a bold, black-eyed girl a year or two older than myself. The highway was white with the summer dust. The locust blossoms, which we were not tall enough to reach, drooped downward over head, tantalizing us with their fragrance. It was so warm the birds had ceased to sing, perching lazily with folded wings; and, looking over the wall, there was something very inviting in the ripe currants and dewy roses under the shade-trees of the little garden.

"I do think the old woman is so mean," said Jane Anderson as we walked along. "She never gives us so much as a hollyhock; and that caraway would be real good this hot morning, to say nothing of the currants. Hey, Mother Margery!" she exclaimed, in a louder tone, as we drew near, "you're picking currants, I s'pose, for your husband and children, and haven't any to spare?"

Mother Margery lifted her gray eyes and gazed full upon her. There was an angry gleam in them, chased away, in an instant, by an expression of wounded feeling, but she made no reply.

I pitied her, and pulled Jane's arm to draw her away.

"Hush!" I said; "you shall not say any thing to pain her. She is old, and she is alone. What if you should be, some day?"

I thought there was a look of grateful surprise in the old woman's face, but she did not speak, and we passed along.

For the next two or three days, as we went by to school, we did not see Mother Margery. But at last, one morning, as I was passing alone, she came out and spoke to me.

"Won't you come in?" she said, in a voice which, though cracked and unmusical, was still friendly. "You are a good child, and I'd like to give you some of the roses I see you looking at. I am old, as you said, and all alone. I have more flowers and fruit than I can use myself."

I thanked her warmly. I had never entered the little garden before, and, like all prohibited places, it seemed a sort of Paradise. The roses, of which she gave me a large bunch, were redder and sweeter than any which grew in other gardens, and the currants and caraway were enjoyed with a keener zest.

After that I went frequently to see her, for I thought it gave her pleasure, and to visit one of whom the world knew so little, seemed to me a rare treat. Often I helped her in her tasks, and read to her the favorite hymns and verses of Holy Writ, which were no longer legible to her dimming sight. She was always kind, but never communicative, though she listened with pleasure to the little incidents of my own life, and it grew, at length, into a habit to confide in her.

At fifteen came my first love-dream. The star which rose then set soon after, or, rather, I discovered it to have been a rush-light after all, and a breath blew it out. But at the time my feelings seemed very real, and I carried them, at once, to my customary confessor.

"Do you love this young man then so much?" asked Mother Margery, rather sadly, when I had concluded my recital.

"Oh yes," I answered fervently, "there never was, and there never will be, another like him."

"Beware, child, of giving all your heart up to a human idol. God never blesses such a love. I will tell you my story. It will not hurt me to call back the long past now, when the blood flows still and sluggish in my veins, and my steps are so near the shadow of death; and, perhaps, it will do you good to listen.

"You can not see in my wrinkled face and dim eyes

any remnants of youth or beauty, but I was young, and fresh, and blithesome once, though I was never very pretty. Such as I was, Harry Pierson loved me, and at seventeen I promised to be his wife. Oh, how I loved him! I was an orphan, and he was all I had. I could not see God in those days, because of His creature of whom I had made an idol. Harry was ambitious, but he was poor. At twenty-one he resolved to go to college. College learning wasn't so common a thing then as it is now, and his friends looked upon it as a great, nay, an impossible undertaking. I only encouraged him. We had been engaged two years then. All that time I had been working at my trade as a tailoress. I went from house to house, with my goose and my thimble, and earned thus a great deal more than was sufficient for my simple wants.

"How well I remember telling him so, one summer evening, as we walked beneath the orchard trees, and talked of his going to college. I had a proposal to make, on which I ventured timidly, for Harry was very proud. Looking up after I had told him how much money I could earn, I said—I tried to say it in a quiet, matter-of-fact way—

"'So you see, Harry, I can help you a little. Besides my clothes, I shall have, every year, more than a hundred dollars that I shan't know what to do with. You shall take that, and pay it back to me in gowns and bonnets by-and-by.'

"He drew me to his heart. Old woman as I am, I thank God that once in my life I have been infolded in a clasp of such strong tenderness. He looked in my eyes, and the tears his manly pride would not let him shed gathered heavily in his own.

"'You are a good girl,' he said—'a good girl, Margery—too good for me, but you must never say this to me again. True heart, pure heart! much as I had loved you, it needed this to help me sound the depths of your nature. Thank you that you have said it; but, as you love me, you must never say it again. Food that your poor little earnings bought would choke me. I would saw wood from door to door before I would use money for which your weak, woman's hands had toiled. But I know how well you love me now, and that will be the best help of all. God bless you, Margery.'

"I saw how determined he was, and that it was of no use for me to try to help him in that way, but I resolved then and there what I would do with my money. It doesn't take much to buy a little cottage and a patch of garden ground in the country, and there rose up, for my comfort, a mental picture of the snug home which should await him when he came from college—which I would earn for my marriage dowry. I had four years to do it in.

"During the next three years Harry's life was a great deal harder than mine. I saw him only once in a year, during the shortest vacations. In the others he taught school. In term-time, besides keeping at the head of his class, he toiled perseveringly in every possible opening for his support. He was literally a hewer of wood and a drawer of water. Every time I saw him the change from his fresh youth startled me more and more. But he laughed at my fears. He was only tired, he said—a little overworked. When he was through college he should get rested and be well again, and I tried to believe him. At the end of the third year he seemed more than ever weak and exhausted, and he was obliged to confess that his labors were almost too severe. At that time we settled it that as soon as he graduated we should be married, and he should open a select school, which he had been encouraged to think would succeed in our native village. I remember when we parted, though we had been discussing these things hopefully and cheerfully, there was a great weight at my heart—a shadow of coming sorrow. He looked so frail, so spiritual, with the gleaming light in his eyes and the glow on his transparent forehead. But I tried to cast aside my fears.

"I was in high health then myself. My three years had been passed so quietly—my toil had been brightened by such blessed hopes. From day to day and week to week I had gone steadily on, laying up my earnings, until now I had nearly four hundred dollars; enough to purchase this little house and garden patch, for the house was not new or fashionable even then, and land was not so high in Ryefield as it is now. The next year I should earn enough to furnish it simply and humbly, in accordance with our modest wants.

"Harry's college life closed in July, and, by the spring before, I had the little brown cottage all arranged to my mind. I hired a neighbor to help me make the garden. We set out gooseberry and currant bushes; we transplanted roses and flower roots; and, when all was done, it seemed the fairest of homes to my love and my fancy. My needle flew very nimbly in those days, for my heart was glad, and quickest fingers could scarcely keep time to its joyous beatings. Sundays I used to go to my little cottage—our home that was to be—to watch the flowers springing up in the garden, or stand at the door of the tiny parlor and fancy my student-husband sitting in the low easy-chair at the open window, and drawing in life and strength from the outside summer of bird, and flower, and breeze.

"Perhaps into those weeks of joyful anticipation was compressed happiness enough for my lifetime. Of Harry's truth I had never a single doubt. Well-meaning persons suggested to me sometimes, in mistaken kindness, that I must not depend on him too much; that he was getting an education which would place him far above me, and perhaps he might find some one who would suit him better. Thank God, these shafts fell powerless.

"Just about a week before I was expecting to see him in Ryefield, a letter came to me in a strange hand. I broke the seal with tremulous fingers. A mist swam before my eyes, so that I could hardly read its contents. With difficulty I comprehended the truth. Harry was prepared to graduate with the highest honors of his class, when, just one week before examination, his strength had given way, and now he lay there, feeble and helpless, praying for me to come to him before he died. There were no railroads then, but I reached him in twenty-four hours, traveling day and night by stage.

"When I stood by his bedside I lost my self-command—though I had resolved to be very brave—and the tears rolled down my cheeks. I had not been prepared to see him looking so pale and attenuated, so much like a spirit. The soul in his eyes beamed brighter than ever, but the bodily life seemed utterly wasted away. He was dying of exhaustion.

"The next few hours were full, in the midst of our

strong agony, of a peace and trust too sacred for words. I remember their every utterance, but no third person can share them; they must die with me. We were married the next morning. He objected at first. He said he would not burden me with his weakness and his suffering—that I should not take his hand to go down with him into the night. Then I showed him my heart, and he knew that all my life was in his love—that it would be best for us both. We were married, and I took my husband home. The doctor said the change could not hurt him, and I had great hopes that native air, and the tender care of one who loved him so, would give back the strength to his failing limbs.

"He was so weak and helpless that he depended on me like a little child. He had never even asked where I would take him. We were five days making the journey, in an old-fashioned chaise which I had hired for the purpose. The afternoon of the fifth day we wound slowly up the hill toward the little cottage. Harry's head lay upon my breast.

"'Look up,' I said, rousing him, 'here is home. That little house is yours and mine, love; I earned it in these last four years for us to live in.'

"He said nothing, but he lifted up his head and looked at it eagerly, with the color coming and going very fast in his wan cheek. Then he sank back again, closer, closer against my heart, and drew my hand silently over his wet eyes. It needed no words to tell me how fully my husband blessed me in that moment, though words were not wanting afterward, of wonder at my self-denial and perseverance—of praise and passionate love.

"I supported him from the gate up to the house door. I led him in, and made him rest on the lounge in the comfortable parlor, and, seeing him there, despite sickness and sorrow I was happy.

"That was the golden summer of my life. Harry did not suffer much pain. He was not very sick, only weak. He loved to sit, as I had fancied he would, at the open window, drinking in the sights and sounds of the beautiful nature outside. I was always near him at my sewing. The neighbors were very kind. They gave me all the work I could do, so that we wanted for nothing which could help to make Harry comfortable. I felt sure, all the while, that he would recover. He was so cheerful, entering into all my plans, and never saying any thing that could dishearten me. He was my idol, but I did not think God would take him from me.

"The summer passed away at last. The apples grew ripe upon the trees, and the grape-vines hung heavy with their purple clusters. But the bracing winds brought no strength to my patient sufferer, and when the leaves fell the light of his life went out. Oh, I can not talk about it. I loved him too well to tell you, calmly, how he died. My arms were round him. His last kiss, his last prayer, his last blessing were for his 'true wife—Margery;' his last breath came faintly against my clinging lips. Oh, I had not thought he could have died and the life-blood still coursed through my veins—I, who loved him so—who was one flesh with him. But he has slept for forty years come next 28th of October in the village church-yard, and I am here still.

"I have lived in this house ever since. I could not

go out again into the world. I had work enough brought me here to keep cold and hunger away from my dwelling, and I asked nothing more. He was gone, and with him earthly hope died, and all of life was memory. Perhaps, I can not say, if I had loved him less, God would not have taken him from me. But the long grief is over now. You said once that I was alone, but that word, which seemed so terrible to you, has no sting for me. Other love could never be to me in place of the dead, and I thank God calmly, at every sunset, that I am one day nearer the time when Harry Pierson shall dwell with me forever in a mansion not made with hands, eternal in the heavens."

I went away sorrowfully and in silence, for I recognized in my own love no counterpart to this long-enduring devotion, which time and poverty could not chill, and death had only power to make immortal.

Mother Margery is dead long ago. I heard the bell toll for her seventy-two years of life, but it sounded to me like marriage chimes, for I knew she was old and gray no longer, in heaven, and in the spring-time of her immortal youth she was standing once more beside the lover of her girlhood.

A stately mansion rises now on the hill which the little brown cottage crowned in years gone by, but no flowers in its well-kept garden are half so sweet as Mother Margery's roses, and all that art and wealth can do for its embellishment fades into insignificance before the simple tale of that true woman's love.

Joanna, the Actress.

And she too, that princess fair,
If her bloom be now less rare,
Let her have her youth again—
Let her be as she was then.
Let her have her proud, dark eyes,
And her petulant, quick replies;
Let her sweep her dazzling hand,
With its gesture of command,
And shake back her raven hair
With the old imperious air.

MATTHEW ARNOLD.

JOANNA, THE ACTRESS.

I.

FROM dawning the rain has fallen drearily, until now it is toward nightfall. Perhaps it is fittest the tale I have to tell should be told on such a day, with such a cold, gray, weeping sky above, such phantom winds wailing ghost-like and pitiful around. And yet, looking backward over the years, the first picture that meets my eyes is a very fair one.

An old English rectory, with broad, smooth lawn in front, and rows of stately trees shutting it away from the main road. On the portico sits an elderly lady, placidly smiling to herself as she knits. She is unmistakably a refined person. Her soft but silvery hair is put plainly away from a brow almost as smooth as in youth. Her muslin cap and kerchief are unsullied in their purity, and the hands so busily plying the knitting-needles are small and delicate. In spite of the mild serenity of her face, however, she looks like one whose prejudices, not easily aroused, would yet be strong as life.

In the shade of the thick trees are walking, or rather strolling, a young man, the Rector of Eversley, and son of the old lady in the portico, and leaning upon his arm his foster-sister, Joanna. She is a girl not more than seventeen, and very beautiful. Her figure is tall and commanding, her complexion a clear olive, and her eyes black, with an intensity of slumbering power in their expression.

She was a legacy to Mrs. Huntington from a dying friend, and the good lady had received her tenderly and carefully educated her. Father, mother, fortune she had none, save this kind adopted mother, and the few hundred pounds which the Rev. Ralph Huntington, former Rector of Eversley, dying, had bequeathed to her.

Ralph Huntington, junior, the present rector and successor to his father, was a young man at least ten years her senior. He had a face outwardly calm, but which yet gave indications of latent strength. He had clear blue eyes, a lofty forehead, well-cut features, and a decided-looking mouth. Just at present he was listening, with a deprecatory air, to his companion's light words:

"No, I won't, Ralph. I won't stay here and be quiet Mrs. Ralph Huntington, No. 2, and sit by the chimney-corner in winter, or on the portico in summer, knitting stockings and cutting out clothing for the Eversley poor children. I tell you I feel within me the promptings of a different destiny. I can not help my fate. Every man, and woman too, must work their own weird. Yours is to stay here and preach, and visit the poor and sick; mine—" and her eyes kindled.

"Yours is to ruin me and break my mother's heart," said Ralph Huntington, sadly.

The proud eyes softened. "Not so, Ralph. You are cruel. You know your mother is dear to me as if she were my own, and you—I *do* love you, Ralph."

"And yet you are leaving me; giving me up voluntarily; putting a barrier between us no love can scale; burying all our dreams of the future; for the sake of what, Joanna? Of hearing from a senseless throng a few shouts, of having a few flower-wreaths thrown at your feet, of being a mark for the pursuit of every titled spendthrift."

The eyes flashed again. "Not so, Ralph; you do me bitter wrong. Your faith and mine are different. Did you not say yourself, when we read Shakspeare together, that I would make a finer actress than had trod the boards since Mrs. Siddons? Did God create faculties, and shower gifts as an idle freak? No! He means me to use mine, and so I will. I am going to London. I shall become an actress—a glorious one. You know that as well as I do, and—then I will be your wife, if you will have me, Ralph."

He buried his face in his hands and smothered a groan.

"Joanna, do you know how you are tempting me? A minister—a clergyman of the Church, to marry an actress! You know it is impossible. I must give you up, or I must give up my vows, my profession, all that my reason and my religion acknowledge as sacred. Joanna, God knows how I love you! I would do all but peril my soul for your sake, but I must not drink the cup you offer me. Oh! will you not turn away from this mad fancy? Is *your* love, then, dead, Joanna? Have you forgotten the days when you first came to us, a sobbing orphan? Then you loved me—then you clung to me, and I sheltered you in my bosom. Oh! I thought to keep you there always. I thought to see you my happy, peaceful wife, lighting up my home with your beauty, filling it with the melody of your voice—here, where I could love you, cherish you, watch over you, guard you from every stain or sorrow of earth. *Will* you go, Joanna?"

The tears gathered and sparkled on her long lashes, but she dashed them away with an impatient gesture:

"I remember all—I know all, but I can heed nothing. I must go; I shall go; I tell you my fate calls me. Selfish! Do not make it harder for me."

"And so you will go to my mother and say, 'Mother, in vain your love has cherished me, your heart has clung to me. I am going away from you into the great world you dread so much—going to be an actress; to win fame that is dearer to me than friends, or mother, or love.'"

How the eyes flashed now!

"Stop, Ralph," she cried. "I will not have you so unjust, so cruel. You know I shall do no such thing. She will understand me better than you do. I shall say to her, 'Mother, my destiny is calling me. I must go out into the world, but I will be pure, I will be good; I will be true to your teachings; and when I have fulfilled my mission, I will come back home better than I went, and be your quiet daughter.' That is what I *will* say, what I *must* say, and she will understand me."

"At least you will not say it to-night? Let her rest one more night in peace. I tell you, Joanna, this blow will break her heart."

"Well, I will wait till to-morrow; and now, Ralph, once more you shall be my audience—my teacher."

The mad girl bowed her graceful figure, threw herself into an attitude, and commenced the recital of the supper-scene in Macbeth. He was vexed — as near angry as he could be with her; and yet there was such fascination in her voice, her wonderful power of impersonation, that he could not stop her. He listened.

They did not go in until after Mrs. Huntington had rung for lights, and assembled her little household in readiness for her son to read the evening prayers.

When these were over and the servants had left the room, she remained for some time talking to her children with unusual tenderness. She spoke of her dead husband; of their happy life together; of the long past time when he brought her to that same peaceful home a bride; of the children that, one by one, had glided, phantom-like, from the shelter of her arms, and lain down in the village church-yard; and then she told her son what a comfort he had been to her all the days of his life; and, solemnly laying her hand upon his head, she prayed that God might pour upon him the fullness of blessing forevermore.

"And you too, my Joanna," she said, drawing the girl to her motherly bosom, "you have been to me as my own in the place of the dead. You have been very good to me, my daughter, and I pray that you may walk through life in the pleasant paths of our Father's peace."

She kissed them both with a strange, clinging tenderness, and then, taking her candle, she went alone up the stairs, to the chamber so desolate now, where her dead husband had slept so many years beside her, where he had died, and whence he had been carried forth to the burial.

"We have left mother too much to sit alone," said Joanna, thoughtfully. "We were out in the shrubbery all this evening, and so her mind went backward to her dead husband and children. I am afraid it's not good for her. When I am gone, you must be with her more."

Ralph Huntington did not answer; he could not; and she went up to him, this strange, impulsive girl, and kissed him. It was the first kiss she had ever voluntarily given him since the days of her childhood. He took her to his heart and held her there for one moment, and then, opening his arms, he said,

"There, go, and may the Lord guide you, Joanna."

That night there came to the silent house a mysterious visitor. No one knew the hour of his coming; but the next morning, when the breakfast was brought in, they waited a few moments for the mother, and then Joanna went to call her. Ralph Huntington had followed to the foot of the stairs. He heard her enter the room, and then, startled at the strange silence, he went up also. The young girl stood at the bedside, with fixed gaze and face pale as marble, and there lay his mother, with the smile frozen upon her placid mouth, her half-open eyes cold and glassy—dead! The messenger, who comes but once to any, had sought her in her sleep.

This great sorrow drew the hearts of those two mourners nearer to each other. It was almost pitiful to see Joanna striving to soothe her lover's grief—quietly, noiselessly taking the place of the departed—superintending the household, summoning the servants for morning and evening prayers, even attending patiently to all the poor of the parish who had been the dead Mrs. Huntington's pensioners.

The year of mourning was fully over before any thing was done to break in upon the solemn calm which had fallen upon their lives. Ralph Huntington had said not one word in the mean time of the love which every day had deepened, and which constantly spoke, in spite of himself, in the tender looks he bent upon her; the nameless attentions and care for her smallest comfort; in the very tones of his voice.

Again it was summer. Prayers were just over, and the two sat together in the rectory parlor. Joanna spoke:

"Next week, Ralph, I shall leave you. I have waited, because I wished to pass this year of sorrow quietly; I wished to help you as best I could to bear it. But my arrangements are all made. I am going to London to be fitted for the stage. I shall reside in the family of a manager who heard me read when I was last there, and who has promised me an engagement. You will not see or hear from me again until I have succeeded."

Ralph Huntington could not have started with more surprise if the earth had opened at his feet. He only turned toward her with a blind, questioning gaze; he only said, in tones half of inquiry, half of passionate reproach,

"Joanna?"

"It is useless, Ralph. Do not let us waste the time we have yet to be together in persuasions or reproaches. My mind is made up, and the whole world could not change it; my word is given; I go to London next week."

"Have you thought, Joanna? You have voluntarily taken my mother's place—in the house, in the parish, with the poor. Does not duty call on you to *keep* it—you, her daughter by love, by care, by adoption?"

"Is that generous, Ralph? Because I have sacrificed my own plans to help you for one year, to call on me to resign them? I am independent. I am eighteen years old now—old enough to choose, and I have chosen for myself. I shall abide by it."

"Yes," he said, bitterly, "you have chosen—chosen sin, worldliness, vanity; nay, ingratitude—chosen to give up home, love, peace."

"You are wrong, you are unkind; but you love me, and I forgive you. I have not chosen as you say. I have chosen to follow the leading of my own genius, to obey my destiny. Instead of ordering dinners and mending linen, to be—myself—to live my largest, fullest life. I *will not* give it up!"

He drew nearer to her. His voice took a tenderer tone:

"Joanna, you *will* not give up my love? Can any other love you as I have loved you—I, who have cherished you all the days of your life? When you were a little, wee, helpless girl, and came here first, a dark, elfin-looking thing, with your black robes, your black eyes and hair, and your pale face, my heart made its election. Do you mean I shall cease to love you now?"

"I mean you *shall not.* I defy you to cease to love me, Ralph Huntington. I *will* have your love. I *will* reign over your heart. You *know* this. I will come back after a while, if you will have me, and be your wife."

"Hear me, Joanna. I will *not* have you. You have well said, I shall love you to my death. My heart owns your sway. I can not cast you off, but I tell you before heaven that, if you are an actress, you shall never be my wife. I may love you so that my heart will break, so that the life will die out of my tortured being, but I will not marry you. I am a priest of the most High God. I will not give up my vocation—I will not bring a stain upon my calling. Nay, I need a wife—I shall even think it my duty to woo and win some other woman to share my life. Will you have it so, Joanna?"

She laughed scornfully.

"Yes, if you *can* do it; but your chains will not be easily broken. You say *you* will not give up your vocation. Neither will I, nor yet will I give you up. I will haunt you. You will see me ever beside you—at nightfall, in the quiet noonday, ay, even in your pulpit, you will look down and see my face in the old familiar pew, and memory will overmaster you. If you seek to woo another, you will call her Joanna by mistake, and the name will summon to your side a spirit—a fierce, uncontrollable spirit, which yet you love, which yet loves you. You do not know how, from a child, this purpose of being an actress has been growing strong within me. I used to loathe, sometimes, with unspeakable loathing, this still, quiet life. In the rectory garden, walking all alone, visions of the great, bright, far-off world would haunt me; I would hear the applause of the multitude like the noise of many waters in my ears, and the purpose has grown with my growth, until, I tell you, I would die sooner than give it up."

Her face glowed with enthusiasm as she ceased speaking. He felt, rather than thought, that she was more beautiful than ever; and with this there came to him a blinding, suffocating, choking sense of loss—a feeling as if something more than his own life was being taken from him, and suddenly he fell down at her feet in the utter prostration of a deathly swoon.

She chafed his hands and bathed his temples, and very soon he recovered. He rose, and she said, calmly,

"Good-night, Ralph," and without another word left the room.

She kept her resolution. The next week she went to London—alone, for she would not permit Ralph to accompany her. He was left to the darkness, the loneliness, the silence of his blighted existence. She went forth in her proud beauty, her hope, her strength, to work out alone her problem of life.

II.

Three years after, the name of Rev. Ralph Huntington, Rector of Eversley, appeared in the list of arrivals at the Globe Hotel. It was afternoon, and the rector sat alone in his room, gazing listlessly into the fire. He had come up to London with no business, no settled purpose; driven by an impatient longing to see, or at least to hear, something of Joanna. In the past three years he was fearfully changed. He was only thirty-one, but he looked ten years older than that. There were already silver threads among the curling rings of his brown hair. His face was thin, his figure slightly bent, and his blue eyes wore a look sad, yet steadfast, as of one who has no more to hope from life.

There was a tap upon his door—then a waiter entered, placed a letter in his hand, and retired. What was there in that bold, yet delicate chirography of the superscription to bring such a sudden crimson to his pale cheek, to make his fingers tremble so as he broke the seal? Inside there were but a few lines, which said,

"Go to-night to the Princess's Theatre, Rev. Ralph Huntington; look well to the stage, and you will see Joanna. Such contact will not tarnish your holy cloth for once, and it is your only chance of seeing her whom I know, as well as if you had told me, you seek in London."

That was all—no date, no signature, no clew to her abode. Those, his parishioners, his brother clergymen, who thought Ralph Huntington such a calm, saintly man, so far above all the passions of earth, would not have comprehended the emotion which, for the first moment, seemed to paralyze all the faculties of his being; which, the next, caused him to press that sheet of paper to his lips; then to sink upon his knees, murmuring a woman's name in tones of adjuration, of reproach, of entreaty; which made him pray to God such prayers for strength as are only borne upward, from our hearts to our lips, by tide-waves of sorest trouble.

That mocking, half-derisive letter was answered as Joanna knew well that it would be. When she went upon the stage that night Ralph Huntington's face was one of the first to meet her eye. What shall I say of her acting? She was determined to convince *him* that she had not mistaken her vocation. She played as she had never played before. Again and again the house rang with applause, and every time her eye sought his, as if in his presence was the crowning glory.

Not once was his gaze removed from her face. In the intervals of her acting, when her features were in repose, he noted her most keenly. To him, the face whose changes he had watched from childhood revealed a history. She had triumphed, but she had also suffered. Her cheek was a shade thinner, her figure the least in the world less rounded and symmetrical. But there was something gone which he valued more than bloom and symmetry—her faith in the world, her trust, her unconsciousness of sin. In her actual life he knew she was blameless. He had confidence no less in her principles than in her love—the memory-spell which would link her to him, to the pure atmosphere of her early home. And yet the delicate green was gone from the leaf, the primrose tint from the blossom. He read this, alas! too plainly in the expression of habitual scorn which sat on her mouth whenever it was in repose. Her love, too, that had changed. Perhaps it had not grown less strong, but it was less active: she had put it under the feet of her ambition. Even now, when they had not met for three years, there was more of triumph than tenderness in the glance she cast upon him. And yet the passion which time had no power to conquer rose up in his heart and struggled once more for the mastery. He was sore beset by a frantic impulse to give up his ministry, his religion; to cast himself at her feet, and pray her to be his wife. But in that hour he shut his eyes and sent his soul forth in prayer. Strength came from heaven, as manna to the fainting Israelites of old. Before the play was over he arose and went calmly forth.

He made no farther effort to see or communicate with Joanna save a note directed to her theatrical name and address. Inside it simply said,

"Joanna, will not this life weary you some time? When it does, Eversley Rectory is open for your return, and so is your brother's heart. Come back, at any time, when you so will. No mother's arms ever welcomed returning child more gladly than I will welcome you. I have looked into your face to-night. You are triumphant, but not happy. May God keep you safely, and bring you back before you die."

That was all. The next morning the Rev. Ralph Huntington left London and set out for his living of Eversley.

III.

There was a new parishioner at Eversley. For some time before the rector's visit to London, workmen had been busily engaged in fitting up and beautifying a fine old estate called "The Grange." It had been uninhabited for some years, and now, report said, had been purchased by a Mr. Duncan, a man of great wealth and high social position. During Mr. Huntington's absence, the family, consisting of Mr. Duncan, his sister, and his only daughter, had taken possession, and the rector saw them for the first time in church on the following Sabbath.

Alice Duncan, the fragile, delicate young girl sitting between her father and her aunt, was a revelation to him of a new order of beauty. Her face, with its saintly brown eyes and exquisitely clear complexion, had more of heaven in it than earth. Unconsciously to himself, she interested him deeply. Her fixed attention was a flattering compliment.

The next day he called upon the new-comers, and after that the acquaintance progressed rapidly. He was an almost daily visitor. Perhaps if Alice Duncan had been more like Joanna he would have liked her less. Two beings so opposite could hardly have been found. To Alice, ambition was a word almost without signification. She lived but in her affections—love to God and love to man. In place of Joanna's high health and bounding exuberance of life, she inherited from her mother, who died young, a sensitive organization and extreme delicacy of constitution. The sentiment Mr. Huntington felt for the two was so unlike that he never thought of comparison. To *such* love as he had bestowed upon Joanna no other had power to move him. He never had felt, he never could feel, a vestige of it for any other woman. He loved her passionately; *sinfully*, he called it, in the stern self-immolation which vainly strove to banish her image from his heart; and it was with a sense of rest he turned to Alice.

This regard at least was pure—pure as a mother's for her child, a brother's for his sister, and yet it was unspeakably sweet and refreshing. It seemed so natural to talk to her of all that interested himself, of his studies, his parish, his poor and sick people, and she assisted him in all that her feebleness would allow.

Her health was failing. He could see that day by day, as he visited her, and it was very pleasant to note how his coming seemed to invigorate her—how it called to her cheek the rose-tint he loved to see, and summoned to her lips her brightest smiles.

One day he had been sitting with her a few hours, and on his way home her father joined him. They walked for a time in silence, and then Mr. Duncan said, apparently with great effort,

"Mr. Huntington, do you not perceive that my daughter is failing? But no, you can not see it. You do not watch her as I watch her, and, besides, she brightens up so at your coming. Mr. Huntington, when life is in danger, above all a life so precious as hers, my last, my only child, it is no time for delicacy. Alice loves you. No matter how I have found out her secret. She knows not that it is in my possession. I think, if you could love her, if she could be made happy, my child would live. I believe your heart is free. Perhaps you have never thought of this before, but—*could* you love her?"

The father paused and looked at the silent face beside him as if more than life hung upon the reply. Ralph Huntington considered the question for a moment. His heart had been so utterly absorbed in his hopeless passion for Joanna that he had never dreamed that his constant visits might awaken in her sentiments warmer than his own.

To one whose affections were free the proposal would have been a very flattering one. But the rector's nature was not worldly or mercenary. He did not reflect for an instant on the wealth and social distinction which would accrue to Mr. Duncan's son-in-law. He only asked his heart the question whether he could indeed forsake all others, and cherish the gentle Alice as his wife. In that hour Joanna's proud prophecy was fulfilled—she *haunted* him. Look where he would, he could see nothing but one dark, beautiful face, with its splendid eyes, its mocking smile, its lips, tempting, yet far away as the apples of Tantalus.

With a struggling attempt at self-command he turned to Mr. Duncan:

"Allow me to leave you now, sir, and in the morning I will answer your question. The thought of winning your daughter had never before entered my mind. I must have time to seek a response of my own heart."

He hurried home. He entered his study and fastened the door behind him. All night long he paced restlessly to and fro, or knelt in an agony of prayer before the low reading-desk where his father before him had so often sought God, not in vain. He considered the subject in all its bearings.

On one hand was his passion for Joanna—Joanna, the actress, separated from him by an impassable barrier—on the other, this young, pure life, ready to distill itself in love for his sake; this life which he could save—a gentle wife, ready to soothe away every shadow from his heart—one worthy, ay, ten times more than worthy of his love—a father looking to him to be the preserver of his daughter. The struggle was a long one. In the end, his compassion, his esteem triumphed.

The next morning he was closeted for half an hour with Mr. Duncan. To him he laid bare his heart. In conclusion he said,

"Now I will abide your decision. You see plainly this Joanna, this strange girl, is separated from me forever. Not for an instant would I dare contemplate marriage with her, nor, if I would, would she give up her calling for my sake. Yet I have loved her—how well, God knoweth. Your gentle Alice is far more suited for my wife, more worthy of my regard, and I can promise to cherish her very tenderly. You shall decide. If, knowing all, you choose to give her to me, I will do precisely as you think best about telling her of this former passion."

Mr. Duncan pressed his hand fervently.

"God bless you," he said; "you will preserve her to me. No: never tell her that any other was ever dear to you. I know her nature—it would kill her. Go to her now. Let her think the proposal comes only from you. Give her the joy of believing herself beloved."

Ralph Huntington went into the morning-room, as one of the pleasantest apartments in the Grange was called. There he found the gentle invalid. As usual, her face brightened at his approach; and he—Heaven help him!—on the very threshold his feet were stayed. An image seemed to confront him—Joanna—not as he had seen her last, scornful, defiant, mocking as she was brilliant, but pale, sorrowful, tender. For one moment he put his hand to his eyes, he breathed a silent prayer, and the delusion vanished. He sat down by Alice Duncan; he took her hand in his; he asked her to be his wife; but he scarcely heard the words of her reply until she said,

"I am not worthy, Ralph—not good enough for a minister's wife—for *your* wife."

Then he looked at her with an expression of agony on his face.

"Alice," he cried, with such energy of entreaty that it startled her, "don't say that again—never say that again. You are ten times too good for me, but I would die to make you happy."

And she, resting her head against his arm, thought, "Oh, how tenderly he loves me!"

Once, however, that the engagement was fairly formed, it began to grow in a certain sense pleasant to Mr. Huntington. It was a pleasure to see how rapidly Alice's health improved; how she grew able to interest herself in all his plans and labors. His daily visits became a habit, a kind of necessity to himself as well as to her.

True, Joanna's presence was very often with him. In the might of her proud spirit she maintained her empire still; but he reasoned as most men would have done—she had given him up, she had separated herself from him, already, quite as completely as any other ties could separate them—his marriage would not widen the breach, and—Alice *did* make him happier. He had commenced by intending to marry her for the sake of *her* life; he was now rejoicing in it for his own.

The day for their marriage had been postponed but a few weeks from their first engagement, and now it was the night before the bridal morning. The rector had lingered with his betrothed until twilight, and now he walked over the fields to his own home. For once he was not thinking of Joanna. Alice, in her youth, her beauty, her maiden innocence, to-morrow to become his own, was in all his thoughts.

He went into the rectory, into the parlor where he had received his mother's last blessing. A figure stood there, tall, majestic, clothed throughout in black. He started back, believing himself to be indeed haunted; but a warm, human hand was laid on his arm; a mocking voice said,

"I got the note you were so kind as to write me before you left London. You told me to come home. I wanted a little rest, and so here I am. Is my *brother* glad to see me?"

"Joanna."

"Joanna, indeed! Is that all you can say? Oh, I came at an inconvenient time. Is that it? You did not mean to ask me to your wedding, and here I am."

"Joanna, you are cruel—cruel not to me only, but to one who is as good and pure as an angel—whose happiness depends upon mine. You gave me up. You separated yourself from me forever, and now you come here to shadow Alice Duncan's life also."

"And is my life nothing, most benevolent man, that you do not take it at all into account? It is false, what you say about my forsaking you. I did not forsake you any more than you forsook me. You were resolved to continue in your profession, I was resolved to cling to mine. But have I not been *true* to you? Think you any other man could ever have won *me* for his wife? I tell you more than one has tried, who would have laid wealth and title at my feet. Is *my* love nothing to me, that you would outrage it, trample on it, kill it, and not even send me word to come to its funeral?"

She paused; her eyes flashed fire through her tears, for she was weeping. He had never seen her weep before since her childhood. The sight moved him. He put his arm about her, and would have drawn her head to his shoulder, but she sprang proudly from his clasp.

"No, I tell you—no, Ralph Huntington. You have wounded me in the tenderest point. After this I scorn your professions. Do not think that I am come to interfere with the happiness of your pure and beautiful bride. I am too proud for such revenge. I shall not trouble you long. I am going to pass this night in my old room, where neither your father nor mother would ever have refused me shelter, and then I shall go to church to-morrow to see the brave wedding there will be, and after that you shall see me no more. Good-night, Reverend Ralph Huntington."

So saying, she swept from the room, just as she had done once before when she announced her fixed resolve to go to London, and the rector heard her climbing the stairs to her own chamber.

Once more he kept sleepless vigil. Joanna was there, separated from him by a few partitions, a few feet of space. He had seen her, talked with her, heard her call his name, and yet on the morrow he was to be married to another! In vain he recalled Alice Duncan's gentle face, her pure heart, her tender love. He felt bitterly that for one kiss from Joanna's lips he could give up all. But the conflict of a strong soul with temptation, the prayer of a tortured heart to its God, are not for the pen to portray. Once more duty triumphed. When he came forth from his study the next morning Joanna was gone.

He saw her again at the church. The marriage ceremony had been performed, and he turned away from the altar with his young wife leaning upon his arm. Then it was that Joanna's eyes met him, as he had seen them in his vision—sorrowful, tender, despairing. At that moment a wail rang through the church as if a strong heart had broken. The rector dared not pause. He hurried from the house, and led his gentle Alice to the carriage that was to convey them on a short bridal tour.

When he returned a week after, he heard the story which was in all the villagers' mouths—how Joanna Montford, the adopted daughter of the late rector, was there at her brother's wedding; how, just as he was leading out his bride, she had given a sudden wail and fallen in a dead faint; how she had been carried home and restored by the rector's servants, and the next day had departed for London.

Somehow, too, this news came to Alice in her bridal happiness. She had remembered the beautiful face in the church, and the cry which startled her on her bridal morning, and had asked the stranger's name of some one who had given her the history.

Three days after their return home the Rector of Eversley entered the parlor, where his wife was reclining on the sofa. He drew up an ottoman and sat down beside her. She brushed back his hair, very full of gray threads now, with her thin hand, and then, winding her arm about his neck, she said,

"Come, Ralph, I am going to turn catechist, and ask you a few questions—may I?"

"What is there that you may not do, Alice?"

"Well, then, when you've told me so much about your parish, and your father and mother, and, I thought, about all your life, why did you never tell me of your adopted sister, Joanna Montford?"

"I—I—she had gone off to be an actress, Alice."

"Well, was that quite reason enough? Didn't she *love* you, Ralph? Forgive me if I ought not to ask," she added, seeing that he remained silent. "But I may ask *this*, mayn't I?—did my husband ever love *her?*"

Not for his own life, not for hers, which in that moment he felt was more precious than his own, could Ralph Huntington have deceived his wife. His face crimsoned; he covered it with both his hands.

"I told your father," he gasped—"I told your father, Alice, and we thought we were acting for the best. Oh, my wife, my precious wife, can you forgive me?"

She comprehended, in that moment, with the quick intuition of affection, the whole story.

"Forgive you!" she said, gently removing his hands from his face and laying her soft cheek beside it; "that word is not admissible from me to you, dear Ralph. I have nothing to forgive. I can only pity you."

He sank on his knees beside her, he drew her head to his shoulder, and then caressing her, he said,

"But I love *you* now, Alice—you, my own innocent darling. You must believe it; and this other—this Joanna, I could never have married her."

But she saw the spasm of agony which constricted his features, and soothing him, and lying there still, with her head on his breast, she won from him the whole story of his love and his sorrow. Alas! he knew not that even then the iron was entering her soul; the heart that loved him was being broken.

IV.

A year had the Rev. Ralph Huntington been married, and now his wife lay dying. Her father had understood her nature. The knowledge that her husband had once loved another was killing her; and yet her death was beautiful as her life had been. During the year that she had been the rector's wife she had not been wholly unhappy. There was joy in being near him, in hearing the tones of his voice, in watching the play of his features—joy above all in feeling that her sympathy added to his happiness. But beneath all this there was an undercurrent. She felt that there was one name to which his heart echoed as it could never echo to hers; one voice which had power to move the deep currents of his nature as hers never could; and in every rose of happiness which her fingers gathered lurked the thorns of despair.

It was a warm summer day, but Alice Huntington was very cold. Her hand was chill as it lay in her husband's clasp. Her eyes were fixed upon his face, and she murmured,

"It is sweet, beloved, to pass away thus, with my hand in yours, knowing, at last, that I am very dear to your priceless heart."

Alas! unsatisfied Joanna, even in that death hour thou must haunt him. A letter was given to him, whose author he knew but too surely. He crumpled the paper in his hand, and then he withdrew to the window to read it. It said,

"Well, Ralph Huntington, proud stoic, Christian

minister, good man, as you think you are, are you satisfied? Are two victims enough? I hear your wife is dying, and I— Well, hearts break, sometimes, that are *strong*. I am still true to you. JOANNA."

A wave of agony rolled upward to his lips, but he choked it back again. He went to his wife's bedside. He was startled at the change which had come over her in his absence, momentary as it was. Death had already set his seal on her fair young face.

"That letter," she said, faintly—"was it from Joanna?"

"Yes, my wife. She has heard of your illness, and she accuses me of being your murderer. Oh, Alice, angel Alice, is it true?" He threw himself upon his knees—he bowed his head upon his hands in anguish. Once more, with a powerful effort of her failing strength, she raised it, and dropped upon his brow a kiss of heavenly peace.

"No," she said, tenderly; "no, my Ralph, my own husband, it is not true. If you had not loved me, if you had not married me, I should have died long ago. Oh, believe this, believe it always. The year that I have been your wife is the happiest of my life. You have been very good to your motherless girl."

"Oh, Alice, if I had! Oh, if I could think so! God knows I have *wished* to make you happy. God knows I would die to save your precious life. I shall die very soon—I feel it, and then, beloved, purified from all dross of earth, we shall meet again, and be united forever."

She lifted her eyes to heaven with a look of faith, of hope, of ineffable peace, and then she said,

"I feel very sleepy. I want to sleep now. I'll talk to you again when I wake up."

For two hours he held her. He sat in a sort of trance. At first his tears fell fast upon that pale, upturned brow. Then that mood passed, and he lifted his heart in sacred faith to the land whither his wife was going. She had grown very cold in his clasp before he realized that the smile which her face wore was but the token left by the angel of Death—that Alice Huntington's awaking would be in heaven.

His grief was not loud, but deep. Three days after, he turned away from the grave under the willows a chastened man, with the path on which he hoped to walk toward the "land that is very far off" stretching out straight and narrow, to be traversed now with solitary, longing heart, by lonely feet.

V.

Alice Huntington had been dead six months, when once more a letter came to the Rector of Eversley from Joanna. This time the chirography was hurried and irregular, as if written by one who was suffering much. It ran thus:

"Ralph Huntington, you are free now—come to me. I summon you by the memory of your dead father and mother, both of whom loved me. I summon you by the love you yourself have so many times breathed into my ears. The barrier is removed. Joanna Montford is an actress no longer, but—she is dying. Come to me at once. Wait a day, and it may be too late. Oh, Ralph, I have loved you with a love that is stronger than life. If it gives me any claim on you, come to me."

The rector traveled all night. The next morning he stood in Joanna's presence. In a stately room, surrounded by every luxury, she lay, but the shadow of death was on that polished brow. She had well said—"Strong hearts break sometimes."

"You have come," she said, the hectic flush deepening on her cheek; "I knew you would—I expected you. The drama is almost over. Soon the curtain will fall. I wanted one last scene. Clasp me in your arms now; kiss me. I tell you I am an actress no longer, and your canonicals wont suffer. I want to see how the kiss will thrill my dying lips for which my living ones have longed so vainly."

He obeyed her. He clasped her to his heart; he could scarcely have helped it had his eternal birthright depended upon it. He kissed her many times. And then she spoke. This time her voice was not mocking, not scornful, but earnest, pleading, thrilling, in its tones of supplication:

"Now, Ralph, you will marry me. The doctor says I have not more than three hours to live, and I am going to be your wife before I die. It was for this I sent for you."

The Rector of Eversley turned pale.

"I can not, Joanna—I can not. My wife has been dead but six months."

"But you were true to her while she lived. Have I not suffered enough for her already? You married her, in the first place, more for her sake than for your own, and now you must marry me, not for my sake only, but for the dear old love. Listen, Ralph. I am not an actress. That barrier is gone. All my pride is gone with it. It is your Joanna—your poor, proud, passionate, suffering Joanna, who is pleading with you to be your wife three short hours. Then I will die, Ralph, and not trouble you any more."

He was vanquished. A groan burst from his lips.

"It shall be as you say, my own first love. Oh, Joanna, God knows I would have you live! Oh, if my arms could shelter you! if my love could save you!"

She smiled sadly.

"It is too late now; but we must lose no time. There is a clergyman in the next room. I got all things ready. I knew you would come. I knew I should be your wife."

Her look was bright and triumphant. In a few moments more the nuptial benediction had been pronounced, and the two were left again alone.

She put her arms around his neck; she drew his head down upon her pillow, and then she said, while her whole face seemed to glow with the fullness of content,

"There, Ralph, I am your wife. I had faith—I always knew this day would come some time. I am dying, but that matters little. My wild heart is at rest. Love me, Ralph, love me."

And he *did* love her. Into the lap of those two hours he lavished the hoarded love of a lifetime. She died in his arms, lifting to his the fading glory of her eyes, clinging to his neck, murmuring his name. Her life had been an ovation at the shrine of her ambition —her death was a sacrifice to her love.

Doubly sorrow-stricken, the Rector of Eversley bore home the dead body of his second wife. She was laid in the church-yard, with a few feet of ground between her and the gentle Alice Duncan. It was not many months before the man they had both loved, grown prematurely old and grief-stricken, laid off, at last, the worn-out armor with which he had fought his Battle of Life, and went to his long sleep between his two wives. Whose shall he be in the resurrection?

The Record of a Troubled Life.

Soon wilt thou wipe away my tears;
  Yesterday the earth was laid
Over my father full of years,
  Him whose steps I have watched and stayed.

All my work is finished here;
  Every slumber that shuts my eye
Brings the forms of the lost and dear,
  Shows me the world of spirits nigh.

This deep wound that bleeds and aches,
  This long pain—a sleepless pain—
When the Father my spirit takes,
  I shall feel it no more again.

BRYANT.

THE RECORD OF A TROUBLED LIFE.

TOLL, toll, toll! I counted the strokes of the village bell until it had numbered twenty-nine. Then they ceased, and unbidden my tears fell—tears of mingled sorrow and joy; sorrow for the long-enduring, patient, troublous life that was over; joy for the glad, new, glorious life that had begun. Bertha Whitney was dead. There were few on earth to whom these words would bring even a passing pang. She was born of poor parents, and she had been poor all the days of her life. Even her childish memories were of suffering and wrong. Her father was one of those men whose names you sometimes meet in the unread annals of the poor; an unappreciated mechanical genius, with a shy, sensitive nature, and a brain full of glorious schemes.

But what might have won him fame and fortune in another sphere was only a curse to the poor machinist. With these splendid fancies running riot in his brain, how could he bear a dull, daily routine of journeyman labor, under some phlegmatic master, who was entirely incapable of appreciating a single one of his far-reaching plans? It was hardly strange that he neglected the daily toil on which his bread depended, to spend day after day alone, inventing a wonderful labor-saving machine, by which he expected to realize a fortune.

His wife was a gentle, trusting woman, perfect in her faith and devotion, thinking no one so good or so gifted as her husband, and gilding in a sweet, unconscious romance all the after years with the sunshine of love and hope streaming downward from their bridal morning. So, with barely food enough to supply the little Bertha's hunger, and keep the life-breath in their own shivering frames, she encouraged her husband in working month after month on his machine, doing only a few days' work outside, now and then, to keep the gaunt hunger-wolf at bay.

At last the labor of months was completed, and Walter Whitney set out to offer it for acceptance to the head machinist of the large Beverley Mills. It was a bright, beautiful morning, and his heart beat very high as he kissed the little Bertha, playing with a few shavings upon the hearth, and departed with the hopeful tones of his wife ringing like a prediction of success in his ears.

For several hours he was closeted with Mr. Meags, the machinist. He explained to him all the minute niceties of his invention, and as he spoke his clear blue eyes sparkled, and his attenuated figure dilated and grew noble with the majesty of thought. Mr. Meags listened intently; his form bent forward, and his small eyes twinkling with suppressed eagerness as he took in every point of the invention. At last he rose and brushed Walter Whitney's little model from before him:

"It is of no use, my good sir," he said, "our wasting any more time over this. Your theory is very pretty, but, more's the pity, this machine has no practical utility about it. Utopian, sir, perfectly Utopian."

"But," Mr. Whitney ventured timidly to remonstrate, "I thought you admitted, half an hour ago, that it would save the labor of twenty men?"

"Of course, if it could be used, nothing more certain. But it can't be used; there's the trouble. Entire want of practical utility. Perfectly Utopian, sir."

Thus saying, the worthy Mr. Meags arose, and the disappointed Whitney understood that he was expected to make his bow and retire. His wife saw him coming home afar off, and burned with eager questions—had his machine been accepted? would it make all their fortunes? how much had been paid him on the spot? But, as he came nearer, her loving eyes read the sorrowful index of his face, and she was quite silent when she met him at their cottage door.

He did not kiss her. He took no notice of the little Bertha, who began tugging at his coat. He came in gravely and sadly, and deliberately set down his little model upon the table.

"There, Mary," he said, "you may put that away. It will be the ruin of me. How much time I have lost over it, and it's all of no use. Put it away; I never want to see it again."

"Won't they take it?"

"No, Mr. Meags says it has no practical use; he calls it a Utopian scheme. At first I thought he was pleased with it. He spoke about its saving the labor of twenty men, but apparently there was something wanting, for he declared he could do nothing with it, at last. Take it away, wife; the sight of it makes me sick. To think of all those wasted days!"

Mary Whitney was a true wife; would there were more of them. She went up to her husband's side, and laid against his her cheek, fair still in his eyes, though the freshness of early youth was gone. She brushed back the thin hair from his flushed and heated brow, and dropped a tender, sympathizing kiss upon it. Then she said,

"Not so, not so, dear husband. The time was not lost. No time is lost when we are cultivating the talents a good God has given us. I will put away the machine with care. I am proud of it—I have faith in it—if it should never be used, you should be glad that you have made it, and, who knows? perhaps it may bring you a fortune yet. It is only to go to work for a while, just as if you had never thought of it. Only have faith, my husband. We shall do very well, Bertha and I."

He took her hand as she was moving away from him, and looked steadfastly in her face.

"Mary, I am not given to many words. I do not very often tell you what I think of you, but I do believe God sent you to me for a comforting angel. I do not think you are made of the same clay as other women."

She turned away in silence when he loosed her hand from his clasp, but the tears were in her eyes.

For the next six months Walter Whitney worked, uncomplainingly, at his laborious, uncongenial tasks. Comfort began to sit smiling at their hearthstone. But the machinist would have been far happier to stay day after day working out plans and models in his attic, dreaming glorious dreams the while of being a public benefactor, of realizing impossible fortunes, and living an enchanted life. After such a day, a crust of black bread would have better pleased his palate than the comfortable suppers his wife now nightly set before him could ever do, coming thus after the work he hated.

One night he came home as his wife had never before seen him, moody and sullen. Neither Mary's tender voice nor little Bertha's playful wiles had power to exorcise the evil spirit. At length he brought down his hand on the table with a fierce oath, the first one that loving woman had ever heard from his lips.

"Mary, I was tempted to step into Green's as I came along, and buy a paper of arsenic. If it wasn't for you, I wouldn't be long in putting an end to my miserable life. What's the use of my living, poor as I am, so poor that every unwhipped sneak under heaven can take advantage of me."

"Who is it, Walter? Who has wronged you?"

"I *can't* tell it—I haven't patience to tell it. Oh, Mary, if I had that man under my heel!"

"What man, Walter?"

The quiet, sympathizing gentleness of her tone seemed to soothe him a little, and he answered her more calmly:

"You know my model that I carried to Mr. Meags, and which he persuaded me wasn't worth a farthing? Well, he has copied it, and got a patent, and *his* invention—they call it his, Mary—goes into operation next Monday at the Beverley Mills."

Even Mary Whitney's calm nature was roused to wrath.

"Surely," she cried, "surely, husband, you will not bear this in silence? Surely you will go to law with him, and get your rights? To think of his making a fortune out of your genius! Walter, you *will* contest it with him?"

"Mary, it's of no use. The right is mine, but the might is all on his side. I must bear it. I can not prove that he had not got his model finished before I showed him mine, or, indeed, that I did show it to him at all. He was a cunning villain. He has made his invention differ from mine in half a dozen unimportant particulars—a sharp knave—he has left no loophole. I could bear it for myself, but oh! Mary, to think this might have made you rich; that you might have held up your head, as you ought, among the proudest of your neighbors; that we might have sent Bertha to school, and cultivated her gift for music. May God forgive me, but I believe I am possessed with the devil. If I had that man in my sight, I could murder him."

"No, you couldn't, Walter." The momentary flush of indignation had passed from the woman's cheek. She knelt down by her husband's side, and looked pleadingly into his face. "No, you couldn't, Walter. Much as he has wronged you, you must bear no malice against him. God will punish him in his own way and time. If there is no legal remedy, just let it go, and try to forget it. Don't think of Bertha and me. We shall do well."

But her soothing words had lost their usual power. That was the beginning of Walter Whitney's downfall. A friend, who had heard something of his story, urged him that night into the village inn, where he recounted his wrongs to an audience at least outwardly vehement in their demonstrations of sympathy and indignation. Liquor was pressed upon him. He drank deeply, and his enthusiastic, excitable temperament was half maddened by the stimulus. For the time he forgot all his troubles, and when the reaction came, he drank again, and fancied himself happy as a king.

At that time Bertha was eight years old, and for the next ten years her father's downward course blotted all the sunshine out of her life. Schooling she had none, for she had neither books or clothes suitable to make her appearance with the other children.

It was difficult for Walter Whitney to get employment now. For this he had been chiefly dependent on the Beverly Mills hitherto; but one day, when his courage and indignation were plentifully stimulated with brandy, he forced himself into Mr. Meags's presence and demanded a reparation from him, taunting him with his perfidy. The result was his discharge from all employment about the mills. He had thus aroused against himself the full venom of Mr. Meags's vindictive, malignant nature; and that worthy gentleman, restrained by no considerations of justice or humanity, lost no after opportunity of paying him back with interest the grudge he owed him.

It was only occasionally that the machinist could get a few days' work to do, and in the interim he drank up almost all he had thus earned at the tavern. His wife clung to him patiently through every thing. Night and day she toiled to make home comfortable, or rather habitable, for comfort was no longer a word in the Whitneys' vocabulary; and when her husband came home, she never failed to meet him with a welcome and a smile. Sometimes her long-suffering patience, and the sight of her pale, wasting face, would touch to the core his heart, not yet quite withered, and he would be moved to a sudden paroxysm of tears, a vague, desperate resolve of amendment. But none of these emotions possessed enough of abiding power to reclaim him. He had drunk at first to drown his sense of wrong, to lighten his crushing weight of despair, and now habit was too strong for him.

As I have said, Mary Whitney struggled bravely to make what headway she could against misfortune. She herself taught reading, writing, and the simplest rudiments of education to her poverty-stricken child. When Bertha was fourteen, the village dress-maker, a slender, consumptive woman, with narrow chest and hacking cough, as genuine a missionary in her sphere as ever Florence Nightingale was in hers, gave the poor child a trade. In her unemployed days, and often in the evening, after a hard day's work, she taught Bertha to cut and fit dresses, and to sew in her own neat and beautiful fashion. There was a sad satisfaction to Mary Whitney in this knowledge of her daughter's.

"You will need it all, Bertha," she used to say, sometimes; "you will need it all when I am gone. You will have to take care of *him* then."

And so the girl grew up with this great, prospective responsibility, this one object, of being able to take care of her father, forever before her mind. Over and over her mother had recounted to her the story of his genius and his wrongs, the sad excuse for his after downfall; and she grew up with an exaggerated idea of him, thinking him at once the most gifted and the most unfortunate of men. And so, day by day, his fatal habit strengthened its hold upon him, and, day by day, slowly but surely, his true wife was fading away.

It was a winter night when Bertha Whitney was eighteen. She had never known what it was to be young. She had had no childhood, and she was not youthful now. There was a certain beauty, altogether sad, in her pale face, her thin features, her sweet yet sorrowful brown eyes. Her figure was slight, but her shoulders had acquired a little stoop from bending so constantly over her needle. She was sitting by her mother's bedside; for, during the last few days, Mrs. Whitney had been unusually ill. It was a stormy night; but, heedless of the commotion of the elements, the invalid appeared to sleep. At length she started up suddenly.

"Bertha, you have a good deal more work since Miss Hurst died?"

Miss Hurst was the kind-hearted dress-maker who had given Bertha her trade. Consumption had at last numbered her among its victims. Bertha looked up with a sigh: "Yes, mother."

"You will be the better able to take care of him. Bertha, I beseech you not to weep at what I am going to say. You have known a long while that I must leave you soon. I am going to-night. I leave *him* in your charge. You know his wrongs and his sufferings. He will have only you in the world. Bertha, promise me, upon your soul's faith, that you will never desert him!"

The girl's head was bent lower. Her eyes could not see for the tears which she was resolutely struggling to force back; but she put her hand blindly forth and touched her mother's:

"Mother, I promise."

"Dear child, good child, I knew I could trust you. When did you ever fail me? I am satisfied."

With those words she sank again into silence, and seemed to slumber. Outside, the rain hurtled against the windows, and the wind sobbed, and wailed, and moaned, and now and then burst forth in a loud, prolonged shriek. And in the night and the tempest, these two women, the dying and the watching, were all alone. An hour had passed in this solemn silence of coming death, when suddenly the outside door was burst open, and Walter Whitney staggered in. His potations had just reached a stage of maudling, sentimental tenderness.

"Well, Mary," he cried, "I'm glad to find you taking your comfort. It's a great thing, my darling, when a man has got a good home and a pretty wife such a night as this."

By this time he had pulled off the wet and ragged garment which did him service as an overcoat, and Bertha had seized his arm.

"Father," she said, in a stern, solemn whisper, "do you not see? Mother is dying."

These words had power to penetrate even to his dormant senses. In a moment he was thoroughly sobered. He tottered toward the bed; he knelt down beside it, and with a groan, a shriek I should say rather, of wild, despairing agony, he cried out,

"Dying! she shall *not* die—she must not die—my wife, my poor, faithful wife, Mary. Oh, Mary, only live—only wake up again! I'll never drink another drop, so help me Heaven. Mary! Mary!"

The wan face turned toward him. Slowly the eyes

unclosed. She could not speak, but a smile, like the smile of an angel, kindled up the death-stricken features. With one last convulsive effort of despairing life she drew his lips down to hers, and clung to them with her dying breath. When Walter Whitney lifted up his head, his wife was with the angels.

By this blow he was utterly paralyzed. He had only mind enough left to remember the oath he had sworn to her in her dying moments. He renewed it at her grave, with his hand upon her coffin. After this he subsided into a kind of simple, harmless, yet melancholy insanity. He would ask every one who came near him, with a touching pathos in his trembling voice,

"Did I kill her? *Do* you s'pose I killed her?"

But he never once showed the slightest disposition to break the pledge he had made at her death-bed. Sometimes he would sit for a whole half day in the sun, in the long summer days, saying over to himself, like the refrain of a mournful song,

"Poor Mary's dead. Poor Mary's dead and gone."

For five years Bertha continued to devote herself to him, finding her only happiness in ministering to his comfort, and in the memory of the dead mother whose last wishes she was thus fulfilling. But at twenty-three love came to her. It was not a romantic love; indeed, in all the quiet heroism of her most heroic life, there was nothing befitting the heroine of a modern novel. James Carpenter had known her from her childhood. He had grown up to manhood thinking there was no one so good and true as Bertha, and, unconsciously to himself, associating her sad yet gentle face with all his visions of the future. Nor was this strange in one who had known her innocence, her truth, her exceeding self-devotion.

James Carpenter, at twenty-four—he was one year older than Bertha—was a thriving young mechanic. He was handsome, with a manly, cheerful face, and a strong, stalwart figure, such as any timid maiden might look to for protection in the rough places of life. I think his love was a great surprise to Bertha. Her ideas of her own attractions were very limited, or perhaps I should come nearer the truth by saying she did not think she had any attractions at all; so she received with as much surprise as pleasure the young mechanic when he came to her one night, as she sat on the door-step of her humble dwelling, singing, as her wont was, in her rich, sad voice, an old ballad tale of such sorrow as had darkened all her own life. There was much of embarrassment in her manner when he seated himself beside her, and more still when he told her of the place she had so long filled in his heart and his dreams, and besought her to tell him whether he might hope, one day, to win her as his wife. For one moment her heart fluttered toward him longingly. For one moment an enchanted garden of delights seemed opening at her feet. For her, so lonely, might be home, and friends, and smiles. But no; what had Bertha Whitney to do with these? She remembered her promise to her dead mother. She closed her eyes on the forbidden picture. Calmly, and not altogether sadly, for a sense of fulfilled duty strengthened her voice, she said nay to his suit. He offered to take her father also; to be as good to him as if he were his own. He told her he had always meant this; he had known her too well even to think she would give up her duty. But still she steadily refused. She would never leave her father, nor would she ever burden another with his care. He must go out into the world unfettered by the sorrow of her life. He would find some one else to love him, and she, looking toward them from afar off, would pray heaven to make them happy.

When at length he found that her resolution was indeed unalterable, he rose to go.

"Bertha," he said, "it may be years before you see me again. I shall go next week to California. Fortunes are being made there, and I was only waiting to know your answer before deciding whether to join a company that will be leaving here next week. But I shall not go with a heart so heavy as I feared. I believe—I do believe, Bertha, that under other circumstances you could have loved me, and I will have hope in the future. I ask no pledge from you, but I have faith that we shall meet again when your heart will be free to make answer to mine."

This was their parting. He sailed for the land of gold, and Bertha was left to her silent life with her imbecile, helpless father. But she had one more memory in her hours of solitude. A good man had loved her—had chosen her, unlovely and unattractive as she deemed herself, to be his wife. He might marry another now she had sent him away, but no one could ever take from her the memory that he had loved her *first.* Unconsciously her voice took a tenderer tone as she murmured his name in her nightly prayers.

She had no scarcity of employment. Ever since her mother's death she had had all the sewing that she could do, and her earnings were quite sufficient to support them in neat and thrifty comfort. For three years longer she lived thus, but all the time her father's feeble steps seemed tottering nearer and nearer to the grave. At last the Dark River flowing between us and the other side ingulfed him utterly. There was a momentary brightening of the intellect, one fond blessing, an almost painless death, a humble funeral, and then Bertha Whitney was alone in the world, while the summer roses bloomed, and the winds rustled over those two graves where her father and mother lay sleeping side by side.

During the lonely year that followed she thought often of James Carpenter. She would have been less than woman if she had not; but I do not think she thought of him expectantly, or even hopefully. Many sorrows had crushed the hope out of her nature. She only did her duty, and waited passively for destiny to draw nigh her; that destiny which had met her hitherto, not as an angel of consolation scattering flowers, but rather as an avenging spirit, whom she could not choose but meet, even though he stood with a drawn sword in her path. Thus passed autumn, and winter, and spring, and again it was summer.

Again under the old locust-tree, in full blossom, hanging over the stone door-step, Bertha sat watching the last sun-rays gild the white tomb-stone above those two graves, and the stars rising slowly one by one, and pacing forth into the night. And again James Carpenter came and took a seat beside her. After their first greetings were over, he said,

"I heard of your father's death in California, Bertha, and I lost no time in settling up my business and hastening to you. I could not have you here alone.

Bertha, I have been in the midst of temptations, but, under God, the memory of you has brought me safely through them. For months I have lived in the bright hope of this hour, when I could sit beside you thus, and ask you to be my wife."

That night the stars and the young June moon witnessed their plighting, and holier vows have never been spoken by truer hearts since our first father wooed our mother in the undimmed brightness of Eden.

Now, indeed, upon Bertha Whitney's desolate life broke the full glory of the sunshine. Who shall say, after all, that our heavenly Father bestows his good gifts in such unequal measure upon his children? Perhaps into the six weeks that followed was compressed joy enough to make amends for all the sorrows of that patient woman. She was sad no longer—lonely no longer. Before her the future stretched out a sunny path, bright with flowers.

Her betrothed was an impatient lover. He could not bear to leave her for an hour alone in that abode of shadows where her sorrowful life had been passed. He longed to lead her out into the light, to have her patient face win a happier smile in the peace and rest of a home of her own. And so, in six weeks from his return, they were to be married.

The day had come. With a strange, exhilarating sense of perfect joy and content such as she had never experienced before, she had adorned her little dwelling with flowers; she had decked herself in her simple but graceful robe of white muslin. Already the minister was there, and one or two of her truest friends. They had come early, they said, for a shower seemed rising in the west. And now it was time for the bridegroom.

For the first time in her life Bertha was nervous. At length she took her station at the door. Soon the rain began to fall, and the thunder to resound with sharp, terrific peals. In the midst she could see him coming, riding rapidly toward the house.

"Too bad," she heard one of the guests murmur, who had also seen him from the window—"too bad he didn't start sooner; he'll be wet through and through."

Bertha said nothing. With her heart in her eyes she watched him eagerly. Oh, heaven! that wild, wild peal; that sudden, blinding flash; that horse rushing franticly by the house; that falling weight. They hear one piercing shriek. A white figure rushes from the door—out into the storm.

Bertha raises her betrothed's head to her bosom, and then once more rings on the air that fearful shriek, and she has fallen to the earth by his side. They bring them in. Alas! her heart is beating still. She must waken to her long agony, her life of misery, but he, her manly bridegroom, is dead. No voice of love, no prayers, ever so long and all-prevailing, can bring him back. Heaven's own thunderbolt has struck the life from out his veins in the very hour of fruition.

It was many weeks before consciousness came fully back to Bertha Whitney. In the touching disorder of her intellect she seemed to live over only the bright moments of that day which should have witnessed her bridal. She would insist on putting on her bridal robes, and waiting for her lover at the window. More than one kind heart hoped that she would die thus—die before she woke to the knowledge that earthly love was gone from her forever; that beside her father and mother, underneath the willows, slept he who should have been her husband.

But the awakening came at last, and the knowledge of her heart's widowhood. Thank God! she who had struggled with so many sorrows did not yield utterly, even to this, the last and heaviest.

"I shall go to him," she said, "though he can never come to me. There shall be no partings *there*."

And so day by day her step grew feebler and her cheek paler. Soon we knew that her words were true; that she was indeed going to him. She lived until the crocus sprang up in the meadows and the spring violets opened their blue eyes in the clefts of the rocks. But when a kind hand laid the spring blossoms upon her pillow, she turned from them, lifting her dim eyes to heaven.

"There are brighter flowers there," she whispered. "Father—mother—James—I am coming."

And thus, in the pleasant spring morning, she fell asleep. Said I not well that there should be joy for the bright, new, glorious life, begun that hour, in the Hereafter? She had closed her eyes on earth, where for her had been twenty nine winters, and only one bright, brief, yet golden summer. On earth few had known, few loved her; but in heaven was joy, unceasing; supernal; and for the tired wanderer, weary and footsore with the rough paths of earth, a long rest.

"Never here, forever there,
Where all sorrow, pain, and care,
And grief and death shall disappear.
The horologe of Eternity
Sayeth this incessantly—
Never—Forever—
Forever—Never!"

Four Letters from Helen Hamilton.

Come they from sinner or from saint,
Cast them in, for the fire is faint;
The fire is faint and the frost is strong,
And these old letters have lived too long.

FRANCES BROWN.

Let us see—
Leave, gentle wax; and manners, blame us not:
To know our enemies' minds, we rip their hearts;
Their papers are more lawful.

SHAKSPEARE (*King Lear*).

FOUR LETTERS FROM HELEN HAMILTON.

LETTER THE FIRST.

Hillside, June 17th, 1857.

IT is a rainy summer day, good Cousin Jane, and that is why I find time to commence my promised series of letters to you. I have been here three weeks already, and have scarcely put pen to paper, save to announce my safe arrival to father and mother; but to-day I have drawn the cosiest of easy-chairs to the pleasantest of windows, and, with my port-folio on my knee, I feel just in the mood for writing to you. A fancy strikes me to make you, who have not seen me during the five years since your marriage, a pen-picture of myself. For once, some power shall give me the wondrous gift

"To see ourselves as others see us,"

and I will make use of this mental illumination for your benefit. Eight years ago, when I was seventeen, you and I graduated at Madame D'Arblay's together. You know what I was then, young, hopeful, enthusiastic, and—you see I am going to be honest—beautiful. What an enchanted life seemed opening before me—a path wherein should be perpetually springing up roses of love and hope, whose buds I was to gather for my bosom, whose fragrance was to surround me eternally. You know, too, what I was three years after, when you were married to Charley Fosdick, and I stood your bridesmaid.

You know that at twenty I had changed a little from what I was at seventeen. Only a little, it is true. My beauty was fresh and riant as ever; still I wore the roses of love and hope in my bosom, but I had found out there were now and then thorns among them. The world did not look quite so much like Eden, and I had learned one lesson—I do think it is the most sorrowful one a young heart can learn—the fashionable measure of social importance, reckoning a man's worth by his dollars and cents.

Since then you have not seen me. We have only corresponded at rare intervals; but I know your old love for me is warm in your heart, and I know you were thoroughly in earnest when you begged me to sit down in this quiet country place and give you an account of myself. I will be faithful, Cousin Jane, no matter how often my cheek may crimson with shame at the unveiling of my heart.

The five years since you went off with Charley Fosdick—by the way, you say you've never regretted it, though he is only a country doctor in that out-of-the-way town—those five years have all been passed by me in one desperate struggle to get married—suitably married—married to please papa and mamma, who have lived, for my sake, beyond their means, and are so ambitious to see me what they call well established.

I said the years have all been passed thus, and yet not quite all. I stopped once by the wayside, in my long climbing up this weary mountain of social position, to dream a dream. I believe I was almost in love. In society I met one who was in the world, yet not of it. How shall I describe Philip Wyndham to you? You know whom I mean, for I remember your writing me, when his first book came out, that you had read it, and how charmed you were with its grace, its simple pathos; how thrilled by the utterances of a deep, strong heart, making itself heard now and then amid the flowers and the sunshine. You can not think how strange it was to see him in the gay circles of our set, with his bright, earnest eyes, his sweet smile, and his calm forehead. Withal, he wore such shocking clothes—a threadbare black suit, always the same. It was at Mrs. Emerson's I met him first; you know what a woman she is to surround herself with lions; and then, for a while, every one took him up, and he was quite the fashion, only mammas took especial care that their daughters should have no opportunity to fall in love with him. They need not have done this, for Mr. Wyndham would have been harder to win than any lady of them all.

I think he accepted the patronizing invitations extended, at first, solely for the sake of studying human life in a new phase. He was miles above their patronage, and he would have been as little cast down by their ceasing to invite him altogether as he was elevated by their extending to him their condescending courtesy in the first place. He was a noble man, Cousin Jane.

I was twenty-three that winter. My nature had become pretty well incrusted with worldliness. I was tired, though, of the dull routine in which I moved. My naturally restless spirit longed for change and excitement. For a time, in his acquaintance, it found both. I don't know how I managed to attract him to my side. That I did so attract him is the proudest thought in all this review of my past life—that I had power to charm that lofty heart, that keen intellect, that sensitive, æsthetic nature. I think he understood all my capabilities. He saw what I might have been, brought up in another sphere, where wealth and style were less omnipotent. And I, oh! Cousin Jane, an angel's wing seemed to brush the dust from my heart, and make it fit for the pure anthems of heaven to echo through it.

For a time I forgot "the world, the flesh, and the devil." I gave up my shopping expeditions; I ceased to frequent Broadway; I went to half a dozen successive parties without a new dress; I returned to my old passion for poetry and music; I went backward over "the glory that was Greece and the grandeur that was Rome." In short, I was well-nigh in love. But what was I, that Philip Wyndham should gild me with the refined alchemy of his fancy—should pour out at my feet the sweet incense of his praise? Those were enchanted months in which I met him so frequently. A new glory lay on land and sea; the skies were bluer and the stars brighter. I never thought, however, of marriage. The idea that he would seek me as his wife never entered my head. Candidly, I should have thought myself as unworthy of the honor as I was unfit to be a poor man's wife.

It was a strange place to listen to the secret of a poet's love, but never did sweeter words flood a woman's heart with joy than his soul uttered to mine one destiny-marked night, in an alcove of a fashionable parlor, with the music of Strauss's aerial waltzes flooding the air, and the silken billows rolling past us in the dance, like a glittering sea of bright and mazy hues, whereon diamonds flashed and flowers were flung with lavish hands, to die, breathing out their fragrance. With this mirth, and song, and dance about us, our souls talked to each other—our two souls, in all that crowd, utterly alone. I say our souls, for the words we said were no lip utterance merely; our hearts forced the naked truth to our lips.

I shall not tell you with what phrases he told me that he loved me. That must be my own cherished secret. I answered him frankly. I was impelled to speak all the truth. I told him what a new joy I had found in his presence. I told him if he had met me when I was less worldly, I might have loved him; but now, style, and fashion, and luxury had grown a necessity to me, and I could not give them up. I should marry, sometime, a man who would give me these, and I should try to forget all that I had ever felt for him. What do you think he answered me?

"I pity you, Helen Hamilton; I pity you far more than I do myself. I have loved you indeed with all the strength, all the passion of my heart; still for me, time and nature will bring solace; but for you—you, who are smothering all your holiest hopes, all your best instincts, under the silken panoply of fashion, there will come, when it is too late, an awakening. I know you better than you know yourself. I know how your heart will cry out, one day, in its despair, for a love cast away and trodden under foot; for you do love me, Helen. I know how you will recoil in very bitterness from the rich and fashionable husband you will choose, and in that hour may God shield you from sorrow and from sin."

I have never looked on his face since that night, Cousin Jane. For months after that I was very sick, scarcely able to leave my bed, and when I recovered he had left New York, and gone I do not know where, for another lion had taken his place at Mrs. Emerson's reunions, and he was nearly forgotten.

Two summers and two winters have past since then, and I am not married yet. I can see mamma is beginning to be alarmed lest I never shall be. Last winter, however, came an admirer after her own heart—Lionel Fitz-Herbert. He had just returned from abroad. He is a son of one of the richest families on Fifth Avenue, and quite the fashion. He certainly paid me a great deal of attention, but he did not propose; nor, though, I confess to you, Cousin Jane, I used all my arts, could I by any means succeed in bringing him to the point. I can draw his portrait for you with ease. It will not be a Rembrandt. There are no strong lights and shadows in his character. This is he—Mrs. Charley Fosdick, Mr. Lionel Fitz-Herbert:

A small, smooth head, with well-brushed brown hair; small, though very regular features; clear red and white complexion; small hands and feet; short, slight figure, dressed in the height of fashion, and an echo-like manner and conversation, formed, you may be sure, in the best society. He has no particular vices, no particular principles, no particular ideas. Add to this a fortune almost unlimited, and the finest turn-out in New York, and you have a very good idea of the young gentleman for whose admiration a score of pretty women—your cousin Helen Hamilton among the rest—have angled desperately all winter.

This spring I became out of patience with it all. I did not want to go to Saratoga; I hate it, the hot, dusty place, and I persuaded mamma—I assure you it was a work of difficulty—to let me come here and stay with Caddie. You never saw my cousin Caddie. She was a splendid girl, educated in Boston, refined, gifted, handsome. We thought, at the time, that she threw herself away when she married William Ripley, young, poor, and resolved to be a farmer, but since I have been here I have changed my mind. Will is handsome, gentlemanly, well-educated—one of nature's noblemen, in short; just the one to round her life into fullness and harmony. I do not think I ever saw so happy a couple. Despite her many cares and her two children, Caddie is as young and gay as at sixteen.

Perhaps you don't know that this village, where their pretty place, Hillside, is located, was my mother's birth-place. Grandfather Weaver's old home, Oakland, they call it, is about half a mile from here. The house is tenantless now, but in excellent repair, and the old oak-trees around it are worthy of an English park. I pass a great many hours under the shade of those trees, or sitting in the wide veranda which surrounds the old house, dreaming strange dreams about my mother's youth; about my own life; the destiny which seems so long in coming to me; which I sometimes have a curious presentiment that I shall meet here.

I had no idea that I should like a country life so well. This is my first experience of it, for Saratoga, and Newport, and Long Branch are not country. I am beginning to think that country people are better than the denizens of the town. They have more time to think. Life seems here a more solemn, a more earnest thing. Wealth and show, satins and diamonds, carriages and point lace, seem so worthless when one walks under the oaks and larches, and looks up through their boughs to the everlasting sky, or hears the clear bird-songs pulsing downward. Will and Caddie seem to me—though their help is not numerous, and they have to spend not a few hours of every day at work with their own hands—to live far more intellectual lives than most of our fashionable idlers on Fifth Avenue. There is scarcely a good book, the utterance of a strong, true soul, that does not find its way to Hillside. There are some of these whose acquaintance I have made here for the first time, for which I feel that I shall be better all my life.

"Helen—Nellie—Nell!" That is Caddie's voice calling me. I guess it is mail-time, and I must run down stairs and see what has come for me. Then I'll come up again and finish my letter for you.

Oh, Cousin Jane, what shall I do? I am in sore perplexity. There was no letter for me, but Will had received two, and there are to be two visitors at Hillside. Whom do you think? The first is he whom I have not seen for more than two years—Philip Wyndham. It seems he has always been a friend of Will's, and he is coming here, he writes, for a little peace and rest, a little of the comforts of true friendship, and to finish off a book which he had promised to give the publishers in September. He does not know that I am here, and as he is coming to-morrow there is no time to tell him. Indeed, if there were ever so much time, why should he be told? It is not probable that he would avoid me. I am nothing to him now. Is it his fault that the sound of his voice should rouse from its long trance a silent sleeper in my heart to mock me with words against which I may not close my ears; to look at me with eyes before which my soul will quiver with agony? But he will never know it. He will never know that this strange ghost of the past is not dead utterly; that it folds its shroud about it sometimes, and rises up in the midnight with its still, accusing eyes. After all, it shall not rise. I will, I must control myself. Philip Wyndham can be nothing to me; I can be nothing to him. I will teach my heart not to quicken its pulses at the sound of his name. Perhaps our second visitor will help me.

Who do you think he is, Cousin Jane? No other than my admirer of this winter, Mr. Lionel Fitz-Herbert. It seems he, too, knows Will; in fact, they were in college together. He has ascertained my whereabouts from my mother, and written to ask Will and Caddie for permission to come down here and make a visit. They are too hospitable to refuse. But he will not arrive till next week. In the mean time, I shall have been seven days under the same roof with Philip Wyndham. But why do I speculate on that? my life-path leads otherwhere.

It seems, then, that Mr. Fitz-Herbert was more impressed with my attractions than I feared. He is evidently coming here solely on my account. The probable result will be an engagement. This will completely satisfy papa and mamma in their ambitious views for me, and it will insure me, for life, the possession of all the luxuries that have become so necessary. Well—I say well, and it shall be well. I will not let my foolish fancies make it ill.

I must close; to send you this letter by the evening mail, but I will write again soon, and keep you advised of the progress of this drama, whose result will determine the hereafter of your cousin,

HELEN HAMILTON.

LETTER THE SECOND.

Hillside, June 19th.

Oh, what a morning it is, Cousin Jane! Your heart drinks in the incense of many such, I doubt not, but to me, who have lived in the city all my life, each jubilant sunrising comes like a new revelation of power and beauty. I wish mamma could look out of my window. The landscape she would see would delight the heart of a painter. Hills, and dells, and woodland, and, in the distance, the bright river winding along like a thread of silver light. Blessed be God for summer. I do not think I have so rejoiced in the dewy freshness of any morning since I have been here. And yet I am not very happy. I rose early to tell you this. I have much to say to you; but, though I have sat here half an hour, my pen has only traveled over these few lines.

Philip Wyndham came yesterday in the ten o'clock train. I was busy all the first part of the morning helping Caddie; that is, I put little beautifying touches here and there which she had not time to give. I filled every vase with the sweet June roses and the other early flowers which thrive so well in Caddie's garden. The parlor looked charmingly when I had thus adorned it with blossoms. I opened all the windows, and fastened sprays of roses in with the ribbons which looped back the snowy muslin curtains.

Then I went to Philip Wyndham's room. I knew he would never know it, and so I indulged myself in making it beautiful for him. I filled it with such flowers as I remembered to have heard him say he loved—bright, sweet-scented ones—roses, and heliotropes, and geraniums. I scattered over the dressing-bureau little articles of *virtu* from my own room, and on the table I put a handsome port-folio full of all varieties of stationery.

At length, when I could find nothing more to do, I went to my room. There I took counsel with myself. I called my heart to account for its foolish flutterings. I bade my fingers cease their nervous trembling. I chided my voice into calmer, less faltering tones. You know I told you that I never loved Philip Wyndham; that is, not well enough to give up wealth and luxury for his sake. I reminded myself of this fact, and then I remembered my other lover. I reflected that a few months would probably see me Mrs. Lionel Fitz-Herbert, and there was no reason I should suffer my fancies to run riot about another. To be sure, I never could, by any possibility, wax romantic about Mr. Fitz-Herbert, but it was pleasant to contemplate the future he could give me—so luxurious, so free from care—to imagine myself presiding in my stately mansion, or driving down town with my liveried servants and my faultless equipage.

"Ah! Helen Hamilton," I said to myself, "you are a girl of sense. Poetry and romance are delightful condiments at the banquet of life, but very unsubstantial as a *pièce de résistance.*" I resolved to meet Mr. Wyndham with calm indifference. I would not even bestow a single extra adornment upon my toilet. I put on a fresh, simple white muslin, with a blue ribbon about my waist. Then I twined a few red roses in my hair. As I did so, the face reflected in the mirror arrested my gaze. It was as beautiful as ever; perhaps a careless observer would have said it was as youthful; but I could see it had grown old and worldly. There was a proud curl to the lip; a haughty, half-sarcastic gleam to the eye, which I did not like. They had come there since Philip Wyndham saw me last. The spirit had not become meeker in the past two years—more chastened, more womanly. It had grown proud, defiant, self-loving. Well, I could not help it. He would read the change, perhaps he would despise it, but why should the future Mrs. Lionel Fitz-Herbert care for Philip Wyndham's scorn?

Just then I heard a step coming up the graveled walk that thrilled me with the old memories which rose, ghost-like, at its echoes. I went down stairs and stood in the parlor as he and Will came up the steps. Caddie met them at the door. I heard her joyful welcome, and then they came in. I thought—perhaps I was mistaken, Cousin Jane—but I thought Philip Wyndham grew a shade paler as he saw me. His voice did not falter. He came to me and extended his hand.

"This is indeed a surprise, Miss Hamilton."

I was quite as cool and self-possessed as he. Caddie knows little of my acquaintance with him. I only told her we had met several times in New York, and I know, shrewd observer as she is, she saw no clew by which to guess our past.

Now, Cousin Jane, that man is nothing to me. When I might have been his wife, I refused him without a moment's hesitation. And yet he has made me more than half miserable with his indifference already. He does not avoid me at all. He talks with me, when it comes in his way, as easily and as agreeably as with Will or Caddie, but he hardly seems to know whether I am in the room or out of it. It must be my vanity that is wounded. We women do not like to find our captives quite so free and heart-whole. However indifferent we may feel to the victim, we do not like to find the chains we forged all broken.

There, he is going down stairs now. I am going down too. Why not? Though he is nothing to me, there is no reason I should not hear him declare what this beautiful morning has said to his soul. I know what a look of inspiration will beam from his earnest face. But, look you, he shall not know this. I will say some provoking, ridiculous thing; something that shall make him feel that what he does and says is nothing to me, even as what I do and say is nothing to him.

I shall not send you this letter yet. I will leave it open till Mr. Fitz-Herbert comes. You shall see how I will welcome him.

June 26th.

Well, Cousin Jane, Lionel Fitz-Herbert came yesterday, by the same train that brought Philip Wyndham a week before. You shall hear all about it. In the first place, you will want to know how I got along with Mr. Wyndham seven mortal days. Well, I had very little to do with him. The forenoons he has spent in his room, writing diligently, as I suppose, on the book which will find its way to your table next autumn. Afternoons he has been for the most part with Will. They have taken together long drives, and been off on fishing excursions from which Caddie and I were excluded. But I have seen enough of him to give me more than one heart-thrill, yet I am unhappy at his indifference no longer. I chose my own path, and I must walk in it. It is strange, though, what an influence this man has over me. If I were with him always I couldn't help being good. His earnestness is infectious. He makes one see life as he sees it. In his presence it seems a solemn thing. Wealth and station look like mere tinsel. They are shorn of charms, and nothing on earth seems worth the staining our souls with its dust. One cares only to live the life heaven appoints—to live it simply, earnestly, honestly, until this life on earth shall lose itself and be absorbed in the fullness of the life of heaven.

You have felt something of this influence in his books; you would feel it still more if you could see him. I do not think I would have him stoop from his lofty height to a poor butterfly of fashion such as I. It would be like the kingly eagle mating with the peacock. I know myself. I could not always live on the enchanted mountains. I should come down into the valleys sometimes, and then I should want the luxuries that he could not give me. You see I must marry Lionel Fitz-Herbert. And this brings me back to his coming.

"I suppose you'll beautify Mr. Fitz-Herbert's room for him?" said Caddie, standing by my side after breakfast. I blushed, for Philip Wyndham had heard her question, and was looking at me keenly.

"Not I, indeed. I'm not sure that the gentleman cares for flowers; and, any way, I have all I can do to beautify myself."

I came up stairs and made an elaborate toilet. I did all that art could do to enhance my attractions, and I was well satisfied with the result. When the visitor came I met him at the door. I received him with much *empressement.*

I could see that he was highly elated. When we walked into the parlor together, Philip Wyndham looked at us both with one of his quick, analytic glances. Then an expression passed over his face which made me angry. It seemed to me it was compassion. I remembered the tones in which he said to me, long ago,

"I pity you, Helen Hamilton."

Well, I think I made Mr. Fitz-Herbert's day a pleasant one. I certainly devoted myself to him with most flattering assiduity. I can see him now from the window. He is walking to and fro in the garden, now and then dashing the dew-drops from a shrub in his path with a dainty cane about the size of my little finger. His complexion looks bright; I guess he rested well. His hair is smooth as the hat he has just lifted to bow to Caddie, who spoke to him from the door. N.B.—When I am his wife I will tumble his hair up. It would kill me to sit opposite to it, day after day, so uniformly smooth.

Oh, I forgot to tell you that Mr. Wyndham dresses better than he used. Will says his books bring him in eight or nine hundred dollars a year now. To be sure, this would hardly find me in silk dresses, but with it he manages to clothe his outer man with a good degree of taste, to say nothing of keeping himself in bread and butter.

But I must go down. My carpet knight has paused in his walk to cast a languishing glance up to my window. I shall send this letter off to-day, and when there's any thing new I'll write to you again. My heart loves, and sends you its blessing with as warm a tenderness as when, on your bridal morning, you kissed through your tears your cousin,

HELEN HAMILTON.

LETTER THE THIRD.

Hillside, July 26th.

Who would have thought a whole month would pass before I wrote you again, you fond, true-hearted Cousin Jane! And now I have so much to tell, but I must tell it briefly, for I have another letter to write to-day.

Will, and Caddie, and I are all alone again. Our two guests are gone. Mr. Wyndham went first. It is a week since he left. We went on, during his stay, much as before. I bestowed my chief attention on Mr. Fitz-Herbert, and yet I listened to every word that Wyndham said. His is a noble soul. I am proud that he loved me once. Jane, when I saw Lionel Fitz-Herbert in the city, I did not know him. I was dazzled by his gold and his name; I did not look into his heart. Give me the country for knowing a man as he is. Under the solemn sky, under the century-old trees, with the free winds fanning the dust from your path, there is little chance for artificial refinements and conventional disguises. Only the true and the real can lift up its face to those solemn heavens.

Well, I saw Fitz-Herbert as he was; nay, perhaps he seemed to me even feebler and tamer than he is when Philip Wyndham walked beside him with his tall stature, his lofty port, his clear, far-seeing eyes; above all, his high, far-seeing soul. But, despite this, I persevered in my resolve to be the rich man's wife. "I never would, I never could marry a poor man," I said to Caddie, when she asked me what I meant to do.

One week ago Philip Wyndham left. He held my hand in his for a moment when he bade me good-by. We chanced to be all alone. He looked earnestly into my eyes, and then he said,

"Miss Hamilton, if I could I would say God bless you in the path you have chosen, but I can not. You will have to account to Him for every crushed down impulse for good, every stifled aspiration. I suppose we shall never meet again, but I know you will forgive my sincerity when you remember how truly I was your friend."

Oh, Jane, it seemed to me, in that moment, as if I would have given every hour of my splendid future, with its station, and wealth, and luxury, just to have been folded to his heart—just to have heard him say, "Helen, I trust you." But he went away, and resolutely I banished this longing. I would marry Lionel Fitz-Herbert. This would make my parents happy. It would relieve all papa's embarrassments. In short, it was the only rational course for me to pursue. That afternoon I went to ride with him. I had never been more lively.

It was three days before he proposed to me. The decisive moment came at evening. We had been over to Oakland, and were pacing to and fro under the trees. I do not know exactly what he said. I was sensible he was asking me to marry him. I had, in my mind, a prettily framed acceptance. Listen to what I said. It was not I, surely; was it my guardian angel speaking through my lips?

"Mr. Fitz-Herbert, until this very moment I have meant to marry you, but I know now that I can not. Do not be angry with me. Do not think that I have done you wrong. I should do you ten times greater wrong were I to perjure myself at the altar—to give you my hand when my heart can never, never love you. If you had asked me when we were both in town—when the gaslight glowed above us, and diamonds sparkled and repartees flashed by us, I should have been your wife; but here, under this everlasting sky, I must tell you the truth—I love another."

I stopped. The influence within, which forced me to speak, was gone. I looked at my auditor. I could not have thought those smooth, small features could have worn such an expression of impotent rage or vindictive hate as crossed them there in the moonlight. May I never see its like again. It passed away as suddenly as it came, and then, in utter silence, he offered me his arm, and we walked back to Hillside. The next morning he left.

Oh, Jane, what shall I say to you? How shall I make you feel the wild, glad sense of freedom that has been with me ever since? Thank God, thank God that I was not suffered to stain my soul with a lie. The scales have fallen from my eyes. All the wealth, all the splendor in the world could not now buy my life, my heart, my free, independent self. Out here where the sun shines, the winds blow, the birds sing, and the dew-drops sparkle brighter than any diamonds, I am glad, I am glad.

And yet, Jane, there is an under-current of sadness. Low down in the deep heart of this mighty anthem of joy which all nature seems chorusing together, I can hear the half-smothered echo of a wail, and my heart joins in it. Not for the vanished dream of pomp, and pride, and splendor; not for the stately house, with its velvet canopies, its gilded cornices, its gold and silver. Once in life I had laid at my feet a pearl of great price. I did not stoop to pick it up, and now it can never sparkle on my bosom. I may go sorrowing and mourning all the days of my life, but I can not light again the ashes of a dead hope. Jane, I know now that I love Philip Wyndham; that I have loved him long with a love that is stronger than life or death. But I will not waste my future in weak repining; I will trust in God, and be thankful that I am not all unworthy of a love that once was mine—thankful that I am still free to cherish one blessed memory; and perhaps, when the shrouding mists of time shall roll away and disclose the distant hills of heaven, standing together on those glory-crowned hill-tops, Philip Wyndham may know my best self for what it is.

I said I had another letter to write. It is to papa and mamma. I am going to entreat them to come down here next week. I must have them share the glories of this unrivaled summer. They love me too well to refuse. After they have been here, you shall hear again from your cousin HELEN.

LETTER THE FOURTH.

Oakland, August 26th.

You will be surprised at the date of this letter, Cousin Jane, and yet not more so than I am. All this past delicious month seems like a dream. I am not awake enough yet to explain it, so I will give you the outlines, and you must fill up the picture with fancy touches.

My parents came. Tears were in their eyes when they kissed me. I think there was a strange sweetness to them both in coming back, after nearly thirty years, to the dear haunts of their days of love, and romance, and wooing. Never have I seen them so happy, so free from care. Their souls asserted themselves here. They grew tenderer to each other, to me, to every earthly thing. They opened their hearts to the blessed influences of sunrise and moonrise, bird-songs and dew-falls. I waited until there had been time for the free country wind to sweep from their memory all the dust and care of the soiling town. Then I told them of Mr. Fitz-Herbert's proposal and my answer. Mamma was the first to speak.

"You are a good girl, Helen. God forbid that we should wish you to give your hand without your heart—we, who know what love is." She looked with filling eyes upon papa.

Then, Jane, I pressed my advantage. I besought

them to give up forever their city life, its toils, its cares, its living for the world, its worriment about ways and means; to come here, where they would have enough to live in comfort, where mother's vacant girlhood home waited for them. They listened with more readiness than I had feared. You behold the result in the dating of this epistle. Father is growing young in his freedom from care and trouble, and dear mother tells me, with tears in her eyes, that this is the best life she has ever known. As for me, I can hardly realize my own happiness. I must lay down my pen now, and go out among those magnificent oaks, in whose tops the golden arrows of sunset are quivering, until I feel through all my heart the exultant consciousness that this dear home is my very own.

Oh, what shall I say to you now, out of my full heart, dear Cousin Jane? It is almost midnight, and yet I must conclude this letter before I sleep. To think that since I laid down my pen, four hours ago, my destiny has come to me. I was pacing along under the trees, my eyes cast down, when suddenly I felt rather than saw that I was no longer alone. I looked up, and there, right in my path, stood Philip Wyndham.

"What! are you visiting now at Hillside?" I asked, very abruptly, saying the first thing that came into my head in my confusion.

"No, not exactly; that is, I shall stay there, but I came on purpose to see you, Helen."

And then, walking by my side under the oaks, he said once more words which you may not hear; which are only his and mine in all the world. Once more my pearl of great price lay gleaming at my feet, and this time I raised it up and placed it in my bosom. It seems that Caddie, that keen-eyed Caddie, did suspect our secret after all, and so she gave him a hint of my rejection of Mr. Fitz-Herbert, and that I had persuaded my parents to come to Oakland to live, and then he came up to see me. I know the look with which Caddie will say to me to-morrow,

"I thought you never would marry a poor man, Helen."

And I shall answer,

"I am not going to. I shall marry the richest man I ever knew; rich in faith, hope, genius, and a millionaire in love."

Oh, Jane, God was merciful. He did not require me to wait till the Beyond for the fruition of my hopes. Even here has He crowned me with the largess of his blessing. Philip is mine and I am his. I ask no more of life, only I pray God to keep my heart meek and pure, a fit temple for the love He has sent to dwell in it.

Before the October moon has waned, you and Charley will come to my simple bridal. I shall wear no costly robes, no glittering ornaments, but truth and love will make me fair to the dear eyes whose light outshines for me all the diamonds in all the world. I shall be crowned by woman's holiest crown. I am happy. There is no undercurrent of wailing now in the great glad chorus of nature—no sheeted ghost in the still chamber of my heart. I am blessed beyond all I could ask or hope. Has not this been the golden summer of my life? And now, at the close of this last chapter of my maidenhood's romance, I must write the name which will soon be mine no longer—

HELEN HAMILTON.

The Phantom Face.

"The soul has inalienable rights, and the first of these is Love."

I too had once a wife and once a child.

BALDER DEAD.

Suffer not woman and her tenderness to sit near him in his darkness. Banish the frailties of hope, wither the relenting of love, scorch the fountains of tears. So shall he be accomplished in the furnace, so shall he see the things that ought *not* to be seen, sights that are abominable, and secrets that are unutterable. So shall he read elder truths, sad truths, grand truths, fearful truths. So shall he rise again *before* he dies.

DE QUINCEY.

THE PHANTOM FACE:

A STORY FOR CHRISTMAS.

I HAD seen her all day long, just as she stood before me that other Christmas morning. Her eyes —those soft brown eyes, wore a timid, appealing look; her chestnut hair fell around her neck in silken tangles. She was clinging to Ralph Humphries' arm. I was no believer in ghosts, apparitions, spiritualism, or any other supernatural manifestations; and yet, all that day, turn my eyes whither I would, I could see nothing but that Face. She was our fifth child—fifth and fairest, Mary said. The rest had all died in their cradles, and it was not until she had been with us a year that we gave her a name, so fearful were we that she, too, would be borne from us into the valley. But when, after that year of waiting, her soft eyes were still bright and beaming, and the smiles still dimpled her rose-bud lips, we named her Faith.

The world had always called me a hard, cold man, money-loving and money-getting; but Mary knew that low down in my heart was a fountain which the angel's wing had troubled, whose sweet waters of tenderness gushed ever for her. We knelt together by our baby's cradle upon her christening day, and I said amen with my whole heart to the prayer my wife's low voice faltered. It was Christmas-day on which the little one was baptized. This was also her birthday; for she came to us, the white, frail thing, with the snows of a Christmas morning, and our fondest pet name for her was "Our Christmas Child."

God knows, as that child grew up, I loved her; perhaps all the more tenderly because she was not yet three years old when her mother closed her eyes, already full of the glory of heaven, and died with her head upon my bosom. I could never have married any other woman. Other men—men far tenderer and more affectionate than I, have done this; but I—no matter; it may have been that there was little of the affectional element in my nature, and what there was, having sprung into full bloom at Mary's presence, left for all after-comers only dead leaves and withered boughs. Faith was all I had, and I loved her well and fondly. I do think I made her motherless childhood and girlhood very happy. She loved me, too, with more than a daughter's affection. As she grew up, she was child, companion, friend—the occupation of all the hours not devoted to business. Why was not this companionship enough for her as it was for me?

I had had, for some years, a young man named Ralph Humphries in my employ. Faith never saw him until she was seventeen, and had left school. Then, one evening, I invited him to the house. I had a very good opinion of him. His business capacities were excellent; his reputation was spotless; his manners those of a gentleman. I knew he devoted his evenings to lonely and indefatigable study. I thought there would be no harm in lending to one of them a little of the brightness which Faith's eyes and

Faith's presence shed upon my own life. I could see at once that the two young people were interested in each other, but I never thought of the faintest possibility that this interest could grow into any deeper feeling.

I noticed with pride that Faith had never looked more lovely than that night. The coldest critic could not have helped pronouncing her beautiful. It was an autumn evening, crisp and cool. She wore a dress of some soft, rich fabric, plaided in bright colors. It was cut in such fashion as just to reveal the contour of her small, white throat, round which her chestnut hair fell in rings of dusky gold. Her loose sleeves dropped away from her snowy and daintily-moulded arms, round which were clasped golden chains. I remember all these things well, for I gloried more in Faith than any lover in his mistress. I enjoyed the admiration with which Humphries evidently regarded her.

He was a fine, handsome, manly-looking young fellow of twenty-three. At first he seemed a little embarrassed. He was not accustomed to meeting beautiful women, surrounded with the appliances of taste and luxury. But soon this *mauvaise honte* passed away, and he charmed even me by the ease and brilliancy of his conversation. He talked well not only, but he possessed the rarer accomplishment of listening well, which is a still surer passport to the favor of a woman.

In the course of the evening it came out that he had been studying French and German, the former with the assistance of a fellow-lodger, the latter alone. I remarked that with a good knowledge of these two tongues he might make himself invaluable to me as foreign corresponding clerk, and at once Faith, who was herself a most loving student of German literature, volunteered to assist him. If she had asked my advice in this affair, perhaps I should have opposed it; but I could not contravene her invitation when it was once given, and, indeed, I saw no great harm in the matter.

Thus it was that Ralph Humphries became almost domesticated in my household, and three or four evenings of every week were monopolized by him and his German books. Quite frequently I left the two young people together. Of the possibility of any love growing into her heart stronger than the tie which united her to me I never thought; but one day, late in November, with terrible suddenness the truth was brought home to me.

I was about leaving my counting-room for the day when young Humphries came in and requested a few moments' audience. I do not remember in what words he told me that he loved Faith, that he was beloved by her. At first my mind utterly refused to comprehend him, but he forced upon me the unwelcome truth. I was thunderstruck rather than angry. I did not rave at him, or even forbid him my house. I only spoke one sentence—

"You have stolen into my home to take away my most precious thing, my one child: it is of no use."

In vain he strove to plead with me. I would neither hear nor speak another word. I buttoned up my coat, went out of the office, and, stepping into an omnibus, I was soon at home. Faith heard my key turn in the door, and sprang down the stairs to meet me, as her custom was. She looked like a celestial vision, clad, as she was, for a dinner-party, all in white; her lips softly and tenderly smiling, her eyes full of welcome. I put my arm around her as we went up to the parlor together. Somehow I felt as if she had never in her life been so selfishly dear to me, and then a fierce anger flamed up in my heart against the man who would fain take my treasure from me. I waited until I had taken my customary seat in the easy-chair, and Faith had established herself on an ottoman at my feet, and then I said, watching keenly her expression,

"Faith, Ralph Humphries has been speaking to me about you this afternoon."

A quick crimson overspread her face and neck; the lashes drooped over her shy yet eloquent eyes. I could see with what fullness of love she regarded him; but this only hardened my heart. I went on.

"Of course I told him it was no use. I could not give you up to any one, least of all to one like him, every way unworthy of you, a mere employé in your father's warehouse."

The girl had my blood in her veins. The flush on her cheek deepened. Her lip curled with pride. Her voice was firm and strong.

"Father, Ralph Humphries is in no way my inferior. You yourself introduced him to me; you told me how unstained was his character, how untiring his industry, how gentlemanlike his manners; I have seen for myself how true and tender is his heart. Father, I love Ralph Humphries, and I shall love him till I die."

I saw that to contend with her roused spirit would be useless. I must endeavor to soften her heart.

"Faith," I said, "my only treasure in life, my dead Mary's last child, would you break my heart? Would you leave your poor old father to die alone? Think, daughter—your mother loved me. She is looking on you from heaven."

She was touched. Tears gathered slowly in her eyes and fell heavily, glittering like dew upon her silken raiment. She knelt at my feet and clasped her hands in a passionate entreaty.

"Father, I do not want to leave you alone. I want to stay with you always; but only let Ralph be your son. He is good and worthy; you are rich enough for us all. Oh, father, you have been so good to me all my life. Do not refuse to make your last child happy now. If my mother could speak to you from heaven, she would join my prayer, for oh, my father, even as she loved you through life and death, so do I love Ralph Humphries."

She paused, but at the door of my heart I heard another voice, a pleading voice that had stolen to my ear many and many a midnight from under the grave-mould. God forgive me, but I barred my heart's door, and shut even that pleader out. I spoke with stern decision:

"Faith, just one month from to-day will be Christmas—your birth-day. We will talk no more about Ralph Humphries now, but on Christmas day you will be eighteen, and you shall choose then between him and your father; for, as God hears me, his wife and my daughter you shall not be. If you go with him, you must leave forever your father's home and hearth."

She made no answer. She looked at me for a moment with her reproachful eyes, and then she rose and went out of the room. After a short absence she came back. She had taken off her festal robes, and was attired in a quiet dress of some sombre hue. She seated herself at the table and took up a book.

"What, Faith," I said, "are you not going out, after all?"

"No, father, I am in no mood for merriment; and as I have not the faculty of dissembling, I will not go among happier people, to make a discord in their mirth."

We passed the rest of the evening in silence.

During the month that followed, not a single allusion was made by either of us to Ralph Humphries. I had told Faith that she must choose between us. After that I was too proud to forbid him the house, or to ask him if he came there. I presumed they met almost daily; but as he never made his appearance when I was at home, I did not take his name upon my lips.

Faith had never been so entirely lovely as during that month. Sadness gave an added charm to her beauty, a tenderer light to her eyes, a more pathetic melody to her voice. She strove very hard to please me—to make herself necessary to me. No sooner did my key click in the latch, than her light feet would steal down the stairs to meet me. She brought my dressing-gown and slippers, she read to me, she sang my favorite songs, she arranged her hair after a simple, graceful fashion, in which she knew I used to love to see her mother's. So dressed, I could sometimes have thought that Mary's self had come out of her grave to walk and sit beside me.

And yet, will you believe it, all this time my heart

grew harder and harder. She was not practicing these gentle endearments, so I persuaded myself, for my sake, but for that of Ralph Humphries. She wanted to make herself so necessary to me that, rather than give her up, I should be induced to accept him. So I steeled my heart against her.

Shall I ever forget that Christmas morning which came at last? I was too full of anxiety to leave the house. I sat in my study, hoping and fearing. At twelve o'clock she came in, and with her Ralph Humphries. Together they stood before me, and Faith spoke:

"Oh, father, will you not relent? Will you not let us both be your children?"

"No, Faith."

"But, father, listen. You have told me, on this my eighteenth birth-day, to choose—choose between you and him. I do choose. Kind father as you have been to me, dearly as all my life long I have loved you, even as my mother left home and kindred to follow you, so will I give up all things, even you, for Ralph Humphries. But, father, if you send me forth, my heart will break. I can not, can not live and bear your curse."

Once more she sank on her knees before me, with her white face, her pleading eyes, her hands clasped in a passionate prayer. But my heart was not softened. I answered in cold, firm tones:

"Remember, Faith, I called God to witness that if you chose him I would cast you off forever. I shall keep my oath. But I will not curse you. Mrs. Ralph Humphries will be no child of mine, but I shall wish her well. Do you still persist?"

She rose. With a sudden, fond movement she clung to her lover. Her eyes met his, and she murmured, in the words of Scripture,

"'The Lord do so to me, and more also, if aught but death part thee and me.'"

He put his arm round her trembling figure and drew her closer to him in my very sight. Then he said, in a firm, respectful voice,

"Mr. Gardner, for loving your daughter I can make no apology. No man, with a man's heart, who had known her as I have known her, could help that; but I would not take her from you to share my humble destiny did I not know that to her pure, womanly nature love is all the sunshine of life. I can not leave her here to break her heart."

I smiled scornfully.

"Since my day hearts have grown strangely brittle; but sit down, both of you."

I summoned a servant, to whom I addressed a few words in a low tone. He went out, and in ten minutes returned, and stood bowing at the door. I motioned him to close it, and then I said,

"You have had a few moments for consideration. Are you still resolved to be Ralph Humphries' wife?"

Her tone was as determined as my own.

"I am."

"Well, then, you must be married before you leave my house under his protection. I have sent for a clergyman, and I will witness the ceremony."

The Rev. Mr. Wilde must have thought it a strange bridal, but he made no comments. As soon as it was over, I placed his fee in his hands and he departed. I turned to the bride.

"Mrs. Humphries," I said, in a mocking voice, "I congratulate you; I wish you long life, an easy conscience, and many happy returns of this day. This is my bridal present."

I laid in her nerveless hand a check for five thousand dollars. Her husband took it from her and placed it upon the table.

"I thank you, Mr. Gardner," he said, proudly, "but I can not allow my wife to be a pensioner on her father's bounty when she is an outcast from his home and love. I have strong hands and a willing heart. You are not afraid to trust me, Faith?"

He needed no answer save her look of entire reliance, of perfect love. They rose and stood before me. I have that picture framed and hung away in my heart. Its colors will never fade until the morning light of eternity breaks over them.

Faith, my daughter Faith, is leaning on her new-made husband's arm. Marble white is her brow; her chestnut hair droops round her pale face with its soft, silken tangles; her sorrowful brown eyes are full of a prayer which eternity itself can never shut out of my memory.

Thus she stood before me for one moment, and then they went out of the room, out of the house, those two young things, so utterly helpless and alone in the world. God forgive me! God forgive me! Every night this prayer goes up from my lips, through the midnight, to the far-off throne. Will He hear me?

Twelve years passed on after that Christmas morning, and I knew not whether the earth still held my child. At first letters had come to me now and then, in her handwriting, post-marked from a distant city, but I was afraid they would soften my heart, and I had burned them all unread. For years none had come, and, in spite of my resolution, my heart had begun to grow sick with fear. All that twelfth Christmas-day after she left me, turn my eyes whither I would, they rested only on Faith. Old superstitions about ghosts and wraiths came to me, but I am no believer in the supernatural—I dismissed them resolutely. I could not so dismiss Faith. Turn wheresoever I might, the Face turned also.

At last, toward night, in very desperation, I seized my coat and hat, and hurried out of doors. Among my tenants in a humble quarter of the city was a pawnbroker. I knew the man well. I had often talked with him for half an hour. Seized by some unaccountable impulse, I went toward his shop. I did not see the Face now, but I had an impression as vivid as it was strange that Faith was walking beside me. I entered the shop. As soon as the man saw me, he left a customer with whom he was engaged, and came toward me.

"I should have come to you to-night, Mr. Gardner," he said, respectfully. "Something has happened in the course of my business which I have been feeling for several days that you ought to know. Five days ago a child came here, about nine years old I should think her, and pawned a locket containing a miniature of you. It must have been taken when you were younger, but the likeness is perfect."

As he spoke he laid the miniature in my hand. It was one I had given Faith fourteen years before, on her sixteenth birth-day. Oh, how the sight softened me. I could not see the Face now, but I heard, stealing up through the silence of twelve long years of estrangement, Faith's voice, calling me father. Was it the tears of some pitying angel which began to soften the hard, dry soil of my heart?

"Do you know where the little girl lives?" I asked, eagerly. He handed me an address, written upon a crumpled piece of paper.

"I asked her," he said, "because she seemed to be suffering. She said that her mother would have been willing to bear any thing but death rather than part with the picture, but it was all she had left, and they could not starve."

I did not see the Face, but I heard that voice still, calling upward through the years. How full of reproach its tones were now!

"I must keep the picture," I said, hurriedly. "You shall have twice its value. It is priceless to me."

So saying, I went out of the shop, and hurried on through a miserable street and along a blind alley to the number indicated on the paper I held in my hand. It must have been but the illusion of fancy, but still Faith seemed to walk beside me. By dint of inquiry I found, in a great, rambling house, a room in which they told me a woman named Humphries lived. My heart grew sick. The hand with which I opened the door was almost powerless, but I did open it, and I stood there looking in, and the Face, oh, heaven! the Face seemed to pause and look in beside me.

On a straw bed in one corner of the room lay a woman's form, and beside it knelt a girl, older than her years, her face, so like Faith's own, frozen into the white stillness of despair. She did not heed my approach. I went up and stood over the bed, and there, after twelve long, silent years, I found once more Faith, my child—dead, dead, dead!

I was possessed by a strange calm. I roused the girl; I said to her,

"I am your grandfather. Look up; you shall never suffer any more."

The tears gushed now from her stony eyes. She sank at my feet.

"Oh, grandfather, you are come here. *She* told me to go to you—to give you this paper. See, she has it fast in her hand. I can not get it."

I loosened the death-grasp of those thin, cold fingers. I smoothed the paper and read, in Faith's handwriting, only these words:

"Father, let death plead for my child: forgive! forgive!"

Oh, it was too late. The tears I rained over that still form could not waken the dead; those closed ears could not hear moans or prayers; but when I clasped her child to my bosom and promised to be a father to the fatherless, in a far-off corner of the room I seemed to see the Face, with a misty, golden glory bathing its hair, and a smile upon its lips, such as I think only the blessed ones of heaven can wear.

I learned Faith's story afterward. It was the old, old story of hopeless struggles with want and poverty; suffering; despair; death. But, thank God, their love never grew dim; their faith in each other never wavered. Ralph Humphries died first, but his wife was not long in following him to the far-off City—

> "Where true love shall not droop or be dismayed,
> And none shall ever die."

T

I will not sadden your Christmas fireside with my own remorse and despair—the agonies of my broken heart. For me, in this world, is no more peace; but, thank God, I have made *her* child happy, and I can see over the Distant Hills the coming light of an eternal morning, which shall break, by-and-by, even for me. Every Christmas day I see, or seem to see, the Face. Wherever I go, it goes beside me. It is bright as ever. No tears dim those eyes of brown. No shadow of age dims the lustre of that ever-shining hair.

Soon will come the last Christmas day on earth, and, I know, beside my bed of death the Face will smile; its lips, its forgiving lips, will be the first to speak my welcome into heaven.

THE END.

HARPER'S WEEKLY.

A JOURNAL OF CIVILIZATION.

A First-class Illustrated Family Newspaper.

PRICE FIVE CENTS.

HARPER'S WEEKLY has now been in existence two years. During that period no effort has been spared to make it the best possible Family Paper for the American People, and it is the belief of the Proprietors that, in the peculiar field which it occupies, no existing Periodical can compare with it.

Every Number of HARPER'S WEEKLY contains all the News of the week, Domestic and Foreign. The completeness of this department is, it is believed, unrivaled in any other weekly publication. Every noteworthy event is profusely and accurately illustrated at the time of its occurrence. And while no expense is spared to procure Original Illustrations, care is taken to lay before the reader every foreign picture which appears to possess general interest. In a word, the Subscriber to HARPER'S WEEKLY may rely upon obtaining a Pictorial History of the times in which we live, compiled and illustrated in the most perfect and complete manner possible. It is believed that the Illustrated Biographies alone—of which about one hundred and fifty have already been published—are worth far more to the reader than the whole cost of his subscription.

The literary matter of HARPER'S WEEKLY is supplied by some of the ablest writers in the English language. Every Number contains an installment of a serial story by a first-class author—BULWER'S "*What will he do with It?*" has appeared entire in its columns; one or more short Stories, the best that can be purchased at home or abroad; the best Poetry of the day; instructive Essays on topics of general interest; Comments on the Events of the time, in the shape of Editorials and the Lounger's philosophic and amusing Gossip; searching but generous Literary Criticisms; a Chess Chronicle; and full and careful reports of the Money, Merchandise, and Produce Markets.

In fixing at so low a price as Five Cents the price of their paper, the Publishers were aware that nothing but an enormous sale could remunerate them. They are happy to say that the receipts have already realized their anticipations, and justify still further efforts to make HARPER'S WEEKLY an indispensable guest in every home throughout the country.

TERMS.—One Copy for Twenty Weeks, $1 00; One Copy for One Year, $2 50; One Copy for Two Years, $4 00; Five Copies for One Year, $9 00; Twelve Copies for One Year, $20 00; Twenty-five Copies for One Year, $40 00. *An Extra Copy will be allowed for every Club of* TWELVE *or* TWENTY-FIVE SUBSCRIBERS.

www.ingramcontent.com/pod-product-compliance
Lightning Source LLC
LaVergne TN
LVHW021141110826
845150LV00005B/1089

* 9 7 8 1 4 2 5 5 4 8 2 3 0 *